SECOND CHANCES

a novel

BOB SCHUELER

For Dolores, Ben, and Erika

PRAISE FOR

SECOND CHANCES

". . . full of puzzling twists and turns. . . . The unlikely heroes of the story include people who have mental health challenges, and some from diverse communities, but each one brings a unique set of strengths to solving the mystery."

—**Patricia B. Nemec**, PsyD, editor of *Best Practices in Psychiatric Rehabilitation*

"The master of the simple title with different levels of meaning, Schueler, the author of *25 Years* brings us his new novel with an equally meaningful title, *Second Chances*.

"People who seek help, their families, and those who seek to help are all around us. Yet their experience is often inaccurately captured in literature. Offering us an engaging story, Schueler offers a story from their diverse viewpoints, accurately capturing their diverse perspectives and evolution as people."

—**Kenneth J. Gill**, PhD, co-author of *Psychiatric Rehabilitation*

Second Chances

by Bob Schueler

© Copyright 2022 Bob Schueler

ISBN 978-0-9973683-2-1

PART 1

1

Paul

When little Harvey David Ellison died and my sister, Cindy, took the blame, no one looked to me for help. It was almost thirty years since I'd generated high hopes as the little teenage reverend, going to be just like his daddy, the pastor of Providence African Methodist Episcopal church in Boston. Cindy was the state family services social worker supposed to be protecting the boy, the little White boy, and I was a crazy, middle-aged man stuck in a group home, there for most of his adult life and, everyone assumed, of no use to anyone.

I'd failed her before. When she was eleven, Mother died and our little family blew apart, Father retreating into his work and yours truly, Paul Abernathy, going wild and then away to the mental hospital. Cindy just put her head down, the only thing she could do, determined to become a social worker—the dream Mother had for her own self, her role as a reverend's wife as close as she'd been able to get.

After that, in my twenties, I'd been angry, enough to drive Father and Cindy away. When I got quiet later on, they figured not visiting had worked best for everyone and stuck with it. They didn't understand how I'd changed—why I was quiet. I'd learned I had to push it all down just to survive. I shrank up and made a world within the four walls of that group home, but no matter how scared I got, they were my only family. I never forgot them.

Father and Cindy probably didn't imagine I'd follow what went on with her and the Ellison boy, but the local news was on the TV every night in the house, and I heard them talk about the young Black social worker and the poor little White boy she was supposed to look out for. What started out as questions became accusations, her White supervisor throwing up her hands, implying, *If only that girl had listened to me and followed procedure, that little boy might still be alive.* Except Cindy's boss never got around to saying exactly what those procedures were that my sister didn't follow; it was all just nasty hints, like she wanted to be more specific but wasn't allowed. Sure.

I learned later that the job had worn my sister down to nothing way before the little Ellison boy was beat up and killed by his mother's boyfriend. Maybe I could have helped, but I didn't know any of that. Far as I knew, she was the married, successful professional, and I was the failure, the embarrassment.

I will say this—when Cindy quit her job and her only-good-for-the-good-times husband walked out, Father took her back to the parish house we grew up in. And he took me back a few years later when I had to leave that group home. Grown as we are, some of his church leaders still criticize him for it, but at least we're a family again. A family whose youngest is finally ready to follow her own dream.

This is Cindy's story, about starting over—her second chance.

2

Cindy

The morning of the interview, Cindy sat in the big rectory kitchen as she had so many times growing up, feeling like a kid. Maybe it was the institutional smell—not like the little kitchen in the apartment she'd shared with her husband, her memory of both faded and worn. Her brother, Paul, was already up, sitting at the table and fussing with the newspaper.

"You couldn't make a pot of coffee? The group home, you never made it yourself?" *It's the smell*, she thought, *making me this sharp.*

"They didn't encourage that sort of thing," he said, with maddening equanimity, "but you're right. I'll try next time. Hell, I'll do it now."

"No, I've got it." She didn't want to suffer through his skill building, not this morning.

"Going to that place today?" He looked up from the paper, frowning, like it was a dumb thing to do. He didn't say anything else, just made a show of turning the page, shaking it out straight, his fingers dark against the white pages. She wanted to say something smart, but another image took over.

Her father's fingers were longer, all of him bigger, but he shook the paper out just that way, on the same table, that morning of her eleventh year when she waited in vain for Paul to come downstairs, for Father to take them to the hospital on their mother's last day. During the cold ride over, all she could think was *Where is he? Why isn't he here?* The big brother she'd depended on wasn't there for her, that day or ever again. First in and out of the state hospital, then planted in a group home, he stayed in his room, in a way, for the next half of his life.

"Go ahead," she snapped, "say it. Your sister's thirty-seven, too damn old to be an intern. Could be putting her fancy social work degree to use, helping the downtrodden, doing the Lord's work, right?"

"I didn't say that." Still not looking up.

He didn't have to. She snorted and, as she turned away from him to reach for the coffee pot, slammed her head into the edge of the open cabinet door. It brought tears to her eyes but didn't make much noise.

He put the paper down. "I know how much it hurts, what happened." He hadn't noticed her accident. "I just hate to see you start over again when you've got an education, a profession. There's got to be a place for you in that world. It's not all child protection. Everyone knows that's thankless."

She leaned back against the sink to keep the tears from running down her face. "So, tell me, what? Mental health?"

"Well, God forbid you should have to hang around more crazy folks, coming back home to me every day. Anyway, I'm moving out, soon as I can. If you weren't so damn stubborn, you could too."

That one hurt, but she'd earned it. "All those damaged folks that won't get on with their lives—I'm the big expert knows how to help them? Next it's going to be 'Momma would have been so proud, she had this dream.'"

"Watch out, now . . ."

Cindy turned and busied herself with the coffee preparation. "I'm not like all those ladies Father has to deal with who just love clucking around, drawn to all that pain, long as it's somebody else's."

"Like visiting your broke-down brother in the group home all those years?"

She turned back to glare at him. "I know, how about this? It's not about you this time. This is something I want to do, and it doesn't involve you, or Father, or Mother and her dreams. Now shut up and drink your damn coffee."

· · ·

Back Door Technologies was an easy walk from Alewife Station, the end of the line on the Red Line subway; good so far. The three-story glass atrium was imposing, as was the humorless Rambo security guard behind the counter, but she made it through to the third floor and Human Resources, hardly intimidated at all.

When the elevator doors opened, a young man, very large and White with a round face and close-cropped hair, filled the opening. His warm smile seemed genuine as he ushered her off the car with a little matador's bow, pivoting his wide body with surprising grace.

"Ms. Abernathy? Steven Henchcliff. I'm so happy to meet you. We spoke on the phone."

Surprisingly light on his feet, he rotated his substantial girth around an erect axis, head tilted back as he glided down the thickly carpeted corridor. An image flashed: *Fantasia*, hippos in tutus. As they sped down a hallway past a graceful wooden counter, the sight of a smiling middle-aged Black woman sitting behind it helped loosen the knot in Cindy's stomach.

Soon they were sitting on old-fashioned furniture among large, leafy plants. A second look at the man's face revealed fine wrinkles; older than she'd thought, maybe fifty. "Now, I spoke with Luiza about you, but I'm not sure how she described the opportunity."

He went on to describe the unpaid internship in terms so vague she had no idea what she would be doing, leading her to suspect he didn't either, but she would be in his department, a combination of HR and public relations. She would be working to design and maintain their internal website.

"Well," he said, "I'm sure that's more than any one person could absorb in one sitting, so let me shift the focus to you. I have to say first, though, that it's been such a pleasure working with Luiza and the others from the Stewart Center. This is my first experience working with a program for the mentally ill, and I was a bit concerned at first, but our founder and CEO, Charlotte, was, as usual, insistent, and I have to say her sense for these things is uncanny. So far, the dishwashers they've placed with us have worked out splendidly."

Cindy heard the far-off tinkle of alarm bells. This was the first time the man seemed to be disengaged from his words and reciting his lines. She wouldn't have noticed had he been more formal in his presentation. What was he telling her?

"And since she recommended you, I could hardly be more thrilled to meet you."

Cindy thought back to the call from Lu, the Stewart Center's job developer. She had encountered the gregarious Brazilian on her weekly visits to the Center with her dog Bruno.

"I tell you, this place is gorgeous—you should see, even the kitchen." She spoke as if they were good friends. "I just placed our second member there washing pots. The first, they found him a job in a fancy restaurant. He did so well, I got them to take a chance on a young man with trouble in his background, but I think he'll do okay. They make some kind of computer software, and all these young men running around . . . Anyway, I know Steven, the HR director, very nice but a little, you know . . . I had to work very hard on that one, but now I hear he is looking for someone in his office, an intern. Should I tell him you might get in touch?"

"Please," said Steven, "tell me a bit about yourself and your interest in working with us."

Later, she could only remember bits of self-promotion, but still enough to make her cringe: her dream of saving kids, career with the state (failures omitted), discovering her talent for design, acing her web classes at the community college, then dropping names of platforms, hosting services, and languages, ending with triumphs like animated web pages for the local vet and secondhand shop. When she gestured toward their URLs on her resume, he didn't even glance down.

Instead he said, "Yes, I have to say I was struck by the fact that you have a master's in social work and a good deal of experience—"

"I know, I'm old for someone aspiring to an unpaid internship." They shared a laugh, and Henchcliff looked relieved, and impressed that she had provided him an out. "But I'm trying to build a new career, and I need a place to start. I know I don't have a degree, but . . ."

He waved a hand. "Oh, our friends in academia can't keep up, so we care little for their degrees. In any case, let me show you where you will be working."

Cindy stifled a gasp at his assumption that it was a done deal. This wasn't just a lark anymore; she might have to make this work.

A peek around as she followed him to a nearby room revealed long worktables with closely spaced workstations flanking each wall. He introduced her to a shockingly young man named JJ along with a woman who might have been pushing thirty, and two more youngsters barely looked up before returning to their screens. Soon Cindy was back in Steven's office, trying to make sense of the disconnected jumble of names and faces.

"And now, for the pièce de résistance." He sailed back in, waving papers in the air before placing them on the coffee table with a flourish. "The inevitable, inescapable paperwork." He collected her license and passport and left her to dig a pen out of her bag. The forms were brief and well designed. The confidentiality and noncompete agreements were indecipherable—whatever. Sign, sign, sign.

She expected to be ushered politely out the door after agreeing on a start date and schedule, noting she had been there less than forty minutes—how could so much have happened so quickly? Instead, he put a hand on her forearm and lowered his voice.

"I should have clarified on the phone, but I had hoped to include an orientation lunch in our cafeteria; it's free. Do you think you could stay a while, uh, into the afternoon?"

Cindy allowed that she could arrange to free herself up—Father could get his own lunch.

Steven seemed delighted, launching into the origin story of BDT, as he called it. "Nearly twenty years ago, Charlotte's husband, a vascular surgeon, died in the crash of his private plane and left her a single mother to Arthur, a thirteen-year-old computer prodigy. A family friend, Vernon Crofter, saw an opportunity. He was a cyber security expert somewhere in the federal government, and together they came up with a plan to use Charlotte's considerable wealth—they call it 'old money'—to found a company built around Arthur's amazing skills, Charlotte's vision, and Vernon's government contacts."

Good Lord, it must be tough being rich and White. How much money must she have had to start this place? Cindy struggled to hold her smile, hoping it read "How fascinating!"

"What you see here"—he swept his arm in a theatrical arc—"is a broad-based cyber-security operation. Charlotte is the CEO, while Arthur continues to be the technical genius. On his eighteenth birthday he officially acquired the title of chief technology officer. Vernon handles operations and marketing, and he's liaison with various federal government departments. You probably know of our private computer and internet security programs for battling viruses, Trojan horses, moles, and the like: No Back Door for the home computer, and Bar the Door for commercial systems."

All news to her.

"This year we're launching a version for smartphones and tablets. But highly classified government work is still about forty percent of our business, and Vernon is a stickler for security, as you've no doubt noticed. And everything, all the jobs, happen in Cambridge and at our packaging-and-assembly plant in Devens, right here in the cradle of liberty."

Who wouldn't be proud to join such a virtuous place, and get rich by doing good? If only they were paying her.

• • •

Later, as Cindy and Steven emerged from the elevators on the ground floor and headed down the hallway to the cafeteria, they were overtaken by a tall woman in a fitted floor-length gown of shimmering green silk with a Chinese print. A smaller woman, apparently attached to her left ear, bobbed along beside her, carrying a leather shoulder bag, as casual and utilitarian as her boss was elegant. As the two swept past, Steven looked up and sang out.

"Oh, Charlotte, I have someone you must meet. This is Cynthia, er, Abernathy. She's just who we've been looking for." *Really?*

The woman stopped and turned, her left palm framing her face, and favored Cindy with an ironic eye that belied her friendly smile. "Is she? Well, if Steven says it, it must be so. I'm so happy to meet you." She extended a limp hand for Cindy to shake. Or was she expected to curtsy and kiss it? "Please join us. We're going down to the dining room to see a demonstration by our wonderful young chef Kaz." She had a low-pitched voice and a plummy accent that sounded affected. "Oh, and this is my assistant, Susan Hayes."

So, this was the visionary gifted with enough money to start her own company. As they moved with alarming speed down the hall, Charlotte commanded their attention as her due, regaling them with her philosophy—something about nutrition as a basis for spirituality.

The speech was wasted on Cindy. The woman's intense gaze had brought on a memory of Cindy's seventeen-year-old self, looking at a similar gown on another ample body. Standing in the church basement, the usual gathering after the service, the gowned woman bent close and pinned Cindy rudely with her eyes and said, "Maybe there's still hope for this one"—compared, everyone within earshot would know, to her disgraced brother locked up in the mental hospital. Cindy's shame was amplified later as she remembered joining weakly in their smug laughter. She stopped attending her father's services after that, her first real act of defiance.

And here was that same feeling: powerless, outclassed, at once dominated and sullied by someone above her. Or perhaps she was being paranoid. The woman had stopped to greet a lowly intern.

As they surged into an elegant dining hall, what appeared to be a display booth turned out to be a small but elaborately equipped kitchen with an open counter on three sides. A crowd of young men in jeans, T-shirts, and running shoes gathered around it, most looking at their phones. On closer inspection, Cindy noticed several women among them. A few were Asian, the rest White except for an older man in canvas coveralls—a janitor, of course.

Behind the brightly lit counter stood two men in chef's whites, one Asian and as young as his audience, the other older, a skinny giant with long white hair peeking out from beneath a white baseball cap. He had a matching mustache waxed up at the ends and held his hands clasped before him. When his eyes fell on their group, he gave them a nod, which seemed a signal for the knot of youngsters to glance at them and give off a ragged little chorus of "Hey, Charlotte." She returned the nod, and all eyes returned to the kitchen.

After a rather pompous introduction by the older chef, the younger one launched into an impressive demonstration of noodle making by stretching strands of dough between his hands repeatedly like a cat's cradle, multiplying and thinning them until he held up a large bundle, which he tossed into a giant pot of boiling water. More workers joined the audience as the demonstration continued, some in collared shirts and chinos. The tall chef blathered on about Marco Polo while the younger repeated the noodle-making process three more times, and then they were chopping and stir-frying, and there was a reference to a "heavenly broth"; she had to admit, it smelled great, and she was starving. When the older chef came by, pushing a cart with steaming bowls, Charlotte called out to him.

"Carlson, dear, do join us when you can." She turned to Cindy. "He and Kaz are essential to the operation, and as you can see, their contribution goes beyond everyday food. Creative flair in everything we do is what makes us special." This orientation seemed an excuse for Charlotte to hear her own voice. "So, my dear, how do you see yourself contributing to our community?"

The lecture had turned into a job interview. Cindy took a breath, then stammered, "I, uh, well, I've been doing some freelance web design, and I hoped to work on the website, internal . . ." She glanced desperately over at Steven.

"Cynthia has a master's in social work as well, and experience in child protective services. And she's a minister's daughter, the African American Methodist, er . . ."

Was any of that relevant? And how did he know about her background? With Paul's help, Luiza had done more to pave the way here than Cindy had imagined. "Actually, it's African Methodist Episcopal, or AME, but . . ." *But what, damn it?!* She looked down at her hands. *Say something!* This time she was rescued by the white-haired chef, who patted her shoulder as he passed behind her to glide into an open seat.

"Charlotte, are you badgering this poor woman on her first day? Cynthia, is it? Steven has told me all about you, and we couldn't be more thrilled to have you join us."

He did? They were?

"I was only getting to know our newest member," said Charlotte, "but I suppose you have a point. Let's relax and focus on this amazing soup. Every morsel is crisp, retaining its distinct character—perfect, don't you agree, Carlson?" The CEO's gaze had turned sharp.

"It's just right for us, but will a clear broth sustain our youngsters through the long afternoon? They'll be eating donuts by three."

The CEO's face hardened, but her voice remained light and musical. "My dear Carlson, must everything be buried in a heavy sauce, barely recognizable? Comfort food is all well and good from time to time, but this is so much more in line with our current philosophy, don't you agree?"

With this last, her voice hardened as well, and she turned her gaze on Cindy, bringing back the chill and allowing Cindy only a glimpse of Carlson's sullen reaction. It was like an old argument between a married couple, but it made her angry on his behalf. Did she want to work for this bully? *Stupid.* She was an intern, a nobody, would probably never get to talk to the CEO again. But the tense exchange had to say something about this place.

Carlson excused himself, and conversation shifted to more relaxed subjects, leaving Cindy's eyes and mind to wander until Charlotte declared an end to their little gathering.

• • •

An hour later, as Cindy followed the winding path back toward the subway, she thought of how ridiculous the boss lady had looked in a shimmering gown among the casual young techies. It reminded her of the outfits the ladies wore to church. *But who wears her Sunday best to work?*

The whole scene bothered her, but she couldn't say exactly why. Could she spend her life with people who'd never had to struggle with poverty and misfortune? They seemed more than welcoming, but she felt like an exotic creature in their eyes—an ornament. A mascot.

A rustling in the grass drew her gaze to the side in time to catch a flash of movement, the white tail of a retreating deer bobbing through the tall grass to disappear into the woods. One more world where she didn't belong.

• • •

Daylight saving still held, so it was dark when Cindy left her sleeping father and brother in the rectory the next morning. The same security guard at the front desk seemed startled by her outstretched hand.

"Cynthia Abernathy. It's my first day. With Human Resources and Public Relations."

He offered her a tight smile that stayed well south of his eyes. "No one from your department's in yet. You can't be up there by yourself. Wait in the dining room." And his eyes went back to scanning the empty lobby. It was a cold dismissal. She wondered whether he was this unfriendly with everyone new, or just with women, or Black people.

The little kitchen in the middle of the dining room was shuttered, but she noticed a bank of snack and beverage machines on one side and serving counters fronting a more traditional kitchen on the other. A brown-skinned man with thick black hair spilling out of his white ball cap bustled about behind the steam table while a few other early birds ate breakfast at two of the tables.

Cindy was far from famished, but the smells of eggs and bacon drew her over to the man behind the counter, who didn't say anything but gestured to the steaming bins with a questioning raise of his eyebrows. She pointed at scrambled eggs, then bacon, sausage, french toast—by now they were both giggling.

"Syrop, is real maple," he managed in a thick Spanish accent. Laughing, she nodded. He seemed genuinely pleased when he handed over the plate. "Bodder, coffee—there." They grinned at each other.

"Cynthia Abernathy," she said, reaching out her hand to shake. "This is my first day."

He seemed surprised, grabbing a towel to wipe off his hand before offering it for a shy shake. "Miguel Solar. Please to meet you." He offered a little wave before fleeing into the kitchen.

What a place. She'd avoided the freshman fifteen at Northeastern by commuting, with the additional help of a tight budget. Being short made every pound show, and getting involved with Ralph, who didn't know how to make a meal that wasn't a feast, hadn't helped. Oh well, it was her first day.

When she finished wiping her plate clean with the last of the french toast, it was time to report for duty. Gloria, the woman behind the counter outside Steven's office who'd helped with her sign-on paperwork, was there to greet her when the doors opened on the HR floor.

"Cynthia, my, you are the early bird. We don't get started here till seven thirty, sometimes closer to eight, but the lights come on at six, and you can come right on up."

Cindy almost asked her to tell that to the guard dog in the lobby but stopped herself. Instead, she tried for sisterly self-deprecation.

"Good thing. I just pigged out so bad I'll probably be asleep in an hour. I can't do that every morning."

"Tell me about it. I'll get your ID picture taken. We'll have your badge ready this afternoon, and you can come and go whenever you like. And I'll wake you up if you need it." The woman looked to be mid to late forties and probably had to struggle with her weight about as much as Cindy.

Gloria brought her back to her new workstation and showed her how to log in to the system, access her email, and change her password. Cindy's log-in brought her to the company's internal website, which, she was thrilled to see, was drab and unappealing. She took a tutorial, noting the interface was barely functional, ugly and confusing. Ideas for improving it began bubbling in her head while the other employees trickled in. Cindy idly ticked off the names Gloria had given her: Estelle something, who was the benefits manager, then Jeanie, Mark, Kimberly (never Kim), and JJ. The guys were JJ and Mark, but she couldn't keep the young women straight. It didn't help that they were all dressed the same, in faded jeans, white T-shirts, and running shoes. After a quick greeting, they logged on and disappeared into their jobs, leaving her to return to her web-based orientation.

The woman who came in around 8:30 and dumped a handbag into a drawer seemed older than the others, perhaps close to Cindy's thirty-seven. Thin enough to look good in baggy black yoga pants and a thin, scoop-neck top, she moved like a dancer. Very short dark hair framed a pretty face, and her eyes held a sort of radical openness, as if she expected Cindy to see into her as she herself saw into Cindy. It was creepy.

She extracted a much bigger tote bag from her desk and was subject to good-natured razzing as she swept through the room, managing to touch and be touched by everyone before coming to Cindy.

She introduced herself as Nicole Arnessen in a surprisingly deep voice as she gently brushed her fingertips across Cindy's left temple to back above her ear, so briefly Cindy might have missed it. She felt something let go inside her, a release of tension she hadn't realized was there. A little crinkling around the woman's eyes—time stopped, the hand came down; she broke off eye contact and was gone.

Cindy caught Mark's eye and saw his smirk. "That would be our Nicki. She's, uh, in charge of morale."

This brought a chuckle from the others, who stayed glued to their screens, where Mark returned his attention. *Morale.* Cindy didn't understand what he meant, or why it should be funny, but it felt like they were laughing at her.

It was a relief when Steven came in and asked to see her in his office.

"Let me show you what we'd like you to work on." He had her sit next to him in front of the large screen on his desk and pulled up the web page. "All our administrative communication is web-based—time sheets, policies, reporting. Paper gets lost, written policies go out of date, and old versions hang around, confusing people. This way we can control and update everything from here."

She was struck again by its drabness. He seemed to read her thoughts.

"It doesn't have to be pretty, but it's got to work easily and intuitively—though if our staff can follow it, it shouldn't be hard for the coders. It's been a challenge for my little team to learn Arthur's platform and language, but they're getting up to speed."

How nice for them. How was she supposed to catch up? She tried hard to look confident. Her boss was so vague about the whole thing, and didn't demonstrate anything on the page, but rather turned brusque and sent her back to her seat with a wave. "You'll find a way to be helpful, I'm sure."

Great. That makes one of us.

• • •

She had been assigned to work with Kimberly and JJ, but though she remembered the young Korean, which one was Kimberly? She decided to try to bluff her way through. "I'm supposed to work with Kimberly and JJ on the manuals on the internal website."

JJ looked up, along with a young woman with a dark ponytail. Cindy tried to talk to both at once, but her eyes settled on the woman as she said, "I'll check it out, but if there's something I can do, please let me know. Do you guys meet or anything?"

Ponytail snorted. JJ looked at the woman and then back at Cindy. "I'm JJ, but this"—he pointed, indicating the woman—"is Jeanie." *The punk rocker must be Kimberly*, Cindy decided. "Anyway, we're kind of busy for meetings. When we get a chance, we'll fill you in. No one asked us if we had time for an intern."

Fuck this. "I guess I'll just check it out myself, then. If you need coffee or snacks, I'm sure you'll let me know."

"Ooh!" No one looked up, and she couldn't tell who said it. It didn't matter. At least they picked up her sarcasm. What mattered was that Ralph had been right, which was worse than infuriating.

She buried her head in her screen and clicked through the web page while the others went back to work and ignored her for the rest of the morning. Around noon, as if by a secret signal, everyone in the room got up and filed out. No one looked at her. It was so blatantly rude she could scarcely breathe. Before she could move, the one named Nicole came in and dumped her bag on a desk.

"Hey, how's it . . . ? Did they invite you along for lunch?"

Cindy looked down, not sure how to respond.

Nicole pressed her lips together and frowned. "Assholes!" She came over and wrapped Cindy in a quick, tight hug. "How about some air? The grounds are pretty neat here, and I can fill you in on who's who."

Cindy felt ridiculously grateful. "Thanks. I didn't want to have them deny me a seat at their table, and anyway, I already ate like a horse at breakfast."

Nicole spoke as they walked through the building to the lobby.

"I'm sorry about the group. Believe it or not, they feel superior to most of the staff around here because they have social skills. They're like the cool kids at school, you know—with it, but dim."

Nicole moved with an easy grace, slow enough for Cindy to keep up without losing her breath or breaking into a trot. When they left the elevator and walked around the back wall of the lobby, Nicole did a little skip as she moved behind the big marble desk and pressed herself up against the big guard, who seemed a bit flustered. Nicole gave a musical laugh. "Craig hates it when I sneak up on him—like an enemy commando."

He straightened even more and moved her aside. She didn't seem offended.

"She just got dissed by the little rats in Steven's office. We're going for a walk."

The guard kept staring straight ahead at the lobby entrance, giving no indication that he'd heard, and Nicole didn't wait for an answer before drifting toward the door.

"Unlike a lot of places, we haven't had interns."

So she kept hearing. *What am I doing here?* Not ready to ask the question and dreading the answer she suspected, she said, "Let alone a middle-aged Black lady."

"Yeah, I suppose," said Nicole with her tinkly laugh. "It might take a bit for everyone to figure out what's going on. What did Steven say?"

"Something about helping JJ and Kimberly with the internal website, posting policies or something like that."

"Are you into systems or administrative stuff?"

Cindy shook her head. "Website design, layout, and graphics. I've been trying to catch up on the programming side of it, but I'm starting to think I'm in way over my head."

"Well, Steven's a good guy. If he took you on, he'll do his best to make it work. I'll check in with him."

They came out of the parking lot onto a curved drive with the other office buildings looming over them. Nicole led them across the street and into a grassy park studded with trees that looked like they'd been planted last week.

"This is part of something called the Alewife Reservation, named after a scummy river called Alewife Brook, which is named after a little fish no one's heard of. The path leads to a footbridge over to a swamp on the other side—oops, I mean *wetland*. It's actually nice; there's birds and things and a boardwalk. It gets a little buggy sometimes, but it works for when you need to get away and chill."

The place had a just-finished feel that was the polar opposite of her family's Jamaica Plain neighborhood with its Olmstead-designed parks and tiny houses mashed together. The wooden bridge, when they finally reached it after an uncomfortably long walk, looked like it was waiting for its first coat of paint. And she couldn't even see their building anymore.

"I should be getting back," said Cindy. "I'm supposed to meet with Steven at four, and I want to be able to say I went through all the HR policies."

As they rode the elevator upon their return, Nicole said, "I'm going to check in with Steven, then I'm off on my rounds. Hey, I know—how about I show you around the place, sort of an orientation tour? I could do it first thing tomorrow morning if that works."

Cindy couldn't think of a reason to say no.

Though she got through all the policies, her colleagues continued to ignore her, and the meeting with Steven was perfunctory.

• • •

The next morning, Cindy was once again grateful for Nicole's modest pace. Her guide turned toward her and seemed to brush up against her side as she spoke. "We'll start back in the lobby."

When they came around the wall behind the desk, Nicole held them back. Craig was occupied checking in two Asian men who appeared to know little English. They looked flustered at his lack of response until a woman hurried over and introduced herself in Japanese. Bows were exchanged before she led them off toward the elevators.

"That's Arlene, from Commercial Network Security. We'll be going through there in a little while," said Nicole, as she skipped over and hip-checked the guard, who pretended not to notice. "Sweetie, tell her how things are set up here. We're taking the grand tour, but you do it the best."

Craig's eyes continued to scan the lobby as he spoke. "The building is set up in three wings. Left and right are commercial and retail. There's a gym in the center section, above the dining room, and above that the secure section, where they do government work. Admin is above the lobby, with the executive suite above that."

Nicole couldn't have told her that?

"That's it? He's the strong, silent type, aren't you, baby?" This last she delivered in a husky voice, batting her eyes. The guard stayed reptile-still.

Nicole broke the moment by dragging her back to the elevators. The gym was large and lavishly equipped. The side floors were open fields of cubicles with concave spy mirrors hanging from the ceiling. Was this what Cindy wanted—an anonymous cubical, a drone in a code factory? At least the offices had glass walls without drapes, and the doors always seemed open. They mostly held guys around her age wearing collared shirts, like the ones she'd seen sprinkled through the crowd at the cooking demonstration.

Everywhere they went, people exchanged enthusiastic hugs and touches with Nicole, but soon the visits became boring. People seemed to have little time for visitors or each other, and there was a tension in the air that Nicole only dissipated for the few moments she was there.

It was a relief when a buzz from the cavernous bag on Nicole's shoulder brought a message and the woman gave her a brief, hard hug. "Time to get back to your team. Look, Cynthia, you're new. Give yourself a chance, and let people get to know you. And not everyone's a kid, including yours truly, so enough with the middle-aged bit."

Cindy was dismayed to think she came off as needing that much reassurance.

· · ·

There was a background hum in the room that Cindy only noticed when it stopped—keyboard clicks, murmured remarks, sighs, grunts of frustration or satisfaction. Once the full team was in place, it wasn't silent. And then it was, and it made Cindy look up without knowing why.

She'd seen the woman before, Charlotte's assistant, but the name wouldn't come.

The woman's gaze darted around before settling on her. Oddly, no one else looked up. "Cynthia? Susan Hayes." She came over and gave her hand a firm shake. "I'm Charlotte's executive assistant. She would like a quick word."

When they got to the waiting room, the tall, older chef, now glassy-eyed, stumbled out the door, propelled from behind by Charlotte's hand on his shoulder.

"Our Carlson," she said once he'd left. "The price we pay for haute cuisine."

This brought a snort and smirk from her assistant. Then Charlotte turned to Cindy, coming over to put an arm around her shoulders and lead her into a large office made achingly bright by two walls of windows framing a table-desk with a pair of monitors even larger than Steven's. If she felt Cindy stiffen at her touch, it caused her no concern. The desk itself was modern and looked handmade. She led them past it to a seating area with leather-and-chrome chairs that were surprisingly comfortable, surrounding a glass coffee table that held a silver coffee service. Cindy hadn't noticed Susan follow them in until she saw her perched off to the side.

Charlotte asked how she was settling in her job, and Cindy got busy making herself cringe. "I still can't believe my luck, happening on a place like this. It's just what I was looking for, what I dreamed about."

The woman surprised her then. "Oh, I think it's we who are lucky, though it was no accident. I was talking to my old friend Martin, the CEO of Consolidated Dorchester Human Services, at one of these tiresome fundraising galas, and I happened to mention that we were pleased with our experience with the kitchen help from his program. He must have mentioned it to someone at the Stewart Center—clever man—and next thing, I get a visit from their jobs person, who tells me about someone looking to go into web design, a social worker and . . ."

Martin Islington, Ralph's boss. Cindy's politically connected father would know him from the gala circuit, and must have shared that tidbit. She felt a surge of irritation and had to remind herself that this was the way things were done: networking.

Charlotte continued while looking out her wall of windows. "We live in this bubble, you see, and these wonderful young people keep coming, but they're either White or Asian, and mostly male. I just can't be satisfied with remaining an enclave of privilege."

Ah. Cindy was the poor Negro, here to make the boss feel virtuous.

Charlotte paused, perhaps noticing Cindy's look, and held up her hand. "Yes, I imagine you're concerned about being a token. Let me assure you, if you can't cut it, no one will cover for you."

Cindy dared a quick peek at Susan, but the assistant stared ahead, unreadable.

"You have four weeks. If you prove yourself, we will offer you a full-time position at a competitive salary. If not, we will wish you all the luck in the world. I won't drag this out; that's worse for everyone. I'm going to have my son, Arthur, check you out." She waved off the poor word choice without apparent embarrassment. "As our CTO, he usually evaluates new talent at some point, and he's been working on the upgrade of our external website, which should fit your expertise, no?" Her eyebrows reached new heights. "He will report to me. But I have a feeling about you, and my intuition is seldom misplaced, so, if that assignment doesn't work out, well, we'll see."

A quick movement caught Cindy's eye as Susan jerked her head around and stared at Charlotte with raised eyebrows of her own before turning back to her blank forward stare. Her boss didn't seem to notice.

Well, Cindy could hardly claim she'd earned the opportunity, and the CEO had promised to hold her to a high standard. She doubted it would take this Arthur four weeks to figure out she was an impostor. Then she would learn what else the woman had in mind for her. Maybe she could greet people in the lobby, like at the home improvement center but hopefully without the smock. She could certainly do better than the creature currently guarding the front desk.

She tried to gauge her feelings toward Charlotte. Despite the affected speech, there was something Cindy was inclined to trust. On the other hand, Charlotte couldn't be much more condescending, and judging by her assistant's reaction, there was something else going on that Cindy couldn't begin to fathom, and that pissed her off.

Still, a full-time job at a salary someone like Charlotte considered reasonable . . . With everyone in Cindy's life waiting for her to fall on her face, she had to make this work.

As she left the office with Charlotte's assistant, Susan leaned into her. "Well, well, eyeballed by the Golden Boy. And she made it sound routine." The woman's expression was hard to read—cool, with a bit of mischief? "This should be quite the experience. And, by the way, I wouldn't put much stock in 'We'll see.' If he gives you thumbs-down, she won't even see you; it'll be my job to give you the bad news. Anyway, let me know how it goes. I'm always looking for Arthur stories."

3

Paul

Saturday morning, I'm enjoying breakfast with Father.

"Your sister's sleeping in today," he says. "I guess she's earned it. You think things will work out this time?"

She's been stuck back home three years now, feeling sorry for herself; and though he's never said anything to her or me, she knows it worries him.

"I sure hope so," I answer, always happy to keep the focus off my own failure. "She helped me when I was stuck in that group home all those years."

"Well, she needed that. You missed the first few years after she left her job and lost her marriage. It was nice to have her with me, but I wasn't sure I'd ever see light in her eyes again. She was closed up, like when your mother died. I kept pushing her to invite friends over, but there was always a reason. The ones from social work school, her pride got in the way, and the others were Henry's friends too. I even got her a puppy."

"Bruno." Hearing his name, the big golden retriever raises his head but then puts it back down. He's used to having Cindy home; this has been hard on him.

"She was mad," said Father, "but at least she showed some life over it. I don't think she ever imagined how many hours of kissing up to the church elders it took, how many promises I had to make—and keep—to get them to let me bring a dog in here."

"I always wondered how you managed that. Cindy must have too."

"Maybe so. Didn't make her any less mad, though."

"That must have been, what, a year before she started visiting me at the group home?"

"Yeah, and I begged her to do it. They'd convinced me my visits would set you off."

Hell, they should have stopped worrying about that ten years before. Guess they didn't want to risk the inconvenience. "I'd been quiet a long, long time."

"I suppose. Maybe I was afraid it would set me off. Anyway, she agreed to a schedule."

"Wednesday afternoons."

"I think at first she thought I wouldn't bug her so much about getting back to work if she got out of the house. It just seemed like the more I pushed on that . . . well, she was angry enough."

"Depressed. That's how some folks show it. You know that."

That gets him angry, but it feels good to get under his skin now and then. He stayed away from me for twenty years, and if he's apologized, I must have missed it.

It takes someone to go in and bring you out, make you feel comfortable, even useful. I can only hope that happens for Cindy at this new place. If I'd gotten that from Father . . .

But Cindy coming downstairs gets me out of thinking that way, thank God. She waves her hand in response to our greeting and stumbles over to the coffee pot.

"So," says Father, "what's the verdict? You like the place?"

I can tell Cindy's not ready to jump into a discussion about something so important while she's waking up. "I don't know. Everyone there, it's like this is what they've been doing all their young lives, and I'm this older lady who only knows a little. I am way out of my depth, and it's nerve-wracking, waiting for them to figure it out."

"Well, they hired you, sort of," Father says with a shrug.

"Oh, Miz Scarlett," I pitch my voice high as it'll go, Southern, fanning my fingers, palms out next to my bug eyes, "I don' know nothin' 'bout makin' no websites!"

Father sprays coffee all over himself. "Look what you done now, boy. Daddy goin' need a whole 'nother shirt." I'm enjoying that too much to notice Cindy draw her fist back, and she gets me a good one on the shoulder. It hurts, but not so much I can't join in as we all crack up.

After a while, wiping tears from his eyes, Father manages, "Just give it a chance. You've got wisdom those boys don't, and maybe this Charlotte'll see that. You'll be more like complementing them."

"'Sides, they's always the washin'," I add, managing to rub my shoulder and duck at the same time.

"Alright, I get it," she says, but the look she gives me is serious, worried. She's remembering the old days, when we were in school. I'd do Father's sermon voice with my chin up in the air and my eyes raised toward the divine light, waving my arms and strutting around. I was playing to Mother, who saw it as the perfect way to keep her husband's head from getting too big, and she made sure he laughed along. After she passed, I did the same things, but by then I was bitter and serious in my disrespect. We'd both end up angry and wouldn't talk for days.

By then, I was going way back into my head, and it wasn't a nice place to be, but no one knew how lost I was until I got suspended from school and ended up in the hospital. After a couple of times, it was the state mental hospital, and I was in "the System." For years, any time I'd get out, my hot mind led to wild outbursts that sent me right back, and soon I wasn't getting out. I can't blame Cindy for being worried I'm headed for another crash.

When Father leaves to change his shirt, she says, "I haven't heard that kind of teasing in a long time."

I can see she's poking around, trying to figure me out. "Yeah. It's got to do with me going down on my meds." I can see that's a shock. "Come on, now, I'm working with Dr. Jamison."

Are you crazy? That's what she wants to say. She fought to get me back to the group home when I wanted to move back here—always had her doubts about me, and I can't blame her.

"Getting to laugh again, that's a part of life I want back; to feel joy, anger, sadness, like I'm alive."

I stuck in the part about the meds on purpose to get her used to the idea. I still take a lot, but I talk to my doctor about it every time I see her, for a whole half hour every two months—more than most people get. Everything that happens in my life gets watched, because you never can tell with folks like me.

It's time to get Cindy off worrying about me returning to my badass twenties, so I excuse myself, tell her I have to go get something to show her.

It's a little roll I dig out of my backpack, a drawing by my gifted love Phyllis, on art paper I got for her birthday. One is of Cindy, and I think I'll let Phyllis show it to her next time she comes over for dinner. I don't know how she got the light in her eyes, using just a pencil.

I show Cindy the one of me. It'll work for my purposes, even though I think maybe Phyllis was mad at me that day. I look hunted, desperate.

"It's you, all right," Cindy says with a wide smile. I realize now that isn't the reaction I was hoping for. Instead of saying how it's exaggerated, she goes on about how Phyllis caught some truth about me. Huh. She did do it early on. Maybe if she does another one, I won't look so crazy. Maybe. Time to shift the focus.

"Seriously though," I say, "I don't imagine first days anywhere are ever easy, and you've been out of the game for how many years?"

I can see by the quick flash in her eyes it was the wrong thing to say, but her smile stays. "I know, but this place, it has this energy. You sense a shared mission. I just wish my job wasn't so vague."

"It's got to be rough going at first," I say, the wise older brother hardly worked a day in his life until a couple of years ago, part-time now at a little desk jammed in the hall, "and it's going to take time. No way to rush it." She's bored already—some of us have the knack. "And you got your own smarts, experiences these kids don't have. Just remember that." See how I helped there?

"Anyway," she says, like she stopped listening a while ago, "I think I'll take Bruno for a long one, try to walk some of this feeling off. I'm expected for dinner." That would be with her boyfriend Ralph, at Grace and Billie's place.

4

Cindy

Cindy had met Ralph at Paul's group home when her brother was in crisis. Somehow she had allowed him to become her boyfriend. Having begun—she hoped—a new career, it was time to take control of this part of her life as well.

He rented an in-law apartment from Billie LoPresti, the retired founding director of the Stewart Center. It had been a relief at first to escape the elegant stuffiness of the parish house to spend her nights in Ralph's bed under the eaves of Billie's two-family house, but it was cramped and shabby, the kind of place she'd long since outgrown. Struggling up the dark, creaking stairs to Billie's front door brought home the contrast with Back Door's gleaming headquarters.

It was tiny Grace, a former nun and Billie's partner, who opened the door on the dim landing, in her usual state of agitation. "Cindy, dear, back at last. It's good to see you. Ralph's in the kitchen fixing dinner." That was part of the deal for his ultra-cheap living arrangement. Almost as cheap as hers; she had no job, while much of his salary went to pay the private college his son attended.

"Cindy's home, Ralphie." Billie's foghorn easily overrode Grace, even from the kitchen. "How'd it go, punkin? Any luck signing up for cyber-slavery? Haw! Come on, lover boy, let's see how she made out."

Though well into her seventies, Billie's energy made her an imposing figure despite her wiry, modest frame. Cindy made sympathetic eye contact with Grace, then went through the dining room into the steamy kitchen as the little woman clopped along behind her in the blocky-heeled nun's shoes she'd never surrendered. Ralph gave Cindy a little stooped-over wave and a muffled hello, barely looking up from the stove. This had become a source of friction, his insistence on fancy—or, more accurately, obsessive—cooking for the three or, more commonly, four of them. His long workday pushed dinnertime close to nine, often leaving him in the kitchen past ten. The Italian sauce he made from scratch bubbled on the stove. Anyone else would have opened a jar.

"Hey, Cindy," he said, still without looking up, "we got chicken parm, linguine, and spinach."

Fresh, no doubt, sautéed in olive oil and garlic. She sighed and tried to sound enthusiastic. Though he made it every few weeks, its preparation absorbed him completely. Sharing the details of her day would have to wait.

Billie jumped in as if on cue. "While he's finishing up, let's go in and get started on the wine."

Cindy began to relax as they settled around the big table in a room filled with old, dark-wood furniture. Grace, whose little face, framed by a choppy, brown page boy, barely cleared the tabletop, spoke in a hushed voice that sounded vaguely conspiratorial. "Just to let you know, Ralph's had a tough day. These risk assessments have him on edge."

"They're ignoring his objections, of course," added Billie. "Dr. Marsha's on the warpath."

Cindy sighed. Ralph was always upset about something at work. He was something of a big deal at Consolidated Dorchester Human Services, better known as ConDo, and the Stewart Center was a subsidiary. Their connection with Back Door through the kitchen job placement made things awkward.

Then Ralph was bringing out dinner, which she had to admit was delicious, though he was frustrated by some aspect that wasn't quite perfect. *God, it's just food!* She thought of Kaz's airy self-assurance while serving more than forty people. Why did this have to be such a big deal?

At last Grace asked about her day.

"It was interesting. There are a lot of bright people there, and I'm not sure where I can fit in. They seem to work all the time, but the place is set up to be really supportive, with great food—and it's all free."

"Which is a good thing," Ralph interjected, "considering you'll be working for free as well."

Was that really necessary? Before she could think of a pithy rejoinder, Ralph had scurried back into the kitchen to start his cleanup. Did he look guilty? Grace, at least, was interested in hearing more, and Billie held her tongue in response to the little woman's glare, so she had someone with whom to share her enthusiasm. She would have to make an effort to stay in touch with Grace from here on.

It was close to ten when a flushed and sweaty Ralph emerged from the kitchen and made an effort to show he was listening as she finished her account. Early in their relationship, he had seemed like a good listener, but that was when he was helping her brother and she was involved in his world. Now, as she followed him through the kitchen and upstairs one more time, she thought he was feigning attention, waiting for her to finish.

His one big room doubled as bedroom and living room. Along with his bathroom, it was cheaply done and furnished. The floor seemed large enough, but the sloping roofline pressed down over her on three sides, making coming upstairs feel like crawling into a tent.

Sitting with him on the bed, she tried again to tell him how excited she was about the internship. It was a stall to avoid the uncomfortable subject to come, but maybe part of her hoped he would share even a little bit of her excitement and bring back her ambivalence.

No. Once again he seized on the fact that it was unpaid.

"We talked about this." She didn't try to hide her exasperation. "It could lead to something paying, and at least I'm not back in school, building up debt. I'm changing fields; the options are limited."

"But you've got a perfectly good social work degree, a license—you could walk into a good job tomorrow." He saw her look and held up a hand. "I know, but that was child protection. There are so many other jobs out there, and you're so talented."

"Look, I need to try something else. I've got to find out if I can make it in web design, and this could open some doors. This is a different world. It's too early to tell whether I could fit in there, but I've got to try."

How could she make him understand that she couldn't go back? She had cared about those kids, wanted badly to help, but everything else about the job had been a struggle. She hadn't liked social work school, doing the research, writing the papers, and writing reports on her families was no better. She hated the meetings, deliberating over whether to take children out of their homes. She had tried to establish trust with the mothers, to give them support, but it never worked; she was the lady who was there to criticize them, looking for reasons to take away their kids. By the end, she'd hated everything about the system and the job.

By contrast, website design had been a revelation. It came to her easily, and she enjoyed it. The work she did actually made people happy and grateful.

Ralph, of course, wouldn't let it go. "But I always felt that was something we shared, that sense of purpose, helping people get a fair shake."

Yes, that was it, wasn't it?

There would never be a better time. She put her hand on his. "Ralph, I'm sorry. You think we have this shared mission, but that's not me. I tried. I don't belong here, with these people—with you."

He stared into her eyes for what seemed like a long time and then drew back and was off the bed, pacing. He ended up hunched over on the edge of the couch, leaning toward her, twisted at an uncomfortable angle. "This has been coming for a while. Go ahead."

So, he wasn't completely clueless.

"I need a break. I need to put everything into this, to find out what I can do, who I can be." She wanted to sound firm, resolute, but instead heard a whine of desperation. She looked down, could only manage, "I don't want to see you . . . for a while."

His ability to read her, to know what was coming, made it harder. She could barely hear his voice.

"I guess I thought—I hoped—we could get through this. I should have known. I've been too wrapped up in myself. I'm sorry."

There it was. She had to fight off the attraction she felt—poor, suffering Ralph, taking responsibility. She remembered the time after he had been mugged—more accurately, chased over a fence and done in by his own clumsiness, but bruised and battered nonetheless. It was when their relationship had intensified. This attraction to pain— it wasn't going to define her anymore.

She couldn't think of anything else to say, and neither, apparently, could he. When he broke the long silence, he still wouldn't meet her eyes.

"Okay, uh, okay. I guess that's it."

That was her cue. She got up and walked down the stairs, past the kitchen where Billie looked around, startled. Cindy got out before the couple could raise any questions, without a goodbye. He would have to explain it to them.

• • •

The next morning was going well. JJ and even sarcastic Kimberly grunted at her when they arrived—progress. Cindy was fully absorbed in the website when Gloria's loud voice came through from the hall. "Hello, Susan."

The little woman stormed in and headed straight for Cindy. "There you are. You were supposed to report to Arthur's area."

Oh. They were off at a trot to the elevators, where Susan held up a card to light the button for four. Then she handed it to her—a new ID. How, then, was she supposed to have reported to this floor?

Susan didn't acknowledge the contradiction, and Cindy decided to let it go, but it smelled like a setup.

Behind the desk in the lobby sat a heavy, middle-aged Black man in a guard's uniform. Unlike the one in the building's entrance, this one looked calm and friendly. Cindy would have been grateful for an introduction but had to settle for an exchange of smiles—his badge said Morris—as Susan rushed them into a large room crammed with people, desks, and monitors.

There were no cubicles and no apparent order or pattern, and the only sound was the clicking of keyboards. No one looked up as they wound through the maze toward the floor-to-ceiling glass, behind which she saw a conference room on the left, flanked by an office. Past these was the glass front of the building.

They reached the open door of the office. The man sat in front of the most impressive array of screens Cindy had yet seen. He was tall, with short, sandy hair and what might pass for formal wear in this place: crisp chinos rather than shredded jeans, an oxford shirt buttoned all the way up, and brown loafers. He held up a finger as they walked in and clicked away for several minutes before standing and peering down at them through black-framed glasses. When it came, the flat voice was pitched higher than she expected from such a tall man.

"Hello, Susan. And you must be Cynthia." His handshake was firm enough, and the eye contact was intense, but he looked quickly away when he dropped her hand as if it burned. "I'm Arthur."

This last was interrupted when a shaggy young man at a desk nearby slammed his palm down hard on his desk and let out a whiny growl. "Aarthuur!"

"Okay, Elmer, we'll close the door." He moved his gaze to Susan, who gave Cindy a look she couldn't read, patted her arm, and was gone, closing the door behind her.

Arthur motioned toward a nearby desk chair and returned to his own. "I'll show you what I've done so far." He pulled out a keyboard drawer and typed rapidly, his eyes on the screen to his right.

Assuming that was where she should be, she wheeled a chair to his side. "I know I'm a bit old for an intern, but I'm changing careers, and I've been working as a freelance web designer for about three years."

"I know," he said, without turning toward her. "Steven told me." *Okay.* "I've been roughing out a new version of our external website. Steven insists we need a portal for the public, not just for our tech customers. I realized I can't think like one of them—the public."

"And that's where I come in?" She wasn't sure she liked where this was going, but she was growing accustomed to that.

"I want to get your reaction, as someone who doesn't know anything, like you were coming upon our website by chance. Tell me if it makes you want to explore."

He moved his chair to the left and invited her to center herself before the big right-hand monitor and take over the mouse. She was confronted by blocks of text, some a line or two, others up to a dozen, some in boxes and some just stuck in space. There was no apparent visual theme, no indication of how they related to each other. The language was mostly indecipherable jargon. She had no idea where to begin, and caught herself sighing and shaking her head.

"It's problematic," he said. "Please be specific."

She pointed at the blocks of texts, mentioned the lack of any organizing principle, how she didn't understand the terminology, how there was no visual theme and nothing appealing to the eye. The explanation went on for a while, but he didn't stop her. He pecked out notes in a text file, then stopped.

When she noticed his stillness, she asked, "Is there some reason you want the public to explore the site? Anything you want to tell them?" He shrugged. She went on to say there was nothing inviting exploration, no place the user was asked to take action. At that, still keeping his eyes on his own screen, he said, "Okay, I've got what I need. Thank you. It was nice meeting you."

He stood and stuck out his hand. It couldn't have been more than twenty minutes, and now she was being dismissed. Worst of all, she deserved it: so worried about appearing incompetent, so intent on showing off her skills, she'd forgotten to be tactful, or even polite. Give a little feedback, then see how he takes it, get his thoughts. Basic awareness, a simple adjustment; that was all she'd needed to do. Now it was back to volunteering her services in the neighborhood—maybe the new dog-grooming place on Centre Street needed a better website.

Out in the lobby, Susan looked up from her phone. "Well, that didn't take long."

Was she laughing at her? Cindy searched her face but could find only amused sympathy. "Yeah" was all she could think to say.

"He's a busy man, our Arthur. And you, after all, are his mother's idea. He may think he has more important ways to spend his time."

Not more important to me, she thought, as they rode back down to her team. "I don't think I did very well, but it wasn't fair. I don't know what he really wanted. And I can't imagine that he could have formed an opinion of me that quickly."

Susan touched her upper arm. "He and his friends in there grew up in front of screens, coding, programming, hacking. I don't imagine it would take him long to figure out that you didn't. It's nothing personal."

"I've got to hope Charlotte will let me stay where I am, at least long enough to learn something."

"Or that she'll come up with something else especially for you, like she promised?" Again the smirk. It did sound ridiculous. "As soon as I hear from Charlotte, I'll let you know where you stand."

JJ and Estelle looked up when she walked in the room. Gloria hadn't acknowledged her on the way in, which was unusual for her.

"That was fast," said JJ. Was that a smirk from him too?

"Yeah," she answered.

"You're ahead of us," added Estelle. "The only time I was ever invited into the sanctum was to talk about their 401Ks. I don't think Arthur even bothered to come."

"Charlotte said that he often evaluates new people," said Cindy. "Is it usually this fast?"

Estelle pursed her lips. "I never heard that." She looked around, but JJ, Kimberly, and Jeannie had nothing to add but shrugs.

"Well, you're here," said Kimberly with a sigh. No one seemed thrilled.

• • •

It actually felt good to get back to the admin website, and she was able to distance herself from her anxieties as she entered her zone of concentration to the accompaniment of the now familiar background hum of the office. That sustained her until five or so, when the thoughts in her head began to intrude again. Would she be able to stay here, and would the team ever accept her? Did Charlotte mean it when she promised to give her another chance at a different role? What could that possibly involve?

The more Cindy thought about it, the more she trusted Susan. The assistant seemed grounded, in contrast to Charlotte and her acolytes. Cindy had been around her father enough to suspect intellectual pretensions, in contrast to her mother's more grounded idealism and purpose. What haunted her most was the feeling that she was close to a wonderful opportunity but could still fall short.

By 7:30, unable to pretend she could concentrate, she decided to go home.

When she surfaced to an awareness of her surroundings, she was in the lobby at the front desk. She'd confined herself to the salad bar for the past few days, but the prospect of losing her source of free food eroded her resolve. The vision of the frost steaming off a chocolate-covered Cherry Garcia Peace Pop fired her steps. Just the thing, a longish chew on something sweet and rich to provide the comforting gut-weight she'd been denying herself. The machines' glow drew her on as she turned left just before reaching the darkened kitchen.

Only, this evening the glow was muted by bright lights pouring out of the open door of the little show kitchen in the middle of the room. *Carlson or Miguel must be doing some prep work for tomorrow's feast.* More temptation to resist, but she was getting used to it. Still, she sniffed the air, teasing herself by trying to guess the ingredient, expecting onions, or maybe something exotic. What she got was vaguely familiar, maybe meaty, but she couldn't be sure. Definitely not onions or other aromatic veggies.

Now she had to know. She walked up to the open door, noting the muddy footprints nearby, out of place in the immaculate dining room. When she got close enough to look in, the fluorescent lights were blinding against the white walls and floor tiles, the glint of stainless steel everywhere else. As her eyes adjusted, she found herself staring at a mound of white cloth on the counter. Breaking the whiteness was a vertical oblong object, black with a glint of shiny silver below it, surrounded by bright red. Her mind was still looking to solve the food problem—what was being prepared here? The odd smell was overpowering, with a disturbingly foul underlayer.

Then, it clicked. A man lay on the counter, staring up at the ceiling light. His eyes, which should have been squinting against the glare, were wide open instead. The man's legs—the familiar white beard and long mustache told her it was a man—were indelicately splayed, and a little red waterfall trickled out from between them, over the curved edge of the steel counter, drip by drip onto the white tile floor, to join a pool inches from her own toes. Now she saw smears and splashes in other places—on the white uniform, spreading from around the very top of the broad blade of an alarmingly large kitchen knife that protruded from the man's midsection like a caricature of an erection.

A lurching tilt brought her eyes sideways and down to the pots stacked on the shelving under the side counter, then to the floor where a small pan lay upside down. She managed to catch herself before toppling over onto that same counter and then down to the floor; was still staring at the body when she found herself back outside the door in the larger room outside, far enough away to break the thread that tethered her. She stumbled back down the corridor toward the lobby.

Craig's cool glance changed when he saw her, and he was at her side, bearing her weight when her legs collapsed. He put her in his seat and pushed her head down between her knees, saying something she couldn't make out over the roar in her ears. When that began to subside, she had to wave her hand to get him to let her raise her head. Then she heard him ask her if she was okay, what happened, was she in pain? The babbling voice that answered didn't register as her own, and probably didn't help him much. He was on his intercom then, and Morris, the guard from Arthur's compound, appeared at her side as Craig pounded down the hallway to the dining room.

The older man looked at her with soft brown eyes. "Was it something you saw?"

Cindy found it hard to look squarely at the question, simple as it was. "The kitchen . . . Carlson, I think . . . has to be . . . blood, drips, splashes, a knife, really big, sticking straight up . . ."

Cindy saw his eyes widen before they disappeared into the buzzing haze, felt his hand on her forearm. Soon his words made it through. "Okay, that's okay, wait now, later. Craig is checking it out; you don't have to say anything. Just stay right here with me." And he was reaching for the telephone, murmuring to someone on the other end. Soon others were arriving, some staying and milling around, others running toward the dining hall or back to the elevators. Charlotte and Steven were there, and Craig, and she heard snatches of his clipped tones as he reported, ". . . the crazy dishwasher . . . blood all over him . . . retrieving his jacket," and "Yeah, right" with a snort from someone. "He went right by . . . could have stopped . . ." Then police burst through the front doors and men were shouting and Gloria was hoisting her up by the shoulders as they stumbled toward the elevators like drunks at closing time.

• • •

Pressed against Gloria on the sofa in Steven's office, Cindy heard herself babbling, only to be cut off. "Honey, you may as well wait and calm yourself. The police will be up here soon enough with all their questions. When they start in, just take your time and tell them everything you saw. Don't try to make sense of it or explain anything. That's their job. Just tell them what you saw, and try not to worry about anything beyond that. I'm thinking we might be here for a good long while. Anybody at home we should call?

Father. A couple of tries and she managed to say the number, and Gloria dialed. After what sounded like an argument despite Gloria's soft voice, the phone was in her hand. She told him there had been a bad accident, that she was fine but would have to be here a while, helping out. He wanted details, of course, but she cut him off. She had to go, would tell him about it later. Gloria was reaching for the phone when she hung up. She thought of apologizing, but she was tired and not really there.

Luiza, ConDo, the dishwasher, splendid . . . The dishwasher, covered in blood. Steven, in her interview—his lines kept running through Cindy's head. How could she explain she wasn't just another placement, one of Ralph's people? They would never want to see her again.

PART II

5

Cindy

Cindy's sleep was fitful, haunted by flashing images, disjointed dreams that, when they startled her awake, left behind no specific memory, only panic and dread. By five she felt groggy and drained but had had enough. Soon it would be time to go to work. Getting up now, she could get coffee first, here, at home.

She felt a deep fatigue in her limbs. Breathing felt like work. Setting her teeth, she thought if she could just get moving . . .

It was all too clear, from the casual remarks between the various police officers. The ConDo dishwasher had killed Carlson and run off. They would find him; only a matter of time. But nothing terrible had happened to her. There was no use wallowing in her feelings. *Just move.*

It didn't help. The hours spent waiting, then telling her story to the uniformed officer, reliving the horror, then waiting some more, then reliving it again when she had to repeat it to the older man in plain clothes, mostly succeeding at keeping at bay old memories of other interviews with other officers following the death of the child.

Showered and dressed now, she sat dully at the kitchen table over coffee, listening to the sounds of her father and brother dressing and getting ready for their days, trying not to think. Lately she had been leaving before they rose. There was comfort in those familiar sounds now. Then the telephone rang, and the memories flooded in.

She'd only recently begun answering the phone again, but now it was back, the icy grip to her gut that came every time it rang, sending her tumbling into the memory, helpless. She was seven years into child protection, a young veteran social worker with a caseload of beleaguered mothers and their children. It had happened so gradually, she couldn't have said when the numbness had begun, but by then she was going through the motions of filling out forms and following rules, presenting in meetings and choosing between bad alternatives. Should she leave the children with the (usually single) mother, to be abused and neglected, and watch the life in their eyes fade and die until they were fully shut down, little zombies? Or would it be better to rip them away to some crowded foster home, likely to be shuffled around every year or two, bullied and preyed upon by the older ones, with the same result?

Either way, there would be nothing to celebrate, and no one would thank her. Mothers, children, foster parents—long ago their hopeless, implacable hatred had left her hollow, emptied of compassion and strength. Still she met with her sullen mothers, sat with their children, gathered information, wrote her assessments and progress notes, followed procedure and relied on her supervisor, her team, anyone but herself, to make the decision.

And then there was David Harvey Ellison, four years old, with his nineteen-year-old mother who was three months sober, maybe, with the boyfriend who was not his father and was somehow never there when she visited. But the mother said he had a steady job, there was food in the apartment, the rent was paid—she wasn't about to rat them out to welfare, and there were others among the eighteen mothers and twenty-eight children she was responsible for who worried her a lot more.

One Saturday morning she was drinking coffee and staring at the little TV on her kitchen counter in the apartment she shared with her husband when the telephone rang. David was in intensive care. The details came drop by drop as she spoke to her supervisor and the police. A blow to the side of his head—a devastating injury. If he pulled through, extensive brain damage. Mother mute. Boyfriend nowhere to be found. Where was the social worker, the one charged with keeping the boy safe? What had she missed?

Most of her never went back. There was an investigation, but she couldn't remember anything from that time. It didn't matter. She knew she had failed. Three months later, while the investigation was going on, the boy flatlined—no brain activity, no possibility of recovery. There was a fight over when to pull the plug, but he died before it could gather steam; the only thing left to do was assign blame.

Though Cindy had already put that responsibility on herself, it came as a shock when her supervisor let slip that "there were questions to be resolved as to whether the social worker in charge had followed all applicable procedures." When pressed, the woman refused to elaborate, leaving everyone with the impression that Cindy had screwed up, that her carelessness had led to the boy's death. Nobody else in the office would comment or look her in the eye.

She had overstayed; that was her mistake—to think she could stay on the dizzying, numbing ride through misery and not screw up. She hated to give up, to admit she didn't have it in her to absorb and carry all that pain, couldn't grow the callouses she needed. She thought she might get there, and maybe she would have, had David not been killed, but she doubted it. She should have left long before.

Now, today, the phone kept on ringing. Cringing, she waited for the talking caller ID.

"This is Charlotte Harcourt calling all Back Door Technologies staff to inform you that our offices will be closed today because of the tragic death of our beloved chef Carlson Reveniste."

Cindy ran for the telephone.

"Hello, Charlotte? It's Cynthia. I'm here."

She flushed with embarrassment when she realized it was a recording. Charlotte's formal voice droned on. "Unless you are contacted and instructed otherwise, please do not come to work until you receive further instructions from this office." Refer any media to her, a new staff log-in on the website would provide news during the crisis, thank you, great sadness . . .

Cindy had the machine repeat it twice but couldn't take it in. Her father had just come into the kitchen by the time she shuffled back to her coffee, weighted by the heaviness she thought she had left behind.

"You're up early," he said. "Did you get enough sleep?"

"As much as I could. I thought I was going in to work, but they called. I'm not essential, so I'm locked out, at least for today. The rest of the week, sounds like."

"Well, that's a blessing. You sit. Paul is just about up. I'll make us some eggs."

The coffee was thin and bitter, and food didn't sound much better, but she didn't have the energy to object. She wanted to go back to her room. Family time hadn't been all that happy lately, but the thought of going back to bed, to the images in her head, kept her stuck to her chair. She tried to make her mind go blank. Maybe one of them would get it and just leave her alone.

Right.

She did get her wish for a while. Her father's humming as he puttered around the kitchen was irritating, so she turned the radio on. Of course, it was on the news, murder at the tech company in Cambridge. She dragged herself up again and turned it off, then plopped back down and put her chin in her hand.

Paul came into the room, gave her a soft hello and a long look. He sat across from her and busied himself with the *Globe* newspaper he had brought in with him. The irritation that rose in her was sudden and overwhelming.

"Look, I'm okay. No one stabbed *me*. It was just a long, bad night, that's all. I'm fine."

Her father looked over. "If you'd like to talk about it—"

"That might not be the best thing, Father," Paul interrupted softly. "Cin, it sucks, what you just went through, and I can see it's not okay, but this isn't the time to relive it. Let's just have breakfast together. You need time and space right now. And food."

She felt a wave of relief. He was right; she'd spent the night telling the story over and over to the police, both in uniform and not. Maybe Paul was more thoughtful than she'd assumed.

"I defer to the expert," rumbled her father. "If you're done with the lecture, maybe you could get us some plates and stuff, and we can eat these eggs while they're hot."

It was the kind of interaction, the grumpy rhythm of their family during its best times, that gave her comfort. After some gentle pressure, she managed to eat a full plate of crusty eggs. Her brother quietly made herbal tea for himself—he was cutting back on caffeine—and, to her surprise, pressed a cup on her as well. He never told her what to do, so she found it impossible to complain now. It was better than the coffee, but when had her brother learned to care for others?

· · ·

Try as she might, there seemed to be no way for Cindy to stop her thoughts running around a short loop. Interspersed with flashes of Carlson lying in his blood was the conviction that now that the dishwasher had murdered Carlson, everyone at Back Door would recoil from all things ConDo, its world of disability and misfortune, and that would include herself. They would call her soon to tell her she wasn't what they were looking for, and Paul and Ralph's world would have reached out to claw her back. She put her elbows on the table, head in both hands.

When the cleanup was done, her father went to his desk in the living room to begin his workday. Paul stayed at the table, reading the paper. She looked over at him, staring until he looked up. "Well, it looks like you'll beat me out of here after all."

"Oh?" he said. "How come? I thought you were going to go apartment hunting as soon as they started paying you. Did something else happen?"

She snorted. "What, you think they're going to hire me now? After yesterday? They found me through the Stewart Center."

"But what's that got to do with anything? You're not deranged like Johnnie . . ." She must have looked blank. "He's the dishwasher from the Center—or me."

She knew she should back off, take it back, but she had a surge of energy for the first time that day, and didn't feel like stopping. "Don't make this about you. They were talking at Billie's about the risk reviews ConDo is making them do. Too bad they didn't start sooner. Ralph and his little group are fighting them every step of the way. It's all about opportunity for them.

"Well, this guy Johnnie got his opportunity, and he used it to murder someone, so don't start in with that bullshit about coercive this and forced that. This is about murder, and me trying to climb out of this rut and getting dragged back by the Stewart Center and Ralph." *And you*—she barely managed to stop herself in time. But his eyes—it was as if she'd said it out loud. "So much for my opportunity. It's gone."

The silence dragged on until Paul pushed his chair back and stood. "First off, I think we should wait before we assume that Johnnie murdered anyone." He wouldn't look at her now. "But I guess you never can tell about us crazy people. Maybe I'll go and shoot up Elder Affairs. That would really hold you back." And then he was off to the Stewart Center to begin his day.

More than his words, she could tell by the way he held his shoulders, the stiffness in his walk, how badly she had hurt him. At least now she had the room to herself. She tried again to make her mind go blank, to avoid the image of Carlson with the knife sticking up like a stamen out of the red bloom of his belly. When the shaking started, she paced. More tea didn't help. Later, when her father came in to get some lunch, she mumbled an excuse and fled to her room.

• • •

Cindy dragged herself like a slug over sand through most of the afternoon while her thoughts continued their slow, sickening tumble. If anyone from Back Door called, her father would get her. When they didn't, she allowed herself a speck of hope, then brushed it aside. Charlotte had more important things to deal with. Someone would get to her eventually. Or maybe they'd just forget her.

The soft knock startled her. Father. Someone here to see her. Would they deliver the news in person?

"Who?" she managed.

"Her name is Emma, says you know her, from ConDo."

Great. The people she longed to see wouldn't have anything to do with her. Like many in Ralph's circle, Emma had become her friend too, but it still felt like the ones she was trying to escape wouldn't leave her alone.

"Tell her I'll call later. I don't feel like talking."

Her father shook his head. "She's come over specially to see you. If you don't feel up to talking, at least come down and tell her yourself."

He left before she could argue, leaving the door open. Getting bossed around sucked. *Got to get the hell out of this house, for good this time.* But not today.

The little woman sat at the dining table, very erect, hands in her lap. Tight dark curls surrounded oversized glasses. She bounced up when Cindy came in and hugged her hard. "Paul called me. I had to come over and see how you were doing."

"I'm okay. I should be at work, but they're, uh, they told me to stay home—that is, all of us, or most, anyway. For now, for the week, I don't know." It was appalling to hear herself whine, but she couldn't stop. Emma locked eyes with her and waited. The stare annoyed Cindy, and that helped her stop. Then she understood. "Is this an official visit—the trauma team?" Ralph's group of volunteers from various ConDo programs helped people get over upsetting experiences at work.

The woman sighed, took a step back. "Can we sit down, at least for a minute? You don't have to talk to me. I'm sorry to barge in, but you've probably heard how this works."

She had, from Ralph, over and over. If you called ahead, only about 15 percent agreed to talk. If you went in person—ambushed them, as Emma had—the percentage rose to 50.

Emma went on. "It's up to you. I'm not going to ask you to tell me what happened. I just want to hear how you're coping. I can tell you the kinds of things you could experience after a shock like this, and some things to do that people have found helpful."

It was hard to stay mad at Emma. Cindy couldn't stay cut off from everyone, and after pushing Paul away, God only knew how she'd make that right. She slumped and gave in.

Emma handed her an information sheet and ran down some of the things people experienced: loss of appetite, difficulty sleeping, irritability, problems concentrating—the list was too long to get through.

"It's the flashbacks, mostly," said Cindy. "I saw him—the body, blood—and I can't seem to get the image out of my head. And I care about those people, but . . . I don't think I can go back."

"I know it can be rough, where you had the experience, but give yourself some time."

"No," Cindy interrupted, "it's not that. They told us all to stay home while they sort things out, but they're not going to want me around, a reminder that a member from the Center—Lu—set me up with them."

"Yeah, Paul said. But is it really clear that Johnnie did it?"

Cindy found herself standing over Emma, yelling. "Oh, come on, Emma. Who else? Craig saw him just a little bit before. The guy said he came to get his jacket, and when he came back out holding it, blood was dripping on the floor. Craig said he didn't know what to think at the time, but he didn't know then. Who else would want to kill him? Lu said he had a troubled background. God, I love the way you people talk. Now I see why you need all the euphemisms."

Emma held up both hands but didn't seem intimidated. "Okay. I'm sorry, that was dumb of me. I can see that being cut off from your friends there is really hard, but I wouldn't assume that people there won't want you back." She paused, then went on even more softly. "Maybe just take one thing at a time, for now."

If the woman was hurt by what Cindy had said, she hid it well. Suddenly tired, Cindy fell back onto her chair, putting her head back into her hands while the soft voice droned on.

"This is a hard thing for anyone to go through. Part of the way people cope is to blame someone, to somehow make sense of it. If it's someone's fault, even your own, the world doesn't seem like such a random, dangerous place; we feel like we have some control over our lives. If Johnnie did it, he did it. But blaming you—the Center, ConDo maybe, but—I don't see it. What you're going through is normal, but things will feel better in a couple of weeks. The images in your head will feel more like remembering, not like you're living through it all over again."

Emma came over and put an arm around her shoulder. Her anger spent, Cindy allowed it to stay there while the other woman went on. "By the way, have you been out of the house at all today? If you can't face people, maybe just a walk? It's important to take care of your body, to let it move and breathe. And eat, even though you don't feel like it. I'll check back in with you in a couple of days and see how it's going—all right?"

Too tired to argue, she agreed. Apparently, it would be harder to drive this woman away than it had been with Paul.

Emma seemed to follow her thoughts. "And I spoke with Paul. He'll get past the . . . words this morning. We've all said things that hurt the people close to us when we were in a dark place. When you talk about how much it sucks, what happened, without laying into the people you love, that's step one on the road back."

Her smile brought tears to Cindy's eyes, and they were hugging again. Shortly after Emma left, her father came in, as softly as a man his size could. Reverend Abernathy never could manage unobtrusive. His voice was uncharacteristically soft, though, as he sat in the chair Emma had just left and took Cindy's hand. "So, have you run enough people off for one day?"

"You were listening."

At least he had the decency to look sheepish. "I worry about you. What you saw, it's beyond what most of us have to go through."

That's when it hit her. She had never told anyone here how she had discovered the body. "How did Emma know? That it was me, who found . . . ?"

"That nice lady from work, Gloria, last night on the phone. God forbid you'd confide in your own flesh and blood." He said it gently, though. "I know you want to move out, and I want that for you, but I'm glad you're still here. Let us take care of you a little—you deserve it. And we'll see how things go with this Back Door place. You're a good judge of people, and you felt good about them. Give them a chance."

He led her into the living room, and they sat together and watched soaps for the rest of the afternoon.

6

Paul

The Stewart Center is downtown, in this old, used-to-be-city building on a side street to nowhere that's more like a parking lot for our neighbor, the Precinct 17 station. That's why people smoking out front don't think it's strange that two cruisers are parked across from our front door with a pair of coffee-drinking uniforms in each one.

But after an hour, word's made it inside, and a few of us nonsmokers are out to have a look. I heard it from Cindy last night—we stayed up until she came home, Father and me—but no one else knows what to expect when Johnnie, our young White rapper, comes jive-walking around the corner. There's a crowd to watch the cops boil out of their cars, all blue black and shiny like roaches scuttling out from under the kitchen stove, two of them tackling the boy and pinning him to the pavement, the other two waving guns at us, yelling, "Stay back, stay back."

The boy has to be at least twenty-two to be in our program, but he looks younger, with a crooked nose he probably got in Bridgewater, the prison mental hospital where he was not long ago, his eyes still blue-shadowed where it happened. I spent time there at his age, and I know how he feels when they come up on him. I see him shut down, just a grunt when he hits the pavement face-first, his arms pulled back already so they can cuff him. One of the things you learn in that place: you put up any kind of fight, it gets way worse. Better to learn that watching someone else's beating. Of course, I learned it the other way, hard, but that's a story for another time.

I can just see his eyes past the cop's knee mashing down the side of his head—empty gray stones. When they drag him over to the car, blood pouring from his nose stands out bright red against his blue-white Irish chin, so the cop pushing his head down has to scrooch back to keep his nice white shirt clean as he stuffs him into the back seat for the short backwards ride up our little street to their basement garage. There's no telling what will happen to him down there. I suppose his white skin might just save him.

It's all over by the time the cries from the crowd mix with the shouts of the bully cops and bring more folks outside, all of us buzzing about what the hell just happened, trying to figure out what we can do, which is, of course, nothing. We feel bad for the guy, but truth is, we don't know him that well. He's one of the sneering young men they send over here, hoping we'll keep them out of trouble. They clump together and practice pushing us around, telling each other they won't become one of us, the chronics folks try not to see. Anyway, he's one of us now. Once you step in the door, you're a member, and we care about you, no matter what.

Everyone standing out here knows life can turn brutal and unfair, and the damage, they know about that too. This is going to touch all of us, even some who got jobs and moved on from this place. Johnnie thought he could get away from a life in foster care, those years in mental hospitals, all the hard time, all that damage. Now, thirty more years in the worst of those places may be the best he can hope for, the young thug, the maniac, the killer.

This is bad for all of us. All the talk of crazed killers you hear on TV and read in the paper, it's come right to our door. When you look in the papers after some killing, the first thing you think is *Let it be one of those others, not someone hears voices, not someone Black*. Maybe an Arab or a White supremacist—that'd be nice, except they'll dig up some kind of history and call him crazy too. First thing they'll ask: Was he in treatment? Taking his pills? Maybe not enough. Who was watching him? Then it's, *We tried to be nice to those folks and look where it got us.*

We're all of us going back to school now, the hard one, get our lessons.

7

Cindy

Cindy slept better that night and, finding herself wide awake at six, made coffee and sat at the kitchen table again, this time reading the paper. *Get out of the house*, Emma had said, so she decided to take Bruno for a walk around Jamaica Pond. The self-absorption of the joggers and dog walkers made it easy to avoid any interaction, and the exercise did feel good.

When she came into the kitchen, her father was finishing his breakfast. "I made us a cheese omelet; saved you some."

It was her favorite growing up, but her father had never cooked it. She was amazed he could pull it off.

"By the way," he said, "you had a call."

Oh God. It suddenly occurred to her it would be him, Ralph. *Fucking Ralph!* It would be just like him to try to weasel his way back to her. He loved to help people; it validated him. He wouldn't pass up the opportunity.

But it wasn't Ralph.

"Gloria called from Back Door," said her father. "I told her you would be back soon, and she said she wanted to come over to see you. I didn't think you'd mind." He said this last without meeting her eyes. He was a hopeless liar; she always thought it a great liability in his profession. Thank God it hadn't been Ralph. Her father would have invited him over. He loved him.

"I've been waiting for that shoe to drop. It's classy of them, to do it in person."

Which made the loss even harder to think about. She hurried through breakfast so she could get cleaned up. Might as well make a good last impression.

As she came downstairs, she heard her father greet someone at the front door. She caught up with them as they entered the living room. Though she should have expected it, Gloria's appearance came as a shock. Her permed waves were a wreck, eyes bloodshot. Cindy hadn't realized the woman wore makeup, but its lack was obvious now, and she looked older without it. Her usually erect posture was replaced by slumped shoulders, and there was a vague, wandering quality to her eyes. She approached Cindy slowly and enveloped her in a lingering hug.

"It was so nice to meet you," Gloria said to Cindy's father after releasing her. "I hope we can talk sometime soon."

It took her father a beat to get the idea, but then he nodded and left the room.

"I'm sorry," said Gloria. "I meant to at least check on you yesterday, but it's been frantic over there. Your father says you're feeling a bit better, but I can't imagine, finding Carlson like that . . ."

Seeing the dark bags under Gloria's eyes, Cindy decided to take control. She hadn't realized the woman was close to Carlson. Gloria looked awful, yet she had come herself, to let Cindy down gently. "And I can't imagine what it must be like for you. It means a lot to me, you doing this in person."

"Steven wanted to make sure. Not just him, the whole team. As you can imagine, he's devastated." Gloria dropped her head, unable to continue.

"They were close friends?"

The woman looked to the side, flustered. "Not friends. Husband and . . ."

Oh. Cindy was shocked, but then, she had never seen them together or heard them refer to each other.

"He's . . . He came in . . . Charlotte sent him home. I'm so worried. There's no one else, and I can't help thinking about him sitting home by himself."

Gloria looked about to cry, so Cindy took her arm and led her to the sofa, to give her some time.

"Charlotte would have come herself, but she's so busy with all this, and she thought, especially where . . ." *What, I would be more comfortable getting the axe from another Black woman?* "She was hoping you'd understand."

Ah. This was her cue to be gracious, to make it easier on everyone. "I understand. I'd like you to thank Charlotte, and Steven. And say goodbye to the team." She hated the pathetic little hiccup as she choked up, tears filling her eyes. She didn't even like most of her teammates.

The woman was startled for a moment, then looked sad. "Well, I was afraid you'd say that, and I do understand. But you must be in shock now. Why not give it a few days? If you still feel—"

"Look, I get it. I came through Lu. I'm the last person anyone will want around."

Gloria looked startled and reached for her hand. "Oh, honey, no one's blaming you. Good Lord, you had to find him. You take a day or two before you start back. I'd understand if you never wanted to, but I thought—I hoped there was a little more to you."

Gloria held her gaze, and Cindy saw some steel come back for the first time since she'd entered. It took a minute to realize what the woman was saying, and to get over her relief enough to realize she was being challenged. Then it was her turn to give the hug, complete with tears dripping on the other woman's shoulder. She was so happy they hardly registered. When she realized what she was doing, she pulled away. What must Gloria think of her, carrying on like this when the woman had lost someone who meant so much?

"Don't worry about me. I'm just thrilled I can keep working with all of you," Cindy said.

This brought a big smile from Gloria, but then she seemed to remember the weight of events again, and the light in her eyes flickered out. "Well, there is one . . . I think, given the connection you mentioned, it might be best for you to stay with Arthur's team for now. Steven, when he comes back—I'll straighten him out, I can promise you that, but it will take . . . Right now, he needs time."

So, her fears hadn't been groundless. How much might she owe Gloria for keeping her job? Things were beginning to get awkward when Father came in, bearing coffee and banana bread on a tray. Homemade baked goods from his church ladies were a cherished benefit of the job. He stayed, and when Gloria complimented him on "his beautiful rectory," he deftly steered the conversation to small talk about his congregation, then to the church she attended.

They chatted away, ignoring Cindy, until he gently broached the subject of Gloria's loss, and there was the Reverend Abernathy in action, doing his condolence thing. Given Cindy's church avoidance, it had been a long time since she'd witnessed him in action, but she had to admit he was pretty smooth.

• • •

Gloria had left with some of the spark back in her eyes, and Cindy was thinking again about how to structure the external web page. She thought of identifying the different audiences, developing a different feel for each interface. What Charlotte said about Back Door being a family—was there some way to work that in, as a unifying theme? Cindy used her laptop to create an organizational chart for the site structure. She couldn't wait to leave for work the next morning. When the doorbell rang, she easily beat her father to the front door.

It was Emma. Wasn't it a bit soon for her to be back?

"Hi, Cindy? Is this an okay time to chat? I know I was just here, but I didn't want to let things go too long."

Cindy was reluctant to abandon her work but didn't want to be rude, so she offered to make the woman coffee.

"I never say no to caffeine," Emma replied. When Cindy shared her good news, the other woman held her gaze, looking thoughtful. "I can see this has made you feel a lot better. These people must be important to you, and that's what you need, to connect with the important people in your life."

That's not exactly it, thought Cindy. It was the job, the opportunity. She hardly knew the people, though she did feel closer to Gloria now.

Emma asked about her sleep, appetite, and exercise, and seemed pleased with the answers. Then she asked whether she had spoken to Paul. Cindy thought it was a funny question, but then remembered lashing out the day before, when she was at a low point. He had run right to his friends for support.

"He and Phyllis came over for dinner yesterday. We talked."

Why should Cindy feel guilty about feeling good? It was her brother, anyway, and she had stood by him when he wasn't exactly a joy to be around.

Before she could think of how to put any of that into words without seeming ungracious, Emma said, "I was hoping he might have spoken to you about, uh . . ." She looked down, then made eye contact, almost defiant. "We need your help."

"We?"

"Me, Ralph, Sophie, Billie. With you going back to work . . ."

She seemed to gather herself, try again.

"We're having a meeting at Billie's tonight. Dr. Marsha was already on the warpath about risk management, and this is going to make everything worse. We have to come up with a strategy. And there's Johnnie. The police will assume he did it. It looks like the higher-ups at ConDo are planning to distance themselves from him and lay the blame on the Center. We could sure use your help."

Cindy sat back in her chair. "So, you're coming to drag me back into your problems, under the guise of checking in."

"Come on, Cindy. I care about you, and you went through an awful experience. It's great that you're recovering, but you're the only one on the inside. If you can't, I'll understand; we all will. I didn't come here just to put the arm on you."

"Okay, enough. It seems like all of a sudden, I'm in demand. But you want me to help your dishwasher, and the rest of you, to . . . to weasel out of this mess. I won't do it." She stared at Emma until the other woman stood up.

"I'm sorry. That was pretty clumsy of me. But people are getting hurt. I'll check back in with you, maybe early next week."

"Don't bother. Really, I'm moving on, just like you said. You guys work on your own problems. I know it's a big deal in your world; it's just different now, for me."

And she watched the door close on her former friend.

8

Paul

Back upstairs at the Stuart Center, I was upset enough about the way things had gone with Cindy and the arrest that I had to talk to someone. In my life, the main people are my father and sister, Ralph, and Phyllis. Ralph got me over to the Center, but Phyllis made me feel capable and useful for the first time since I was a kid. As I gained her trust, I started feeling smart, and folks were finally starting to appreciate what I had to offer.

A couple of years back, in my first days there, I was sitting on the fringes. Mostly it was a place to stay indoors during the day—I was sleeping at a homeless shelter, and they didn't let you hang around all day. I'd been at the Center less than a week when they started asking me to help out in the kitchen, and to escape that, I needed a place to blend in and disappear. Stewart Center's got this area on the first floor called Communications, where folks get together and do a newsletter, outreach, take attendance, all that kind of office work. I went down to check it out one afternoon, this big room with computer desks around the outside and long tables filling up the middle. Tables seemed exposed, so I grabbed a chair in front of a computer, which is how I met Phyllis. She came over and kicked me off, and I had to go sit at the tables after all.

She was there when I walked in the next morning, but I still thought she was nobody special. This young staff guy, Frank, runs the meeting that gets everything set up every morning, and Phyllis never said anything. It took me the rest of that week to figure out that she was into everything, and a while after that I realized she ran the show. My first couple of days there, she left me alone. The third morning, she came over after the meeting.

"You might not remember, but I spoke with you the other day about collating the newsletter and getting it ready for mailing." She must have said something about that when she kicked me off my seat by the computer.

She was thin, White, around Cindy's age, in a sweater buttoned all the way up the front and a skirt over her knees. Reminded me of a substitute teacher, ready to try but worried things weren't going to go well. She waited for me to say something, but I just sat there, so she had to be the one. "I'm sorry, I don't mean to push. You looked like you might like to get involved."

Where'd she get that idea? Still, I could see it was hard for her to look at me, and her voice was quiet enough I had to strain to hear, so even then, wrapped up in my own head, I could tell she was making an effort, and I didn't want to be mean, so I said sure, whatever.

That's when she did the thing with her hair. It's straight, dark, falls over her face. Where most people would be moving the hair away from their eyes, she does this thing with her fingers, like she's pulling it back in front, and that's when she looks at me full on, through the hair. I didn't know then how I'd come to love it, the hair thing.

She got me to volunteer that morning, and once you do that, it's all over for you at the Center. I wasn't able to say no to Phyllis anyway—still can't—and being the ruthless type, she wasn't about to let me off the hook. I liked her right away, but I think at first she just kept coming over because I didn't screw things up as bad as some of the others. She's nice to everyone, but I noticed this thing she does with her lips, pressing them together just for a beat or two, that says you messed it up and she's going to have to fix it. She'll do the lip thing and then say, "Thank you, that's great," and that's how you know she's not pleased.

I always work hard to make sure she never says that to me. If you do it right so she won't have to do it over herself, she'll just take it, do the hair thing, and give you a nod before she turns away and goes back to her work. It's not her way to gush. She'd say it's not her place, she's just a member in the unit, but everyone there knows better. She runs the newsletter operation, the literary journal, all the creative stuff.

Once they got me the job at Elder Affairs, I was away from the Center most of the day. I started missing her, and I had sense enough to do something about it. I asked her out to dinner, big man with the paying job, and she said yes. It's been a year and seven months since I started that job, and I only stop by the Center once or twice a week, but she comes over to eat with Father and Cindy and me two or three nights and always on Sunday, so I guess you could say we're together. I'd love to get our own place, but then her disability check would get cut back, and with me still only working part-time . . .

Someday, though, we're going to do it. I'd like to see her working and out in the world—anyplace would be lucky to have her.

We talk this morning about Johnnie's arrest and what it might mean for all of us, and then I start in complaining about Cindy before Phyllis stops me. "That doesn't sound like her. Was she upset about something?"

I know right then I'm in trouble, but I don't see a way out, so I tell her how Cindy found the body.

"And just when were you going to tell me that part? After you got over your bruised feelings?"

Some people say you pick a woman to match the ones you already have in your life. Mother wouldn't stand for any nonsense, and Cindy's the same, so of course I went and found one of the same variety. I guess I'm going to have to take care of my own bruise, because Phyllis is hell-bent on coming over this evening to check on Cindy. Just as well she stopped me before I dug myself in deeper.

We find Cindy and Father watching TV. Cindy seems a lot calmer, and the fact she won't look at me makes it better somehow, like she knows things went badly. Phyllis is shy and normally not a hugger, but she holds on to Cindy, and they both cry without saying much. Father looks relieved to have someone else for Cindy to hold on to, and he orders fried chicken, and we sit together in the kitchen and eat without anyone saying anything worth remembering. I volunteer to clean up. There isn't much, and I have the sense I might need the points. When I get done and join them in the living room, Cindy has out the drawing I showed her, and they're both laughing.

Phyllis: "He does look kind of shifty."

Cindy: "Like in that movie, *The Fugitive*."

Father: "More like the older one on TV, kind of hunching down his shoulders, flinching, like someone was going to hit him."

Phyllis sees me come in. "I did that one early on, a couple of days after I met you. You were a sorry sight, but interesting. It was my first portrait since school. Still lifes are safer."

"You mean he doesn't look like a hunted animal anymore?" My sister. I'm thinking she doesn't look so great herself since yesterday, but I'm sure nothing like that shows on my face.

"Don't worry." Phyllis touches my shoulder. "You're still my muse."

I go upstairs then and bring down the one she did of Cindy. Phyllis gives me a dirty look when she sees it, but it's too late now. I unroll it for Cindy, and she loves it, I can tell, in spite of what she says.

"Oh. Are my cheeks really that round?"

"That's what they call artistic license," says Father. "You look cherubic; my little angel."

I point out the way she gets her eyes, that spark they have, and Phyllis looks pleased, before she frowns and looks down.

"If I'm a cherub," says Cindy, "you can do one of Father with a white beard, looking mean, like the Lord."

"Like in the Old Testament," I add.

Father stares at the ceiling with his hands clasped together. "Lord

Jesus, where did I go wrong?" It's quite a show, and helps us get through the evening, until Phyllis gives me the look, and I take her home. It's not even eleven when I get back, but the others have gone to bed.

• • •

The next morning I find Cindy in the kitchen, working on her laptop. It's weird, like the last couple of days never happened. I'm not sure that's good. She goes on a while about how she's being welcomed back, how excited and relieved she is, how fair minded they are, how they believe in her. Almost seems to have a manic edge, but then, who am I to talk? Now that I don't have to feel sorry for her, it should make my job easier.

"Look, I see now why this place is so important to you. I'd be excited too, but I don't get why you've got to turn your back on friends and family. We've stood by you too," I say, knowing full well I wasn't there for her when she needed me the most, "and we need you now." I know it's not fair, but I try not to let that show.

"Oh, Paul, it's not . . ." She looks sympathetic, sorry herself, just for a moment. Then her mouth sets, her eyes flash, and I get the other sister. "Don't make like it's my problem; that's not fair." Damn, she worked it out. "You're not Johnnie Christopher. You and your friends aren't killers, of course I get that, but it sure looks like this guy is. You're my brother. I love you. I'm proud of the way you brought yourself back, and I appreciate all the things your friends did for you, but you managed it without killing anybody."

"But I was like him, young and angry. I could have been accused of something like this. Would you want folks to assume that I did it, just because of who I was and where I'd been?"

"What does it matter what I think? It's got nothing to do with me. I'm an intern, that's all."

"You might be able to help. All I'm asking is that you come to Billie's tonight, have a meal and some wine, talk things over."

"And then say no to Billie, Emma, the whole crew, along with you, when they ask me to screw up my chance at a new life by advocating for the guy who murdered Carlson? Is that all?"

"I know I owe you, not the other way around. You stood by me, kept coming back to visit your pathetic brother in that stupid house when you could have just done like everyone else. More than that, tracking me down at the shelter, connecting with folks at the Stewart Center—no way I can even that out. You were willing to put yourself out for me, even if it wasn't easy."

I can see her eyes roll, but they're softening.

"You believed in me, and it made all the difference, but Ralph, Sophie, Billie—they believed in me too. I'd be back in that group home, counting the steps and watching TV with Archie, if it wasn't for them." I don't need to remind her that she pushed me to return to the group home instead. "I can't turn my back on them now, just like they won't abandon Johnnie."

"That's different."

"Not really. Everyone deserves a second chance. It was my turn then. Now it's his."

"And what about me? What about my chance?"

"Of course you get your chance too. Everybody on the team is behind you, and they're going to stay there. Don't forget, we wouldn't be having this conversation if Lu hadn't turned you on to Back Door."

I've got to say, I'm proud of the way I saved that one for last. It pushes her over. And I didn't mention Ralph, who we both know will be there. That has to be a sore point—I know he misses her a lot, so it won't be easy for him either.

"Okay," she says with a sigh. "Help me get something together for Father to eat when he gets home."

I try not to look pleased with myself; can't pull it off. She laughs, so do I, and then she punches me in the shoulder, way too hard.

9

Cindy

When they arrived late and walked into Billie's living room, most of the take-out containers had been cleared away. Ralph met Cindy's gaze, then looked away, but not before she saw the spark of hope fade in his eyes. Everybody greeted the siblings when they came in, but only Billie was willing to hold Cindy's gaze. Even Spot, their little adopted mutt, seemed cooler than usual. Ralph's family had closed ranks. Emma was on the love seat. The seat next to her was vacant, but Cindy wasn't ready to make peace with her. Instead she took the frayed wing chair on the other side of their little circle, and Paul sat next to Emma while Billie and Ralph occupied sagging easy chairs and Grace bustled in and out of the room.

Billie brought them into the conversation. "Ralph's been bringing us up to date on the fallout from the murder."

"It's hard to say what's happening," he said, frowning. "There's obviously a lot going on behind the scenes, but no one's saying much. Except, of course, Carolyn has told me how important it is to refer all media inquiries to Martin's office. No one else is supposed to say anything to anybody: keep quiet, they're working on it, let them handle it. Johnnie, by the way, is in custody, but that's all I know. I don't know if he's been charged?"

Everyone in the room looked at the others.

Emma asked, "What does Sophie say?"

"So far, not much to report," said Ralph. "She promised to get here as soon as she could get away. It must be wild at the Center." Then he turned toward Cindy, his eyes focused on her knees. "Uh, thanks for coming, Cindy. I'll get you some dinner."

"Thank Paul," she said to his retreating back. This drew a bitter smile out of Emma, so she added, "And Emma."

Billie's rough voice came next. "Yeah, you *should* thank them. I was gonna come over next. Trust me, no one would want that."

The chuckles of agreement were a bit forced, but they lightened things a bit. Then she grew serious.

"Let's not forget our biggest problem. We've got a member in jail. Someone's got to support him, make sure his rights are protected, keep him from getting screwed. He's already lost his case manager, and my guess is no one else outside of the Center knows him very well."

"Worse than that," said Ralph, "Sophie says he hardly knows anyone there. He's in this group of young men who stay on the fringe."

Emma added, "I know him, and I agree. Trust doesn't come easily for these young guys. Five years out of foster care, no family—he must feel so alone right now."

Billie said, "He's going to need a good lawyer, if they charge him."

"He needs one right now," said Ralph. "They'll want to get him talking before they charge him. A lawyer told me once, nothing you say to police is likely to help you; it's always best to stay silent."

"He probably won't want to talk, but if he's scared enough . . ." said Emma.

This finally got to be too much for Cindy. "But he did it. Well, didn't he?"

This got a gasp from everyone. Cindy felt all their eyes on her, but anger overrode her discomfort.

"Carlson. He had a name. He was a nice man. Everybody there loved him, you could see it, even the member who had the job before Johnnie. My first day, he went out of his way to put me at ease. He was lying there, this huge knife sticking out of him, blood—"

People were making conciliatory, calming noises now, but she could barely hear them.

"Johnnie ran away. And he was covered in Carlson's blood. He should just confess. You can get mad at Martin and Carolyn all you want. I know they're pretty awful sometimes, but this isn't their fault. I don't care how alone he feels now. He killed a kind, wonderful man, and I don't feel sorry for him. I can't."

The silence that stretched out was broken softly by Emma. "Not all of you know, Cindy was . . . She found the body, pretty soon after it happened."

There were gasps from Grace and Billie, but no one seemed to know what to say. Grace, though, stood and put her arm around her shoulder. "Oh, my poor child, how awful."

Only Billie seemed able to meet her eyes. Her tone was almost gentle. "That's the thing, Cindy. Just because he ran doesn't mean he's guilty. He could have come on the scene just the way you did. You could see how he could get blood on himself, freak out, and run."

She hadn't thought of that. It seemed unlikely, but not impossible.

"Paul tells me you're going back tomorrow, so you got to be one tough cookie—like we didn't already know."

The door banged open then, and Sophie strode in. There was always a formal dignity about her, but now she seemed so angry she was on the edge of control. After perfunctory greetings, and another plate of food hastily assembled by Ralph, she sat next to Emma on the love seat. Everyone waited to hear her news.

"I'm sorry to be so late, but the place is on fire. Martin showed up with Carolyn and Marsha—when was the last time those three came to any of our events? They told me to stop everything and bring everyone together. Then the pronouncements started, crazy things. No warning. I find out along with everyone else; no way to comment or object."

"Fucking bastards!" growled Billie. As the founding director of the Center, she would understand better than anyone what it would mean to have Sophie's authority undercut in front of her staff and membership.

"All employment placements suspended pending review by Dr. Marsha."

"A fucking witch hunt," said Ralph.

"They are focusing on the decision to send Johnnie onto a job placement. Lu has been suspended pending 'a complete and thorough investigation of our screening procedures.'" Under other circumstances, Sophie's imitation of Carolyn's prim cadence would have been funny. "All the while they're staring at me like I would be suspended as well if they had their way. Martin, on the other hand, wouldn't meet my eye. Oh, and Shepard Linsky, Johnnie's case manager on the outreach team—a nice young man, he comes often, used to meet Johnnie in the dining room—he's suspended as well. I tried to get Lu to come here with me, but she's too upset."

"They're running for cover," said Billie, "throwing out a couple of scapegoats to appease the big shots."

"You mean, all those people on transitional employment can't go to work?" said Emma. "That's not fair. They'll lose their jobs?"

"And we'll be combing through everyone's clinical records now," Ralph added, "searching for anything they did, however long ago, that could look bad. If we find anything, they won't be allowed back to work. And they'll want everyone clamping down, making sure they're taking their medications, monitoring and documenting their every move. It's CYA time."

"Shit," said Emma. "It's a good thing they can't get their hands on my old records: I'd be out on my ass. But that's probably why Carolyn is too busy to meet with me, and I'm totally out of the loop. It just brings home the basic conflict: are you working to help us in our recovery, or is your job to protect everyone else from the crazies?"

For the first time that day, Cindy felt some sympathy for the woman. It must have been uncomfortable being the first person with a psychiatric disability in a leadership role at ConDo. She'd always had to be careful, but now they would want her to choose sides.

"Okay, kiddies," said Billie, drawing herself up straighter, "it's no more than I expected. Management is in damage control mode. Awful as it might seem, there's no way we can fight them on it directly. That means pledging full cooperation, going back through Johnnie's records, talking about Marsha's wonderful initiative, which will now be described as an inspiration for us all."

This was greeted by groans and shouted objections, which Billie raised her hand to silence. She wasn't done.

"If we take a stand on that, we'll lose. We've got to look at what we *can* do. Sophie's going to have to reach out to all the employers, try to get them to hold those jobs. Where it's a crisis for the employer, staff's gonna have to fill in, at least some of the shifts. And it's going to be that much harder with Lu suspended."

Sophie nodded. "There's thirty-four of them, and I've got nine staff—eight without Lu—and she's the only one who's met some of them. Suspended or not, I'm going to have to work with her, even if I have to visit her at home."

Ralph added, "It might help her to feel she's still engaged in the process—if she's willing to do it, despite being a scapegoat." Then his face clouded. "I wonder if they understand how this could screw up her work visa—she's on an H-1B, waiting for her green card. If she's not working, she'll be in violation—ConDo is her sponsor."

This was too much for Gracie. "They never stand by you. I've seen it again and again, at the firm, in the order. The big shots can't say enough about how wonderful you are when it doesn't cost them anything, but when things get a little rough, when you need them, they run for cover. Judases!"

That drew a little gasp from everyone except Billie, whose smile, could he have seen it, would have frozen Martin Islington's blood. "You said it, Gracie—cocksuckers!"

• • •

For some time, Cindy had heard only snatches of the conversation over the roaring in her ears. She was back in the bright-white kitchen with Carlson's body, the knife, the blood, the smell. So like the smell in the hospital room all those years ago, when they pushed her eleven-year-old body up to the inert form that had been her mother and told her to say goodbye; that awful moment that lasted forever, until they must have given up and dragged her out into the chilly white hall, down the elevator, and out into the snow.

She pushed her plate away.

1 0

Paul

My sister is quiet through all this. I can see she's somewhere else. Ralph asks Sophie, "Have you heard anything more about Johnnie?"

"He's in Bridgewater getting assessed for competency to stand trial."

Bridgewater. For all its progressive reputation, ours is the only state that puts its forensic mental hospital under the Department of Corrections rather than Mental Health. Remembering any of my time there gives me a cold feeling, even twenty years later. Anger landed me there in my early twenties, but it's where I learned to contain it—by going dead inside. I stayed that way for years. Makes me feel sorry for Johnnie, despite my experience of him.

My first encounter was in the stairwell at the Stewart Center. He was hovering behind this big young dude who had me cornered, demanding a cigarette. I don't smoke, but that didn't satisfy the guy; he'd settle for my money instead. Sophie had to come along and rescue me. The second time was in the clerical unit when I'd come by to see Phyllis before my shift at Elder Affairs. Johnnie was standing there talking to her, and right away I was thinking I'd have to go over and back him down, but when she saw me coming, Phyllis gave me her sweet smile—you won't see it unless you know what to look for—and introduced us. I was ready to back him off, but he looked embarrassed and let me stare him down. Turns out she'd been encouraging him, planned on featuring his raps in the Center's literary journal.

That's about it. I figured he'd moved on—the young guys don't usually last long at the Center—but I guess he must have started his job at Back Door. Not before Phyllis got to know him, though.

"These young guys," she said one day, "they hate to seem sensitive. It makes them feel vulnerable. You must remember that, right?"

I sure do. It's hard for most women to understand how little choice we've got in the matter at that age. Of course, Phyllis isn't most women.

"He works hard, though, making lists of rhyming words, and for a rapper, his stuff isn't that angry. It's trite, and his vocabulary is limited, but there's some heart comes through."

I've told her how angry I was at that age, and she's heard Cindy and Father back me up on the subject. It's almost like she's saying *He's been through more than you, foster care and a crackhead for a mother, and he didn't get all angry, so what was your problem exactly?* Or maybe that's just me being paranoid. The thing is, after that first time, I never worried about the guy being around Phyllis. She always talked about him as this sweet, lost kid.

Back in the meeting, Billie's back in charge. "They get him a lawyer?"

"Public defender," says Sophie, checking her notes, "one Sam Shapiro."

Billie nods. "Probably some hack, got the job from his father-in-law, a bailiff or something, put in a word with his state rep."

Sophie. "This guy's no kid. I looked it up—he's been there more than ten years."

Billie huffed. "Might be worse. Staying on that long, he's probably not the brightest, or he's lazy, sloppy, or all three. Still, someone's got to talk to him, and Paul, you're going to need help getting in to see Johnnie so you can hold his hand through this. What?"

What did she just say? Emma's waving her arms around.

"I'm sorry, Billie," she says. "I haven't had a chance to ask Paul." Then she turns to me. "It's just that we don't have a lot of options. No one who works for ConDo can get near him without getting in trouble."

"But I—"

". . . haven't had that much experience," Billie finishes for me. "I know, but you've had some training, and you're a natural. You've been in Bridgewater and had some of the same issues."

I've been an angry young man, yeah, I know. Never mind I never came close to winning a fight, never pushed anyone around or tried to make anyone feel small. Gangsta Paul. Sure, I'm just like this White rapper.

I'm trying hard to come back with something—anything—when my sister steps in. "You can't send Paul into this by himself. Less than two years ago he was afraid to leave his room in the group home. It's too much."

Billie turns to reply. "You're right, honey, it's not fair, sending him there by himself. Someone needs to go with him." She pauses, squinting. "How about you?"

Damn. Cindy glares at me, like I knew this was coming and tricked her into being here. I've got to say something, but she finds her voice first, looking right at Billie, hard. "No. It's not that I'm not grateful for all you people have done for my brother, but I've seen how you operate. You think you can add me to your little band of followers, but it's not going to work. I'm not on the team."

Now, I'm proud of her for standing up to Billie, and in a way, it's inspiring. I could do that too, but the thing is, Billie's showing me respect, asking me to do something important, and Cindy's still acting like I'm a helpless wimp, like my church ladies are always saying.

"That's okay," I hear myself say. "I'll go talk to this lawyer, and I'll do my best by Johnnie when I get in to see him. Emma will coach me up. I'll be fine."

Emma's smiling. "I know we're rushing you, but you know what it's like there, and I think you could really help him."

"None of us," says Grace, "can know what the Lord will ask of us. Some say He never asks for anything we can't bear, but that's a line those smug priests feed you. I'm not at all sure what you're asking of Paul is reasonable, Billie, dear. I know it's not fair. And none of us has been through what Cindy has endured these past two days. I think that's enough for one evening, for both of them. I'll give them a ride home."

This is a side of Grace only those who worked with her at Stewart Center have seen. I've only heard stories. But have any of them ever seen her take control away from Billie? Their eyes slide over toward their leader.

Billie chuckles. "Well, fuck me, she's done it again!"

11

Cindy

The vaulted atrium was empty and silent when Cindy used her ID card to unlock the door. The night had been full of restless flashback images of Carlson dripping blood interspersed with Nicole's confusing touch, Grace's kindness, and Ralph's wounded eyes. The only thing left was to keep going, to ride the subway to work with the early-bird hospital workers and paralegals who had become her tribe.

Desperate as she had been to get back here when it seemed certain she would never again have the opportunity, her bad night brought back the fear and doubt of her first encounter with the place without the hope and excitement. The front desk was empty at this hour, and the hallway behind it that led back to the dining room gaped at her. She hurried to the elevators. *Don't feel, just move.*

A subdued Gloria looked surprised to see her, and not in a happy way. "What in the world are you doing here? Aren't you supposed to be working with Arthur's team now?"

Of course. Gloria had warned her to avoid Steven. She stammered her apologies, only to be waved off. "None of us is all there right now. You have a good day now, honey."

Apparently her evaluation wasn't over after all. So it was back to the elevators and up to the secure floor, where Morris's deep voice greeted her. "Well, it's good to see you back." The warm smile from their first encounter was back. "Go on in. Arthur's expecting you."

Fewer than half of the desks in Arthur's bullpen, as he called it, were occupied, all by scruffy-looking young men who looked up and stared at her without offering any kind of greeting. She wondered what they were thinking.

"Cynthia, uh, hey." Arthur stood awkwardly, twisting toward her without moving his feet, his eyes looking everywhere but at her. "Welcome back."

When the large man sitting just outside the office, the one with a bushy beard and an unruly nest of hair who had complained the last time she was here, slammed his hand down on his desk, the CTO rounded on him with shocking ferocity.

"All right, Elmer, that's it! I don't give a fat fuck about your concentration right now. If you can't do your work without absolute silence, put on your fucking headphones."

The other two grinned and slow-clapped without looking up. It was scary, though, seeing wooden, flat-affect Arthur explode, but he motioned her calmly into his glassed-in office and shut the door.

"Sorry. I've set you up in here with me, but the door'll be open most of the time. Try to ignore Elmer. We met in fifth grade. He's our highest paid coder, but he could get more somewhere else if he had any social skills. I know, pretty funny coming from me. He's quiet most of the time, keeps his head down and pumps it out—code."

Set her up where? Apparently at a little workstation across from his desk. "You, uh, want me here?"

He had turned back to his screens and was motioning her to bring the other chair over.

"I need you to look at this. Without all the others around, I got some good work in. You saw things I'd never thought about, got me going in, like, a new direction."

"Wow," she said, "this is way better." It was. Though still a jumble, she could almost follow it, and ideas of how to organize it visually were hitting her.

"I suck at the graphics, so I left that for you. Here, I set up your account so you can sign into our area every morning—if you insist, I can let you change the password, but it would have to meet our standards, so you're better off using the one I wrote down for you. Memorize it and then swallow the paper. Oh, that's a joke. Because of the work we do."

A smile might have clued her in, but he remained stone faced as he brought her over and showed her how to sign in. Just when she thought he was kidding, he held his hand out and waited. She looked at it again and did her best to memorize it before he put it through a huge shredder that lurked against the wall.

"This thing reduces documents to powder. Remember the hostages in Iran? I was just a kid, but it was in that movie with what's his name. Kids sorted out the strips of paper from the shredders in the embassy and reassembled their pictures; almost got them." He was staring off, then abruptly returned to his screens and proceeded to ignore her, which gave her a chance to absorb what had just happened.

He was weird, there was no doubt about that; not unkind, just clueless in particular ways—probably on the mild end of the autism spectrum. He wouldn't be able to read most social cues; she would have to remember to spell things out, and be literal and concrete in what she said. No sarcasm—that would be a challenge.

But he had listened to her, and she had passed at least the first test with him, which meant he could take criticism, probably better than she could. Still, she had better watch herself.

As she began exploring the structure he had outlined for the site, ideas came to her, for a theme and the basic layout, and sub-themes for each of the seven branches. She would have to learn more about each branch's constituency in order to match them thematically. After digging around a few hours, she was able to work up an improved design with a coherent visual theme and a structure that made sense.

She managed to get his attention, and after looking at her screen and following the links while she held her breath, he said, "This is better. Thanks." And returned to his screens.

She tried to contain her excitement. She was working with the CTO.

Later she heard the door shut and saw him looking at her. "Time for a break," he said in his flat voice. "Steven says they're important. And I wanted to get to know you a little. Mother said you discovered Carlson—the body. It must have been bad."

"Don't worry about any of that," she replied. "I'm just glad to be able to come back."

"Oh, I wasn't—worried, I mean. Sad, though. I've known Carlson my whole life. He named a special burger after me for my fifteenth birthday." He trailed off, looking confused.

"It's just that Charlotte said you were going to evaluate me, and here I am, back, I mean, even though I got here through the Stewart Center. So I guess if it weren't for you bending over backward, I'd be home, looking for a job."

"Oh, you mean the kind that actually pays you money?" He held up his hand. "I know. We'll get that fixed, I promise. It's just that right now, Steven—"

"And Carlson were married. Gloria told me. God knows how he must feel about me."

"I think he's more upset with Lu, but anything to do with ConDo— he thinks, like, if he hadn't gone along with bringing Stewart Center people in . . . Anyway, Charlotte's not going to ask Steven to process your paperwork, not now. Maybe next week."

"Look, I wasn't promised anything when I came here. I'm just happy to be back. But I'm not sure how I'm going to do my work. Steven was checking in with me every day."

"And did he really look closely at your work? He doesn't understand anything we do, you know. We can send him weekly updates, summarize stuff at a level he can follow. You're going to be useful, but I can't spend time with you today. Vernon . . . We lost a week of work because of all this, and now he's in a frenzy. Look, I've got to go kiss Elmer's ass so he'll get back to producing instead of pouting out there. There's coffee and snacks in the kitchen—fresh fruit, donuts, tonic—help yourself."

A virtuous apple and a Boston cream donut later, she was back to work, immersed in the website. It almost filled up her brain enough to chase out the images that tormented her. She barely noticed when Arthur returned and sat clicking away in front of his screens.

Around eleven, there was a *bing*, and a lunch menu filled her screen. She swiveled around to look at the back of Arthur's head.

He spoke without turning. "Gloria said you might not want to go back to the dining room yet. They usually bring us lunch here anyway. It used to be just during deadline pushes, but lately—fucking Vernon! Mother wants me to *mix and mingle*," he said, with a credible imitation of Charlotte's voice, "but this saves time."

By two, she felt herself nodding off. Free food was particularly dangerous when they brought it to your desk.

Maybe she would leave on the early side today, get back into things gradually. She was certain her family, at least, would approve. It occurred to her to thank Gloria first, and see how she was coping.

She found her in her usual spot behind the curved counter, staring straight ahead. Gloria didn't seem to notice her until Cindy asked how she was doing. "Thanks, I'm okay," she replied. "Steven's still at home, and it's just so quiet here."

"How's the group doing?"

"I'm worried about Nicki." Gloria stared, her message clear: *Do something.*

"I can talk to her," Cindy said.

"Would you? She said she was headed to the gym."

It was no accident that Cindy hadn't been to the place since the tour on her second day. If Claude recognized her when she asked after Nicole, he didn't show it but nodded toward the mirrored studio. Nicole was there alone, sitting on a mat, legs folded in the lotus position, eyes closed. Not wanting to disturb her meditation, Cindy took a mat from the pile and brought it over to the mirrors. Sitting against them was the best way to avoid her reflection.

"Cindy."

The toneless voice was barely recognizable.

"I don't need to disturb your meditation," said Cindy. "I just wanted to say hello."

Nicole turned slowly toward her but stayed on the floor, halfway across the room. "That's okay. I don't seem to be getting anywhere."

This was a different Nicole, awkward and unsure in her movements, with her usual animated voice a monotone. And her eyes wandered everywhere, never settling on Cindy's, despite her own attempts to engage them. Cindy moved to sit next to her on the uncomfortably thin mat.

"Are you okay?"

"Oh sure, yeah." Nicole was looking away now, though she had to twist to do it. Cindy reached for her shoulder. She didn't have a plan, but words weren't getting her anywhere. She put a hand on her shoulder, and Nicole's head dropped.

Some level of reserve broke inside Cindy, and she reached out her other hand and pulled Nicole into a hug, felt her stiffen for a second, then go slack, then raise her arms and hug her back, hard. When the sobs came, it was Cindy's turn to have a wet shoulder.

After a while, Nicole stopped crying but continued to hold her tight. "He was such a sweet man. Why would anyone want to hurt him.?"

"You knew him well?"

She nodded. "When I got here, there were only about twenty people. Before they built this palace. No one understood why Charlotte hired me, not even Carlson, but he was welcoming just the same, and when I told him how I work, he was so open."

"Like you were with me when I got here."

"Thanks. He made you want to be like that. He loved new people. Places like this can become cutthroat—like our lovely Human Resource team—but Charlotte never wanted that. She and Steven

. . . I think it's why they want the website, to link us to the outside. You know, I never thought of it, but maybe Carlson understood my role better than I thought. I could have been his idea."

At last she broke away, but this time her eyes were back on Cindy's, searching. "Why would anyone want to kill him?"

"The dishwasher—"

"It's not like he was ever harsh or critical. I'm sure of that."

"Well." Cindy wasn't sure why she was implicating the young man from ConDo. "A young guy, maybe insecure about his sexuality . . ."

That seemed to deflate Nicole. "He was temporary, from outside, so I didn't reach out to him. I could have helped with that; I know it."

Cindy thought of Emma's words. "I know in some ways it feels better to try to make sense of this, even by blaming yourself, but that's a stretch. We don't know what was in his head."

"You're right. And I suppose I'm making assumptions; it could have been anyone."

It seemed clear to Cindy that, for whatever crazy reason of his own, the dishwasher had killed Carlson, but if it made her friend feel better, she wasn't going to argue.

"Look, thanks. I needed that hug. Right now, though, I need to go for a run. You?"

"Have to get back to work." Like she could keep up with this woman for more than a block.

She headed back to check in one more time with Gloria. By then Nicole would be out the door and it would be safe to go home without being caught in her lie. It felt good to pay Nicole back for her kindness. Maybe Cindy could fit in here after all, when things settled down. Even Craig's failure to acknowledge her on her way out didn't dampen her spirits.

12

Paul

If I'm going to meet with Johnnie, I need something they call "standing." Emma can't send me because that would connect back with ConDo, and she'd lose her job, so the idea is to get Johnnie's lawyer to help. A good thing about working for the state in Elder Affairs is that there's folks who know how things are organized, and a friend there pointed me to the Committee for Public Counsel Services where the public defenders work.

I figure this Sam Shapiro is probably working off his conscience before he goes about getting rich. I can't get through to him by phone, but the secretary there is nice, once I reach her—my job with the state is digging up resources for old people, so I know how to work the phones with state offices—and she gives me an appointment to meet with the guy. She even confirms that he's representing Johnnie when I tell her I'm a friend from ConDo, and she even sounds a little bit excited.

His office is in Malden. I find 6 Pleasant in one of those older brick buildings you see all over, could just as well be in Jamaica Plain where I live. Only problem is, I can't find an entrance to the offices upstairs from the storefronts. I give up and ask in the Army recruitment office, and it turns out the door is right there next to it. For some reason, the guy doesn't try to sign me up.

Things get easier once I get inside and find the elevators. Seems they've got the whole top floor of the building, and there's a counter right there when I get off. I ask for Attorney Shapiro.

This elegant woman comes out, maybe Cindy's age but thinner and darker and, I have to say, dressed better, especially since Back Door came into our lives. The other thing I notice is her hair; shorter than mine, and that's saying something. I keep mine cut low so the bald parts aren't so obvious, which doesn't seem like a problem for her. She's got hoop earrings and a little gold stud in her nose. "Mr. Abernathy? We spoke on the phone." She shakes my hand and leads me back through a maze of cubicles to a little conference room, and there's my man—gets up from the table to greet me. He's older than I pictured, maybe fifty, with a bad comb-over and a gray suit that fits like a sheet thrown over a worn-out chair.

"Mr. Shapiro," I say, "thanks so much for seeing me." I'm thinking I'm handling things pretty smooth, so I'm not ready when they look at each other and start laughing.

When you've been branded crazy most of your life, you have to get used to some things: everybody questioning your judgment, the discomfort of the people close to you any time you get emotional or excited, lots of little everyday things others wouldn't notice. But not laughing *at* me; any hint of that, and I'm gone.

She says, "I'm Sam Shapiro, Mr. Abernathy. It's short for Samantha. I'm Mr. Christopher's lawyer."

"And I'm James McCarthy," says the guy, "the lead attorney in this office. You'll have to excuse Sam; she loves surprising people. Most of the judges take it well, but they all know her now anyway. She's our most experienced defender." And with that, he's gone.

Time for a second look, while I get myself calm, which isn't easy. I can see now, her shirt could be real silk, and the necklace she's got on looks too expensive for a secretary. I can see where it's a game they like to play, catching folks making assumptions, but I don't like it. Doesn't make a damn bit of difference to her, though, and I'm the one needs something. She motions me to sit, then gets right to it.

"I understand you're from Consolidated Dorchester Human Services. I have to say I'm a bit surprised." When she looks down at her notes, I notice she's got those fancy nails you see all over these days, though nothing too loud. "Do you work with my client? Mr. Linsky"—that's Shep, Johnnie's case manager—"said he was forced by his superiors to break off contact with us and Mr. Christopher."

"I don't actually work for them. And I've only met him—your client—a few times, around the Stewart Center. He's a member there, and even though I'm working for Elder Affairs now, I still go there sometimes."

"So, you're . . ." She looks like she's waiting for more, maybe waiting for me to start making sense.

I'm thinking good luck with that, lady, while my mouth's still going. You see, I didn't think this through at all, and now I'm stuck. How do I tell this hotshot lawyer who I am without her writing me off? Sure, we've got the same color skin, but she's not going to listen to me once she knows where I come from. I've got no time now to work out a slick story, and anyway, I'm not smart enough to fool this lady.

"I'm what they call a peer, not a peer specialist yet—that is, not certified or anything, but I've had some training, and with them dumping the guy, there's folks at the Center, at ConDo, asked me to get in touch and, uh, offer my services." Maybe she'll give up trying to figure out what that all means and move on.

After a bit, she sighs, making it clear what a disappointment I am, but she's going to hang in there anyhow because she's such a dedicated professional, and fair minded. "Your services . . ." She says it like she can't imagine what those could be.

"Look, Ms. Shapiro—"

"Please, Sam," she says.

That's better. "I won't lie to you. I was a client with ConDo, in one of their group homes, more than twenty years. When I was Johnnie's age, I was a mess, worse than him, and I still hear voices. But now I'm a resource specialist with the Office of Elder Affairs—you can check with my supervisor there. Johnnie's in Bridgewater now, right? You ever been there?"

"As a matter of fact, I was on the attorney general's task force. I was there every day for eight months, rotating through the wards, interviewing inmates."

Interesting. I take a look at her again. "I don't imagine it has changed much in the twenty years since I was shuttling between there and Mass Mental, before I landed with ConDo. I'm just saying that I know where he's been. I didn't kill anyone, but it wasn't because I wasn't angry enough back then."

That wipes the smile off her face. Here I was, thinking I might be getting somewhere, but now she's giving me a hard look, and her voice takes on an edge. "I'm not ready to make any assumptions about my client. As far as I'm concerned, he hasn't killed anybody. He's been charged, that's all. If you can't accept that, then I'm not going to help you gain access to him. There will be enough folks assuming he's a murderer."

As that speech goes on, she's leaning over the table at me, and I'm back so my head is touching the wall. "Whoa, okay. I'm not assuming anything." I don't know if it's my words or my fear that makes her lean back. "I'm just trying to say that I have a sense for the young man's situation, and I could talk to him if he's willing. If not, then I'm not involved. Anything he says to me stays with me, too. I've had enough training where I know how that works. I've got to figure he doesn't have a lot of friends right at the moment, and I know how that feels."

I'm starting to think this one's willing to fight for him. Maybe he could do a lot worse.

That stops her. She looks down at her notes, thinking of where to go next with this guy sitting in front of her. "Well, if you don't work for ConDo—"

"How come I'm here?" She nods, so I tell her about Billie and the team, and just a bit of how Ralph and Cindy stepped in when things went bad for me at Farnsworth group home. Somewhere in there I mention that Cindy works at Back Door now.

It's not until then, when she snaps her head around, that I notice she's been spacing out on me. I was too into my story, didn't see it. Emma would be laughing at me—*The story's for them, not you*, she'd say. *Pay attention.*

"Your sister—at Back Door Technologies?"

"She started as an intern, just a few weeks ago; something to do with web design."

She opens the folder in front of her for the first time, starts to rummage through papers. "I should have recognized your name. Cynthia Abernathy found the body. Would she be willing to meet with me?" So much for peer counseling and my story. "I'll get formal access to her later, but I'd like to talk to her while it's still fresh."

What the hell did I say that for? Of course, she should have put it together by now, and most likely would have anyway before we were done.

"There's so much I don't understand about that place," she says, "and most people there aren't going to be inclined to cooperate with me. I'm sure they assume if the police charged him, he must be the killer. It's easier for them that way—temporary kitchen help, not one of their own. But your sister's new there."

Why am I shooting my mouth off to this woman? My story had her glazing over, but now she's all excited about my sister the intern who discovered the body. After all, my sister's not crazy. Which is why it's the last thing Cindy will want to do.

1 3

Cindy

Her father gave Cindy a questioning look as he handed her the phone. The public defenders' office, a woman named Shapiro—said she'd met with Paul, suggested meeting the next morning at Back Door. That way Cindy wouldn't be taken away from her work for long, which had sounded good.

The woman had been friendly, barely mentioning the crime, her focus on Cindy, the fellow Black career woman, how difficult but important her child protection work was, the lawyer's own experience as a foster child. She was so impressed that Cindy was able to change careers and become a pioneer, opening up the tech world to women of color. Even though Cindy wondered how the woman knew about her child protection experience—from Paul?—the glow from the conversation lasted a good half hour. Then it occurred to her that meeting at Back Door might not be a good idea. What would they think?

She was aching to light into her brother, but he had the good sense to spend the evening with Phyllis. Her father was mildly interested in the woman, even asking about her church affiliation. For all Cindy knew, she was Jewish.

Cindy hated feeling like a patsy—like she could be led about by anyone with strong convictions or the will to dominate an interaction.

The next morning she was buried in her screen beside Arthur, determined to match his focus and feeling like she was succeeding. He answered his phone with irritation: "What?" Then, covering the mouthpiece, "It's Craig. Were you expecting a visitor?"

Oh shit, the lawyer. She should have mentioned it to Arthur but hadn't known how to explain it without coming under scrutiny. She muttered she wouldn't be long and bolted for the elevator.

Upon exiting the elevators on the ground floor, as she was about to round the wall behind Craig's desk in the lobby, Cindy heard his voice first, then Nicole's. He sounded angry.

"I just wish Charlotte—"

"She knows what she's doing."

"Sure, she's found a governess for Arthur. I thought teaching him social skills was your job."

Cindy had never heard Nicole hiss, but there was hurt underneath. "You of all people should know better."

"Okay, okay, but Vernon—"

"Our little Napoleon get to you?"

". . . says having someone we don't know so close to Arthur, and in the secure work area—"

"Well, I trust her. And she's been through a lot. You told me how she looked after she found the . . . Carlson."

"But she's from ConDo, and we put her at Arthur's elbow? With his, uh, limitations, he could be compromised. Vernon's worried. We can't afford any more distractions."

She heard Nicole's grunt of frustration but was unprepared when the thin woman rounded the end of the wall and nearly ran into her. Cindy felt lucky when Nicole merely nodded a greeting and hurried past toward the elevators.

When Cindy came around the wall into the lobby, Craig favored her with a worse glare than usual—anger replacing indifference. Then he turned to face the bench under the ficus where a slender, stylish woman with an ultra-short afro sat erect with her hands folded in her lap. When she noticed them looking, she smiled, hoisted a large leather satchel over one shoulder, and approached. Sam.

She looked at Cindy and said, "Ms. Abernathy? This gentleman wanted to know my business in coming here to visit you, and I explained. I understand"—she seemed apologetic, but directed it toward Cindy rather than Craig—"this is a painful time for everyone here. With the possible exception"—turning toward the guard—"of the murderer."

Craig's stony stare made Cindy step in. "We'll go for a walk, shall we?" She took Sam's arm and began to steer her firmly toward the door, then looked back at the guard. "I'm sorry, Craig. I should have put her on the list. I'm just overwhelmed right now." The tight smile didn't make it to his eyes.

Neither spoke until they were through the revolving door. "Okay, am I under arrest?"

Cindy realized she had been holding the woman's arm with most of her strength while she propelled her through the lobby. "I'm sorry. I guess I'm not handling this very well. I should have suggested a neutral site."

The woman rubbed her arm. "It's okay; it takes more than dirty looks to put me off. Did they always have a thing about security, or is it just since the murder?"

"They do military work." Should she have shared that? "I guess security goes with it."

The lawyer sighed and seemed sincere when she said, "I'll try to keep this from spilling over on you too badly." She paused, gathering herself. "I have the police report, so I know you found the body, and I've reviewed what you told them. Right now, I'm more interested in background on this place." She pointed with her eyebrows and a cock of the head. "Your brother said you just got here, as an intern."

"Two weeks. It's all new to me, and these people are so smart. And they've been good to me, really."

"I suppose you're one of the only sisters?"

Cindy had to laugh. "Or brothers, unless you count Indians and Koreans. Not to mention feeling old. My boss is still in his thirties, the CEO's son. He has his own issues"—*Whoa, don't go there*—"but he's been more than gracious." She led them to a picnic table shaded by maples.

The lawyer pulled a yellow pad from the satchel, reminding Cindy of social work, but the buttery leather would have made Cindy a target between home visits. Within fifteen minutes, the lawyer had extracted what felt like every bit of her knowledge about the company's mission, business plan, leadership, and staff. Cindy found herself wanting to give her more, despite a very distant voice telling her to shut up. When she heard herself saying that Steven Henchcliff was not just the HR director but Carlson's widower, she caught herself.

It was as if the lawyer had been waiting for it. "Look, Cindy. This is my job. Johnnie's entitled to a vigorous defense, and I *will* ruffle feathers in the process. I'll turn over more than a few rocks; people will get hurt, and they'll blame me for embarrassing them, or worse."

"They'll blame you, but I'll be collateral damage. Regrettable, but unavoidable, right? My career gets shot to hell so you can say you did your fucking job."

"Miss Abernathy." The lawyer didn't seem bothered by the outburst. She would do well at the Stewart Center.

"I know," Cindy went on, "every killer gets a defense, and you're it. Go for it. But leave me the hell out of it. I've got to get back to salvaging what's left of my new career, along with some friendships that matter to me."

Cindy didn't look back until the revolving doors, only to see the woman staring at her, not even starting to gather up her papers. When Cindy got to Craig, Susan was standing next to him, shaking her head.

"Not smart, Cindy." *And hello to you too, Susan. How are you holding up?* "That woman shouldn't be in the building, and no one should talk to her. If she needs information, she can contact me, and I'll handle it. Is that clear?"

So she was speaking for Charlotte now? Cindy hated it when anyone talked down to her, but she was at the bottom, a lowly intern—nobody. "Yeah, I'm sorry. I guess I wasn't thinking. She said she just wanted to know a little bit about the place. I should have thought—"

Susan's manner softened. "Okay, I can see—an African American career woman around your age; it would be hard to say no to a *sister*."

The condescension stung. And was that what it had been? Explaining further without implicating her connections to ConDo and the killer seemed impossible, so Cindy gritted her teeth and gave the meekest nod she could manage as Susan went on. "But now that you know our policy, please report any further overtures to me immediately, and don't, under any circumstances, speak to her again." With that, she gave them a stiff smile, turned, and headed for the elevators.

Craig's voice came softly as Cindy watched the woman hurry off. "Cindy, I'm—I had to let her know about your, uh, visitor."

At least he wasn't glaring at her anymore. "It's okay," she said. "I should have let you know ahead of time."

"Just as well you didn't. They would never have let you talk to her. And now that we know what she looks like, I'll be running her off if she shows up here again; no one else will be allowed any contact."

Well, look at that, Rambo can talk. Were they having a friendly conversation? Could she have misjudged him? "Yeah, I know. And thanks."

"But she's right, you know," said Craig.

"I know. It's reasonable for them to want to handle this carefully."

"No, the dishwasher. He's going to need someone to stand up for him."

What? They hadn't spoken until they got outside. Was the picnic table bugged?

"Don't worry, I wasn't listening in. Before you got down here"—did she imagine the smirk?—"Ms. Shapiro reminded me of that fact. The kid probably doesn't have anyone else. Lu called to apologize. Said she's been suspended, and ConDo's dumped the kid."

．．．

It was disorienting to hear Billie's foghorn upon entering the rectory. "That you, Cindy? Come on in and join us." She was sitting with Paul on the dainty upholstered chairs, each with a discreet plaque on the back, *In memory of . . .*

Billie wore her usual plaid flannel shirt, blue jeans, and untied work boots, but her short hair was freshly spiked with mousse. Paul was looking shifty.

"I brought beer, but your brother insisted we drink out of these," she said, raising one of the chunky white mugs from their kitchen.

Cindy peered through the french doors in horror. The dining room was packed with deacons and church ladies. At the head of the table, her father wore the formal face he used to mask his frustration. He would need his secret scotch when this was over.

It seemed like there were only two body types among the women— those who weighed almost nothing and looked pissed about it and others who were alarmingly large and *you got a problem with that, honey?* As it was, Cindy imagined the doors bulging out, straining to contain all the brightly colored fabric and perfumed flesh.

One of the smaller women's hands disappeared briefly as she poked the one beside her and both turned to stare. Cindy wondered what they made of Billie. No wonder Paul had them drinking their beers out of coffee mugs. She hoped he'd remembered to hide the bottles.

Billie's growl brought her back. "God, these chairs suck. What a fussy place. Grab one and join us."

Cindy had never seen Billie outside her Savin Hill apartment. What had it taken to bring her out?

"Gracie's in the car. The church lot's full, and she won't leave it on the street in this neighborhood. You see," she addressed Paul in a hoarse whisper, "Jamaica Plain is a nest of anarchists and nonbelievers—I quote."

Gracie took great pride in their massive, early '80s American sedan, but Cindy suspected the ex-nun didn't want to come into a non-Catholic rectory, let alone encounter leaders of the heretic church.

"I suppose you're wondering why I happened to wash up on your beach—haw: limited options. We got a problem, and most of our solvers are off the table. I figured something like this was coming."

"Something like what?" For the second time that day, Cindy wanted to say something snippy like "Fine, thanks, and how are you?" but there was no shaming Billie.

"Johnnie's been charged, first-degree murder." Cindy knew that. "And Martin has staked out the ConDo position, which is as far away from the poor kid as he can get. He issued an edict: no ConDo staff member is to have any contact with Johnnie or anyone associated with his case, so as not to interfere with the ongoing investigation." She knew that, too. "Our Ralphie got a written warning from Carolyn put in his file, will be subject to termination. You, me, and Paul here are all the guy's got. At least he was assigned a decent public defender from what Paul says, but they always figure to try and cop a plea. That's what Martin's praying for. He wants it out of the news fast, and if it goes to trial—"

"Wait, wait," said Cindy, "I don't think you understand. I can't get involved in this. I'm trying to work there. And anyway, what would I do?"

"This lawyer," said Paul, "she seems to care about Johnnie. She's not assuming that he's guilty."

"You can see why she's still stuck in the public defender's office," said Billie.

Cindy gave Paul her best glare. "And you figured, no way will I get my sister to go along with this. I'll have to bring in the big gun."

Her brother looked down at his hands while Billie replied. "Someone's got to look into things."

Paul said, "Sam went to see him, and I went with her, to this jail in Billerica. An hour drive, and I didn't get past the lobby—some form had to go in a day ahead—but Sam said he seems lost: just shakes his head, looks around, doesn't understand the trouble he's in, keeps saying how much nicer the jail is than Bridgewater, how the food's better, how he likes his roommate. Didn't look nice to me, and they treated us like dirt just for visiting, or trying to. I'm worried he could get himself killed in there."

Cindy only half heard the words as they went by. "You want me to—what?"

Billie jumped back in. "Look it, Cindy. I can't get around so good anymore, and I'm, well, you might not know this, but I don't do that well with authority figures. And you're there, on the inside."

They would want her to find another suspect, someone with a motive to kill Carlson. If she succeeded, it could tear the company apart. But it did sound like Johnnie had few allies, and with his limitations . . .

Paul spoke again. He and Billie were a tag team. "I could help out with some things, but you're there, at the scene of the crime. You can find out more about what led up to it. Even if it is Johnnie— and I can't see it, really—we'll at least know more, understand what happened. Maybe an insanity defense."

This brought a snort from Billie. "That never works, but what's the difference anyway? Bridgewater over Shirley"—the maximum-security state prison. "One thing, though: I know a guy, sort of family, used to be a police detective. He's in assisted living now, got time on his hands. I think I could get him to help. Uncle Sal's a little rough around the edges." *Compared to Billie?* "But he likes the ladies. I think he'd help us if you came with me. Then, when you hear things, you can bring it back and we could, you know, analyze it together."

Cindy looked at Paul. This was important to him. Six weeks ago, she would have done anything to please her older brother, and to impress Billie. How could she make them understand what this job meant to her?

"Look, I know this is important to you, and I appreciate your faith in me." Even though it was more a matter of where she worked, and the lack of better options. "But I have a chance at a new career, in a place where they value me. I'm not just someone's sister or girlfriend there. I won't do anything to jeopardize that."

She saw Paul's shoulders slump, but Billie seemed unfazed. "Of course. No one expects that. You have to stay in good there, or you won't be able to help. Just keep your ears open, maybe ask a few questions, and report back what you hear. Hey, it'll help you out, getting to know people. You're kinda shy, after all. This'll give you a push in the right direction."

"I guess I thought," said Paul, "where you were there for me—"

"You were my brother. I visited."

"But he's got no one but us. It would help so much. Please, Cindy."

She was still adjusting to the fact that her brother was no longer the fussy, helpless man living out his days in quiet futility. He'd been talking about full-time work, going off disability, even moving to his own apartment. It had been a long while since he had asked her for anything, and the support he offered her recently reminded her of the big brother she had worshiped when she was ten and he was in high school. She found it impossible to look at him and say no.

"Okay. I'm not going to play detective, but I could listen and report back what I hear."

There. She had met them more than halfway. Billie grumbled, called her naive, but Paul looked satisfied, even grateful, and that was the important thing. Even Billie seemed to realize she had gotten the best deal she could and left soon after.

• • •

When Cindy came in, Nicole was hanging out at the front desk with Craig, and she bounced over to give Cindy a quick, hard hug, then turned to the guard. "Okay, big guy. You're on."

"I, uh." The man was visibly uncomfortable, avoiding her gaze. "I'm sorry, about yesterday. I should have warned you about Susan." He seemed relieved to have gotten it out. Cindy assured him that she understood, repeating that it was her fault for not alerting him.

Nicole said, "How were you supposed to know the policy?" Then, turning to Craig—"And . . ."

"I could have covered for you."

Cindy was trying to think of something to say when Susan came from the elevators and sailed past them with barely a nod. They turned to watch her go, and Cindy noticed a rather impressive black limousine that must have pulled up while they spoke. Susan opened the back door to greet a man in a dark suit, and after a moment they walked back toward the elevators. Neither seemed to notice the group at the front desk, which made it easier to stare as they swept by. The man was old for their building, perhaps early fifties, tall and lean, expensively dressed, with graying hair. The way Susan bobbed along beside him reminded Cindy of the first time she saw her walking beside Charlotte.

"Well, well," said Nicole, "the money man makes an appearance."

"Susan sure gave him all of her attention," said Cindy.

"Yeah. I think she knew him before she got here. He's the type that expects it. Never gives a look to the small fry, either. He's a big shot on the board. Things get tense whenever he's around."

"Well, some of us," explained Craig with a head tilted toward Nicole, "are a bit insecure."

"And as close to invisible as I can manage and still do my work. But it's easy for you to say. Everyone needs security, but I'm so discretionary," she said, flipping a hand behind her ear.

"Well," said Cindy, "I've got to find a way to thank Charlotte for allowing me back."

Her plan was to follow Susan up to her office and try for an appointment. When she explained, Nicole gave her a searching look, her head cocked sideways.

"Hm. Craig, sweetie, is that, like, what do you call them?"

"Social skills?"

"That's it. Bye, Cindy. Good luck!"

Cindy sat at her desk for a fidgety two hours—long enough, she hoped, for the meeting to be over—before going to Charlotte's office. Susan's desk was empty, and the doors behind it were closed. Worried her resolve might weaken, she decided to sit and wait.

And think. Nicole seemed able to tame the beast at the gate. He behaved like a human around her, but it was so different from his previous conduct that she didn't know which version was the real Craig. And the idea that he could cover for her with Susan seemed odd. She had the sense that she was stepping between two warring factions, and that at some point she might be pushed to choose sides.

Both doors of Charlotte's office burst open at once, and Arthur's long strides carried him across the room before Cindy could do anything to gauge his mood. A short man in a gray suit followed. With lips pressed together and eyes fixed forward, his short legs pumped almost comically as they carried him toward the elevators. *Vernon.* She wondered whether he always looked so angry.

When he emerged from the office, Steven looked dazed. His walk showed none of his usual grace and was slow enough for her to notice the sheen of sweat on his pale cheeks. None of them acknowledged her. When the office doors shut, she was left to decide whether she dared approach Charlotte now. Whatever had happened in there, she had no desire to get in the middle.

When the doors opened again twenty minutes later, Susan emerged next to the limousine man. She looked at Cindy, then turned back to him. "I just need a moment, Ash." Then, to Cindy: "If you were waiting to talk to Charlotte, this isn't the best time. I'll check in with you later, in Arthur's office." She turned without waiting for an answer, but she stood next to the man as they both watched Cindy get on the elevator.

Sitting in her usual place, back-to-back with Arthur, Cindy wondered what he was thinking. Was he evaluating her? How was she doing? There was no way she could ask, and his calm demeanor as he worked at his screens told her nothing. All she could do was wait for Susan, and it was hours before the usual silence accompanied her entrance into the bullpen. When Arthur made his decision, calm and grounded Susan would be the one to tell her.

Cindy couldn't decide which she preferred: Susan's distance could be jarring, but it felt appropriate, while for all her warmth, Nicole's openness and intimacy made Cindy uncomfortable.

She could almost relax as Susan spoke. "I suppose you're wondering what that was all about. It wasn't as bad as it looked. Ash—Mr. Whitaker—is a major investor, our biggest stakeholder outside the originals. His hedge fund underwrote this building and enabled us to branch out into commercial and retail operations so we aren't totally dependent on government contracts."

"Hey," said Arthur, "it's still our bread and butter."

Susan laughed. "Don't worry, Arthur, no one's about to take you and your team for granted. I just want Cindy to understand Mr. Whitaker's role, and why he commands respect." It had looked more like fear. "He challenges Charlotte about some of her, uh, inspirations, but she can handle it."

"Mother can handle anybody." Arthur's flat voice made him hard to read. Was he angry or anxious? Bored?

"Ashton brings a world of business experience to the table," she said, almost as if she were talking to a child. "It's hard when someone comes in and questions the way things are done, but it's necessary."

Cindy had thought of that as Vernon's role in the organization. Charlotte, Steven, Vernon, Carlson—they had looked like a tight group, balancing each other. She'd never seen them uncomfortable until now, but everyone had seemed shaken after the meeting. Could Carlson's death have upset the team's balance? Or was it this Mr. Whitaker character, "the money man," shaking things up?

There was something condescending about Susan's description, especially coming from Charlotte's assistant, but she was one of the few people here who seemed calm and balanced, and Cindy was inclined to trust her judgment. She would have liked to hear more, but Arthur had turned his attention back to his screen, and she didn't want to appear nosy. It wasn't until Susan left that she realized she had learned almost nothing about the meeting and had forgotten to set up her audience with Charlotte.

• • •

Around eleven the following morning, Cindy sat in the waiting area outside Charlotte's office, trying not to stare as Susan pecked away at her keyboard. She had waited until what she thought was a reasonable hour to come to the office, eight forty-five, to request the meeting. She got the expected response from Susan—what was this about, why was it so urgent, it would be better to let her handle it—but Cindy had remained firm. Being asked to return now seemed reasonable, but the wait had been difficult.

Her two priorities didn't mesh together: she had to express her gratitude for being accepted back despite her connection to Johnnie and ConDo, and she had to ask permission to meet with staff, under the guise of offering support. That would remind Charlotte of her background as a social worker, just as Cindy was trying to break from her past. And Susan's chilly manner made the wait even more awkward.

When at last she emerged, Charlotte's appearance was shocking. Wearing black jeans, a dark-blue, man-tailored shirt, and hiking shoes, she had shrunk to ordinary size. Though she greeted Cindy warmly, her manner brought home what recent events must have cost. She offered Cindy coffee as they sat on the leather sling chairs.

"Cindy, it's so good to have you back. How are you?" The plummy accent was gone.

"Oh, I'm fine, really. I wanted to thank you for bringing me back."

Charlotte seemed not to have heard her, but her pain was so apparent that Cindy didn't take offense. Instead, she pushed on.

"But this must be so awful for you. I know Carlson was one of your original hires, and I remember seeing him come out of your office earlier this week, before our last meeting. I can see this has been a blow."

Before this, she wouldn't have dared such familiarity, but the woman's pain pulled at her.

Charlotte broke her gaze and looked down. "You're so right about that. Carlson had been going through a rough patch with us, but he was a dear friend. This place wouldn't be what it is without all the things he brought: the craft, the caring, the loving attention to every task, everything and everyone around him. It's awful that his last days with us were painful. I could have done something about that." She waved the thought away. "I can't believe he's gone."

They sat in silence. After a while, Charlotte continued.

"Carlson touched so many people here. In many ways, he was the heart of this place. I lost touch with that, somehow."

This was going to be hard, but Cindy would never have a better opening.

"I was wondering if it would be okay with you, uh, for me to speak with some of the people here. About . . . what happened."

"Oh, dear, that is so like you to reach out—I really do appreciate it."

"I know I'm just an intern, but I've had some training in trauma recovery, and people I know"—oh God, she had almost mentioned ConDo—"that is, I have some professional support." She forced herself to stop there.

"Well," said Charlotte, "people are awfully upset."

"I'd be careful. I wouldn't push anyone to talk, just listen, offer some information, resources for coping, things like that."

"Well, I suppose, now that the police are done with us."

That must mean they believed they had their killer in Johnnie. But wasn't it early to stop asking questions? Cindy took a breath. "Do you get the impression they're looking beyond the dishwasher? I mean, it would be easy to assume, because he has a mental illness—"

"And ran away, covered in Carlson's blood?"

"But it was mostly on his jacket. For them to have finished here so quickly . . . I just wonder whether they might be jumping to conclusions without doing a thorough investigation."

"I see. You think they should be camped out here, perhaps in numbers, questioning everybody repeatedly, looking for inconsistencies in their stories?"

Maybe it was the woman's flat manner that kept Cindy from reading the danger, and led her to argue the point further.

"I'm just saying, it's possible it wasn't Johnnie Christopher. Just because he came from the Stewart Center—"

"Of course, it might not have been the obvious person, a young, disturbed man with a violent history. It could have been someone else. Perhaps someone who worked with him, maybe for years, someone from our family, chose to murder him. Is that what you're saying?"

Uh-oh. Cindy willed her voice soft and calm. "I wouldn't think of doing anything without your blessing. That's why I'm here. I'm just worried about a rush to judgment."

"Is that what I'm doing? This maniac comes into our family. Kind, gentle Carlson takes him under his wing, gives him private instruction, every encouragement—"

"It's just that my brother, Paul, knows Johnnie. He doesn't believe—"

"Ah, the one who suffers from a rather severe form of mental illness. That brother?"

Did I tell her about Paul? She didn't think so. Her own anger choked her voice. "My brother has had more than his share of challenges, but he's smart, sensitive, and a good judge of character. He's lived in that system, he understands it. You've never met him, but you think you can write him off . . ." She realized she was leaning forward, almost yelling at her new boss—not a great idea.

But Charlotte's face and voice softened. "Yes, I'm sorry, that was uncalled for. You're offering your support, and I accept it gratefully. But you're not to go poking around and upsetting people further. We'll just let the authorities handle the rest, if that's okay with you."

A cold rage settled into Cindy's gut, but she kept her face bland. There was no way to push the issue, and she had what she needed—

permission to talk to people. Why had she said anything about the police? It should have been obvious that any questions, even casual remarks, might set these people off. And she was still on a trial period. It might not be a great idea to make a nuisance of herself when she could so easily be brushed aside.

But she'd always had trouble keeping quiet. Working in social services, it wasn't until she had been slapped down repeatedly that she learned to shut up and go along. Now she understood for the first time the role that surrender had played in crushing her spirit. Her focus had to be on proving herself and finding a place, maybe even a career, here. Could she afford to squander her prospects on Billie and her team's crazy enterprise? On the other hand, did she want a career among people who could devalue her brother? What would she have to compromise to stay in Charlotte's good graces?

1 4

Paul

The visit to the jail shook me up, even though I didn't make it past the waiting room. At first I thought the shaky feeling would go away once I got out of there, but I had it bad last night, and now, in the morning, I remember that I have to go back to that place, go inside this time. I'm not sure I can face it.

"You okay?" That's Father.

We've come a long way since he invited me back into his life, but not that far. "Yeah. I didn't sleep so well, that's all."

He doesn't push. He's not ready for that sort of thing either. It's enough to get me thinking, though, that I'd better talk to someone. I can tell Phyllis some things, but this'd upset her. There's Emma, but she pushed me into this; I'm afraid she'll feel bad about it, and I don't want that. Ralph's the other one. I've been meaning to ask him what's going on with him and Cindy anyway. Something happened, and she's not talking.

It's a nice evening when he meets me after work, so we go for a walk in town, in the Public Garden. We had a warm September, but the flowers in the manicured beds are spent now, their brittle, brown stems broken on the ground. I find us a bench facing the empty pond; the real swans are gone, the boats tied up.

"I went with that lawyer to see Johnnie, like everybody said I should."

"Bridgewater?" Ralph knows what that place means to me.

"No, the county lockup out in Billerica. Drove out there with Sam, the public defender. Middle of nowhere."

"Yeah, who goes to Billerica? Still, I imagine it brought back memories." Ralph knows how to get to the point.

"Huh." I nod. "The guards, the smell, swaggering guys giving you looks. And I didn't even get past the waiting room—some permission form I had to file ahead of time. I thought I'd be okay once I got out."

"Sure, you would've been fine if it'd been your first time in a place like that. But it wasn't."

He looked at me, waited. I had to look away before I could start up again. "Back behind those bars and metal doors, with those desperate guys. I was that way, angry, restless, all that energy and no place for it to go. When you're that age and caged up, only thing you can do is what gets you in trouble."

"A smart guy like you, watching it happen—must have made it that much worse."

"You lash out, get beat down by the guards, the inmates, doesn't matter which. Just gives you more rage, so you do it again."

"No way to get away from it, I suppose."

"For me, it took a while, but when I started to see the ones who would play with you, do little things on purpose, you know, to set you off, it got me thinking. And thinking, after a while, got me a way to pull back on the rage, to stuff it down. Saved my life, I guess."

Ralph just waited, knowing he didn't have to say anything now that I'd got going. "There's the feelings I had at first, the rage, the terror, wanting to jump out of my own skin. Then there's the feeling after I learned how to hold it in, like my head was stuffed with cotton, with a big, heavy knot in my gut."

"You shut down."

I nod. "That's the way I was when I woke up this morning. That's what kept me in that group home all those years, that and all the pills."

"For twenty-three years, five months, and eighteen days," says Ralph. He's laughing at me, but I've got to join in. I used to count everything, my crazy way of holding my world together. He's short by eight months and twelve days, but I get the point. Then he gets serious again. "You know how it goes. When something comes up that pulls you back to the place where the trauma happened, it's like going through it all over again. I'm glad you called; honored." He puts his hand on my arm.

I explain to him why I didn't go to the others—I don't want to give him a swelled head. Then I turn it around, ask how things are going with Cindy.

It's his turn to look away. "More like not going." My turn to wait. "She, uh, put me on hold, the way she put it."

I nodded but couldn't come up with anything useful.

"I know what that means." He looks back at me. "I've been dumped before. With everything going on, I doubt she's giving me much thought."

"You giving up?"

He looks off and sighs. "Shit, I don't know. Almost. Maybe. It's not like she owes me anything. It's just, it felt . . . like she was right there with me. Thing is, if I'm that clueless, I must not have been paying attention. Hard to blame her."

We're quiet for a bit. The man's hurting, and I don't know if more news is going to make it any better, but for some reason, I'm sharing it anyway. "You hear Billie paid her a visit?"

"Wow, they brought out the big gun. Seems like Cindy loves that place. I hope she doesn't let herself get pushed into anything. She needs this."

"Hard to say no to Billie. I feel bad now—I set it up."

"Aw, shit, man—"

"That lawyer was pushing it, and I knew I couldn't talk her into it."

"So you punted, to Billie, of all people. I should call Cindy. But I guess I can't do that, can I." His eyes are moving around, and I can see the pressure building, like he's mad as hell but doesn't want to put it on me.

"My sister, she doesn't always appreciate what she's got. I know you care about her, but—"

"She's got her own ideas. I was an asshole, got cocky, teasing her about not getting paid. I guess I was afraid of losing her to someplace new and shiny, with things I couldn't understand. I should have respected her for her courage, but I ran her down instead."

I couldn't disagree, but then, he wasn't the only one. "Thing about my sister, though, she'll do what she thinks is best. She won't let anyone, even Billie, push her around."

"Yeah. I wish I could help, though."

We run down after that. Ralph's back into himself, and anyway he has to make his old ladies their dinner. He let Grace and Billie know to expect him late, but instead of offering to cook for themselves, they said they'd have a snack and wait. Man, he's spoiled those two. I head home to see how Cindy made out at Back Door.

Father's home when I get there.

"Dinner is served," he grumps. "Spaghetti and meatballs. Sauce is from a jar, meatballs out of a plastic bag—please don't beat me, sire."

"I'll let it go, seeing as how you're all humble and everything, but don't make a habit of it. Any word from milady?"

"Oh, this is way too early for our Cindy to get home. She might have to eat with us, and wouldn't that be a shame." He won't admit it, but he's lost the most, not having her around the house.

"She was going to try for permission from her boss lady, do some kind of outreach, help them deal with the murder."

He gives me a serious look. "So she's going to use her training after all. I hope they appreciate what they've got in her. Long as she doesn't try to play detective."

"Who said anything about that?" Damn, the old man's nobody's fool.

"Well, Billie was over here the other night for something. I figure she's worried about Stewart Center and that dishwasher they sent over to Back Door. That boy's goose is cooked anyway, I imagine."

"I don't know. This lawyer he's got is pretty sharp."

"Well," he says, "here's hoping they pin it down, and he's the one who did it."

That shocks me. "Why would you say a thing like that?"

He shrugs. "Think about it. If it's not him, it means somebody who's still there put a knife in that chef, and Cindy's there every day with him."

1 5

Cindy

Cindy walked in around eight thirty to find her father and brother in the living room, watching TV. They said they'd saved some dinner for her.

She knew she should eat something, and going into the kitchen helped her avoid talk about her day, which had sucked. She hadn't been able to think, work, eat, or talk to anybody after the meeting with Charlotte. Even Susan seemed preoccupied when Cindy passed her by the elevators, and Arthur was absorbed in his screen. Nicole came by around one to see if she wanted any lunch, but Cindy sent her away. She wasn't getting anything done at her own screen but was afraid to leave and make it obvious how useless she was, so she fussed aimlessly for the whole long afternoon and evening, until more than half the team had drifted off and she thought she could sneak out.

She wondered if Charlotte would talk to Arthur about their meeting. Would he care? Would Charlotte interfere with her work there? It had been hard enough, trying to fake her way into a job in that place. Now she had promised to use her questionable skills as a trauma counselor while she tried to wheedle information out of people. And the image of Carlson bleeding on the counter kept coming back, washing away any coherent thought, leaving her edgy and empty.

But she slept through the night without any nightmares and felt better sitting at her workstation the next morning. So much of Back Door seemed off limits now: the dining room and her old work-team room in Steven's suite. She wasn't yet comfortable with the A team, but at least they weren't openly hostile.

Then Arthur came in and actually spoke to her before turning to his screen.

"Hey, good news. Steven liked your work. He, uh, thinks it came from the team; Mother said not to bring up your name." If that made Arthur uncomfortable, it didn't show. "It was hard to keep his attention, but then, he was never interested in the technical side. I hope enough got through. I'll take it to Mother today. Then to Vernon, I suppose. He'll find fault with it—it's what he does. I'll handle that."

The phone rang, and after a curt greeting and a "Yes, she is," he extended the receiver her way.

Gloria. "Cindy. I was hoping to catch you." Where else would she be? "Charlotte said you were going to be helping people, uh, get over it, the shock and all. I promised her we'd help, so if you come to Steven's office now, we could talk it over."

When Cindy walked in, Gloria must have seen her anxious look. "I sent him home. He was in no condition, poor man," said Gloria. She spread her hands, palms up, and tears leaked down her cheeks.

Cindy was embarrassed by the other woman's lack of self-consciousness and shamed by her own charade. At least she could try to help. "Did you know Carlson well?"

"Well, of course, I've been over to their house any number of times. They're both so warm, especially Carlson. He used to bring my girls into their kitchen at home, get them involved in cooking, baking, even got them laughing over the dishes—something I never managed. After they separated, they both tried hard not to put me in the middle so they could both stay close." This time she had to hide her face, shaking her head. "I'm sorry. I guess I'm not quite ready for this."

Cindy had no opportunity to digest the news—married, now separated—and put her hand on the other woman's. "I know. The pain you're feeling, that's what will help you recover. Is Steven . . . ?"

"It's like he's in a trance. Worse. You look in his eyes and it's like he's not in there. You know men. He's not denying it or anything, but I haven't seen the tears come yet. Of course, when he's home, it might be different."

"Is there anyone else, outside of here?"

Gloria shook her head. "I don't know. His generation, when they came out, a lot of their families pulled away. His never came back. Maybe some of Carlson's . . . He had a daughter—married young, before . . . She's in New Mexico now, with young kids. I've talked to her, and she'll be here in a few days. There's not a lot of money, so I think she'll be invading Steven's place. I'll have to help him put some of his prized possessions away before they hit town." The thought brought out the first chuckle and smile. That was good to see. Then her smile got bigger. "You know, you are your daddy's child. You're not bad at this. Not as good as him, maybe, but not bad." She looked off past Cindy's shoulder, eyes focused somewhere else.

Oh my, Cindy thought, *she's falling for him.* The deep voice, the soulful eyes—she'd seen ladies in the church react this way, and watched their husbands squint. Of course, just because she found him attractive . . . *Time to do some digging.*

"How about your family?" She hoped it wasn't too obvious. They *had* been talking about Steven and his sources of support.

"Oh, well, my Arnette is about to graduate college—North Carolina. I don't suppose she'll be back here anytime soon; she's got a boy to follow. And Cecile's got little ones of her own, in Springfield. I'm on the phone with them every Sunday. They're good kids."

"You and your husband must be very proud."

"Oh, he was, but Matthew's gone now; be eleven years this summer. Way too young."

"I'm so sorry."

"There's just no sense to it, no matter how I look at it. He was a churchgoer—we went to the West Medford Baptist. I hardly go now." How did church come up? *Oh, yeah.* "The minister's all about sinning, heaven, and hell. I don't know."

That stuff never worked for Cindy either. It wasn't Father's style, but even so, she hadn't found a home in his or any church.

Gloria asked, "How about your mama?"

"Oh, she passed before I got to high school."

"You know, then. It's hard when they're too young to understand but old enough to remember, to miss them. And old enough to worry when we fall apart. Those were hard times, oh yes, they were."

Cindy liked the woman. If Gloria set her sights on her father, he could do a whole lot worse. Then she shook herself. *What an imagination!* "When do you think Steven will be back?"

"I really don't know. I can't imagine what he'd be doing now, sitting at home. Do you think I should go get him?"

Cindy wasn't sure how to respond to that. It turned out she didn't have to.

"Oh, I'm forgetting—the daughter and her two littlest ones, two and five, they'll be here tomorrow. No need to worry then. He'll be back."

"I'd like to meet with him when he does." As the bereaved husband, he topped both her lists: one for suspects, the other for those in need of support.

Gloria raised her eyebrows and gave her a long look.

1 6

Paul

I'm sitting at the kitchen table, staring at the paper without seeing, let alone reading, when the phone rings. It's not even nine, but it's already been an eventful morning. Father has gone off on a visit to one of his deacons, and I was just stumbling down the stairs when Cindy left for work. She made sure to share the news about her new assignment from Charlotte, her boss. She's still mad at me for setting her up with Sam, and I can't blame her. Blaming me for Billie being on her case, though, I'm not so sure about that. I can't help who I am and where I've been. It's all cooking around in my head when I drag myself up to stop the ringing.

"Reverend Abernathy's residence, Paul speaking." Yeah, I know.

"Paul." It's Phyllis, but it takes me a beat to recognize her voice. Something's wrong. "I can't stay on the phone, but I had to let you know. Sophie came down, and she's crying. I've never seen her like this. She says everyone's getting a call this morning telling them not to go to their jobs."

"You mean, like, in the units?" I'm not usually this slow. I think I know what she's saying; I just don't want to hear it.

"From their regular jobs—all of them." You see, a lot of the members at the Center have jobs like Johnnie's, scattered all over the area. It's what helps us get our lives back. "They're even calling people at work, telling them they have to leave. That Carolyn Doyle"—ConDo's director of mental health services—"she's standing around with her arms folded, glaring. There's going to be a meeting at eleven. I've got to hang up— they need the phone."

I tell her I'm on my way, to hold tight, whatever that means, but it isn't until after I hang up that I realize they might mean me too. I've been there a year and a half, though, so I figure I should be okay. That's how dumb I am. I'm thinking it's just as well I'll only get to hang around the Center until I leave for work around eleven thirty. The whole way in on the subway, I'm thinking I'll be giving support to other members along with Phyllis.

Phyllis is in the middle of the communications room, standing, alone. I've never seen her like this. When she's in that room, she's always busy. I rush over and put my arms around her, and we hug each other hard. I hear this little cough and feel her go stiff. It's Doctor Marsha, ConDo's top shrink. Used to be my doctor. I've heard she's been pushing to make it so members aren't allowed to touch each other, but so far Sophie's been able to hold her off.

Phyllis is already pulling away, so I stand back and turn to the woman. She's taller than me, with wavy red hair. We didn't part on the best of terms because I refused to go back to the group home, and I've made trouble for her by "stirring up" the other residents.

I'm not backing down today either. "You got something you want to say to me?"

She's got on this nasty smirk, her happy face. "Well, Mister Abernathy. Still using some of our services, I see."

By this time my hands are balled up at my sides and blood's pounding in my head. If she thinks she's going to drag me back down . . .

"Paul, honey," says Phyllis, at my side and pulling me back by the upper arm. She can't finish because Sophie's there.

"Why, Doctor Obermann, how nice of you to come by for a visit." Everybody here knows it's not a social call, and Sophie's not feeling nice about it. "You know Paul Abernathy, and this is his good friend

Phyllis Dietz, who edits our newsletter and literary journal, along with many other responsibilities."

I realize I'm sweating now, and it's a blessing when that woman turns her glare on Sophie.

"Thank you. I'm happy to be here." Right. "But I also need to make sure that our policies are being carried out."

"Yes, I suppose you do," says Sophie. Then she looks at me. "Paul, may I see you for a moment?" Then, to Dr. Marsha, "Please make yourself comfortable. I've much to do, but Phyllis can answer your questions about what happens here." She's too caught up in the nasty stare-down to notice Phyllis's desperate look. I tell her I won't be long and give her hand a quick squeeze.

"Paul," says Sophie as we huddle in a corner of the busy office, "I tried to call you half an hour ago, but there was no answer. I suppose you were on your way here."

"Phyllis called to tell me about the meeting with Carolyn. When did the good doctor get here?"

"Just a few minutes ago. I don't have much time. You know the order to pull everyone off their work placements? They're insisting I include you."

"But I'm not transitional. I know it's not a regular state block, but I've been there well over a year."

"I know. I think because it's a state office—"

"Or maybe because I said no to their plans for me?"

"Well, perhaps that too."

Bastards. I can't believe they could get away with it. Then I'm thinking, maybe they can't. "I'm going to call my supervisor, see what she says. If they want me to go to work, I don't see how ConDo can stop me. They could maybe keep me away from here, I suppose."

"Well, give it a day or two—let's see what we can work out. I called Billie, and we're going to have a team meeting this evening. For some reason, she wants it to be at your place."

The rectory? What's that all about?

It can't have been more than five minutes, but when I get back to the main room, Phyllis is standing in the same spot as when I left, alone. Her shoulders are slumped, her head is hanging, and she's shaking it back and forth. When I reach her and touch her shoulder, she peeks at me through her hair. I don't like the look in her eyes.

"Let's get out of here," I say, and lead her to the door.

She doesn't say anything until we're a few blocks away, on a bench on the edge of the big plaza in front of city hall. Now that my arm's tight around her, I can feel her shaking. Her voice barely reaches me over the traffic. "She said schizophrenia is a hereditary condition and offered to arrange for genetic counseling."

We've talked to Emma and done the research together, and even though that was the thinking for years, there's never been evidence of a strong genetic link. My doctor agrees with that too; I remind Phyllis of all that.

"That woman is evil," she says. "She destroys people, crushes their spirits."

"We'll just have to keep her away from you then. I'll talk to Sophie about it."

"Don't you dare patronize me, Paul Abernathy." That's better. "I can handle this myself."

That's what I figured she'd say. I'm not always clueless.

"Did she tell you they're pulling me out of Elder Affairs?"

She whipped around at that. "You're kidding! That's not fair; that's your job now."

"That's what I thought. I want to call my supervisor, but Sophie asked me to hold off a day or two—or at least until the team meeting tonight. Billie's coming over to the rectory. You want to come?"

"Oh, I don't think so." I figured, but wanted to ask anyhow. She's willing to go to an early lunch with me, though, at this soup place across the street. We don't talk about it anymore, but we both want to stall until the big shots have their meeting and clear out. Some folks may stay home after they get the call about their jobs, but others will come in, and we agree it's important to be there for them.

Back at the Center, we see folks we haven't seen for a while, there now after being pulled out of work. It's good to check in, and we all try to act like it's a temporary thing, maybe for the rest of this week at the most, but underneath we all know it could get worse. A few folks are bitter, but the worst is the feeling you get that we're used to it—yanked back down yet again when we're trying to climb up and out. You could almost hear them thinking, *This place again—shit!* Most of them look numb, and staff members are standing around the same way. This is always such a calm, happy place. Not today.

After I've had about as much as I can stand, I try to get Phyllis to come home with me, but she turns me down. "I'm going to stay here. Sophie said they'll fix an early dinner. After that I'm going home and getting in bed."

I stay around until they get ready to serve dinner, when it's time for Billie's meeting. Though that's not going to be fun, it will be easier than sitting with all this pain. I tell Phyllis I'll see her here in the morning, but I'm thinking if she's not here by nine (more than an hour later than her usual), I'll have to go get her.

17

Cindy

Cindy couldn't believe it. Instead of the congregation, the big meeting room at the rectory held Billie, Grace, Emma, Sophie, and Ralph—Team Billie in all its ragged glory—along with Father and Paul.

"I got a tip," Billie explained. She was famous for her connections. "ConDo was on *Boston Chronicles* this evening. We don't have one of those recording things, so I called Eugene and asked him to tape it."

The show was on public television every weeknight and featured interviews in a magazine format. The host, Alec Barber, introduced the show.

"Three days ago, Carlson Reveniste, the chef at Back Door Technologies in Cambridge, and apparently a beloved figure there, was brutally murdered, allegedly by their dishwasher, a mental patient placed in the job by Consolidated Dorchester Human Services."

He swiveled his chair to the left to face three guests arrayed on the other side of his desk. "I'd like to welcome Martin Islington, the CEO of Consolidated Dorchester; Dr. Marsha Obermann, their medical director; and welcome back a frequent guest on *Boston Chronicles*, state senator Margaret Finney, who serves on their board of directors. Thank you all for joining me. Starting with you, Doctor, are we ever going to get a handle on the mental patients who commit these brutal crimes?"

Islington interjected: "First, if I may, I'd like to express our profound sympathy for Mr. Reveniste's colleagues and family—"

Barber: "I understand his husband works at Back Door as well."

Islington: ". . . in their grief over this terrible loss. Everyone at ConDo feels awful about what happened, and we take full responsibility. Thank you for giving us the opportunity to make that clear to your viewers."

Obermann: "Let me assure you, Alec, that we are doing everything we can to address the issue you raise. Serious mental illness is far more common than people think, and the job of monitoring all the people who have the potential for these kinds of acts can seem overwhelming, given our limited resources. The hard work of mental health agencies, in this community and around the country, to monitor disturbed individuals and keep them in treatment is often overlooked. We have very effective medications that, in the vast majority of cases, can prevent this sort of tragedy."

Barber: "So what happened here, Doctor? This man was in treatment, no? It seems reasonable to ask why this obviously dangerous individual would be placed in a setting where knives were readily available."

Islington: "While we don't presume to encroach on the district attorney's activities, our own internal investigation has resulted in the suspension and discipline of two of our staff who were responsible for the screening that should have occurred prior to this individual's placement."

Barber swung to his right: "Senator, ConDo is a private organization, but they receive state funds to perform this work. What's the legislature's responsibility in this?"

Finney: "Alec, let me say how sad it is that we have to have this conversation only after such a tragedy, when hundreds of dedicated staff at ConDo and agencies like it throughout our commonwealth do heroic work every day with little or no recognition, and for very modest pay. It's a shame that the negligence of these two has taken over the spotlight. I know how hard Martin and Dr. Obermann work to prevent this kind of tragedy. Unfortunately, human services will always be subject to human error."

Barber, with a wave of his hand: "Okay, so these individuals are gone. Is anything else being done?"

Obermann: "We've decided to suspend all job placements such as the one this individual was participating in . . ."

Barber, looking down at his notes: "Transitional—"

Obermann: "Yes. Our Stewart Center, which oversees these placements—"

Barber: "And where one of these folks worked, is that correct?"

Obermann: "That's right. The Center will be stepping back from such placements for the foreseeable future. The idea that seriously impaired people should work regular jobs may be an unrealistic expectation in the majority of cases. We are going to sharpen our focus to monitoring treatment compliance, to make sure nothing like this is ever allowed to happen again."

Islington: "It's a matter of responsible stewardship that goes with the mission of any nonprofit community agency. I think it's too early to tell whether we will be eliminating these placements entirely"—unlike the cameraman, he seemed unaware of Obermann's glare—"but we will be performing a thorough evaluation involving highly qualified experts from within and outside the organization, in close consultation with the Department of Mental Health."

Barber: "Yes, the department that funds these services. I should mention that we invited Commissioner Celestine to join us, but she had a prior commitment." He didn't hide his disdain—how could anything take precedence over his show?

Finney: "I want to say again, Alec, that I have complete faith in ConDo and their leadership to do the right thing here. And I have to acknowledge that it is all too easy for people in my position, in the legislature and elsewhere in state government, to underestimate the terrible toll mental illness exacts on our families. I hope that one thing that can come of this awful event is a commitment to support

ConDo and other agencies in their critically important work. I intend to introduce a bill for supplemental funding for these services, and to streamline regulations to enhance access to treatment."

Soon Barber was shaking their hands, turning back to the camera, and moving on to his next story, and Eugene switched the set off, leaving a heavy silence in the room. It fell to Sophie to break it. "Isn't that wonderful. Everybody's brave and hardworking except two negligent staff and all the dangerous mental patients. We just need more money to keep them in check."

"Would it have been so hard," asked Emma, "for them to say anything to balance it out? Like how we're no more violent than anybody else, and way more likely to be victims?"

Billie said, "Not gonna happen. That was all damage control, for ConDo and for the state. It's a huge problem, so many crazies and so little money, we're doing the best we can, and we're weeding out the bad apples in our staff. We're tough—no bleeding hearts here."

Paul spoke up for the first time. "Get rid of the ones that believe you're good for something, the ones'll give you half a chance. Damn!"

"And did you catch the code?" said Ralph. "Enhanced access to treatment is a euphemism for outpatient commitment."

"Forced medication," growled Billie.

"And now it's public," said Sophie, "so no chance of rescinding it. All our members lose their jobs, and we're supposed to stop encouraging them to go back out there and try. She trashed our whole approach. We're supposed to give up on our members because they'll never amount to anything, never be more than full-time mental patients. Our job will be to follow them around and bully them into passivity."

Billie said, "You gotta admit, that was pretty slick. Now it's not enough to work on Martin to get Marsha to back off; we have to help him go out and create a whole different narrative."

"Before this, anyone who asked for a job got a chance," said Sophie. "How are we supposed to approach employers now that this is out there? Our own psychiatrist says our folks are too dangerous."

"Well," said Billie, "it all hangs on whether Johnnie did it. We don't think he did. We manage to clear him, there's some hope to push this all the way back, and chase Dr. Marsha back into her hole."

"I have to say, as the daughter of a labor organizer, it would be handy to have a union involved," said Emma. "I know you hate them, Billie, but it's just not right, what they're doing to Shep and Lu."

Paul said, "Someone's got to reach out to them."

Sophie answered, "I'll talk to Lu. I'm sure others at the Center will as well. We won't forget her, I can assure you."

Billie said, "How about the other one—Shep? I don't trust the people on that outreach team to take care of him. They'll be intimidated by the bitches." Meaning Dr. Marsha and Carolyn. "And, Ralph, you have a memo in your file. It would be like handing them a gun to put to your head."

Cindy was trying to picture that when her brother spoke. "I'll do it. I'm likely the closest one here to that system, being at Farnsworth all those years. Nothing much those two can do to me now. And it looks like I'm going to have some time on my hands."

Cindy was shocked. "They wouldn't do that, would they? You're not transitional anymore. It's been, what . . ."

"Eighteen months." *Of course he would know the exact amount*, she thought. In the old days, he would have given her the number of days. "And they already did it," he said, turning to Sophie. "No reason to wait now. I'm going to my supervisor at Elder Affairs, see what she says."

"I'll give Martin a call," said Billie. "After all, he still wants to be buddies with Rev Eugene here." She was the only one to ever call him that. Remarkably, Cindy's father didn't seem to mind. "And it won't cost him anything."

"We'd surely appreciate it, Albertina. Thank you," said Father. Was that really Billie's name? Trust her father to dig up that nugget.

Cindy took a deep breath. "I've got some news too. I talked to Charlotte, the CEO at Back Door, and offered to reach out and offer trauma support to the folks who knew Carlson best. I'll have to be careful, but I can let you know what I hear."

"Holy shit," Billie shouted. "That's great! I know it's got to feel overwhelming to take on, but I think Uncle Sal could help with that. He's over in the assisted living on River Street. Course, he's not that strong anymore—thank God—but he's still, well, about as sharp as ever. I'll get back to you after I talk to him."

That seemed to be the signal for the group to file out, buoyed by the only good news of the evening. All because she agreed to listen? She didn't get it. When she said as much to her father and brother, Eugene pulled her into a hug.

"It gives them hope," he said, "that's all. Right now it's all they've got."

• • •

Back in Arthur's office, it was time to get busy on the site and prove herself, and Cindy focused well enough for a few hours, when something truly odd broke through. A voice, deep and in tune, started singing "Ol' Man River." She looked up as others joined in, singing about sweating and straining, searching for the song's source, only to see a small figure in a gray suit wind briskly through the desks. He was certainly not singing. A few snickers rippled among the coders, though none looked up.

"Hey." Arthur stood hunched over with his hands in his pockets as the man strutted in. It was the man who'd followed Arthur out of the meeting; had to be Vernon.

"Good to see you too, Arthur," he said in a formal tone. "I won't take much of your valuable time, just . . ." He paused and glanced at Cindy.

Arthur waved an awkward arm in her direction. "Vernon, this is Cindy. She's designing the external website."

Vernon was well proportioned, but she barely had to crane her neck to look into his sharp gray eyes. "Ah yes, the social worker." After shaking her hand, he looked imploringly back at Arthur, then shrugged and turned back to her. "Ms. Abernathy, Steven has explained your, er, assignment. We should speak privately. Please give my secretary a call." Then he turned back to Arthur. "Our NSA friends are in need of a progress report."

"Tell them it's going fine."

"They want details. Give me something."

"Look, Vernon, my team is the best they're going to find. We're on it. That's all I can tell you or them. I could say something meaningless, like we're this or that percent along the way, but it wouldn't mean anything. Some parts go fast. Then we hit a problem and we're stuck until we solve it. Then we go fast. My guys will keep at it until it's done."

"Our friends are concerned. It's not like you and your team to have these kinds of . . ." He seemed to grope for a word. ". . . issues."

"I know. It was a stumble, but we're back on track now."

"And are you any closer to knowing what happened?"

"I've got an idea. No proof—yet."

"We've got a deadline—"

"Which we just might meet; or not. It depends. When it's done, I'll tell you and you can tell them."

"Unless," said Vernon, in a tone Cindy heard as condescending, "you'd prefer to tell them yourself?"

Arthur didn't seem fazed. "You tell them or I tell them—it's all the same. If I could explain it to you . . . It's all code. When we're sure it works the way it's supposed to, I'll tell you. And them."

Her boss had remained calm, if slightly condescending himself, through the whole interaction, but Vernon had by then dropped all pretense at patience. Clenching and unclenching his fists, he threw his chin out and up, with index finger raised. "Very well. I've warned you. I'll do what I can with our government masters, but if you find them on your doorstep, DO NOT blame me."

The singing resumed as Vernon left. *He jus keep rolling, he keep on rolling, he jus keep rolling a-long.* Everyone joined in laughter and applause as he stormed out the door.

"Now you've met Vernon," said Arthur.

"He doesn't seem popular with your team."

"They like to have fun. He always wants to know what they're doing. He used to look at their screens and ask them to explain, and some of them tried, but he doesn't have the background. Then he'd get pushy. They don't like that. Oh." He looked embarrassed. "I hope you weren't offended—by the spiritual. We're so White around here."

It was old Broadway, but she let it go. "That's okay, I wasn't offended. I would like to get to know the members of your team better, though."

He gave her a puzzled look and pointed. "There they are."

Somehow it had been easier with Steven's crew; there were fewer of them, and though they thought highly of themselves, they hadn't been billed as a team of geniuses. These were the elite of the company, and smelly Mount Elmer sitting just outside their door was an added barrier. The obvious place to mingle was the kitchen, but so far, she had only managed to resist its siren song of donuts and muffins, candy and ice cream bars by staying away.

Someone here would know what lay beneath that cryptic exchange between Arthur and Vernon; maybe one of them would tell her. The kitchen held only one young man, powering down potato chips from a large bag and following them with Coke. With dark curls, a prominent Adam's apple, and skinny jeans ending inches above his running shoes, he looked like an exceptionally tall twelve-year-old, yet to fill out after his growth spurt. She stuck out a hand and introduced herself.

"Oh, yeah, we know who you are." Despite the deep voice, it came out more childlike than unfriendly. Could this be Ol' Man River, the *Show Boat* soloist? "Freddy."

"I'm working on the website."

"That's good. Arthur needs the company. He's not naturally social, even for a coder."

"Is there some trouble with Vernon?"

Apparently unfazed by her abrupt prying, he nodded. "Not normally, but we've had some problems. The projects get broken down into pieces, and they get passed out to us, like, in pairs, to work on. We turn our product over to Arthur to stitch together and proof it. Chips?"

She grabbed a handful and started feeding them into her mouth, one after another.

"Last week he brought us together for a meeting—we never do those—told us how important the work we were doing was, to the company, to the country—duh—and then said start over, just like that." He extended the bag again, raising his eyebrows in encouragement, and she got another load. "So, we're way late and Vernon's pissed. Can't blame him."

The chips were gone. How many were there—twelve, twenty? Probably a lot more. *Shit.* She thanked him and got out of there. So, the A team wasn't infallible. That must be a shock to their young systems. It made her feel better—another guilty pleasure.

• • •

Cindy hunched into the collar of her jacket as she trudged to Alewife station. The winding dirt path had three-foot-high light posts set ten yards apart, with fins around the tops that cast little pools of light downward and all around, illuminating the path and the tall weeds alongside while leaving the scrubby woods beyond in darkness. There was always rustling in there, no doubt the sounds of rats or other woodland creatures.

Then, something strange. One by one, the lights began to wink out, starting a half dozen lights ahead and progressing back toward her. She stopped and stared, too self-conscious to turn and run. Just before the light directly ahead winked out, she thought she saw a faint silhouette, a person dropping something on top of it. In the next moment something hit her, knocking her backwards onto the ground. Her breath was driven out, and her hands scrabbled to push the weight off until larger hands pinned them above and on either side of her head. Then all his weight—a knee or shin—was on her chest, squeezing out her remaining air so she couldn't scream, despite the pain.

A rough beard scratched the side of her face, hot breath against her ear, the voice hoarse. "Not a sound, sweetie. Not one word. You don't belong at that place, you know that? I catch you around here again, you won't walk away."

With that he raised his weight off her but kept hold of her arms. It turned out he was just rearing back to drive his knee into her, just under her ribs. The pain was mammoth, the inability to find breath terrifying. When he released her hands, pain kept her pinned to the ground until he kicked her hard, three times, first in the ribs, then her kidney when she curled up on her side. Then it was over.

It seemed to take forever for the first shallow breath to make its way into her lungs. She finally identified the pathetic, high-pitched moan as her own, every time she exhaled. The first blow hurt her badly, causing a deep ache in her pelvis. The pain in her kidney was worse. Her ribs and lungs hurt with every gasping breath as she spit dirt out of her mouth.

She wasn't sure how long she lay there whimpering, but when she could move her arms, she decided to get out of there. All the lights that had winked out were on again, but she was much closer to Back Door than the station, and she couldn't face going deeper into the woods, so she began a hunched stumble back the way she had come, moaning with every step of her right foot, dragging her left. The blow to her kidney had taken all the strength out of that side of her body.

When she reached the doors, she realized that she had dropped her purse with her entry card back on the path. She pressed a hand on the glass wall, slipped slowly down to her knees, and began to cry. She didn't know the young man who discovered her lying on her side. He looked down at her and said, "Are you okay?" The universal stupid question, then, "Wait here," which almost made her laugh; like she was going to get up and run off.

Then Craig was kneeling beside her, an arm around her shoulders, supporting her head with his chest, asking her what had happened, where she was hurt.

"Guy kicked me" was all she could manage.

He coached the young man hovering nearby through a two-man carry, and soon she was floating through the lobby, down a hallway, into one of the little relaxation rooms, and lowered down onto the bed. Craig was beside her, talking into his shirt collar, and in a few minutes, he was replaced by Charlotte, with Susan's concerned face hovering in the background.

By this time, the pain from breathing had localized in her ribs and grown sharper in her lower abdomen. At least she had managed to stop moaning by the time Charlotte came in and demanded every detail from her. She lacked the strength to fight her off, and her presence was reassuring, even while Cindy flinched at her intense stare. She gave her everything—it was all too vivid in her mind.

Charlotte turned to Craig. "We'll talk in a minute. We cannot have this." Then, to Susan, "Bring her to Mount Auburn." The hospital across town. "I'll call ahead." Turning back to Cindy: "I'm on the board there."

Susan used the dashboard touch screen to recline the leather passenger seat of the surprisingly fancy German car. "I should have warned you. Now that it's dark so early, those woods aren't safe. There's an encampment in there; rough characters, they panhandle in the intersection where the highway starts. The way I heard it, when we moved here Charlotte tried to get them cleared out, but this is the People's Republic of Cambridge—bums have rights. Oh, excuse me, *the homeless.*"

Hm. On another day Cindy might have challenged that, but she didn't have the strength or desire to stick up for the bastard who had mugged her.

"You might want to start driving to work."

That wasn't an option, but Cindy lacked the energy to argue. Couldn't she just leave her alone and drive? Apparently not.

"I've been lobbying for a shuttle van, but Charlotte keeps saying it's an easy walk—just over a quarter mile—and she wants people out moving, being healthy. This might tip the balance, though."

"Look, Susan, you're all being very nice, but—"

"Hey, we look after our own. We'll work something out."

Cindy was no stranger to emergency rooms. Fortunately, she had been too young to accompany Paul on any of the meltdowns that led him there as a portal to the state hospital, but she had often been called in to them as a social worker, so she was prepared for at least two or three hours' wait. She didn't realize how the one percent experienced health care.

Susan called the hospital on her hands-free phone, and when they pulled to a stop under the shelter above the Emergency Department doors, a nurse with a wheelchair was waiting to whisk her past the glares of the ordinary folks in the waiting room into a private curtained area. She dug out her insurance card (someone had retrieved her purse from the path), and it was taken from her by the nurse, who said, "I think we have all your information, but if we need anything else, we'll let you know. The doctor will be with you shortly."

Seven familiar little words that in Cindy's experience meant anything from one to four hours, but this time a doctor—an actual adult, not some fuzzy-cheeked resident—was at her side before she finished the thought.

"Well, you must be special," he said, with a friendly smile. With skin and hair as white as his coat, he could have stepped out of a soap opera.

"I'm not feeling special, but thanks for the royal treatment."

He gently asked her for the whole story again as he helped her out of her clothes, thankfully allowing her to keep on her underwear. She jumped when he probed her bruises, though his touch was light and he grunted his sympathy each time. Then it was into a smock, onto a wheelchair with her clothes bundled on her lap, and off to X-ray, which did involve a longish wait—there were limits to Charlotte's influence. Then she was wheeled back to a little room off the ER, where a muscular young policewoman with a dirty-blond ponytail insisted she repeat the story all over again.

Cindy couldn't describe her attacker except to say that he seemed quite big and strong, with a short, stubbly beard. When the officer made a face, she explained how very dark it was in the woods after the lights went out one by one, and at this point the policewoman drew back and raised her eyebrows.

"And you're sure this wasn't someone you know?"

It couldn't have been more obvious. The cop didn't buy the story about the lights going out and figured Cindy was covering for someone. Probably a domestic, she would say to her colleagues back at the station, shaking her head.

Then the doctor was back. Her ribs and kidneys were bruised, but no broken bones. She should call if there was blood in her urine, which was likely but only a concern if it persisted. He seemed relieved when she turned down his offer of oxycodone—she would make do with ibuprofen. They sent her home in a cab, courtesy of Charlotte.

Her father and brother were there to greet her—Gloria had called to fill them in—and Father wanted to know what had happened, but she couldn't face going through all the details again. She was bruised and sore, but the doctor said she'd live. That would have to suffice. When her father opened his mouth to demand more, Paul broke in to tell her that was plenty of information for now, and stared his father down, which was quite a sight. He did allow Father to bring her a rather large brandy, which burned all the way down but helped her get to sleep less than an hour later.

1 8

Paul

When I get up the next morning, Cindy's bedroom door is closed. Downstairs, Father pauses on his way out the door.

"Gloria called, said to tell her not to come in today, take as much time as she needs. She feels bad. They didn't think of that path as dangerous, even after dark, lit up as it is."

"Huh. I guess they know better now."

"Well, now, things happen," he says. "You can't always know what to expect. Anyway, they're having some meetings, figure out how to make things safer."

"How'd Cindy take it?"

"Relieved. She's frustrated more than anything, but you can see she's sore in a bunch of places, and her eye's swelled up. She'll heal in time, but after the other thing . . ."

"I'll come back early this afternoon, look in on her." I figure to stop in on Phyllis at the Stewart Center later this morning.

When I look in on her at the Center, Phyllis insists on going over with me, and we find Cindy in the living room. "Thank God you guys are here. I couldn't stand any more email or Facebook. And the soaps are all set in hospitals."

That brings a rare smile out of Phyllis. Cindy shuts down the TV and volunteers to make tea. Phyllis, of course, thought to pick up some scones on the way, and we sit down to pack on a few pounds—it's what Abernathys do. It's not an issue for Phyllis, but then, who ever said life was fair?

After we tuck in for a while, Cindy makes a growling noise. "Better. Much better."

"So," says Phyllis, "do you feel up to talking about it?"

I look around at that. Phyllis hasn't had the trauma training. You're supposed to let the person decide when the time's right. But Phyllis has instincts about these things.

Cindy seems calm enough when she answers, "It wasn't much, actually. This big guy knocked me down when I was walking the path on my way to Alewife yesterday evening. Got right on top of me, then kicked the crap out of me."

Phyllis: "Did you get a look at him?"

Cindy tells us the story about the lights, and Phyllis buys it; I guess I do too, though it's hard to picture.

Then she tells us what he said.

"Don't belong there." I ask, "Could he have been from Back Door?"

"I don't think so. Susan, Charlotte's assistant there, said there's a place in the woods there, like a homeless encampment. Maybe I got too close and he felt threatened."

"But why you?" I press. "Must be lots of folks walking through there every day."

"Actually, by that time, most everybody still at Back Door drives. I guess they know better than to walk through there after dark."

I can't let it go. "But why would he see you as a threat?" Turns out that's the wrong thing to say. I should stop pushing her, pay attention to Phyllis's hand squeezing the hell out of my arm.

"Why? Maybe because he's a paranoid schizophrenic, like the ones they used to keep in the hospital so they wouldn't be sleeping in the woods and attacking people."

You see, there's a reason they teach us not to press for information right after someone goes through bad shit. Of course, no one needed to teach Phyllis not to push like that. Did I deserve to get that thrown in my face? I don't know. It feels better when Phyllis puts her arm around my shoulder and I feel her hair brush my ear.

19

Cindy

The Stewart Center people hated Back Door, her new work home. They wanted it to be someone from there. *Nice try.* Cindy's resentment kept her from feeling Paul's pain, even when she saw the effect her words had on him, the flicker of anger, then coldness and finally distance that came into his eyes. It made her tired more than sad. But Phyllis put her arm around Paul, murmured something in his ear, then tipped her head onto his shoulder. Paul looked off past her, but his shoulders relaxed; he nodded and put his arm around her, hugging her back.

The surge of jealousy surprised Cindy. Paul had someone now, while she was left alone to slog through the swamp of her own thoughts. There were calmer, sweeter waters. Still, a murmur at the edge of her awareness: something about the homeless guy, the should-have-been state-hospital lifer, didn't fit.

Hearing a rustling, she turned back to Paul's sour smile. "We best be going," he said. "You need your rest. Going back to that place tomorrow?"

"I think so. Gloria said Craig would walk me to the station, for a few days anyway. I can't sit around here much longer without biting someone's head off." That earned her a smile and a hug.

"It's okay, little sister. As this one never stops reminding me, I've made more'n my share of messes you've had to clean up. She says we'll straighten you out later."

It was hard to tell whether Phyllis tripped him by accident on their way out, but he did hit his head on the doorframe and yelp in pain, and she seemed not to notice. Cindy felt ashamed. Nothing to be jealous of there; nothing but support, from both of them.

Did she have it right? Did she get too close to the lair of a paranoid homeless guy? Paul might not want to hear it, but it fit.

• • •

As Cindy pushed her way through the revolving doors into the orange-gold-infused lobby, she concentrated on evening her gait. It slowed her down, but she thought she pulled it off as she headed toward Craig's desk and the elevators behind. It wasn't until she got close that she realized the big man was chuckling—it was there in his eyes, plus a slight vibration.

"It's good to see you back," he said. "You can relax—limping is allowed." He must have seen the astonished look on her face. "I know that walk, from the Rangers. Don't let them see any weakness. We were always beat up some, all of us."

She couldn't believe it. The stone face had softened, and it looked like a smile struggling to break through. It was the best possible reaction to what she knew from the mirror was her mess of a face; the respect and trust in those few words felt great. She gave him the cheeriest wave she could manage as she set off toward the elevator, groaning with each hobbling step.

Pushing off the elevator into the lobby on Arthur's floor got her another warm greeting, this time from Morris. The older security guard was up at her side, asking if she needed help. She waved him off, but it felt good all the same.

It was more of a challenge to weave through the desks, but for the first time many of the young coders looked up and called out greetings. Not, conspicuously, Elmer, the last desk to pass before walking into

Arthur's office. The sharp smell that hit her as she passed him set off a little tingle in her head, a stray thought that evaporated before she could grab it.

She let out a grunt as she plopped into her chair, just as Arthur came in from the kitchen with his coffee and a pastry. She had to struggle to take her eyes off it and keep the drool off her chin so she could greet him properly.

"You're back," he said as he folded his praying mantis body gracefully into his chair. "I'm glad."

Back to work. Despite her aches, Cindy couldn't remember a time she felt better.

Around one, someone cleared his throat so near her ear she jumped in alarm.

"I am so very sorry to have startled you. It was insensitive of me, given your recent experience." The voice went up and down in pitch, almost like singing. "I am Neerav." He patted his chest, then swung his head around. "And this skinny fellow is Freddy."

"We've met." She waved her greeting. The one called Neerav was Indian or Pakistani. Their desks were together, she remembered, off to the side, somewhat removed from her route from the entryway to Arthur's office.

"I am from Calcutta." He emphasized the first syllable. "But since the age of fifteen I am from Lynnfield. My name, Neerav, means 'silent.'"

"The irony isn't lost on anyone," said Freddy.

"Yes, so my father often points out. In any case, we wanted to welcome you back with a celebratory lunch in the dining room. Would you be able to get away soon?"

"How about now?" She wasn't going to pass up a friendly invitation from her new team.

Though she thought virtuously of salads, when her new friends headed for the kitchen, she followed, ending up with a steaming helping of creamy chicken on rice, with extra sauce courtesy of a beaming Miguel, who treated her like a long-lost friend, asking reproachfully where she had been.

"We wanted," said Neerav, when they were seated, "to make sure you understood about Arthur. He can seem abrupt at times. It is his way. When you are around him a long time, you get to see that his manner doesn't reflect a lack of kindness or consideration. He does everything to support and protect us."

"He can't help it," said Freddy. "He's just a little weird is all."

"He's been very kind to me," she said, "but I'm glad you invited me down here. It's such an intense place. You guys work hard."

"Ah, yes. We have to earn our way. We are, after all, what you would call the A team, the elite. We don't want to be sent down to the minors, you see."

She laughed. "Yes, I suppose I do. I guess that's why everyone seems so focused."

"Hey, even by tech standards, this is a great place to work," said Freddy.

"This one"—Neerav pointed to Freddy, whose plate was piled with seconds—"eats twice his weight each and every day. Costs them a fortune."

It was the most relaxing time she had spent at work. There was no need to offer more than the occasional nod or grunt to keep them going. Having fought successfully against the urge to fill her plate a second time, she was sorry when Freddy was finally finished and they had to return to work.

2 0

Paul

You might think it's strange that I meet Ralph for lunch every Thursday now that Cindy's dumped him—oh, right, put him on hold—but he's my friend. Even more than my father and sister, he's the one who believed in me, and folks at the Center can tell you how important that is when you're trying to get back on your feet. He deserves to hear about this, and it's not going to come from Cindy.

There's this courtyard inside a building—you'd never know it was there from the outside. Has a fountain and some metal tables behind a sandwich place; Korean, but with a salad bar. It's near his office at ConDo, and Ralph doesn't like to be away long, so it's our usual spot.

I bring my salad and water back to where he's sitting with his usual bowl of bebop or whatever, the fried egg on top about the only thing I recognize.

We start out with the usual chit-chat, and it's easier to talk about his work, which isn't going great, than about you-know-who. He helped me get out of my rut, and I want to tell him there's other jobs he could go for, but he never seems to want to move anywhere. He's been with ConDo longer than as I have, and I guess he can't see himself anywhere else. Of course, I had help getting me going—some guy trying to kill me. I guess it's like being in a hole deep enough where you have to jump to see out of it. Throw a snake down there, you might just figure a way out.

Anyway, I give Ralph the short version of Cindy's story. "Some homeless guy jumped Cindy. It happened over by Back Door. There's a path through the woods, takes you to Alewife station." He just puts his fork down and stares at me. "Folks there told her there's some kind of camp in the woods where they sleep rough. It was dark, something going on with the lights, and he was able to sneak up on her."

I've never seen this Ralph. He's intense, angry, asking me all kinds of questions—*how late was it, why was she working hours like that, weren't there lights on the path, wasn't anyone else around?* But I've already told him what I know. He starts yelling, like it was my fault, till I stop him.

"Look it, Ralph: she was starting to, you know, go back there, in her mind. I wasn't going to push her for more details."

He's the one taught me about reliving bad things and how it doesn't help you get over trauma, so he stops and sits back. The look on his face when the anger leaves it, that's going to stay with me. When I was fifteen, before the voices took me over, Mother sent me out on a house call with Father. A boy—went to my high school, younger but I'd seen him in church—walking with some other boys, was shot down. Police made it like he was in a gang, like they always do. Anyway, we went to see his ma, and when she looked from Father to me, I saw that look: helpless, mad, sad, horrified, all together.

"She went there," he says, "looking to get away from troubles, and it's been one thing after another. She needs to get out of there." This from Mister Stuck-in-a-hole-and-don't-know-it.

"She says folks like her there, and she's making her way."

He lets out a breath, looks down. "Yeah, I guess. It's her life. Just bad luck—not her fault. Or yours."

He's gripping the side of the table, starts shaking his head, slow, doesn't look up. I can't think of what to say. Then he looks up.

"I've got to get back. Thanks for, uh . . ."

Then he's gone, doesn't even clear away his lunch. I finish eating and sample his before I clean up. Why waste a fried egg?

• • •

Billie and Grace drop me at a Jamaica Plain hangout on Centre Street to meet Shep. Like me, Johnnie's case manager is locked out of work and has time on his hands. I'm looking for a thin guy about Cindy's age wearing a knit hat and bright-red T-shirt. The Work-day Grind is a classic Jamaica Plain coffee shop: community bulletin board, posters with fists taped to the walls, beat-up old tables and chairs packed in any which way, lumpy baked goods in an old-fashioned glass case, tattooed and pierced counter girls, one with blue-and-orange hair, the other shaved on one side and spiky bright yellow on the other. Classy. Mostly young folks staring into laptops fill the tables; eleven in the morning, and they look like they're settled in for the day. A line snakes through, waiting to order.

It takes me an extra minute, standing in the crush, getting attention I don't need, to find Shep. He's just like they said, wearing a bright-red T-shirt, a reddish brown buzz cut and matching soul patch on his lower lip. He's up from a sagging old sofa stuffed into the corner, waving, and I work my way over through the crowd and reach out a hand.

His T-shirt says *IWW: Industrial Workers of the World.*

"You're a Wobbly. I did a paper on them in school. They were quite the group."

"One of a dying breed," he says with a smile, waving his hand around, "hiding here among the yuppies, entrepreneurs, and other phonies."

"What can I get you?" I say, with the brash generosity of the underemployed.

"They make a great latte here."

At least the line moves along. I get our order in while he saves our spot.

When my ass drops down by my ankles next to Shep, I'm brushing an overhanging tree branch out of my hair. After a while, I give that up and just tilt my head to the side.

"They call them laptops," he says, "but everyone wants a table anyway, so I can usually get a spot on this beast. Billie filled me in. I really appreciate what you're doing. It can't be much fun—I've made visits in Nashua Street before."

That's the jail for Suffolk County, in Boston. "He's out in Billerica," I say. "It was Cambridge, where it happened."

"That place? Even worse. Out by 128, all those companies and malls—that's the belly of the beast right there. At least at Nashua, you can walk out into a city, not a mess of highways. You're a good man to go there, let him know he's not alone."

"An injury to one is an injury to all—isn't that how it goes?"

That gets me in with him. He grins and holds up a clenched fist, then twists around so I can see the back of his shirt, which sports the same motto.

"Right on, brother. I have heard Back Door is a good place to work—free food and other bennies. Not exactly fertile ground for organizing."

"How about ConDo? Anything happening there?"

He waits for the server to drop off two soup bowls with handles and our scones, like we're plotting something. "Union activity, you mean? Every once in a while, local 302 makes a run, but those guys are pathetic. I'm not interested in adding another good-old-boy network to the mix—not my thing. Which means at least I didn't have a target on my back going into this mess."

"So, how come you're sitting here instead of doing your job?"

"I guess they looked around for somebody to blame and came up with Lu and me. I don't know what I was supposed to do, though. The guy was on his meds, and he was beginning to like the job."

"No sign that he might go off like that?"

"Look, people get the wrong idea about Johnnie. He's young, and a rapper, always pumping out rhymes—and they can sound pretty rough. If you want a place in that world, you have to go there, sound tough, establish your cred."

"Least he ain't Black," I add.

Shep looks uncomfortable for a moment, but then seems to get that I'm not offended. In fact, I'm getting to like the guy. He's kind, friendly, and upbeat despite his suspension—a gentle anarchist. "Thing is, he's off in his own world. He's always beating out rhythms, going over rhymes in his head, putting them down on these lists when he can. Like a lot of our young guys, he's been through the mill: beaten and neglected to start, special ed because of a learning disability, passed around shitty foster homes, minor trouble. I mean, he's grandiose, thinks he's going to be a star, dreams about the bling— like a lot of the young guys."

"I get it. I had dreams of my own when I was that age. Got me angry, thinking folks were trying to take them away from me."

"But that's just it: Johnnie's not an angry kid. He's cheerful. Plus, he's tuned out, in his own world."

"You've never seen him lose it?"

"I never have, no. I heard he made a scene down at the rep payee office at ConDo a couple of months ago, but that was mostly my fault. I should have gone down there with him. That rep payee shit makes them all mad, and you can't blame them."

"I know. It's like they assume you're too stupid to count your own money. Makes you feel small all the way down."

Shep nods as he swallows some coffee. "It sucks. This office full of clerks gets your check; they pay your bills, you don't even see them. How do they think poor folks manage—by paying all their bills on time? Right!"

"They give you an allowance, like you're a kid." My old anger's coming back, kissing me on the cheek, whispering in my ear.

"Johnnie's in a furnished room," he says, "no real kitchen, so he's got to eat out. In this town, it's just not enough. These guys coming out of foster homes, they don't have a clue about money, bills, setting up house; it's like, goodbye and good luck, you know? I'm trying to teach him how to manage his money, but he never sees his checks or the bills. He was doing better than most, but he wanted this little amp and microphone to go with it, thought he could set up in Nubian Square by the bus station and do his rapping, make a few bucks."

"There's lots worse things young guys get into." I can picture it, some kids hanging around in a knot, people hurrying by to get their buses, dropping in the occasional quarter or buck. But a White kid— maybe in Andrews Station in Southie, not Nubian.

"He thought it would lead to his big break, you know? It gave him some focus. It was a crime to crush that hope. He saw the amp in a pawn shop downtown, wanted it so bad. I had to tell him we'd have to request a check two months in advance, assuming he had the money in his account. I submitted the form, told him there was no use arguing with them—he'd have to wait."

"I bet that went over big. Did he blow his top?"

"Not at all. Oh, he got upset at first, said it would never last that long—he was probably right about that—but he calmed down after a bit, and I thought he understood. Maybe he didn't, though. He just mumbled something, smiled—might have been tuning me out. I should have gone down there with him, have them explain it to him, but they hate to come out from behind their plexiglass.

"Next thing I hear, he was down there pacing back and forth in front of the window, yelling. Doctor Marsha came by, made out like it was a big deal. She said he was making threats, but I think he was rapping. He was loud, and you know what rap lyrics are like, standing up to the man, all the swearing. Carolyn Doyle came along and got him quieted down, and that should have been the end of it, but they'll probably say it shows his violent temper. Bullshit!"

"Well, I guess it could look bad." I have to say, I'm not all the way convinced. Maybe because Shep hasn't been bullied at the Stewart Center by the guy's friends. The thing is, Johnnie was hanging back, like he was embarrassed, maybe even ashamed.

Shep's still going. "I just can't see it. It just doesn't sound like the kid I know."

"Did he ever sound angry with Carlson, or threatened somehow? Was he having problems with the job?"

"It wasn't his dream gig; he was pretty clear on that. But he told me he liked Carlson. Said the man was funny looking and weird, but Johnnie appreciated the support he gave him. The guy was trying to get him interested in becoming a cook, said he had a talent for it. You know, that's a big deal for Johnnie. His life hasn't exactly been filled with encouragement and praise."

"Sounds like he hit the jackpot with you, though." I've seen enough mental health workers to know a good one when I see one. Shep took the trouble to get to know Johnnie, and sees him as a person, not a case. My words seem to embarrass him, though.

"We get along. He's just a sad kid, a lot less angry than most, or than he has a right to be. I always thought he had a long, rough road ahead of him, but there's a core, some resilience, and warmth. He's a nice kid. Maybe you'll get to see it."

"I hope so." I can't think of anything encouraging to say.

"I can't . . ." He looks up, almost like he's trying not to cry. "It's not like there's anyone else on the team he trusts. The young guys, they're kind of my specialty; too scary for the wimpy-assed professionals on the team. Ah, I'm sorry. The other staff are okay. They're just young. It's just—"

"I know. I'm sorry too. You don't deserve this. I can't believe ConDo is acting like this, so . . ."

"Cold? How about you? Didn't you get pulled off your job?"

We share a smile. I saw this side of ConDo when I went against their wishes by moving out of the group home and changing doctors. Why does it seem like the ones with integrity, who try the hardest and care the most, always get in trouble? And why are the needs of ConDo's clients never their top priority? I find myself wishing for Shep some of the resilience he saw in Johnnie. They're both going to need it.

As for me, I called my supervisor at Elder Affairs, and she promised to look into my situation. She's mad as hell.

2 1

Cindy

Cindy was at her desk, back-to-back with Arthur, when her phone buzzed in the handbag she'd stuck by her feet. Who would be calling her at six? Everyone was still working.

Billie. "Listen, we've gotta go talk to Big Sal. *Gracie!*" She yelled so loud Cindy grunted in pain. "She'll take us over there. When can we pick you up?"

When she asked, Arthur said, "You've been here ten hours—go!"

Cindy told Billie she would meet her out front in half an hour.

"Great. I'll fill you in on the way over."

So it was set, and Cindy found herself in the back seat of the cavernous old sedan with Billie while Grace hunched over the wheel in front.

"The thing is, Big Sal likes his ladies—the younger, the better. Oh, you're plenty young, don't worry about that. Just, you know, watch his hands. They're still quick, and he's a crafty old bastard."

Grace spoke from the front. "He's a loud-mouthed blaspheming devil. Does she really have to go see him?"

Billie softened her tone. "I know, darling, he's a nasty piece of work, but he knows stuff; he worked homicide. Anyway, Cindy can handle him—right?"

"Sure, I guess."

"He worked vice," spat Grace. "His buddies cooked up that phony promotion at the end to boost his pension. And that's not the half—"

Billie cut her off. "He's the best we've got."

"Just watch his hands," warned Grace as they got out of the car. *Jeez, I've got it!*

Cindy and Billie walked into the big converted hospital building and checked in at the desk while Grace parked the car. Cindy expected to wait for Grace in the lobby, but Billie shook her head.

"If she came in, all we'd do is watch the two of them go at it."

The place was spartan but clean, with light-green tile halfway up the wall and a disinfectant smell that made her eyes water.

"Sal's got his own room, at least. He'll probably tell you, the food sucks. Thing is, he can't get around much anymore, between the arthritis and COPD, and the way he smokes, he was gonna blow his place up and kill all the neighbors, so he's been stuck here since 2013."

The snarl that greeted Billie's knock on the door was anything but friendly, but the grizzled little man folded into a wheelchair seemed pleased enough to see them when he opened the door. There was just enough space to squeeze past him into a room barely wide enough for a single bed, a little desk, and chair. It reminded Cindy of Paul's bedroom at the group home, but this one was far less homey, despite the incongruously large flat-screen TV that covered most of the only window. With a plastic tube in each nostril, his body resembled a twisted, empty plastic bag. Big Sal couldn't weigh more than a hundred.

She wasn't sure he even saw her until she felt a hand squeeze her ass, which she quickly slapped away. She had been warned.

"All right, you old goat," said Billie, "that's your last chance. If we didn't need your help, we'd be out of here right now. As it is . . ."

She reached out and handed him a plastic drugstore bag, which he tore into with surprising ferocity. An e-cigarette emerged, with a package of refills and a bag of Junior Mints. He switched the tube on and puffed hungrily at it, tossing the rest of the bag's contents onto the desk. His voice was a faint, reedy rasp. "Ah, bless you. The nicotine gum tastes like shit."

"Yeah, well, make those last; they're not cheap. Look-it, this is Cindy, the one I told you about."

The little man squinted at Cindy, then back at Billie. "Didn't say she was colored."

"Okay, that's it. Let's go." Billie grabbed for the cigarette cartridges, but Sal wrenched them away with unexpected strength and held them tight to his body with both hands, elbows out.

"A'right, a'right. Didn't mean nothin'; just sayin'. Siddown, would ya?"

"Listen, asshole. You want to stay here, stare at the walls all day by yourself, fine. You want us to visit you, bring you shit, then mind your goddamn manners."

"Hey, I'm old. I get to say what I want. S'all I got left. Don't gotta be nice to assholes no more, neither. Don't mean I won't help you out. She talk, or is she just gonna sit there an' stare?"

"Just watching family catch up on old times. I gotta say, all this sentimental stuff is embarrassing, though."

This brought out a laugh from the old man that ended in a coughing fit. "A'right, shoulda known if you been around this one, you'd have a mouth on ya. So, what's the story?" His look was almost friendly.

Billie broke in. "We got a situation. A murder, happened where Cindy works, so she can do some poking around, but we need some advice." And Cindy took over and filled him in with everything they knew. His few questions were pointed enough to suggest he was taking it all in.

"So, you wanna play detective, like that show *Murder She* whatever, with the old writer broad?"

"Kinda like that," Billie admitted.

"You don't think the cops know what they're doing? Like you can do better? Jesus fuckin' Christ!"

"They think the guy from my program, the dishwasher, did it,"

Billie replied. "We're not so sure, and we don't trust them to break their asses looking at other possibilities."

"Well, there is a sayin': if it looks simple, it probably is. I mean, usually, you look at the wife first—"

"In this case, the husband," said Cindy.

"Well, a'course. Fucking Cambridge, what else? Not faggots anymore—husbands."

"But?" Cindy managed to get in, edging herself between the other two as she felt Billie about to blow.

"That's the rule," he continued, "but when there's a wacko, they jump ahead. And when they got blood on 'em, and run . . ." Either he had listened to her account or he knew about the case from the giant TV.

"Right." Billie had composed herself. "That's what we figure, but we wanna make sure they don't take the easy route and railroad the kid."

"Well, you gotta like him for it. Trouble is, the guys on the job these days, they're in the squad room most of the time, staring at their damn computers. How's that supposed to work? You need to know your victim inside out. Go out, talk to everyone he knew. Open him up, spill his guts out, and roll around in there till you can smell him in your sleep."

Yuk! As he spoke, the old guy's eyes took on a ghoulish glow.

"Yeah, I know, I know, but the point is, ya can't be delicate, hold back. Everybody's got some kinda shit. This guy's got 'im killed. Ya gotta find it, whatever it is. If it's not the wacko, then there's gotta be something. You don't find it, you're fucked. You have to talk to everybody, see who feels, like, off, you know? There's some pretty bad shit you're gonna step in, make you wanna puke—that's okay, that's the job. You don't get what you need from a damn screen. I'm telling you now, it's the nastiest parts of the guy's life, that's what's gonna lead you to your perp. You follow the smell."

At that moment, Cindy couldn't imagine anything smelling worse than this old man and his funky cell, but at least his voice had lost its nasty edge. "Hell of a job, what it is; leaves a stink on you won't wash off."

"The setup is," said Billie, "Cindy's going to do some trauma counseling with the folks there so she can feed us some information; then you and I could figure it out."

"You? I guess. Well, they won't be lawyering up, at least. Maybe they'll tell you some little thing they don't think matters, 'cause they're relaxed-like."

"Okay," said Cindy, as evenly as she could manage. "What else?"

He gave her a satisfied smirk. "That's enough to get you started. Don't wanna have too much running around that pretty little head. Come back in a few days, tell me what you found. And bring me some of these." He pointed to the nicotine cartridges. "Some nice fruit flavors or something, and maybe some Mallomars. Now that ya know the way, don't need ta bring this one," he said, cocking an eyebrow at Billie, who was not amused.

"Like hell, you old prick."

They left on that pleasant note.

"Gracie's right," said Billie as they gulped down fresh outside air. "He always was a manipulative bastard. Sorry about the racial crack. I tend to forgot what an asshole he is—always was."

"I've dealt with worse. You think he can help?"

Billie shrugged. "I don't know. Seems like he'll try."

22

Paul

Phyllis comes by for dinner tonight, like she does every Wednesday now and most Sundays. She brings part of it, I cook something, and sometimes Father helps clean up. When we're done eating, he says, "I'm off. Got to get my mind right before the ladies come over for Bible study." Oh well.

Most times Phyllis comes over to dinner, he'll find some excuse to go off and leave us some time alone. It's a bit obvious, and always makes Phyllis blush, but I know it's his way of being kind. I always wondered what he really does—Cindy and I never got the praying habit. This time I hope he's praying this woman will stay with me. I like Ralph a lot, but I'm not looking to mope around along with him, have a we-got-dumped party. Different situations, I know, but it reminds me not to assume I know what's on Phyllis's mind. It looks like there's something on it tonight, so I'm relieved when she pulls a rolled paper from her shoulder bag and spreads it out flat on the table.

"I haven't seen him for a while; had to do this from memory." Johnnie. She's good; you can always tell who it is in her drawings, even though they're just pencil. This one's amazing. You can see the cocky kid, the smirk, but somehow the fear comes through too, like he's balancing on something skinny, trying not to fall. "You've got to help him, Paul. What I hear, there's no family, nobody else." She gives me the look, the one says *I know you'll do the right thing.*

Because if I don't, she won't think as much of me. She likes to keep her thoughts to herself, but not with me. I like to keep my thoughts private too, except with her—and Cindy. Well, she'd read them anyway.

There's something else about the drawing, something not there. "He doesn't look tough, or mean," I say, thinking out loud. "It's like he's playing a part, and not pulling it off."

"I was thinking about that. I've watched him sit in the corner some days, doing his raps, writing them down, waving his hands the way rappers do, lurching around in his chair."

"Huh. Never seen that."

"If you hung around the Center more . . ."

It's an old argument between us. She's been there seven years, runs that communications unit—not just doing the work, but getting others involved, folks that won't talk to anybody else. Gets them out of their heads, at least for a while. She could be out working a job, earning money, getting on with her life. I've told her more than once, but when I try, she just goes quiet, shuts down. That dead look, I know that way too well—seen it on so many folks I should be used to it by now, but I can't take seeing it on Phyllis, so I don't bring it up anymore. She'll have to figure it out for herself, which is the way it's supposed to work at Stewart Center. I suppose that's the only way it works anyplace, for anyone.

Now, her wanting me to hang around there, instead of working so much—I'm hoping to get up to full time at Elder Affairs soon as I can—that would be an argument too, but she knows it's going to lead to me saying *why don't you get a job*, so she holds up her hand. "Okay, yeah, I know, the job. Anyway, I was getting to like him before he started at that Door place. When I talked to him about printing his lyrics as poetry in the literary journal, he was thrilled. It made me think that gangster routine of his is like playacting."

I have to agree: he can't have done anyone the way someone did Carlson. And I'll do what she says, the right thing.

"I was sorry to see him go to that job," she says, "but he wanted the money."

I've got another thought. "I should show this to Cindy. She still thinks he's a thug."

Phyllis gives me a hug. She knows I'm all in with her now, that I'll go see the boy, do everything I can, anything she wants—big surprise.

Then she pulls back, excited, which is another thing not too many get to see, and pulls a couple more papers out of her bag, spreading the first one out for me.

It's Billie and Grace. Phyllis was there when they still ran the Center. Billie's facing ahead, got that scary smile you can't ever look away from, with her arm around little Grace, who's looking up like Billie's someone holy. She gets their love for each other into both their faces; the pride too. It's amazing, what she can get out of a few lines. It looks so simple the first time you see it, but it's got everything it needs.

I tell her if she gives it to them, they'll hang it up in their home. I offer to get it framed.

"We'll see," which means no, not now, but I'll keep after her.

I'm staring at the drawing when I feel her hand on my arm. "Paul, this is me. It's not just what I do. It's who I am. I've found a place where I can be myself. Your sister is trying to find that; Ralph too, though I think he had it and then lost it when things went out from under him. He's trying to get it back. Maybe that's harder to go through."

It's just like Phyllis. When she finds the right time to argue back, she wins, and manages to do it without making me feel bad. I could go on for hours and not say near as much.

2 3

Cindy

It felt funny walking into the HR/PR area. Cindy greeted Gloria, and the older woman jumped up from behind the big reception counter to squeeze her so hard it hurt. "Go right in, baby, he's expecting you," she said, as Cindy struggled to regain her breath.

Cindy knocked softly on the open door and eased into Steven's office to give him a chance to see her coming. He rushed out from behind his desk, enveloping her right hand in both of his and looking into her eyes, but only a quick glance. As he motioned her to one of the little old-fashioned upholstered chairs and offered her the usual coffee, his eyes never met hers.

Until now, she had never seen him uncomfortable, but the light grace had left his body and hands. Despite his awkwardness and her anxiety, she couldn't detect any hostility. As he began speaking, his eyes darted about, but his voice seemed calm and measured.

"I know you're here to complete your paperwork so we can get you on the payroll, but I wanted a word first. I've spoken to Charlotte, and I know she has asked you to reach out to the people most affected by Carlson's death. I just wanted to tell you that I'm grateful you're willing to help. I realize it isn't what you came here to do."

"I really appreciate that. I'm not sure I can be of any real use, but . . . I know this must be a horrible time for you, and I was concerned, with me having come here through ConDo."

"Gloria was worried about that, but Johnnie was here months before you arrived. And I am sorry, by the way, to hear that Luiza is in difficulty over this. It was her job to find work for these people, after all, and I'm sure whatever their screening procedure, there must have been others involved as well."

He was working hard at fairness, at grace. This was going to be delicate. Cindy started out by describing her role, beginning in general terms about traumatic experiences and loss, and how people recovered. She handed him an information sheet with the things that could be expected at first, ranging from loss of appetite to recurring upsetting thoughts, hopelessness, and difficulty concentrating. She didn't go through each item but suggested he review it at his leisure. Then, she took a breath and plunged in, hoping her purpose wouldn't be obvious.

"You and Carlson were—"

"Married, yes, as no doubt you've heard. We had been together for more than ten years."

She noted the tense. "Until . . ."

"The middle of last year, we separated. I suppose it was a long time coming, but . . . it was his idea. I was hoping he would come back. I think he would have." At this point, Steven faltered and turned away, walking over to the table to refill their cups. By the time he carried them back, his hands were steady, the cups firm on their saucers.

Cindy knew she should probably wait for another time—but didn't. "I know this must be a very difficult time, but could you tell me about Carlson, and how he got on here? I mean, to have this just happen . . ."

This seemed to amuse him, and he spoke with some of his old assurance and flair. "You mean, did he have any enemies? That's what they ask on television. It's hard to imagine anyone wanting to kill Carlson. Oh, he was passionate, dramatic—not everyone's cup of tea, I suppose. He could get under your skin sometimes; perhaps I know that better than anyone. And there were parts of his life—one couldn't cage a spirit like his; it would never have worked. Well, I suppose I tried, years ago, but . . ." His gaze drifted off with his words.

"Parts like other, uh, relationships, here?"

He met her eyes for the first time. "Very good—sharp! Yes, given what happened, if this is to have any bearing, it would have to be someone here, wouldn't it? And yes, thank you for your attempt at delicacy; there was one in particular."

He paused so long she had decided he wasn't going to tell her.

"All right, the young man's name—younger, at any rate—was Marshall; Marshall Simmons. A coder on the home user floor. Maybe two years ago, they fell hard for each other, though each in his own way. Simmons simply could not understand what it meant to Carlson, a fling with a younger man. The poor fellow thought he had found *the one.* You can still find naïve queens, believe it or not. Oh, sorry. You are a good listener. I usually don't share my cattiest thoughts with women.

"And of course, you may have heard of his issues with Kaz. Charlotte brought him on to bring a lighter touch to the cooking. Well, I kept telling Carlson, with Claude and his gym, Nicole and her yoga, he was going to have to adjust. His penchant for classic French, Italian, Viennese—it was beginning to seem out of place, most importantly to Charlotte. But Carlson was so passionate about his food. It was a real blow when Charlotte brought Kaz in. It was a sign, and not just that she was determined to impose her will. It was personal, a betrayal. I think Carlson feared that his days here might well be numbered. Or worse, that he would be pushed aside—patronized." He shook himself and moved on even faster. "There, you see, I seem to need to talk about it all with someone. And you did volunteer."

"Wow. From what I've heard about Carlson, that would have been devastating for him. He lived and breathed this place, didn't he?"

The big man waved this away with a pudgy hand, recovering some of his old style. "Charlotte was never going to let him go, but something had changed in their relationship. He sensed she'd moved on in some critical way. And there were some structural changes. But I just can't see what that could have to do with what happened."

"Well, I appreciate your sharing, and at a time like this."

She had run out of questions (rather quickly, she thought), and anyway, she shouldn't badger Steven at a time like this. Still, Sal had made a point of it: look at the closest family first, and here was the husband, cuckolded.

"This affair, with the coder . . ."

"Was a long time ago. And not the first, I'm afraid."

"Still, it must have—"

He met her eyes now. "Bothered me? Ah, I see. And then I went to the kitchen to confront him, and, full of jealous rage, I stabbed him"— she wanted desperately to look away but couldn't—"with his own knife. And left him to die. Is that what you think?" He wasn't shouting, but he was leaning toward her, biting off the words, quivering. "We're done here. Or rather, you're done. I don't care what Charlotte says." He turned away so that she could barely hear his choked hiss. "Get out!"

When she got out into the hall, Gloria was standing behind her desk with an expectant look. Cindy could only keep going. She thought of running for the stairs to avoid waiting for the elevator, but that would be too obvious. She heard the woman move around her desk, but to her relief, Gloria headed back to Steven's office rather than following her.

During the ride down on the elevator, Cindy realized she was in no condition to go back to her seat next to Arthur. Instead, she rode down to the main lobby and hurried past the front desk without looking at Craig, on out into the air, where she could cry without attracting attention.

Intruding in people's lives with obnoxious questions brought back her days in child protection, turning over people's personal rocks, bringing the bugs and worms into the light. The hurt, rage, humiliation, and resentment in Steven's eyes, it had been the same with those mothers. The resentment that flooded her then, toward Billie, Ralph, Emma—even Paul and Charlotte—was overwhelming. Reinventing herself as a web designer and proving herself in this challenging environment wasn't enough; she had to pretend to be a something else. She had long since proven to be a lousy social worker and had no business playing therapist, let alone detective. It wasn't just that she lacked the skill and was certain to fail, but all the feelings that had paralyzed her for years came rushing back. And her new career would be stillborn.

She resolved to dive back into her work on the website, and not think about anything else for the rest of the day. And then she would give her notice to Paul and Billie; Detective Abernathy was hanging it up, for good.

But she found, when she got back to her desk, that she couldn't face any of it. Instead, she hurried out of the building and onto the winding dirt path back to Alewife subway station, to the rectory, and home.

2 4

Paul

Until I hear from my supervisor in Elder Affairs, there's nowhere to go but back to the Stewart Center. It's crowded here now, and it feels lousy, trying to push my way into helping Phyllis with her projects. Before they drift away throughout the day, I can see that lots of others here share my frustration. I didn't do anything to lose my job, but it feels somehow like I'm not as capable as I was a couple of days ago. It's nice to have more time with Phyllis, but I feel like a puppy competing for her attention, so I just go off to the side and sit as the afternoon drags.

At four, I head home, thinking about the drawing Phyllis did of Johnnie, the way she saw the little boy who hoped to please and impress but wasn't sure he could pull it off. And Phyllis looking at me, like *this is what you've got to do, for me, for yourself.* But thinking of that jail makes me shaky inside. I get the idea maybe Cindy could go with me. Wouldn't she want to talk to him? It couldn't hurt her investigation. I almost convince myself I'd be doing *her* the favor.

I figure I'll ask her tonight when she gets home around eight, but when I walk in, she's sitting at the kitchen table with a cup of tea, looking dazed. It's all set to jump out of my mouth, how she should do this thing for me, but the look on her face stops me and I ask, "You okay?"

Next thing, she's hugging me and crying. I'm still not used to my big brother duties, but I owe her. A lot.

"I can't do it. I'm sorry, I can't, I just can't." More of that, but it's all the same words, different combinations, sobbing.

When she starts to run down, I get her down into a chair and sit in one next to her, still with an arm around her, pushing a tissue from my pocket into her hand. I'm all teared up too, even though I don't know what it is she can't do—okay, I could guess it has to do with this murder investigating. "So, take your time. Tell me about it."

And she does, about the business in Henchcliff's office, how it was like her social work nightmare all over again. I know about nightmares, my own and hers. "Like being back there," I say. Reflecting, they call it. It's all I know how to do so far, but it seems to work.

"It's like you sneak into people and poke around where it hurts the most. You pretend it's for them, but it isn't, never was, and then they figure it out. I said I'd never do that again. I can't." And she's off crying again. "I can't, I can't, I can't."

"He's the husband?" Sounds stupid when I hear it come out.

"That's what Sal said, look at the family first. And Gloria, she suggested I talk to him. I'll bet she didn't realize what a mess I'd make of it."

"Sounds like you started off with the hardest one, when you'd never done it before. If you'd had the experience, you'd'a known that."

She pulls back and looks at me. "But I'm stupid, clumsy, naive—that what you mean?"

Now, that's my sister coming back. "Means you're no detective. Not yet, anyway. But you went and stuck your neck out and tried to do it right. You must have known it could cost you."

That finally gets a chuckle. "I did that, didn't I? When Sal talked about walking around in people's guts"—say what?—"I thought I knew what he meant, but I never imagined how it would feel."

Now I'm getting into it. "It's one of those things where you find out where they hurt, and you feel it. I don't imagine this Big Sal is the sensitive type. Probably rolled right off of him."

"I guess. Look, thanks. It really helps, talking to you."

"Yeah, we Abernathys do take our lumps. Still, there's someone else you could be talking to about this. I know he'd want to help." Well, he is a lot better at this sort of thing.

She stiffens at that, and her voice gets hard. "Big brother, do not go there. You been talking to Ralph?"

Shit. I can't hold her eyes, so I've got to pretend there's something interesting on the table. "The guy cares for you. I don't get what he did that's so bad. He told me how sorry he is that he teased you about being an intern. He'll tell you himself, you give him the chance."

"He go all mopey on you, get you to talk me back into his life? Well, you can forget it. That man just . . . brings me down. It's always some outrage, someone getting picked on, or someone's picking on him, and he wants me to be all sympathetic. I'm turning that page; it's over."

I don't know why that set me off. I guess because that word, *mopey*, keeps popping out of her mouth, and I've got to figure she thought the same about me all those years I was stalled out in that group home.

"I'm sorry, but it feels like more than that. You want to get away from people like me, all of the ones who struggle, like we're going to drag you down. Your father and his ministry, Ralph, me and my crazy friends, all those messed-up people who stand up for the unlucky ones."

She stares at me, her mouth hanging open. I don't blame her. What am I doing, popping off at her like that when a few minutes ago she couldn't stop crying? I guess I couldn't stand being the older brother anymore, had to turn useless again, maybe remind her not to depend on me for anything but making trouble for my family.

My sister, though, doesn't back down—never does. "Now, look, I've tried living in that world. You were going to be the minister, follow in Father's footsteps. How'd that work out? Going from one bereaved family to the next, in the company of those ghoulish church ladies who love to be around suffering, long as it's someone else's. You think being in line for that had nothing to do with what happened to you? It was Mother's dream for you, wasn't it? Just like it was her dream for me to be the little social worker and go save all those broken kids. She was good at sending other people out, but she hardly ever did it herself, so she never knew how it felt. Well, it hurts. And anyway, it doesn't work."

"You made a difference, to some at least. You did your best."

"It wasn't near good enough though, was it? Sure, once in a while, could be I helped one, maybe a little bit. But how about the ones I hurt—dragging them out of their horrible homes into a string of worse foster homes till they got dumped out, ended up in prison. I'm sorry, it was a nightmare, and I'm done with it. I'm finding out what I was meant to do. It's not about turning my back, or hurting you. It's not about you."

"No? It sure seems like you want to get as far away from me as you can. And Father. And Ralph."

"Is that what this is about? You his agent or something?" Now she was yelling.

"Okay, look. You've decided he's not the one. Of course you get to make that choice. You're entitled to your own life, I get that, and I know I shouldn't take it personally. But we really need your help on this. All those years you visited me, never gave up when Father stayed away . . . I guess I thought you could hang in there a little longer. I know I've got no right to expect any more from you, but Johnnie—I saw him around the Center. And I talked to Shep, his case manager. And Phyllis—"

"He drove a knife into Carlson and left him to bleed to death. That's your Johnnie, the guy who murdered someone everyone in my new world loved and admired. How can you ask me to help him?"

"He's one of those kids you tried to help, the heartbreakers. Beat up at home, one foster after another, no stability, no anchor. Makes me feel lucky to have grown up here, in this museum. Much as I railed against it when I was his age, it's made it so much easier to have this family to come home to. He's got nothing; no family, no one but us. Everyone assumes he's a murderer. The people at ConDo who believed in him, they'll probably lose their jobs over this. There's no one else. And the police—this works for them. It's just too easy."

"But, Paul, what am I supposed to do? You guys expect me to solve this, but I don't know how. I've already hurt someone there and made things worse. I can't stand it."

"I know, but it's not for nothing. You picked at that man's scab today, and maybe it means something, and maybe it doesn't, but you can't hurt him any worse than he's hurt already, losing his husband. He's still got it better than Johnnie ever has. The others, they won't be so bad."

"You're not listening! There are not going to be any others. I'm done."

"Didn't you promise Charlotte you'd reach out to folks? Just listen while you're at it, and let Billie and that uncle of hers do the rest."

That gives her pause. "When Charlotte hears what a mess I made, she'll see that this has all been a mistake. She can hire a counselor, someone qualified. Hell, she can probably call ConDo, and they'll send Ralph and Emma. I can only hope she'll let me go back to my job with her son, Arthur." I see her stop then and squint at me. "Wait, is that—"

"Yeah, plan B." I can see that really pisses her off, but then, the prospect of having Ralph at Back Door would have to horrify her. I hurry on before that hits her. "Okay, I get it. And I'm sorry I blew up like that. Sometimes a piece of the old, angry Paul pops out, and I don't see it coming." She looks at me and squeezes my hand. She's used to forgiving me. Just like old times.

Then there's the other thing. I must be desperate to bring it up again, but out it comes. "There was something else I was going to ask you—a favor. I've got to go see Johnnie, in that place."

"The jail? Oh, Paul."

"Yeah, well, that's the only place he's going to be for a while. I was wondering if you'd come with me, just like, to be there. This Saturday?"

"That pretty young lawyer not doing the trick for you?" I know that smile—means I'm in.

2 5

Cindy

The call came around five the next day. Arthur answered, called her name, and extended the receiver. Gloria.

"Steven would like to see you in his office."

"You mean, now?" *Duh!*

"Mm-hm. He talked to me about your meeting yesterday. He has something he wants to say."

Cindy told Arthur she had to go see Steven.

"Now? Haven't they finished with the paperwork yet?"

"Well, not exactly." And now they never would. "I wanted to thank you for going out of your way, to give me this chance."

He looked puzzled. "Oh. Okay." Then he turned back to his screen.

When she walked into Steven's suite, Gloria rose with a sigh and came around the counter to greet her. "Well, come on then," she said, and motioned her to follow into Steven's office. To Cindy's surprise, he was sitting on a chair in the grouping in front of his desk and waved her onto the couch without rising. Gloria took the other chair facing her.

"At a time like this," he said, without quite meeting her eyes, "it's impossible to be at one's best."

Gloria took over. "What Steven's trying to say is that he's sorry he blew up at you yesterday."

Cindy stumbled around for something to say. Nothing came out.

When he looked at her, she couldn't avoid his eyes—bloodshot, with bags underneath, but there was no anger in his voice. "This has been such a shock. I thought you were accusing me—"

"I'm the one who needs to apologize. It came out wrong."

"Did it? Well. The thing you said, about the police. I realize they've earned a level of mistrust in certain communities—yours *and* mine—but I see nothing to suggest they have an agenda here."

"I wasn't . . . well . . ."

"The thing is, I fully support your mission, to reach out to people who may have been affected. I know it's unfair to ask this of you, but we trust you. In a short time, you've shown us you belong here. We're not comfortable bringing in an outsider. They would never get our particular culture. I understand that in the process of, uh, working through issues, you might occasionally make some of us uncomfortable. Whatever is best for our staff in the long run . . ."

The trust he expressed in her made it harder to meet his eyes. How had she gotten herself into this spot? What came to mind promised to sully her further, but something pushed her on. "It's been a struggle for me too, finding the—Carlson—like that. I appreciate your trust, especially that you see me as an insider."

"Part of the family," he said.

"And I'll try to do a better job going forward."

"I'm sure you will." The direct look, something unsettling in his eyes—but then the moment passed. "I assume you'll want to speak with all the originals: Charlotte, Arthur, and those who worked with him most closely—Kaz and, uh . . ."

"Miguel," said Gloria. "Miguel Solar."

"Ah, yes, thank you. And Gloria, of course."

"You should speak with Nicole," said Gloria. "She might as well be an original."

"Oh, she is that," said Steven, with a weak smile, "in her own way."

By this time, his assistant was beaming at him. Cindy realized that she had prepared him for the meeting and was pleased that he had come through. Gloria asked, "Would it be alright if I sent a note out to all the staff with your number here? There are others who were close to Carlson."

Was that the start of a glare from Steven? If so, he covered it, saying, after Cindy had murmured her agreement, "I suppose we should get you on the payroll." And then, to Gloria, "Could you help her complete the paperwork? I'll call Charlotte."

Nodding, Gloria said, "Speaking of originals, you forgot Vernon."

"Did I? Well, they were hardly close. Carlson represented everything Vernon wants us to move away from—Charlotte's softer side, if you like. And he never managed to be comfortable with the two of us, together."

The man's face seemed to fold down onto itself, and Cindy sensed she had exhausted him and her welcome. Gloria must have reached the same conclusion and ushered her out.

She turned on Cindy when they reached the counter outside Steven's office. "You're welcome. It wasn't easy getting him calmed down after your mercy mission yesterday."

Gloria waited, but Cindy had no idea what to say. The older woman shook her head, then let out a sigh. "I guess it's done now, and you're back at it."

"Look, Gloria, I'm doing the best I can."

"Never mind, child, I know. It's just, this has been such a hard time for Steven, even before. He was trying so hard to convince Carlson to come back. They were talking more and more, and Carlson even seemed excited, about something, anyway. But he was being mysterious, almost teasing, and it hurt Steven, not knowing what was going on. He had laid himself open, begged him. You see, Carlson was always the exciting, popular one. Steven's more thoughtful, shy. I worried Carlson was just playing with Steven—he was almost feverish, and I thought, that couldn't be about a reconciliation. It didn't make sense."

"What else could it have been?" *Something that got him killed?*

The woman seemed to read her thoughts. "This isn't fun for any of us. Just try to go easy now. I know your father would want that."

How did Reverend Abernathy get into this?

"Maybe there's a reason I'm trying to break into web design, huh?"

That got a chuckle out of Gloria, and the first smile of the day. "All right, all right. Let's get these papers sorted out and get you paid for making all this trouble." As she dug out papers from the file behind her counter, the phone rang. "Yes," said Gloria, with unusual sharpness. "Okay, she just needs a few minutes. We're doing her sign-on—" Then, with a roll of her eyes, "Oh, all right, I'll send her up."

That didn't sound good.

"That was Susan. Charlotte will see you now," said Gloria in her best doctor's office manner. Then she added—under her breath, though Cindy could still hear as she headed for the elevators—"No, not in a few minutes, right now. Bitch."

Upstairs, Charlotte led her over to her seating area and pointed to the couch and said, "Steven said you wanted to see me?"

"He listed off people who were most affected by Carlson's murder. Your name was at the top."

"After his, I presume." She waved at imaginary gnats in front of her eyes. "Of course. I'm being pedantic. And uncooperative as well, I suppose."

Time to jump in. "I know this has been a painful shock for you, as much as anybody here." Cindy was aware of Susan's quiet presence behind her right shoulder, at a discreet distance—far enough to give the illusion of privacy without interfering with her eavesdropping.

"Well, at least I was spared the sight of his body. That must have been awful for you."

Cindy was surprised at the light buzzing in her head, the blurring around the edges of her vision, that followed. She shook her head; it helped. "The people I need to talk to all knew Carlson so well, and I'd barely met him." She wasn't sure why she said it. It sounded whiny.

But Charlotte was looking out the window and didn't seem to notice. "Ah, Carlson. It's so hard to sum up a human being that you've come to know so well, who is—was—so much a part of our lives. He had this tiny restaurant in Arlington, the kind with no menus, just two or three choices on a blackboard, something different every night. Arthur was a baby when we started going, so it was more than twenty-five years ago. It wasn't the kind of place you brought an infant, but Arthur was a quiet baby, and Carlson always made us feel welcome. There was one waiter and Carlson in the kitchen, and while you were having dessert, he would come out and sit with you—with me, at least—and chat, about food, children, life."

Cindy nodded. She could picture it.

"We kept going back, the two of us. It was adult conversation, a great treasure to a single mother." Her voice got quiet then. "We sat together and talked about everything, even men. It was wonderful. He was like a doting uncle to Arthur. When I began sharing my ideas for Back Door, for building our community, he lit up. He knew about starting a place of your own, all the little decisions, the excitement, but I think he was getting tired of being tied to that tiny place. As soon as we got big enough to have our own food service, he came on board.

"By then we'd planned the whole thing out, and we were both so excited. He helped design this building; he has such an eye, a gift. It's hard to imagine this place without him. The whole idea of creating a community to support the whole person, that was his idea as much as mine. In those early days we shared a vision. He just glowed, sharing his passion for food, giving his little demonstrations, always checking in to see what would make our youngsters feel happy, excited, loved."

It fascinated Cindy, picturing this powerful woman as a young, single mother finding someone to share her dream. No wonder Carlson meant so much to this place.

"When we were still a little start-up in an old warehouse in East

Cambridge, Carlson met Steven, and after a while he suggested I bring him on. I suspected they might be lovers, but we were tiny and building a family; I wasn't thinking in terms of rules and boundaries. I've never regretted it. Steven's ability as a publicist helped us grow, and when that happened, he was the one who saw the need for an operations person.

"Vernon enabled us to go further with product development and build teams that really produce, and his government contacts . . . Of course, he's never fully bought into my vision for our community, but he's seen our people develop exciting collaborations, so he grumbles, but he goes along. He's a partner now, part of the team, as is Steven, but Carlson—it was our vision, together. There'll never be another one. If I have to be honest, without his encouragement, his faith, I wouldn't be sitting here."

Charlotte looked off in the distance, the animation leaving her face and voice. "Of course, there were some points of contention. After a while. Carlson became more skeptical of some of the things I brought in, perhaps no longer as motivated to do battle by my side with Vernon. The gym, yoga—Carlson is a bit Euro-centric. It didn't help when I brought on young Kazuhiro." She chuckled. "Ah, the elemental struggle, East and West, young and old. It seemed so important at the time. Now, to have fallen out over that, seems so sad."

Cindy kept very still, willing Charlotte to keep on with her narrative. She wanted to know everything about this place.

"I wanted a change, something lighter, healthier. And less European, more diverse. Kaz represents a new adventure, but to Carlson, it was a betrayal."

"You no longer shared a vision."

"It's still my company, you see. He was going to have to adjust, but he was a vain man, and it hurt him, that I didn't care more about what he believed. When our ideas diverged, I would never have wanted him to leave, but he needed to defer."

This seemed like the right time to bring up the little scene in the waiting area outside the office. "The other day, when Carlson was coming out of your office, he seemed upset, even downcast."

"Ah, you don't miss much, do you? That was a discussion we'd been having for over a year, since . . ." Her voice rose as she pulled herself more erect, chin thrust out, but then she stopped.

She was silent for a while. Cindy waited.

"We have a major investor now, and he's brought with him some business acumen, much needed—at least, according to him—and he started asking questions. You see, we were all together from the beginning, Vernon, Carlson, and I, and later Arthur—as a sort of executive committee. He looked at our roles: CEO, Finance and Operations, Technology, PR and HR, and chef. As they say on Sesame Street, which one doesn't belong? I had to give Carlson the news that he was voted off. He was hurt, humiliated—one couldn't blame him. But we're no longer a start-up, you see, and we can't act like one."

So, his death was a personal loss for Charlotte and the others, but perhaps not a loss for the company. Were some secretly relieved? Even if someone wanted him gone, was that enough reason to kill him?

It was starting to feel like there might be a motive here somewhere, for someone, but Cindy felt very far away from finding it, and she couldn't think where to begin. There had to be something she should ask, but nothing came, except the realization that had been with her since she started here. She wasn't of this culture or part of this family—not yet.

This time Charlotte broke the silence. "So, what next?"

Oh. This time Cindy caught herself, she hoped, in time. As she launched into her speech about the effects of trauma, the typical recovery period, possible short-term effects, Charlotte affected a little smile, as if these trifles were for weak people with time on their hands. Cindy couldn't wait to escape, to think about all she had learned.

Susan followed her out.

"That is one strong lady," Cindy said.

"Strong and powerful, which is not always the same thing. It's the latter you have to watch out for." Cindy stopped walking as Susan continued. "She likes you, which is great—as long as you do what she wants."

Oh?

"Just remember what happened to Carlson."

"You mean I'm in danger?" It seemed ridiculous.

Susan just stared at her for a beat, then shook her head sharply. "No, no, that came out wrong. Charlotte assigns people roles in the organization—I mean, that's her job. She expects people to keep to those."

"Like, stay in your lane? Stick to your knitting?"

"Exactly. She sounded mellow about it in there, but when she was dealing with Carlson and he was pushing back, she lost patience with him, and it wasn't pretty."

"If she really lit into him, she must regret that now."

"Oh, I don't know. You heard her in there."

"It's my company. He had to defer." Yes, Cindy could see how that might have sounded, when Charlotte felt it necessary to remind Carlson. "Okay, I hear you. I'll be careful."

"The problem is, when you're around her a while, you see that what she wishes today will shift and change tomorrow. It's about calling the shots, and she doesn't always . . ." She stopped, gave her head a little shake. "Well, I should let you see for yourself. Just remember, I'm here, and I'll stay with you when she moves on to other things. For now, focus on getting in with Arthur."

Now the woman took both Cindy's hands and looked steadily into her eyes. "Don't get so caught up with this that you neglect his work. And don't assume you will continue to have his support. Arthur is, well, practical. It's nothing personal, but it's best to keep your head down and let the bullets fly by."

That made sense, but there was more there, behind the words—a look bordering on pity, even more unsettling than Steven's earlier attack. Fitting in around here was starting to look more daunting, even without her secret mission.

2 6

Paul

My sister kept her word, as usual.

A blown head gasket doomed Cindy's old heap a couple of years ago, but she has a credit card, so she booked us a car to take us to the Middlesex County lockup. The driver's nice enough, promises to come back in two hours to take us back home. I've already paid Cindy back for the ride. The mood she's in, I'm not about to hold out on her till the bill comes.

Sitting in the grimy waiting room, it's strangely reassuring to see my sister's discomfort. We checked in moments ago with the sour woman behind glass that's got to be an inch thick—the speaking hole is covered with another thick piece, raised a half inch or so above its surface by heavy bolts.

"Two of you? You'll have to go in separately," she said.

"We got authorized to go in together," I said, holding the letter up in front of the glass. "It's a reasonable accommodation."

The woman heaves a sigh. We're making her already difficult day of sitting on her ass, staring at a room full of losers, unbearable. Somewhere around my age, with red circles on her powdery white cheeks setting off dark-red lipstick, she looks about to bust out of a dress that must have fit her thirty pounds ago. "Take a seat," she says, waving us off with a knuckle. After having another go at her magazine for a while, she heaves the receiver to her ear and turns sideways.

While she's whining on the phone, a skinny White teenage girl comes in holding the hand of a small Black boy, maybe ten years old. They're like brother and sister, an unmistakable warmth coming from the girl, responding to the frightened boy with a smile and a hug. I look at Cindy because it feels like the way she's there for me, but when she leans over and whispers, "Look at the bag," I have to adjust my view.

The fraying canvas satchel over the woman's shoulder screams social services, and I realize I'm not the only one getting flashbacks to an earlier time. A fresh-faced child protection worker, a recent graduate—a young Cindy. I can see my sister looking at a little boy like that, holding his hand, being there for him. Maybe she's thinking of what lies ahead for him, or maybe for the girl. I know those things still haunt her.

The social worker sits the boy on the bench at right angles to ours. After looking in his eyes and squeezing his shoulders, she turns away from him to stand in front of the receptionist, who holds up a fat finger behind the window without looking around. When the receptionist manages to drag her attention away from her magazine, she waves the social worker away and beckons to Cindy.

"It's gonna be a while, miss. Takes extra security for the two of you."

At last the young woman manages to get attention through the glass, asserting in a quavering voice that she too has authorization to accompany her charge into the room, only to be greeted with the same resentment and delay.

"It's routine," whispers Cindy with an incredulous look. "She's accompanying a minor. Why are they jerking her around?" She smiles at the fidgeting boy on the bench, bringing out a shy grin. The young woman notices, nods, and smiles. Then comes the familiar chime, and the woman digs into her bag.

"Hey, hey!" It's hard to believe that much venom can make it through the heavy glass. "No phones in here. Read the sign."

The woman looks around in panic. This must be her first time.

"I'll sit with him," Cindy says, approaching the boy. "What's your name?" She was always good with kids.

"Marcus," comes the little voice, the boy stealing a quick look at her, then away.

"You here to see your daddy?" The boy doesn't look up. "Your first time in here?" That brings a little nod. "These places can seem scary at first, but they're okay." Cindy's smooth when she says it, though she always talked about how she never got used to lying to the kids.

Maybe he senses it anyway, or maybe he just has to move, but the boy bounces up and goes tearing around the room, touching some old magazines on a table, bumping into a chair, then returning to the magazines and waving one around so that the pages flutter and an envelope drops to the floor.

"Hey, kid," comes a growl from behind the glass. "Yeah, you know who! Sit down! Now! And keep your grubby little hands off the magazines; they're not for you." Then, to Cindy, "You watching him or what? Since you assigned yourself the job, do it!"

Uh-oh. There was a time Cindy'd had all the fight beaten out of her. I know that feeling real well, but hers has been coming back. I wondered whether getting mugged took the fight out of her, but I should know better. The look on the boy's face, though, I've seen that at Bridgewater—the dead eyes when they go somewhere else. It hurts me to see it on this beautiful young boy.

Cindy's standing in front of the glass, leaning down with her mouth angled into the speaking hole. "The kid's waited long enough to see his father. I worked family services for eight years, bringing kids to places like this, and I've seen a lot, but you're the saddest excuse for a human ever." She lowers and slows her voice. "Now listen carefully: you will not yell at that child, and you're not pushing me around. Look at me! He gets to be a boy, and you will not speak to him again. I will look after him."

They stare at each other for some time, until the woman flicks her fingers in dismissal and returns her attention to her magazine.

By that time, I'm thinking someone's got to do something with the little boy, so I go over and ask him if he knows the slap-hands game, where you hold out your hands palms up and the other guy covers them with his hand. You try to flip a hand over and slap one of his before he can pull it away—*you know that one?* The boy learns it real fast, and before long he's whooping and slapping me pretty good, and I'm not even close to getting his. Of course, he might be trying harder. We're both laughing, but that woman is staying quiet behind her glass, pretending we're not there. Round one to Cindy.

Then the young social worker's back and kneeling in front of the boy. "Marcus, I'm so sorry. Something has come up, an emergency, and I'm going to have to bring you back to the home. We'll have to reschedule the visit to your dad."

"Look," says Cindy, "I can bring him in. I was at the Beverly office. I've done tons of these. I'll stay with him until you can get back or send someone to take him home."

Now, she's got to know that will never fly. Right there, I can see why child protection was never going to work for her.

It wakes up the beast behind the glass. "Oh no, that's not going to happen. The kid goes with you, lady."

"I can stay with him and bring him in there," says Cindy. "You've already got my paperwork."

"Oh, really? You related to the kid? I heard you say you used to work child protection. So what? She goes, the kid goes. End of story." The woman's smiling for the first time. It's not pretty.

By now, the mean guard must be desperate to get Cindy out of her face because we're ushered into the security area a short time later. Once we get wanded, they show us into a tiny room with a large glass window and three plastic bucket chairs. Another guard comes in, pulling on Johnnie, who's all fitted out with metal cuffs on his wrists and ankles connected up with thin chains, his jive walk making them rattle and clank. At least they left his hands in front. They pull them around back, means they're planning on tripping you, knocking you down on your face—they don't want you to break your fall.

Means I can hold out my hand for a shake, long as I reach in close.

"Paul Abernathy. I don't know if you remember, from Stewart Center?"

"Yeah," the kid says, but his face says he's just going along.

"This is my sister, Cindy. She's helping me out." Whatever the hell that means. He's not curious enough to ask, just nods and looks down at her feet.

I can't believe this young man, swallowed up in these overalls, ever scared me. He's tapping out a rhythm on his thighs, *clink-a-clink clink*, his head swaying back and forth a little to a beat only he can hear. I look over at Cindy, and she's staring at him—easy to do with his eyes down like that.

Brilliant, helpful things don't come to mind. "I'm a member at the Center, mostly working now over at Elder Affairs. Thing is, ConDo put out the word that their staff can't talk to you—your lawyer tell you that?"

He shrugs, a tiny movement that makes me sad. Now that he's stopped drumming, he seems even smaller.

"There's some of us want to make sure you're not facing this alone. They picked me to come talk to you, make sure you're okay. Cindy here is working at Back Door—you might've seen her—and she's looking into things there, find out what happened."

That gets him to look up at Cindy, but she's busy giving me a hard look.

"I didn't kill that dude. He was weird, but nice . . . to me." Then, under his breath, "Nice, the dude was nice, like in paradise got a price, throw the dice, once or twice." He's back to the tapping.

"I found the body," Cindy says. I'd have thought that would shock him, but I can't see any reaction at all. I'm wondering what I'm doing here—might as well have stayed home. "They said you were there to see him but then you left."

He's still again. "Not to see him, exactly. I went back to get my jacket. It's my favorite, from when I was working with this band. I was there earlier. After my shift. He was showing me stuff."

Cindy again, "So, you went to get your jacket. Did you find it?"

"Yeah, it was on a table near the door to the kitchen."

"You mean on the counter, right?" she says.

"Nah, not in the kitchen; outside, on a table, where they eat." There's a flash of impatience, arrogant. "I didn't go into the kitchen. Didn't need to, once I had my jacket. I just split."

"You didn't notice the blood?" Cindy's expression is stony.

His fingers are drumming again, *clink-a-clink clank*. "I knew it was wet, you know, but it's like a dark blue. Everything gets wet in the kitchen, where I figured I left it. Someone cleaning up put it there on the table, probably get it out of their way. I was mad, thinking maybe I'd have to wash it, but I didn't think about blood. Once it dried, kind of crusty, you know, then I'm thinking damn, now I know I'm gonna have to wash it. That's why I left it behind, you know, where I was staying, when I went to the Center the next day."

"So you never saw the body?" Cindy's lost the hard look by now. The boy shakes his head. "Lucky for you." It must be the softness in her tone that makes him look up.

"Was he a friend of yours?"

My sister shakes her head. "Only met him a couple of times."

"He was a nice man. This sucks."

It's hard to tell exactly when a mind changes. I can tell Cindy doesn't think she's looking at a killer anymore. I might not have been sure either, until now. This kid didn't kill anyone. Going out into the parking lot of that awful place, we don't talk, but it's what we're both thinking.

2 7

Cindy

When Cindy arrived at her desk Monday morning, there was an email from Gloria waiting for her. "Please check in when convenient." She sent back an answer: "Lunch?" Gloria wrote back, "How about eleven, before the rush?" It sounded like nothing but a social call.

"Thanks for joining me," said Gloria, who looked uncomfortable as they sat in a far corner of the big cafeteria. "I just thought I'd check in, see how you were doing."

"Fine. Pretty well, anyway."

For some reason, Gloria wasn't looking at her or acting interested in her answer. It was hard to take offense, though, when the older woman was twitching with discomfort. Cindy couldn't figure out how to offer her relief, and decided to wait. Then Gloria brightened visibly.

"First off, congratulations. Your first paycheck."

The woman was obviously pleased, but more subdued about it than Cindy, who would have let out a whoop if they weren't sitting in the dining room. As it was, Cindy let out a "Yes!" and pumped her fist. Then she noticed Gloria's discomfort return, and the woman spoke in a softer voice.

"I, uh, I've been meaning to chat to, you know, get to know you a little better. I mean, that's my job—was, anyway, until they moved you down to Arthur's group. And you being the other sister and all."

Okay, that made sense, as far as it went, but didn't explain Gloria's discomfort. Cindy tried to look sympathetic, but patience wasn't among her gifts.

"I've been meaning to ask how you came to us, you know? I mean, I know you're changing careers, going into web design, and social work didn't—well, I don't need to know about that, what happened."

She took a breath, looked away.

"It was a change for me too, coming here. I married young, at least by today's standards, to a good man. Had my girls right away. Matthew was a fireman. Seemed like he worked all the time, but the overtime made it possible for me to stay home with the girls. When he was home, he treated us like jewels. The girls worshiped him, couldn't wait for him to come home, tried to keep him up when he needed sleep. He acted like he didn't mind, but I could tell he was dead tired."

She smiled, a twitch that was gone before it could take hold.

"And then, one time, he didn't come home."

Gloria looked up at her, proud tears in her eyes, defiant. It was touching, but strange. Was this why Gloria had wanted to meet, to share this with another woman?

"He was looking to save two young vagrants, squatters, when the building came down on him. Turns out, they weren't even in there, and might have started the fire, leaving the place with their candles still burning. My girls were thirteen and ten when it happened, and even though we had his pension, I had to go to work part-time for us to keep the house, so they had to go from all of me and a little of him to just a little of me. The fact that they were able to survive all that and go on to thrive—it's because of him. They did all right."

"I was eleven," said Cindy, "when my mother passed. I'm not sure I ever thought of it like that, but I think you're right. Having those years with a father and mother—mine was at home with us too—made all the difference, even though it wasn't easy."

They sat in silence, comfortable, for some time. Then Gloria looked up at her and spoke. "I talked to your father. About you."

Cindy couldn't believe it. Or maybe she could.

"He's worried about you."

"Well, you know fathers," said Cindy, trying hard to stay calm. Why was this woman talking to her father? Had he called her? Did he think she was a child? No, that didn't compute.

"Eugene . . ."

Good Lord, he's Eugene now?

"He's a fine man, your father." Gloria looked down, stopped talking, turned away and stared off, blinking.

Oh. Then it hadn't been her imagination.

"You mean, you and Father . . ." Cindy started to laugh. Somehow, stifling it just made it worse. "I'm sorry, I don't mean—"

"He's not that old, you know. He's got a right to his own life, and I—I do too."

Now Gloria had her chin up, and then she too was trying not to laugh. Cindy gave up first, and pretty soon they were both laughing, and holding each other's hands across the table. When the giggles subsided, though, Cindy wanted her hands back but didn't know how to detach without offending the woman. To her relief, Gloria let go, but neither seemed to know what to say.

There was so much to think about. Cindy needed to be away, by herself, but Gloria was looking at her now, waiting, apparently, for her blessing. The best Cindy could do was smile and nod. She almost felt sorry for the woman when the look of relief passed over her face. *My God, there must be some way out of this.* A talk with her father, Gloria had said.

"You started out saying he was worried. I hope you can understand how awkward this is for me. I'm no kid. This is my job, and I wasn't planning on my father being a part of things here."

"Of course, dear, it's just that, what he told me, about you and your friends trying to clear that young man . . ."

Oh shit. What had Father told her? *How did he find out? Paul? Ralph?* That's right, she remembered now—Paul.

"It's not like I'm playing detective. I just said I'd keep my ears open."

"And how convenient," Gloria said, "to be on this mission of mercy."

There wasn't much she could say to that, but Gloria seemed to take no pleasure in springing the trap. "Since you spoke with Steven, we've talked it over. What you said, about the police not looking hard, it's been worrying him. He can't leave it alone, the idea that someone here, someone he knows, might be involved. He wants to talk to you."

He does? This was making her dizzy.

"Your father, on the other hand, wants me to put a stop to it, keep you focused on your computer work. He's afraid you'll get hurt again."

Cindy had to laugh. "So you're trapped, just like I am."

"Sure looks that way."

Maybe there was a way out. "Okay, how about this. You tell Father not to worry, you're taking care of it, and I'll talk to Steven." *And I'm okay with you seeing my father.* She was relieved she didn't have to say it.

"And you'll be very, very careful this time." It wasn't a question, but it was a deal.

• • •

Steven rose to greet Cindy and shook her hand formally. Once again, no hostility there, but no warmth either. If anything he seemed deflated as he waved her over to the sofa and sat facing her across the coffee table.

"Thank you for seeing me. I've been thinking about what you said, about the dishwasher. When Gloria told me about your, ah, assignment . . ."

Cindy turned to the other woman, who wouldn't meet her eyes.

" . . . I thought, maybe that's not the worst thing. And I must say, I had to admire your nerve." He held up his hand to quell her objection. "I mean that in a positive way. You're new here, and you discovered the, uh, Carlson."

"I'm doing the best I can, but it's obvious I don't know what I'm doing. I could use your help."

"And I too will do my best."

"You see, I've been to the jail to see Johnnie. Did you have a chance to get to know him?"

"Ah. You are taking this seriously." When she stayed silent, he went on. "I didn't know him, thank God. I may have met him once, at the beginning. You see, it was always through Lu, and the agreement was that she and her colleagues would do the screening. Everyone was to get a chance—it seemed so hopeful, so right when she said it. I had no idea . . ."

He started to cry quietly, with a quiver of his shoulders the only indication until tears began leaking down both cheeks onto his lap. Gloria moved to his side to rub his back, but he pulled away, walked to his desk for a wad of tissues, and stood facing the windows. All they could do was wait.

"I don't believe he could have done it," Cindy said softly when he had returned to his seat. "That's why I have to keep going with this."

"Ah, yes, I see. And I—I would like to be sure. If it could have been anyone here, anyone I know . . . I can't get it out of my mind." Gloria put a comforting hand on his shoulder, which he accepted this time.

"Since our talk," Cindy went on, slowly, "has anything else occurred to you? Anyone here who might have reason to want Carlson out of the way?"

Steven looked down and shook his head.

"This guy, Marshall." The name popped out, but she wasn't sure what she wanted to ask.

"Carlson's last conquest," muttered Steven.

"He was a strange one." Cindy and Steven both turned to Gloria in surprise. "There were complaints from his team. His work was sloppy. They may dress that way, but they take pride in the work. When people pointed out errors, he didn't seem to get it, like he was unprepared. And he was in retail security, not the most high-powered section."

"He set his sights on Carlson," said Steven, "and, well, nobody's perfect. Carlson hadn't had that sort of fling in years, but, like all the other times, it was over after a couple of months. He tried to let the young man down gently—usually they were ready to move on anyway, but this one made a fuss. And then he was gone."

"You mean quit, fired?"

That earned Cindy a glare from Gloria. "Just stopped showing up," she said. "No one in his section was sorry to see him go. It's like that, sometimes. Companies are always looking to steal our people, though I'm not sure why any of them would want Marshall. Maybe he figured he wasn't going to make it in this line of work and moved on to something else."

This sounded like a dead end to Cindy. Then a crazy thought. "I keep hearing about how Charlotte's vision pervades every aspect of this place. You explained how important Carlson and his work were to the community she wants to build, but what about Vernon—does he buy in?"

The question seemed to surprise Steven. "Certainly not in every respect. Charlotte and Carlson are idealists, and they fed off each other. Vernon's feet are planted firmly on the ground, and he makes sure the place actually produces value. I don't think he was a big fan of Carlson—nor of me, I should say—at first. While I wouldn't say he's a full-on homophobe, there is a lingering discomfort."

Cindy hurried on, afraid he would start crying again. "Did he find Charlotte's ideas extreme? Nicole . . ."

Here he managed a laugh, though it ended in a sour expression. "Charlotte's little stress reliever? Vernon's made no secret of his disdain for her mission, and the thinking behind it."

"I can imagine."

"Unlike some of his generation"—pointing to himself—"Vernon is of the old school. Stress is part of work, he would say. If you're worried about the job, work harder. The idea that people might need strategies to help them cope strikes him as symptomatic of a weakened society. I imagine he begrudges every penny Charlotte spends on people like Nicole, on the gym, and yes, anything above basic cafeteria food.

But he's come to accept all of it. As far as standing in the way of his goals, I'm afraid it's hard to imagine Carlson would be high on his list of obstacles."

She gave him a long look but found nothing more, no darting eyes, no twitches, his gaze steady, tired and sad. But everyone here was unwilling to consider that their family harbored a murderer. It was still easier to think the threat came from outside, from the temporary, disabled dishwasher.

• • •

Around four, after several hours working in Arthur's office, Cindy heard what she now thought of as the Susan hush.

"Arthur," Susan said as she slid through the door. He gave her the usual finger waggle without looking up from his screen. Then, to Cindy, "Are you able to disengage for a bit? Charlotte wants to see you. Something's bothering her, but she's not saying what."

Uh-oh. Cindy thought back to her interview with Steven. Would she be criticized for making him cry?

Susan must have noticed her concern. "It's okay. Whatever it is, I'll be there with you."

It was good someone had her back.

Cindy knew something was different when Charlotte didn't rise but motioned her to a chair facing her across her desk. "I'm afraid I have to give you some bad news. When you started, I told you that you would have a limited period of time to show us you belonged here. Four weeks, I believe I said, but that was the outside limit. Since we've ample evidence to make our decision, I've decided your services will no longer be needed. I do hope the experience has been helpful to you."

Cindy struggled to breathe. There hadn't been a hint from Arthur, and wasn't he the one to make the call? They had been working on the website together, collaborating. He appreciated her work, the design and organizing sense she brought to it. He'd said so, hadn't he? She tried to bring back his words. But Charlotte made it sound like he hadn't been involved. Cindy pushed down her panic and tried to sound reasonable. "Was there something Arthur said, uh, about my performance? I know I was on a trial basis, but I could use any information, uh, for next time." Her voice sounded alien to her, but it could have been the buzzing in her head.

Charlotte put her hands down flat in front of her and rose up, leaning toward Cindy. "Listen carefully, Ms. Abernathy." The reasonable tone was gone now. "There will be no next time, not at Back Door and not at any of the other tech shops in town. It's a small club."

Cindy's found herself standing to face down her boss. "What are you saying? What's happened?" Was Arthur upset with her? Was he that obtuse, or wooden, that she could have been unaware of it?

"I thought, you being a *social worker*, that it wouldn't be necessary to tell you about my son's condition. I assumed you would have the sensitivity, or at least the decency, to treat him with respect."

As her head cleared, Cindy noticed the hint of a smirk and, behind it, something ugly, an implacable hatred that struck a familiar chord.

"They used to call it Asperger's syndrome. Surely you've heard of it. Now they say he's on the autism spectrum. He's especially vulnerable because he can't read social cues, like facial expressions or tone of voice."

Anger helped Cindy find hers. "Of course I know what it means; I suspected as much." *Get to the point.*

"The years in school, the ignorant teachers, the bullying. This place has become his home, his world. He's capable here, so I forget how fragile he can be."

"He seems very much at home with his team."

"Why, then, am I hearing about you snickering, making little jokes at his expense? It's so easy, you could do it to his face and he'd never know, but no one has ever done that here."

Cindy could only stare. It took too long for Susan to come to her rescue.

"Charlotte, I told you." They had discussed this already? Susan must have known what was coming. "I couldn't see Cindy doing that. There must be some mistake, a misunderstanding."

Though the words were supportive, Susan's wheedling tone betrayed her. Apparently no one here was willing to take on Charlotte.

"Our young people," said her boss, "many of them have had their own issues, in school, growing up—I suppose that's why I allowed myself to grow complacent. But perhaps it's different where you come from." The ugly smirk was back as Charlotte extended a finger at Cindy's face. "Well, I will certainly be having a talk with Martin. When he told me about you, it sounded so good, to help our diversity, and put someone on Arthur's team with a clinical background, to support him. What, did you think we needed someone with your *skills*, designing cutesy websites for the neighborhood dry cleaners?"

Okay, enough with the reasonable tone. "So, it was all bullshit, what a great fit I was. Of course, I was worried I'd be a token here, but this is worse. I was supposed to be, what, Arthur's support animal?" She thought of her earlier flash to wearing a smock as a greeter, but this was a further descent into humiliation.

It just made the other woman angrier. Charlotte actually hissed. "You pretentious brat. I'm going to make sure you never work in tech again. It's not like you're anything special."

Cindy looked back at Susan, who perched on the sofa, staring straight ahead. The assistant was right there with her, but now only in body.

Charlotte wasn't done. "Things didn't work out so well at the Department of Social Services either, did they? They let you resign, I understand. You must have been quite something for them to show you the door. I guess even the union couldn't save you. Exactly what happened there? I can find out, you know." Then she flashed from smug to weary. "Never mind, it's done now." She flicked her wrist as she sat down. "Go."

There was an inscribed glass paperweight on the desk, no doubt a trophy from some collection of Charlotte's rich and privileged friends. Cindy thought it might serve as a weapon, but the images of blood spraying from Charlotte's head as she pitched over backwards brought Cindy out of it. She thought of leaving quietly and putting the place behind her, but that seemed worse. She settled on one last try at reason. "I don't know what you think happened, but this isn't fair. I get along fine with Arthur, and I've worked hard. I would never make fun of him, or anything like that. Who said I did?"

Charlotte failed to look up. When it was obvious she wouldn't answer, Susan came up behind her and touched her arm. Cindy shook her off angrily, looked back at Charlotte and slammed her hand flat on the desk. The other woman didn't look up, but she jumped, and that was enough. "Whatever lies you've heard about me, if I hear you're spreading them around . . ." She would do what, exactly? This woman had power; she had none. Cindy stalked out with Susan following close behind her. The first thing she saw was her coat and purse in a pathetic pile on Susan's desk.

"Cindy, I'm sorry," Susan said, after the office door closed. It sounded sincere.

"Really? I didn't know you had already discussed this with her. You could have warned me."

The other woman's shoulders slumped. "She only hinted at it. At the time, I didn't realize how seriously she was taking these rumors."

"Who could have fed her that bullshit? I can't imagine anything I've said to Arthur that could be misconstrued like that, and I don't talk much to the others. I'm not really part of their group, and with everything else going on . . ."

"Of course." Susan put a hand on her shoulder and looked into her eyes. "It's so unfair. I tried to warn you—it's what she does when something sets her off." She took a business card from a desk drawer and wrote a number on the back. "Here's my cell."

So that was it. She was being fired. For what? Some sort of bizarre misunderstanding, a rumor. That was bad enough, but to learn she had been brought on simply for support, like a teacher's aide in special ed, rather than for her skills was much worse. And could this woman really prevent her from getting another job in her field? She posed the question to Susan.

"I'm not sure. She'll probably cool off in a few weeks, so it might pay to wait a bit before you apply anywhere. I'll do what I can. When the dust clears, I'll talk to Arthur about giving you a reference. She doesn't have to know. I have to ask you for your Back Door IDs, though."

Cindy stared at Susan until it registered. Pulling the lanyard over her head, she held it, dangling, until Susan took it from her hand.

"I'm sorry, Cindy, really."

Cindy could barely make out the words as she stumbled toward the elevators. There would be no confronting Arthur—she couldn't even get onto his floor. Without thinking, she pressed the button for the administrative floor, and found herself standing before Gloria's counter, mumbling a goodbye.

"Not feeling well?" She looked sympathetic.

"No, I . . . guess I'm done."

Gloria stared at her, but Cindy couldn't risk a further betrayal. She had to get away, and ran past the elevators to the stairs. She saw the other woman hurry from behind her desk and head toward Steven's office. Part of her was disappointed that Gloria didn't chase her, demanding to know what had happened. She must already know.

She managed to make it outside without bursting into tears, and when they started to leak out on the way down the winding path toward the subway, she hoped the people she passed would attribute them to the chilly October wind. But why care what they thought? Every face seemed to mock her on its way past. *You're nothing. We belong here; you don't.* The sandy path with its fancy lights through scrubby woods failed to hide the ugly swamp. She wouldn't miss this place.

Every time she thought she was standing on solid ground, her feet would slide. It was like ice skating, something she had only tried a handful of times. You were okay, as long as you didn't think about what you were doing, but when something happened to bring your attention to it, like hitting a crack or someone skating in your path, you were frantic, trying to stay upright while everyone else glided effortlessly past. Would life always be like this?

She had blown her opportunity, but how? It hadn't been Arthur; Neerav and Freddy had been friendly, and the rest of the team seemed indifferent to her presence. That didn't mean someone didn't harbor resentment toward the new girl with dubious credentials moving right in to work at Arthur's side. Someone who'd worked hard to get onto the team, someone far more accomplished than she, might well feel jealous, even to the point of lying about her. Or was she the uppity Black trying to push in where she didn't belong? Could it be that simple?

· · ·

It was five by the time she got home, and her father and brother looked surprised when she walked into the kitchen.

"Don't say it," she said. "Don't say anything!"

She related the story as calmly as she could. Their looks were a mixture of sympathy, outrage, and fear.

"Anyone make any plans for dinner?" was the best her brother could do.

Reverend Eugene to the rescue. "We were thinking takeout from Arnold's. Something substantial, like meatloaf."

"Lots of mashed potatoes and gravy, collards," added Cindy with relief.

"Maybe some corn bread," said Paul. "I'll call it in."

It wasn't until the food came and they'd destroyed most of it that they circled back for more details from Cindy. With time to work himself up, her father's outrage was something to see.

"I don't care if you were just an intern."

She'd been put on the payroll but didn't have the energy to correct him.

"They owe you more than that. I can't see you doing anything to bring that on; no one who knows you could ever believe something like that."

"Well," said Paul, "someone accuses you, and you're new—"

"And Black," Cindy added.

". . . then you're not getting the benefit of the doubt."

"All that shit about me being such a find, a great fit. That never did feel right."

"That was all for her," said Father, "the great White lady, make her feel righteous. Didn't mean anything. Never does."

"I can't believe I fell for it."

Talk ran down after that, and they sat in front of the television in sullen silence for the rest of the evening.

• • •

When the phone rang the following morning, Father answered, looking Cindy's way as he employed his deepest voice. "And why, exactly, do you think she would want to speak with you?"

It was tempting to let Father protect her, but she still had a shred of pride left, so she walked over, raised her eyebrows, and held out her hand.

It was Steven. "Cindy? Did you get the message that Gloria called?"

She had been lying in bed, feigning sleep, and her father hadn't disturbed her with it.

"Yes, Steven, my father left me a note."

"Look, I called Charlotte as soon as Gloria told me you'd left. I want you to know, that's not the way we do things here."

"Well, your boss made her feelings quite clear. She also enlightened me on the reason why you thought I was just the right person for the job."

"Oh?"

"If I'd wanted to do job coaching or whatever she had in mind, I could work for ConDo. I applied for an internship in web design."

"Yes, well—"

"Do you know what she said? My web skills were garbage, and I was naive to think I belonged at Back Door. I don't think there's anything more to say. Of course, I never in any way made fun of Arthur. Whoever told you different is lying—you should deal with them instead of wasting your time calling me. Arthur was very fair to me, and I enjoyed working with him. Please tell him that."

She was pleased that she placed the receiver gently back into its cradle. She was so tired. The shock of yesterday's meeting had settled into a dull ache. The only thing left to fight for was her status as an adult in her own family.

"Thank you, Father, but I really can handle this myself."

"Damn well, too. There's got to be other, better places."

"Charlotte threatened to blackball me with all of her friends in the industry. Looks like I'm back to freelancing."

She noticed the flinch that drew from her father, but he covered it well. It was hard to envision when she would make enough money to afford an apartment. He was stuck with her.

"Look, I'm not going to grovel to that bitch or any of her people."

"I know, but there's got to be a personnel director there, and he'll understand that she can't get away with that."

"You mean the guy I just hung up on?"

She had tried HR at Family Services, back when the little boy died, and her supervisor set her up to take the blame. *When you're radioactive*, she thought, *none of that works*. Just as it was then, folks wouldn't stick their necks out. She'd let herself forget that the radiation stayed with you, ready to contaminate anything and anyone you touched. It wasn't smart for anyone to stand with you.

Her father had gone to his desk in the next room, leaving her to her despair. She opened her laptop to go through her files with the intention of getting organized again. Her website, CynthiasWeb. com, was badly in need of refreshing, and she had to figure out what businesses to target next, but her mind wouldn't stay focused, and she was about to give up when Paul walked in.

He said, "You hear anything from Back Door?" She squinted at him. "Well, you had friends there. It's not only this Charlotte."

"Did Father tell you?" His blank look wasn't convincing—he was almost as bad a liar as his father. "Steven called, from HR."

"And?"

"And nothing. He didn't seem to have much to say, so I ended the call."

"Why'd he call then?"

"He said he was sorry—that's not the way they do things."

"He offer you your job back?"

"What?"

"I mean, Gloria called this morning, and now this was her boss, right? So they want you back."

"They're just nervous, don't want to get sued or something. Charlotte would never have me back."

"I can't believe they think you would act like that, making fun of someone with a disability."

"Hey, believe it."

"I mean, it's got to mean something. First you get attacked, now someone spreads this phony story. Someone wants you out of there. Ralph said . . ." He stopped.

"Ralph! You told *Ralph*?"

Cindy's shouting brought their father out. Was he going to tell them to use their indoor voices?

Paul backed up and edged toward the stairs. "Look, you saw Johnnie. He look like a killer to you?"

"I don't know. Maybe."

"Come on, Cindy. I was with you. And if he didn't do it, someone else did. Someone who works at that place."

Cindy nodded. "Yeah, someone in the family."

"So they'd be on edge, defensive. Stands to reason. And you're there, asking questions."

"Pushed into it by you and your friends—"

"But not anymore, not unless you go back."

Cindy stared at Paul. "You want me to go back, after what they did, after what she said, so I can keep playing detective? Forget it."

"That's for damn sure," added their father. "I can't believe you would pressure your sister to go back to that place. After the way—" He was interrupted by the doorbell. "Looks like duty calls, but you haven't heard the last of this." After a brief stare-down with Paul, he turned and stalked off to the door. Cindy and Paul were having their own staring contest when they heard him say, "In here."

She had never seen Arthur outside his office or apart from his team. She was struck by how strange he looked, how diminished. His tall frame was hunched over as he stared at his feet. Without any of the confidence he showed at work, he glanced about hesitantly until his eyes found Cindy's shoes. Then he hurried over to her, hands stiff at his sides.

"Cindy," he said, his monotone more obvious than before, "I need to talk to you."

All she could do was stare. First Gloria, then Arthur, in her house.

"You need to come back. To work."

Cindy saw her father edge over, ready to back Arthur off. Without turning, she held up her hand toward him, heard his frustrated sigh. "I don't think so, Arthur. Your mother made it clear I wouldn't be welcome."

"Oh, I took care of that. We, uh, talked, last night. At home. You work for me, not her. She, uh, forgot."

"Look, Arthur," said Cindy, "I wasn't hired to do web design for you. She was looking for something else." She couldn't bring herself to confront him with the rest of it. She wasn't that angry, not with him.

"She told me. She still thinks I need someone to take care of me. I don't."

He was still looking at her feet, but the words spilled out faster now.

"On the website, you see how things look to people, and you set things up so anyone can understand. I can't do that. The guys in my room, they're coders. They don't know how to look at that stuff. You've shown me a lot already, and now that I see what you can do, I get why we need it, but I still can't do it. And you make it look nice."

It was more words than she'd heard in all their time together. But he had two more.

"Nicole's waiting."

"She's . . . what?"

"Outside. In the car. She drove me. I don't. Drive. We came to get you."

That was too much for her father. "Now, hold on, young man," he rumbled, "no one's taking Cindy anywhere. That place you're running, people getting stabbed, your mother with her crazy ideas, accusing my daughter of all sorts of nonsense. You go back and tell her—"

Cindy stepped in front of him but still faced Arthur. "I guess you're not the only one stuck with an overprotective parent. You're serious? About my work?"

He peeked around her at her father as he spoke.

"You're good at this. We don't have anybody else."

That was all Cindy needed to hear. Somebody valued her work. And not just anybody: Arthur, the chief technical officer. She hadn't imagined it.

Out in the parking lot, Nicole ran over and gave her a hug, and they piled into her boxy little Korean wagon and, with Arthur somehow folded into the back seat, set off for Cambridge.

"Thank God for GPS," said Nicole. "I could never have found this place. Are there any two-way streets around here?"

"You guys, you showed up. I can't thank you enough."

"Well, it was so unfair," said Nicole. "We had to straighten it out. Arthur—"

"What you said in there," he said, "it's been an issue for a long time. Mother thinks I'm . . ."

"Vulnerable?"

"Is that what she said?" Nicole broke in. "She can't seem to let go. Arthur does fine. He's not fragile."

"No," he said, "but our house . . ."

"What happened?" Nicole's tone was stern.

"The door to the patio broke. It's glass. It was, anyway. Technically, I didn't break it. It was the chair."

"What?" Nicole yanked her head around to look at Arthur, and Cindy had to grab the wheel to keep them from swerving into the parked cars. "What chair?" Nicole was smiling as she got the car under control.

"Uh, the one from the kitchen. The one I threw."

He had on a goofy grin. Then all three were laughing.

• • •

When the trio entered the building, Craig greeted her warmly and restored her IDs, Nicole peeled off with a wave, and Cindy and Arthur went to the secure floor and got back to work. Gloria had left a note on Cindy's desk, apologizing "for what happened" and imploring her to be patient. There would be no heartfelt apology from Charlotte or official welcome-back from Steven.

The next day, sitting back-to-back with Arthur, Cindy was finally able to concentrate on her work—until her mind bounced out in response to a swelling in the ambient sound. She peered out to see Nicole pinball a graceful path through the desks and bodies of the bullpen. The thin woman waved with both hands above her head as she came into their office, bounded over behind Arthur, and jumped onto him, wrapping her arms and legs catlike around him from behind.

"Not now. Middle of a thought. No no no." Arthur was swiveling back and forth in a futile attempt to shake himself free.

"Phooey," she said, coming over instead to wrap Cindy in a hug. "Ooh, so tense. Come here, baby." Nicole got behind her and began to knead her shoulders, rubbing her thumbs up and down Cindy's neck.

She felt the difference immediately, closing her eyes and letting herself drift. After some time had passed, the woman let go and kissed her softly on the temple, then said, "Arthur, I need to borrow her."

Getting a finger wiggle in return—Cindy was surprised he'd heard her at all—Nicole grabbed her hand and dragged her up and out of the office.

"Bring her back in one piece," someone called out, which brought out whoops and giggles. It felt nice, like she was at last part of the group. Susan's warning to beware of Nicole didn't make sense. Cindy would trust her own instincts.

"Ladies," said Craig as they passed him. He didn't even crack a smile, which led Cindy and Nicole to giggle and feign teenage embarrassment. Then they were outside.

Their breath was just beginning to steam in the mild breeze as they headed down a path Cindy had never walked before, past a flock of malingering geese onto a wooden bridge over still, brown water, then winding along a dirt path with clumps of tall golden grass that sprouted from its sides. Behind these, tall bushes were turning a deep crimson. After following a boardwalk across a pond, then back onto a dirt path, they finally turned right on a side path and popped out onto a T-shaped platform extending out into a smaller pond. When they could go no further, they stopped to lean side by side, resting forearms on the railing to stare at a small island floating among reeds. Just below them, a boulder several feet wide just cleared the water, an echo of the island a few yards away.

Cindy welcomed the shelter Nicole's body provided from the chilly breeze, only wishing her friend were wider.

"This is lovely. I never realized it was here."

"Folks back there don't get out enough. Even worker bees in the hive get to go out and smell the roses—hey, I like that!" Nicole giggled.

"Yeah, it's the drones that live out their days in the hive, tending to the queen."

"Charlotte? That's what she is to a lot of the coders. She knows it, too. That's why she hired me. Open them wide, that's what she said. I try. Of course, that pisses Vernon off. You've encountered our Napoleon, our Dick Cheney?"

"Barely. I need to talk to him, I suppose."

"Why? Nobody does, if they can avoid it."

"He's on my list of people who knew Carlson best. I promised Charlotte I'd do trauma support."

"Is that what you did, before?"

"Not really, but I've had some training. But I keep bumping into things. Everyone else knows they're there, and they watch me step in them or kick them over. I feel like I'm making things worse."

"That is so unfair."

"It's part of my job now."

"But is it what you want? I mean, you didn't stay in that kind of work."

Cindy didn't want to get into it, but Nicole continued.

"You're so amazing, to be back at work like it's nothing. It's not, you know. You shouldn't pretend it is."

Tears formed in Cindy's eyes. She tried to wipe them away discreetly—as if she could fool this creature. "I'm fine, really. It was no big deal, just a couple of things that happened. I'm not letting it get in my way."

"The mind is a liar," Nicole intoned, "but the body keeps the score." Cindy stopped, pulled back, and stared at her. "Bessel van der Kolk, runs the Trauma Center. I did yoga training there."

"I've heard of that place," said Cindy. "They do great work with kids."

"Yup. Big people too. This padding"—she put her hand on Cindy's round belly—"may not be the best means of protection."

Cindy slapped her hand away, wishing she could dismiss the woman's words as easily. She knew Nicole wasn't just referring to her weight, but it still felt like criticism.

They were silent for a while. "I need your help—with something else," said Cindy. "I visited Johnnie in jail, and I can't stop thinking about him."

Nicole looked startled. "Oh, Cindy. Why would you do that?"

"With my brother, Paul. He's a peer counselor—someone who's been in a mental hospital and now helps others who are going through it. It's hard for him to go back to places like that. Anyway, I just don't see Johnnie as a killer."

"What, is this a gift you have—like, I see dead people? I mean, he must have had some serious problems to be in that program."

"My brother is from that program, and at his worst, he wouldn't have done anything like that." It was the first time Cindy had seen Nicole look embarrassed. "Okay, look, forget it. I'm doing this thing, talking to people most affected by Carlson's, uh, death. Kaz is next, after Vernon."

"Huh. Well, you've got the yin and yang right there. Kaz is great—a fully realized being, in touch with himself. Vernon is, well, a short man. I suppose he has a hard job, keeping the gears turning, but he's all left brain, no balance—nothing like Kaz. Arthur is always trying to shield his team from the pressure. He thinks it's counterproductive, and he's right, but Vernon's never going to listen."

"I witnessed one of their go-rounds. But I have to talk to them."

"You can find Kaz in the kitchen most times—after six is probably good, when all the cooking's done."

"And Vernon?"

"I've got nothing for you there. I'm a distraction, and that's what he says to my face. If he had his way, all of Charlotte's innovations, her dreams of building a community, would be tossed out. That includes me, Claude, the gym—and we'd have some contract food service, or maybe a food court with burgers and a Speedy Wok."

"Don't forget pizza and subs. And fried chicken."

"Why do I sense you're not fully converted to our virtuous lifestyle?" That was worth a final giggle and hug.

A gust of wind easily made it past Nicole and hit Cindy. The little woman seemed immune, but she saw Cindy shiver. "You're freezing. We've got to get you moving. Can you jog—just a little?" Nicole's expression was hopeful, or tried to stay that way as her eyes scanned down over Cindy's body.

Cindy shook her head. "But it's time for me to get back. I need to produce, for Arthur. He's all business, isn't he?"

"Who, Arthur?" The slant to her head suggested deep thought, not something Cindy associated with this sprite. "Nah, that's just his way. The guy lives for his work, and he'll never look into your eyes and bare his soul, but there's a heart in there. And you're good for him."

Cindy stopped to stare open mouthed at her.

"I can tell," said Nicole. "He likes you. Hey, why wouldn't he? Having you there, it's opened him up." Then, without warning, she said, "Race you back," and took off running. Backwards, so she could make teasing faces at Cindy. Once they were on the main path, she turned and loped off.

Cindy was left to trudge back and wonder: was anything as it appeared in this place?

When the front of the building came into view, she saw the long black limousine glide to a stop in front. The rear door swung open, and a woman slid out, pulled hard at her dress and top to straighten them, then finger-combed her hair into place before looking up and around quickly. Then she turned away and hurried around the car and into the building. Susan. Had she seen her? Cindy couldn't tell.

• • •

Cindy decided to try Kaz first, braving the dining room alone for the first time since the murder. This time the lights in the vast space were left on, revealing the yellow police tape around the show kitchen. *Could it have happened only eight days ago?* Giving the crime scene a wide berth, she passed by the vending machines and went to see whether the kitchen could still serve her some real food. To her surprise, Kaz sat at a table in front of the serving counter, slurping noisily at a large bowl of something. As she approached, a wonderful smell surrounded her.

"Hi, Kaz? Cindy. I don't think we've met. I've been here about three weeks, working with Steven and Arthur."

"Ah, yes, the famous Cynthia Abernathy. What a pleasure. I understand you've found yourself in the middle of our little family drama."

"Yes, well, I—"

"Found the body? You will have noticed by now, there are no secrets here. It's our great strength, and our curse. Would you like something? There's still some tom ka gai—Thai chicken soup with coconut and lime."

Her look must have been answer enough. He bounced up and glided quickly behind the counter, returning with a steaming bowl.

"Please, join me." He continued while she tucked in. "It is a remarkable dish, the way the flavors blend—coconut, lime, lemon grass, ginger, cilantro, galangal, chili. The trick is getting the right balance."

Cindy nodded and grunted, wiping a dribble from her chin. The soup was thin but full of flavor; light, but more substantial than a clear broth.

"But I am being immodest. I have been working on it for some time, though, and this, I think, is the way I imagined it to be."

"It's amazing," she managed. "You take pride in your work."

He gave her a little seated bow.

"As I am sure you do, Cindy. To work here, that, I think, can be assumed."

Was there a hint of challenge in his gaze? That intensity—something was going on underneath. "It makes it a bit intimidating," she confessed. "I'm just starting to learn my job."

"Which is?"

"Oh." Apparently, that bit of information wasn't a high priority on the grapevine. She pushed aside questions of what that might mean. This guy was too intense to let her mind stray. She told him about her work on the external website, and her vision for the multi-site algorithm.

He laughed and held up his hand.

"Okay, I get it. Too much technical stuff for this pot monkey. And in case you're wondering, I am all too familiar with the experience, arriving here as one of Charlotte's prize recruits, wondering what I got myself into and how I could manage to fit in."

It was awfully nice to laugh about it with someone else who understood. Why not take advantage of the moment to dig a bit deeper?

"You were supposed to bring lighter, modern cooking—crunchy veggies, simple, clean flavors—the anti-Carlson, isn't that right?"

For a second she feared she had gone too far, but he threw back his head and guffawed.

"Touché! Yes, I figured that out in short order. And made an enemy, I'm afraid. I felt bad for Carlson. He's an amazing cook. When he's in his wheelhouse, no one's better. But those rich sauces and glazes, all that butter and cream—it's more appropriate for special occasions, not every day. For him, though, it was sharing his art. And I suppose, young as they are, it didn't hurt them to eat that way for a few years."

"It would have killed me. After my first breakfast, I had to stay out of this room as much as possible."

"It was what he knew; he couldn't change. And, being a generous soul, he liked to see himself as a mentor. I had no interest in his style, of course, but Miguel—he can do all of Carlson's dishes. He's been his sous chef for years now."

They shared a companionable laugh. She liked him. "But you brought a different vision and aesthetic?"

"Just like Carlson does what he does, this is what I do. Charlotte brought me in for that purpose. So to be fair, I used to say, 'That Carlson, why won't he adjust? Is he too old?' But then, I'm not sure I could change my vision. It just so happens that it's Charlotte's as well, at least for now."

"Along with the exercise, yoga, massage—the whole lifestyle bit?"

"Yes, a sound foundation for her young charges, in their nest; or should I say hive?"

"Buzzing around their queen." Which brought to mind her job. It was easy, then, to turn her expression serious. "You may have heard on the grapevine that Charlotte's asked me to reach out to the people who knew Carlson best." He looked at her calmly, waiting. "I know I had to avoid this place"—she swept her arm around—"after I found him. How has it been for you, coming back to work here?"

"Difficult, at first. But then, it's what I do, and I have people to feed."

"So, you did take over, as . . ."

"Ah, you mean the ambitious young man, blocked from promotion, takes matters into his own hands."

This was getting weird. "What? No, I—"

He laughed, one big loud yelp. "I'm sorry. It's one of the ways I've kept my sanity, to think what really happened."

"You mean, you don't believe—"

"In Johnnie as the crazed killer? I don't know. You probably never got to meet him." Cindy kept her face neutral. "He's a strange kid, but it's hard to see him as a killer. And like that, such a violent attack."

"So I've heard." It had just slipped out, but it got his full attention. "I—you see, my brother knows him from the Stewart Center."

"Oh, he worked there?"

"He was a member. My brother's had his problems, and just got out of a group home a few years ago."

It was always interesting to see people react to the news. Kaz seemed interested, but neither shocked nor put off. "Ah. Anyway, he seemed spaced out, not caring much about the place. It was all about his raps, you know? I kept thinking, who would hate Carlson that much, to kill him that way—the spurned lover in a heartsick rage, the abused and resentful underling? Or perhaps someone had a more dispassionate reason to kill him." Now he did look embarrassed. "I know, it sounds terrible, but it gives my mind something to do."

"And did you come up with anything?" After all, he had brought the subject up. Cindy was just being sympathetic.

"You mean, a better suspect than Johnnie? Like me, the next in line? I love it here, but I have other plans—my own restaurant, for starters, maybe more than one someday; teaching, even some writing. No, even though I'm willing to be pressed into service as Carlson's replacement, I'm not thrilled about it."

Of course, she couldn't even remember one thing from his list of suspect categories. There had to be two or three more, if she could just get her mind to function. Then she realized she had gone a bit far from her comforting role, but her stupidity seemed to amuse him. That was annoying.

"Ah, right," he chuckled. "The spurned lover."

"Marshall?"

"I see you've acquired some sources of your own. Yes, Carlson talked about it. The young man was bitterly disappointed when their little fling failed to blossom into commitment. Sad. But he should have known. Carlson liked the younger men, but he was committed only to Steven."

"Faithful in his way?"

"Exactly. I think it surprised Carlson. He never set out to hurt Marshall. It was never serious for him, that's all."

"It sounds like you got to know him pretty well, even though you were rivals."

"You know, it was a strength of his. We both knew where we stood, but it was never personal. It wasn't like either of us had any control over Charlotte and her vision. It was just that, lately, I was in."

"And he was out?"

"I know it sounds cold, but it wasn't personal for her, either. She would never have abandoned him; he would always have had a place here. But it still hurt. He had already lost a great deal. He told me how close they were, in the beginning. Food as a foundation for health, health as a foundation for work, for community—that was all his, in the beginning, to hear him tell it. I think he thought it would last forever. But nothing ever does, does it?"

Carlson least of all. At last, deep sadness broke through his glib facade, and they shared a few moments of companionable silence. He had given her so much to think about, more than she could process without retreating somewhere on her own.

He broke the silence. "It's been wonderful meeting you, talking to another one of Charlotte's chosen." Then, he was up. "I'm sorry, Cindy, I seem to have outlasted my cleanup crew. By the time I get home, it will be time to come back."

"Often the case around here, I gather."

She couldn't remember a more interesting conversation. It was a bit frightening to think how much she enjoyed these people; she still didn't feel like she could trust any of it, trust that it would last or that they were who they seemed to be. Walking out into the lobby, she turned to say goodnight to Craig only to have him come out from behind his desk.

"Hey, Cindy. Heading home? I'm your escort—to Alewife, anyhow, to the platform." Cindy started to object. "Charlotte's orders. No arguing."

They walked in silence, leaving her to her thoughts, which were spinning. It started out as a tickle—something she should have thought to ask. When it came, it was obvious. There had been three kinds of suspects he mentioned, and they had discussed only two. What was the third? Something about a subordinate, unappreciated, exploited, something . . .

And she had been feeling so smart. She rarely saw her friend Miguel since her first day, since she tried to avoid the lure of the dining room, but what Kaz had described didn't make him sound abused. Apparently, Carlson had gone out of his way to mentor him, teaching him how to prepare all his dishes.

But if Miguel could prepare all of those dishes, he could step into Kaz's old role on weekends. He would be in line for a promotion. Cindy was a bit shocked to realize how easily she had slipped into Kaz's way of thinking. It seemed cynical, but how else was she to proceed? If not Johnnie, someone had to have a reason to kill. It was unsettling, though, the way she was beginning to adjust to this snooping. Was she even having fun? Maybe a little of that would be okay.

2 8

Paul

My first time visiting Johnnie, Cindy took over and I didn't get to talk to him enough. This time I get Sam to bring me. It takes some doing, considering how it went with Cindy at Back Door, but I convince Sam it would be good for him to have me to talk to. I guess I'm a last resort, but I'll take it. My form's been sitting in their system for a while, and I think the lady at the desk is just glad I don't have Cindy with me, so it doesn't take too long to get into that same little room.

One look when they lead him in and Sam's out of her chair. "What the hell happened to my client?"

His right eye is puffy with a fresh blue stain all around it; and he's limping. When he goes to sit down and put his hands on the table, there's blood and scabs on his knuckles. Sam says, "Paul, could you talk to Johnnie for a while? I've got to find out what's going on."

"She's cool, huh?" The young man is smiling, like there's nothing wrong here at all.

"Yeah, she is. But what happened to you? A fight?" No answer; he doesn't even look my way. "Look, man, you got to keep your head down. Don't meet their eyes, you know?"

"Head down, don't frown, beat down, write them down, go down, wear a crown . . ."

He's coming apart. Maybe there *are* worse places than Bridgewater. I'd been in trouble at his age but never spent more than one night in a jail.

"Write this down," he says. "I need to write this down."

At least now he's looking at me, but I don't know what he means. I'm worried he wants to rat out whoever did this to him. That could get him killed.

"My rhymes. I always write them down so they're there when I need them. I got notebooks, back in my room."

"Oh, I get it. I'll have to talk with Sam, your lawyer, about that. She'll be back in a minute." I sure hope that's true. Try again. "What happened to you?"

"Got jumped. It's okay, though, I got a friend now. Big dude, lots of tats—cats, mats, fats, rats—talks about the master race, being strong and pure."

Oh Lord, the Aryan Brotherhood? He'll be eaten alive in this place. I've no idea where to start trying to support him. Reflection, my only friend. "Some guy, uh, came to your defense?"

"Big dude. Said I could join his group, they'd look after me. Stay pure. Put a beatin' on the guy did this. Bam, bam, bam." He punches the air, his fist angled downward, showing me, chains flying. The big guard to the side frees his arms. Great! Then Johnnie's staring off again, tapping out a beat with his fingers that makes his cuffs jingle. "Wham, bam, thank you, ma'am, Sam I am, eggs and ham, in a jamb, on the lamb, cram it down, goin' down, with a frown, write it down. You get me my notebook out of my room?" The guard leans back against the wall, folds his arms again but doesn't look happy.

"Yeah, I'll see what I can do. If not, I can probably get you a new one—and a pencil or something."

"I like a pen, I'll tell you when, just say when, in the pen, that's where I am—hey, that's not bad. Come on, man, I gotta write this down."

There's a pause, and I'm not sure where to go from here. He's looking a lot better, though, no more panic in his eyes, sitting back now.

"I had a line on this amp but they fucked it up, wouldn't give me my money. I had it, too, but they said there were rules."

"Yeah, Shep told me."

"I thought he'd be here, you know. He always said he'd stick by me."

"Yeah, well, ConDo suspended him, won't let any of their people near you."

"No one else there's worth shit. That's too bad, though. Soon as I get out of here, he'll be working for me, part of my posse, you know? You get me that writing stuff, I'll take care of you too."

"Hey, thanks. I appreciate that. I've got a job, though; think I'll stick with that. You need anything else?"

Just then Sam comes back, slams herself down into the other chair. She takes right over like I'm not there; pulls out a paper, goes down the list of his medications, asking him is he getting them. He is—they're paying that much attention. Then she's talking about hearings and next steps. Doesn't look to me like he's understanding much of what she's saying. He's tapping out his beats, *jingle, jingle, jingle.*

"Yeah, yeah," he says, waving her off, "but when am I getting out of here?" He's trying to act tough with her, but the desperation's showing through in his eyes now—she's got to see it.

Now she looks at me, like maybe I'm worth something if I can deal with him. I look back at her, like, *that's your question to answer.* I'm not the lawyer.

"Well, you have to understand, Mr. Christopher, with a murder charge . . ." She takes a breath. "This next hearing, I could ask for bail, but it gets complicated." He looks at her, waits. His eyes—he's shutting down. "ConDo still controls your funds, and I can make sure they keep paying rent on your room if that's what you want, but to go back there alone . . . "

"That'd be great." He's getting excited now. "I can take my DVD around, get my deal set up."

"Well, we'll have to see how it goes in court. The next date is in three weeks, but I'll be asking for a continuance."

He looks down, like he shrinks up—in a small voice says, "I . . . okay, three weeks. I can make that work."

"I have to tell you, Mr. Christopher, you've been charged with first-degree murder. It's very serious."

"But I didn't kill anybody, so it's your job to make it right." He's looking at her, like it should be obvious, and then at me, like he's asking why doesn't she get it. "You tell them that."

She looks at me again—I shrug—and says, "We're working on it, Mr. Christopher."

"You can call me Johnnie, or Mad Johnnie, that's my handle. Or just MJ."

"Why don't we stick with Johnnie for now."

It's over before too much longer, and we're on our way out of that place.

"I'm glad you could come," she says. "He seemed more relaxed, willing to talk."

"You think he'll be okay in there?"

"You mean, will they beat up on him some more?"

"He seems so lost in that jumpsuit."

"And he's likely to run his mouth," she says, looking worried.

"I don't know. He seems out of it, but he's been in Bridgewater. I saw him get arrested." That gets her attention. "The way he handled that made it look like he knows when to shut his mouth, when to look away. You learn that fast in those places. But now he's got a friend, some White supremacist gangbanger."

It's like she doesn't hear that last part. "He has no idea how serious this is. He's the only suspect—they never looked at anyone else. They said he was competent to participate in his own defense, but the longer he's in jail . . ." She gives a little shake. "I just have to hope they can't scrape up enough to convince a jury. I've got my ears open, but I don't get the sense they're interested in pleading this down. This kind of case could make a name for a prosecutor."

"And a defense lawyer?"

She gives me a glare, then a bitter laugh. "You mean, one like me, in danger of becoming a PD lifer?"

"I didn't mean—"

"Yeah, sure." It's a quiet ride back into town. I guess that was the wrong thing to say.

2 9

Cindy

The next morning, Cindy waited until nine before going to the executive floor to see Vernon. The woman behind the desk was older than Cindy, gray haired and severe. When Cindy introduced herself, there was none of the warm interest that most people at the company projected, just a kind of watchfulness. Cindy stumbled describing her role as a would-be trauma counselor. The woman was unimpressed but had finally turned to her screen to look for an opening in her boss's busy schedule when a voice came from the open door behind her.

"Oh, just send her in, Martha. Let's get this over with."

The office was big, but held none of the drama of Charlotte's or the fussy decor of Steven's. Drapes covered all the windows, and a ceiling projector hung over a conference table and chairs facing a big whiteboard. A machine resembling an oversized photocopier was flanked by a bank of monitors that showed views overlooking office cubicles.

Vernon rose behind a large old-fashioned desk. Shaking his hand, Cindy realized she was looking straight into his eyes. Even accounting for her modest heels, he wasn't much taller than she, and his trim body was encased in a gray suit with white shirt and muted striped tie. He motioned her to a straight-backed wooden chair next to his desk and went back to the old-fashioned, dark-red leather chair behind it. There was no sofa in sight, nor any comfortable chairs, and no offer of tea or coffee.

"Charlotte says I am to give you my full cooperation. Well, I'm past being surprised at our leader's occasional flights. I don't suppose you have any particular qualifications in this area?" He didn't wait long for a reply. "I wouldn't have thought so." Though his chair was padded and extended above his head, he sat erect and unmoving, his hands folded on the desk, his shoulders barely turned in her direction.

What could she say? Was he referring to her limited social work background, or had he somehow divined her true purpose? She decided to let it go. His attitude was annoying, but she couldn't say it was unreasonable.

"Well, I suppose," he went on, "we are in similar positions, unable to say no to Charlotte. I can hardly hold that against you."

It was time for her to begin. "I appreciate your seeing me without any notice. I'll try to get to the point. Charlotte has asked me to reach out to everyone who knew Carlson well. I do have some background in trauma support, and this has to have shaken everyone here. Were the two of you close?"

There was a flicker of something at the mention of her name, apparent only because it was his first show of emotion. "Surely you have met with Charlotte and heard about her vision, for a community, a family dedicated to excellence. My role is to operationalize that vision, to turn this assemblage of young talent into a productive team. As we've grown, that challenge has grown ever more daunting. Ours is a balance of complementary forces. By now you've heard how I came to join the organization."

Her blank look was answer enough.

He continued after a snort of impatience. "Our leader had the good fortune to be born into lots of very old money, and she didn't marry badly either, but when her husband died, she didn't see herself as a stay-at-home mother. She had studied computer science at Wellesley, and—well, it's a long story, but she found me at Wang Laboratories, just when their fortunes began to fade. Recruiting talent is one her gifts."

"That must have been—"

"More than twenty years ago. It's a shock to many of us to be seen as the old guard, swimming among all these start-ups, but it happens quickly in tech. I will say, Charlotte's vision for a supportive community has helped us attract and retain young talent as we've grown. She's the queen bee around here, and that suits me just fine."

Hm. Cindy couldn't help thinking of Dick Cheney, but there was something honest and straightforward about this man that made her want to trust him.

"On the other hand," he continued, "I believe you have to push people to realize their full potential, both individually and collectively. And our success depends on setting ambitious goals. We are in a competitive arena—who isn't these days? We have to promise extravagantly, then deliver reliably. That's not easy; and it requires more than fancy food and yoga."

"Are you saying that Carlson was, in some sense, in the way?" It was out before she could think how it might sound.

"Ah, I see." He did? That made one of them. "I will say that I had grown tired of our young people nodding off in the afternoon after heavy meals. I applauded Charlotte for turning to Kaz for lighter fare. But you have to understand, we're at war. Not just this company, all of us."

Was he teasing her? There was no humor in his eyes. The intensity there made her nervous. It could have been worse. His military posture and bearing made her think she didn't want to see him angry. "We are?" The question came out before she could stop it.

"Cyber warfare is no less real for being invisible and bloodless. Our infrastructure is shamefully vulnerable, and now, the way our cravenly indifferent populous get their news, through this infotainment, even our election apparatus is at serious risk of mischief by our enemies. You sit there, doodling with your website, in the middle of a team that is protecting us, so yes, we are at war, and the stakes are terribly high."

"But surely, the government, the Army, CIA—"

"I'm sure you've heard of Blackwater. Do you really think a bunch of twenty-two-year-olds brought Iraq to heel? These days, it's all about public/private partnerships. We have been the tip of the spear, and I intend to keep it that way, which means we need to stay determined, lean, hard. Yoga, massage, fancy French cooking . . ."

Well, she needn't have worried about Vernon's heartbreak over Carlson's death. Maybe she could use that to her advantage. "Yes, I see," she said, with what she hoped was an easy smile. "I'm afraid I'm not very good at asking these questions. Does it concern you, that a murder could happen here at Back Door?"

"On the contrary, that's a clever question. A different sort of threat, clearly, and, normally, not my problem. How do we protect ourselves from impulsive insanity? I could speculate our anything-goes culture is to blame, but I prefer to let the police sort that out."

"But you won't miss Carlson." Something about man's glibness, and maybe the swipe at people like her brother, forced her to fight back.

He didn't seem offended. "Oh, he was nice enough, in his peculiar way, but life goes on. War exacts casualties; life adds random ones. I will not allow us to be deflected.

"And now I'm afraid I have work piling up. Martha has been holding my calls." He took a business card out of his pocket and scribbled on the back. "If you hear anything I should know, get in touch. The best way is to email Martha; she'll fit you in."

On the way out of the office, Cindy glanced at the bank of monitors and noticed that the images in each one changed every few seconds.

"I couldn't help noticing," she said, waving a hand.

"Ah. I do like to keep an eye on things, and yes, these are recorded as well. Unfortunately, we didn't see the need to cover the dining room. A pity."

As she stepped into the hallway in front of Arthur's area, a figure jumped at the corner of her vision, making her flinch and stumble to the side: Susan, tight fists by her sides.

"Where have you been?"

"Fine, thanks, and how are you?" It came out before she could bite it back, and it brought a satisfying flinch out of Susan. Cindy pushed her irritation aside to answer with a steadiness that surprised her. "I just got through talking with Vernon. Yesterday afternoon, after we met, I spoke with Kaz. They're on my list."

"Yes, of course. And how did it go?" With a shift so sudden it was eerie, the old, supportive Susan was back.

"Fine, I suppose. It's always interesting, the way different people react to the same event. Shock and grief are so personal." Susan looked at her intently, as if willing her to go on, as if she didn't understand that these sorts of things weren't to be shared by someone in Cindy's position. After a longish pause, she suggested they go for a walk outside.

Cindy waved and made eye contact with Craig as they passed through the lobby. Susan paused as she did but didn't make a move to acknowledge him.

"I wanted to talk with you about Nicole," said Susan once they were outside. "She's quite, well, seductive." She seemed to notice Cindy's look, and went on. "I know that sounds weird, but you need to know some background."

Cindy's head wanted to know more, but her gut wanted it to stop. She wanted to feel comfortable in this place.

"You already know that Charlotte set out to establish this supportive community. What she doesn't talk about, outside of her own inner circle, is eugenics. Are you familiar with the term?"

Cindy nodded. It was covered in social work school: the late-nineteenth, early-twentieth-century movement came out of Darwin—progress from natural to intentional selection, improve the human race through selective breeding. Where could this be going?

Susan continued, "Prominent figures—Charles Lindberg, Winston Churchill, Teddy Roosevelt—were adherents. Before the war, it was mainstream thinking, here and in Europe. It was about getting the best people to reproduce and preventing people who were defective or inferior from breeding."

Cindy also knew the downside: mass sterilization of people with mental illness and other disabilities right here at home, including women whose poverty confirmed their "inferior stock"; involuntary sterilization of Black women in the South persisted through the 1950s.

"Charlotte's idea was completely positive, though. She was gathering these exceptional young people, in her eyes the best of the breed, but she looked at these studious, introverted guys and wondered whether they would reproduce. They were spending all their time here, after all, with very few women around, but more than that, she worried they might not be capable of finding mates, and, you know, performing."

Well, at least it seemed more in keeping with the people Cindy had encountered so far. Much more so than Vernon's hard cases—the tip of the spear. Cindy had to laugh, but caught herself when Susan didn't join her. "You mean," she said, "all that good food, the fitness, wellness . . ." It began to dawn on her as Susan continued.

"She found Nicole, I'm not sure where. Cleaning up at her gym, dancing in some bar—there are different stories. She was a runaway, apparently, doing the best she could, and she became another one of Charlotte's reclamation projects."

Had Cindy also been one of those projects, she wondered.

"Her job here is to, uh, help things along, as kind of a, uh—"

"Surrogate?"

"Well, I didn't say that. But she did get Charlotte to convert these closets. They have beds now."

"The relaxation rooms?"

"Ha! Yes, I suppose that's what she's calling them. Haven't you noticed how she's got her hands on everybody?"

That was certainly true, but it always seemed playful, even innocent. Was Susan referring to sex? It seemed unbelievable, but what else could she mean?

"Of course, this could be the first job the woman's had that involves a paycheck and regular hours. Unless she worked in a brothel; that would come as no surprise. Charlotte's moved on to other things—she brought in Claude to get her boys in touch with their bodies, more of a wellness approach—but Nicole is part of the family now."

Susan rested her hand on Cindy's arm and lowered her voice.

"If that's not bad enough, she's an ungrateful little weasel, spreading lies, disrupting operations, undermining morale. I wonder, could she have had something to do with sending Marshall Carlson's way? That's absolutely her style."

Cindy tried hard to take it all in. Nicole? Her friend?

"Charlotte would love to get her away from Arthur. She tried once, but the poor man had a meltdown, couldn't function. Even though Charlotte's gotten over her eugenics obsession, she needs to keep him happy. Vernon would love to get rid of Nicole, but his job depends on a happy and productive Arthur. She's still here, doing her thing, making sure to play up to Arthur—crafty little minx. But that doesn't mean she gets to screw around with you."

The woman actually blushed slightly and waved a hand in front of her face.

"That didn't come out right."

"She seems nice enough," said Cindy, feeling like she needed to stick up for her friend. "She's been very kind to me. She cares, about people."

"Nicole Arnessen is tolerated, but she certainly doesn't have anyone's respect. How could she? And for God's sake, don't trust her! She's manipulative, finds little ways to undermine people, to hurt them. She draws them out and she's devious, a real sociopath. You're still new here, at the stage where people are getting to know you. You simply must stay away from her. And don't, for God's sake, tell her what we talk about. I hate to give you the impression that things are this bizarre around here, but I know you. I can't ask you to do something without explaining exactly why."

It was almost a relief when Susan moved on to Cindy's talk with Vernon. She didn't give up easily. Cindy had to tell her something. "He helped me understand how the place got started, how it works."

"You'll only find out what he wants you to know. Secrecy is in Vernon's DNA. It has to be, given his role."

"Oh?" Cindy wasn't really surprised, but she wanted to hear whatever Susan had to add.

"I'm sure I shouldn't tell you this, and it's essential that he not find out I did. Vernon came to us from the NSA—the National Security Agency."

"You mean, as in Edward Snowden? That NSA?"

"Snowden was a contractor, and Vernon was an executive on staff, but yes, that's the one. Back Door's ties to them go back to the beginning. That's why Arthur and his team have their own security. They know what they're working on, but no one else in the organization does. We all pray they can keep their mouths shut around Nicole—Vernon is especially vigilant about that. Fortunately, the little slut doesn't have a head for such things."

The harshness was shocking, so out of character for Susan, who always seemed reasonable.

"The sensitive government work is all under Arthur, part of his, uh . . . I'm talking too freely here, but I think I have to trust you. As a youngster, he was caught hacking into government computers. He was only a child, twelve or something, and Charlotte made some kind of deal, so now he works for Vernon. You can probably sense that he's not always thrilled about it, and Vernon has to push him to get what he wants."

Cindy had witnessed the tension and Arthur's bridling at Vernon's pressure on his team. It made sense.

"Could Carlson have gotten in the way, somehow? Vernon didn't seem to be a fan."

Susan waved a hand again. "I've been talking way too much. I'm not used to being around a professional listener. I hope it helps you understand this place, though, so when you stumble upon things, you can put them in context." Which happened to be just what Cindy needed. "It might help keep you out of trouble. Just remember, stay away from Nicole—she's poison!"

As they were about to reenter the building, Susan stopped Cindy with a hand on her upper arm. "Charlotte wants a report. Tomorrow at eleven. She cares about her people. And I want to make sure this goes well, for your sake." This last was punctuated with an intense, lingering look.

It was a lot to take in. If Cindy couldn't trust Nicole, at least she had a better understanding of Arthur and Vernon. And Charlotte. Cindy felt further and further out of her depth, and with the stakes this high, she couldn't afford to let her guard down. Her mind kept wandering, though, to fantasies of Nicole stealing in and out of those creepy little rooms, servicing young coders with messy hair and questionable hygiene. The woman was the last person she wanted to see, so of course she was hanging all over Arthur when Cindy got back to her desk.

Nicole detached herself from him and put her hand on Cindy's shoulder. Had it been that obvious before, how she was always touching people, brushing up against them, always in their space? Until then, Cindy had only half believed it, but it fit with the discomfort Nicole's physicality engendered in her. "Hey, Cindy." Nicole must have felt the cringe she got in response and couldn't have missed Cindy's downcast eyes and quick step back. "Oh. Is everything okay?"

Cindy spent the next few minutes squirming with embarrassment, thinking, *My God, I'm going to have to be prepared for the next time I see her.* If she was to stay out of this woman's trap, she would have to be smart, nimble. Arthur, of course, missed everything. He gave her a finger wiggle and went back to his work.

3 0

Paul

Father's moving slow most days, looking tired. Used to be he was one of those big men could carry it. I've only been back living with him a little over two years, but it's hitting me now that he's aged in that time. Today, though, I see some of the old energy.

Phyllis has a class at adult ed, something to do with perspective in drawing, so I'm home all evening with him, and I'm cooking for a change, which means simple. I got us one of those rotisserie chickens from the market, did some instant mashed potatoes and frozen vegetable medley, showing off everything I learned all those years in the group home. Father doesn't complain. He wants to talk about Cindy and Ralph.

"I'm wondering where things stand with those two," he says. "I hardly see either one anymore. That boy was getting to be part of the family."

"Not anymore, if Cindy has any say in it."

"I guess she's got *the* say. It's a shame, though. He's a good man."

"For a White boy?" That gets a laugh out of him.

"All those years without a man." He's looking off now. "I was hoping this one might stick."

"It's this thing in her head, starting a new life. He's not happy about it, but she's pretty clear—he's on the shelf. I'm going to stay in touch with him, though. I haven't forgotten what he did for me, and, well, he's a friend."

"I feel the same way. I don't suppose she'll like it much if I reach out, though."

"Maybe after a little while. Won't help him move on, though."

"I suppose not." Father gives this sigh, shakes his big head. "Young folks don't settle down like we did, that's clear. Breaking up, moving around—having kids without ever marrying or making any kind of commitment."

Young folks—Cindy's thirty-seven, and Ralph's close to my age. "We gettin' old, Pops."

"Now, don't you start." But he's laughing. He always did get my humor, even when I was a boy. Not that many people do, even now. Especially now.

I've still got young Johnnie on my mind. "Speaking of which, that White boy they charged with the killing . . ."

"Come from the Stewart Center?"

I nod. "He's into this rap music. Thinks he's going to be famous with it."

"What do you think?"

"Huh—not likely. It's his dream, though, and I know enough not to step on it. He doesn't seem to get where he's at, though, what's coming down on him. It's like everyone needs him to be guilty, and wants to get the whole thing over with, and he's in there working on his rhymes."

"Might be a blessing. Cindy seems to think it's pretty obvious he did it."

"Not now that she's met him." Father looks surprised. "She went with me, to the jail, my first time. Just to hold my hand, but it turned out she did all the talking, made a connection with him before I could."

"I'm not sure I like either of you getting involved in this, let alone both."

I explain: we both were trapped into it, but now we're all the guy's got. "You know, it's different when you sit there with him. You just get the sense it's not in him."

"These rap lyrics, though. Pretty violent stuff."

"Yeah, I get it, but this young man—it's like he's just a boy, like he's playing with it, that's all. Got beat up himself, pretty bad, but now he's cocky again because he's got this skinhead protector."

"Not one of those Aryan Nation hoodlums? Well, may the Lord have mercy on him, then."

"Him and Cindy, you mean."

"Careful now, son! I'm still the reverend in this house." He laughs, though, so I do too. "But you've got a point; he could do a lot worse than have our girl on his side."

"And there's this Sam."

"Ah yes, the African American Jewish princess."

"Yeah, I went out there with her this time, got to talk to Johnnie, for a while, at least, while she went to yell at folks. She's impressive. I think he did okay there."

"Well, let's hope so." There's more to Cindy's role, of course, but Father looks worried enough as it is, and I can't bring myself to load that on him.

The doorbell rings, and it's Ralph, hunched over more than usual, like he knows he's not supposed to be here. He's relieved to hear Cindy's not around.

"I, uh, this will be easier without . . ." We wait. It takes the man a while to get going sometimes. "I've been worried about Cindy, after what happened."

"Well," Father says, "she has had a spell of bad luck, that's for certain."

"Yeah, well, when she was attacked—on that path—you said there was word of a homeless encampment, there in the woods." I can't think of where he's going with this, and Father's looking as puzzled as I am. "The last few days, I've been going through there— the woods, I mean. There's a lot of tall grass, but those areas are too swampy to walk in. There's trees around, even a couple of grassy clearings where you can hear the traffic on Route 2, but you can't see anything. I'd been through all of it, but I went back over it all today, just to be sure. I even went on the other side of the stream. There's only a little bit of woods there; the rest is exposed."

I feel Father shifting his big body around next to me, impatient. I'm getting there too, but Ralph's got to go at his own pace.

"There's no camp. No trash around, not even an area where the grass is beaten down.

"So?" I say. "The subway's right there." Always someone panhandling in the stations.

"I suppose so."

"A path through the woods," says Father. "I'm surprised it doesn't happen more often. They should patrol it, maybe even set up cameras."

I say, "Cindy says their security guard is walking her to the station, for now."

Ralph won't let it go, though. "What if it's not random? What if it's connected to this investigation she's doing?"

Uh-oh. He's got a point, but when I told Ralph about what Cindy was up to, I didn't think he'd be bringing it back to Father. Cindy and I'd agreed not to worry him with it.

"She's doing what?" Father's deep voice is magnificent in outrage.

Ralph looks at me. "She's looking into what happened."

"What about the police?" A fair question.

I come to Ralph's defense. "It just seems like everybody wants it to be this White kid, the dishwasher."

"Okay, but I don't like it. She's been through enough. I'm not going to allow this to continue."

Ralph and I share a look. It turns out he's better at keeping a straight face. "Well, now," I manage, before the smile breaks through and I start to chuckle. Even worried as he is, Father can't help but join in. "You going to tell her to lay off?"

Father's shaking his head. "Best way to keep her going. I see your point."

Just then, Cindy walks in fast, until she sees Ralph and stops. He can't look at her, mumbles. She looks at Father, then me; we look at each other.

It's Father who speaks up. "Ralph stopped by to visit. I let him know he's always welcome here."

31

Cindy

Cindy wanted to be angrier, but she was too tired. *There will be another time*, she thought, *without Ralph skulking around*. Without Paul either—it was easier to take them on one at a time.

"Long day," said her father. *Duh!* "You hungry? I could heat something up."

She shook her head. Surely he knew by now about all the food at work.

Paul said, "You learn anything interesting today?"

She gave him a hard look and he hunched away. So much for his promise not to tell Father. "Not that I know what I'm doing, but I am learning something about the place from Susan, Charlotte's assistant." They just stared at her. "And I could use a cup of tea."

Ralph waved his hand and scuttled into the kitchen ahead of them, clattering about as they all trouped in and sat around the table.

"Apparently Charlotte is obsessed with eugenics—or was, anyway. She hired this woman, Nicole, as a sort of surrogate, to help the young nerds get their mojo on, so they could make smart babies."

"Did she now," said her father. "I hadn't heard."

Why would he? The interjection was odd enough that she tried unsuccessfully to catch Paul's eye. "She thinks they're, like, superior beings because they can write code." She tried for a dismissive tone, partly to see what would happen. Sure enough, the reaction was far more positive than when she sang the woman's praises.

First Paul: "Well, I guess it's better than sterilizing us."

Then Ralph: "Or the ovens." The voice of Judaism.

Her father looked more thoughtful. "The talented tenth."

It took Cindy a minute to make the connection. Paul was faster. "W. E. B. Du Bois. Your thesis, right?"

"Mm-hmm," the reverend said. "To quote the man himself, 'The Negro race, like all races, is going to be saved by its exceptional men.' Sorry, honey, he was old school. 'It is the best of our race that must guide the mass away from contamination by the worst.' Something like that. Lot of famous people bought into that movement."

Of course, Ralph had to join in. "The whole eugenics thing passed for enlightened science in the first half of the twentieth century, even got intertwined with the women's movement."

"Father wrote his doctoral thesis on W. E. B. Du Bois and his connection to eugenics," Cindy added. "Tell them what else he said, or is that hard to remember?"

"Harder to live with. 'The mass of ignorant Negroes still breed carelessly and disastrously, so that their increase, even more than the increase among Whites, is from that part of the population least intelligent and fit, and least able to rear their children properly.' That one appeared in Margaret Sanger's *Birth Control Review*."

"Even more than the increase among Whites. Huh," said Paul.

"But," put in his father, "you have to understand the context. Du Bois was criticizing the Atlanta Compact. Booker T. Washington had agreed to a deal: the Jim Crow lynching would stop, along with seizing back the property folks got in Reconstruction, and there would be universal public education for Blacks. In exchange, the education wouldn't be equal. Black education would be limited to the trades, and what they called a classical education, one that would prepare you for a profession, would be Whites-only. It was a fantasy anyway; didn't stop the seizures or the lynching—divided Black folks and made it all worse."

Paul picked it up. "DuBois was talking about where the leaders in the Black community would come from, arguing for access to that classical education for the talented tenth. Later he recognized that it's often the people who struggle who have the most to offer."

This seemed to excite Ralph. "Yeah, it's the whole differently-abled thing."

Here we go, talked over and discounted again. "God, how very PC," Cindy snorted.

"No, really," said Ralph. "It's why we're so focused on resilience in the recovery movement. It's not about selecting and privileging the best people; it's about finding ways to get the most out of everyone. Experiencing a major challenge, persevering in its face, getting over—it's the opposite of eugenics. Look at Paul. After wasting years in that fucking group home"—wait, didn't he work for ConDo? didn't they run the fucking group home?—"he's working at Elder Affairs. He's inspiring people at the Stewart Center."

"Amen to that," added her father.

This clearly embarrassed her brother, who rose from the table. "Think I'll clear these things, start in on the dishes. I need to reconnect to my humble beginnings now that I hear how great I am. Least we got to do that at Farnsworth"—his group home.

Hey, what about me? she wanted to shout. *I bounced back, and I'm getting paid now, full-time!* Sidelined again; she wondered what she could ever say that would make them appreciate what she was doing. She went into the kitchen to fix her nightly hot milk, ready to turn in early, as usual, when she saw it sitting on the table: one of the Back Door Technology pens she had seen in a jar on Gloria's counter.

It was hard to find them anywhere else; coders had little use for pens. Could Cindy have left it there? She had taken one the other day, to fill out her paperwork, and it could have ended up in her bag.

She was too tired to worry about it now.

3 2

Paul

First, he's not big. Sal, that is, Billie's uncle.

His state-run assisted living place is in one of the renovated buildings at the old TB asylum on River Street. I was worried; he's a retired police detective, and I haven't had great luck with cops. But this shriveled old guy—there's room for two of him in the wheelchair.

His eyes go wide when he sees me walk in behind Cindy.

"Who's that?" His voice is high, whiny.

While Cindy introduces us, I realize with a start that he's afraid of me. And she hasn't even told him I'm crazy yet. When I shake his hand, tell him I know Johnnie from the Stewart Center and I'm trying to help him out, he seems to relax a little. I can't blame him, though. Billie, Cindy, and I are crowded around him in this tiny room. The ladies are sitting on the bed, so I've got to stand over him in his wheelchair. Smells like an animal died in here. I breathe through my mouth.

"All right," says Billie, "enough formalities. What have you got, Cindy?"

"I'm stumped, Sal," she says. "I've started interviewing people, mostly just to find out more about Back Door—"

"The high-tech place, where it happened?" Shit, he doesn't even remember that? How much help can he be?

"Yeah. The boss has been good about telling people to cooperate with me, and offering them support is working out okay; they seem happy to talk."

"That's good. But I been thinking, since last time: it's hard not to like the kid for it—you know, the dishwasher."

Yeah, the crazy guy. I can't let that rest. "Look," I say, and he does, a little of that fear back in his eyes, which feels nice, I've got to admit, "Cindy and I have both met with the young man, in the Middlesex County Jail, and he just doesn't seem like the type."

He says, "I'm not saying you never follow your gut. You got to sometimes. But with these crazies, you can't tell. They can flip, turn animal on you. You'd never see it coming."

The guy's looking off, in lecture mode, and Billie gives me a look like *let it go or the old man'll clam up.*

"But okay, I get it. You want to check out everyone else, which is what the cops would be doing if it wasn't for all the damn cuts. Let's go over what you've learned so far. Take me through your interviews."

She does, and I've got to say, I'm impressed. The guy has a way about him, like he wants the job done right, and he'll take the time to dig in. Cindy starts with her meeting with Steven.

"The guy, the whataya call, husband? Jesus!" But he slows her down, wants every word, which is good, because I'm hearing most of it for the first time too.

After she goes through it, she says, "I know I blew it. I made him mad, and he cut off the interview."

"And you let him? You gotta ask, right? Nothing wrong with that. What did you see when you hit him with it?"

"I, uh . . ." She looks at me. I shrug. What do I know?

He looks impatient for the first time. "Were his eyes shifting around?"

"I didn't notice." Embarrassed now.

"Hey, look, this was your first, your . . ." He looks at me, stops right there. "Maybe I shoulda given you more last time. Anyways, here's what you got to watch for: who's nervous; who tries to undermine someone else, you know, cast expursions?"

He takes a breath, like talking tires him out, like running up stairs. He's into it, though, not whining anymore. "Most of all, though, you watch their eyes. They go up, to the side, means they're thinking up something, about to spin you a line. Doesn't matter what it is, you know they're lying, probably hiding something. They look down, to the side, means they're not going to tell you everything, so they're hiding something, but at least they're probably not lying, unless it's a story they've already told so many times they don't have to think about it. That's psychology." He smiles—real proud.

"Well, I didn't notice, but I'll remember that."

"Was he, like, twitchy?" She shook her head. "You'll have to go back to him. He's your best bet, other than the kid. That's the thing; when you get them mad, you can't run. Stare them down. Don't blink, that's the rule, and watch. Makes them mad? Nervous? Good! That's what you want. Make them squirm, you're doing your job."

"Well, that's the thing. I do want to keep working there."

"Yeah, I forgot—that's not going to be easy. Anyways, the other things you're looking for, besides shifty eyes and twitchy—if they're smooth, they can hide all that—is if they don't answer you direct, like they change the subject. Cutest trick is if you find yourself answering their questions. Sometimes you don't even realize until after, when you go to write it down. You are writing this stuff down, right?"

Now my sister is hanging her head while she shakes it.

"Jesus. Okay, do that, soon as you can, everything you can remember. Now take me through the others." He shakes his head, but then he's leaning forward, nodding as Cindy goes on.

She goes through the list: this guy Kaz, Vernon (turns out he used to be with the feds, but Sal just shrugs that off), Nicole. She talks about the help she's getting from this Susan. None of it gets Sal excited. I'm thinking maybe it's getting on time for his nap.

Then he asks, "So, what did you learn about this Carlson guy, the vic?" Her blank look gets him going, makes him raise his voice for the first time, high as well as loud. "What'd I say? About gettin in their guts? It's fine to learn all about the company, but you gotta get close to your victim, always." And he stares at her, like he's waiting to hear her plan, but she's got nothing. "Okay, look-it, who's gonna be able to tell you? The husband? It's a place to start. Who else knew him?"

"I did get some information from Kaz."

And they go back and forth a little longer, but they're both looking tired, so I guess it's all she's going to get. I'm surprised she got as much as she did. The guy was working it.

Then Billie speaks up for the first time, which is amazing, because she mostly takes over any room she's in. "So, what have we got? Who would want to kill the guy?"

"Nyah," says Sal, more a growl than a word, "still too early. We don't know shit, not yet."

Which gets Billie going. "Look, asshole, she's doing the best she can. Help us out here."

"I am. Jesus, calm the fuck down! You don't want to jump in right away. You figure who you like for it, yeah, but too early and it shuts your mind down. And we ain't even started on the crazy kid."

"We both talked to him, Cindy and I." He doesn't seem scared when I speak up this time, but he looks ready to fall asleep. I go on, more for Billie than him. "He's, like, unfocused. He got beat up pretty bad, but he's not even angry, looking for revenge. He's stuck in his own head most of the time—hard to picture him grabbing that big knife and sticking it into anybody."

By the time I finish, Big Sal is snoring softly, slumped over in his chair. Billie sets the drugstore bag with his candy and vaping cartridges on the bed, and we file out.

On the way to the car, Cindy says, "Thanks for coming with me. He was a lot better behaved than last time."

"Well, it's tougher to be an asshole with big brother in the room."

"Yeah, the big scary Black man," says Billie, and we share a laugh.

"Still," says Cindy, "I wish I'd talked to him back when I was doing child protection. I realize now that I shied away from making people uncomfortable, let them back me off. And I didn't know what to watch for. Maybe if I was better at reading people, I could have saved those kids some grief."

I don't know what to say to that. That job, that failure, still eats at her, and nothing I say is going to change anything.

3 3

Cindy

It was 6:30 when Cindy got up from her desk to leave for home. Now that Craig walked her to the station, she had to leave at a regular hour so he wasn't on call for her all evening.

The first time, she was too embarrassed to say much, and he was silent. Since then, she had used their walk as an opportunity to learn more about Back Door, and even though that didn't produce much, she had grown to like him. One evening she stumbled on the key, asking how he'd come to Back Door. His pride was obvious as he described a career in Army special forces and the bond with his fellow soldiers. After a promotion placed him in a leadership role, he found those bonds threatened by the conflicting ambitions of people jockeying for influence and promotion, both his peers and superiors. When a few members of his unit left to sign on with Blackwater, he went with them.

"They offered us more for being a grunt than I was making as an officer, and I thought I could get away from the bullshit, back to the way it used to be. Everyone knew the score—we weren't kids anymore—but I missed the old feeling of shared mission, of representing your country, and the cynicism got to me after a while. It made the dirty parts of the job harder to take."

He was recruited by Vernon, a friend of his former commanding officer. That had opened the door to questions about the operations manager, but by that time the short walk was over.

Tonight, Cindy decided to return there. She might not have the chance again, now that she was in Charlotte's doghouse. "What can you tell me about Vernon?"

"He was an officer in the Rangers; ended up in tactical, then switched to military R and D, I think."

"Susan said NSA."

"Did she? I don't know about that."

"One day, when he came in to see Arthur, things got pretty tense."

"Well, guys on that team like to razz him, from what Nicole says. I don't know if anyone knows much about what Arthur feels about things, but he does support his people."

They were halfway down the winding path now, and went on in silence a bit further, until Cindy decided she had to poke a bit more. "From what I hear, it seems unlikely Vernon would buy into Charlotte's vision. What does he think of Nicole?"

The guard stopped walking and looked at her. "What about Nicole?"

"Well, you know, her job—it just seems like it's outside what he would approve of."

"I suppose so," he said, returning to their leisurely walk. "But I think he appreciates the long hours people put in. Nicole helps them tolerate all that. In their own way, each of them is important to keeping the place going."

Not for the first time, Cindy marveled at the casual way people referred to Nicole's work—screwing as stress management; sex as a motivational tool for Vernon, to improve the breed for Charlotte. It made her dizzy. She was a minister's daughter, and she had to admit she'd led a staid life without a lot of sexual adventures, but she never thought of herself as a prude.

Now they were at the station, a five-story concrete parking ramp with buses at ground level and subway below.

"Thanks for the chaperone service."

"No problem. See you in the morning." He stood and waved at her as she descended the stairs.

It was one flight down to the turnstiles and a second to the subway platform. This was the end of the line. Trains came in on either side, and a lighted sign indicated which would go out next. There were a few broad wooden benches in the center, backed by system maps.

Both tracks were empty, and thirty or so passengers waited on the platform. The station was still busy at this hour; each train would disgorge a crowd of frazzled commuters headed for the pickup area, the buses, or their cars parked in the garage, to continue their journey home to the suburbs. The stairs let her down on the end that worked best for her, the rear of the train.

At first, the man escaped her notice, but then something about the way he rolled his shoulders as he turned around set off alarm bells. She had seen that before, just after he dropped the hood over the light on the path, when he turned toward her before tackling her to the ground. Or perhaps she was being silly, jumping at shadows.

She could see him now in the bright platform light, a big, disheveled hulk dressed in a grimy and frayed quilted coat that was light green once but now had darker, greasy patches that shined in the harsh light. When he turned toward her, his face was also smeared and grimy, the skin pale against dark stubble. It was his stare, though, and the smile, the aggressive eyes, that gave her a chill.

This was the guy, the mugger; she was sure of it. She looked away—too late—and began to move away from him, toward the other end of the platform. After a few feet, she glanced back. He hadn't moved but continued to stare at her. She turned away and continued her slow walk, as if she were idly moving down the platform, weaving her way among men and women chatting with each other or buried in their phones. When she stole another look, he was the same distance from her as before, following.

The automated woman's voice sang, "The next Red Line train to Braintree is now approaching." Cindy was almost to the end of the platform now, by the stairs that led up to the other side of the station. These were seldom used, as they offered no access to busses or the parking ramp, leading only to a seldom-used path that twisted through trees, past a park with athletic fields. It would be dark and deserted at this time of night—not a good option. She would have to wait for the train.

"The next Red Line train to Braintree is now arriving."

She peeked back to see the man moving toward her, elbowing his way through the waiting passengers with clear purpose. Cindy looked around in panic. Then he was on her, wrapping her in an obscene bear hug, the familiar stubble scratching her cheek as he hissed in her ear.

"I told you to get lost. You think I was kidding, cunt?"

His voice in her ear grew to a snarl, but it didn't draw much attention because the train was roaring its arrival. As the man danced them toward the edge of the platform—he was so strong that her feet were suspended in air, her arms pinned to her sides—his intention was clear. He was going to throw her in front of the train. She had led him to the exact place he wanted her to be, where it would be traveling fastest as it broke out of the tunnel.

She took a breath to scream, but his hand clamped down over her face. She tried to toss her head, to butt his, but his hand easily prevented her. She started to kick out at him. At least she should be able to attract someone's attention. She heard a man's voice— *"Hey!"*—but it was faint, far away. She felt herself lifted onto his hip, began her tumble over her head and toward the tracks.

Then a force hit her from the side, and she was down on the platform, her head snapping onto the concrete floor. The sound inside her head was so loud and sickening it was almost worse than the pain. For a moment, the roaring in her ears and the sparkles in her eyes were all she could see or hear. She felt herself pressed down by a hand, while elsewhere on her body the pressure of the other man's weight left her. She rolled onto her back, then back on her side as the glare from the overhead lights hit her eyes, but then she recoiled as the train roared inches past her nose.

As other sounds came back, she was able to raise her head,

thinking it was time to get the hell out, away from the man who had tried to kill her. He was occupied, though, grappling with another figure about ten yards down the platform. They were fighting with a savage intensity as other passengers shrank away. Then the man fighting her assailant paused for a second as he drew back his arm for a strike, long enough for the bastard to land a huge punch that knocked her rescuer off his feet, allowing the other man to take off at an impressive sprint down the platform and up the stairs.

Holding his jaw, the man clambered to his feet and came toward her. She flinched involuntarily at his approach until she recognized Craig through the blood trickling down his cheek. She thought he was dragging one leg along but couldn't be sure, as faces of people much closer filled her field of vision, yelling stupid things like "What happened?" and "Is she alright?"—barely audible over the buzzing in her head.

Craig pushed his way through, saying, "It's okay, I'm a friend, thank you." He got down on his knees next to her. The gathering crowd pushed closer as the doors to the train opened and people poured out and hurried for the stairs. He asked her where it hurt.

"Just my head, when I fell."

"Sorry, that was my fault," he said with a wincing smile. His speech was lisping and slurred; something was wrong with his jaw.

"Yeah, thanks. But why were you here?"

He looked embarrassed. "I was watching you from the top of the stairs. I'm supposed to see you safely onto the train. I wondered why you decided to walk down to the other end, and when I saw the guy follow you I came down to check it out."

"Well, thanks for that."

"Was that the guy?"

"From the path?" *Brilliant, Cindy.* "I think so—his size; the way he moved; his voice." She couldn't bring herself to mention the obscene intimacy of his stubble.

"That's plenty to convince me. I, uh, got a good look at him."

"I saw you hesitate, before he, uh . . ."

He looked more than embarrassed now—ashamed. "Yeah, I fucked up. It was just, I thought I . . ." Then he shook himself and turned brusque. "We need to get your head looked at."

She was about to say something like "We've got to stop meeting like this," but stopped herself in time. She wasn't able to suppress the giggle that escaped her. It sounded almost crazy to her ears, and apparently to his as well. He put an arm around her, and they moved slowly toward the stairs. Taking his phone from his pocket, he made a series of calls, and this time it was Nicole who appeared with a car.

After he deposited Cindy in the front seat, he spoke across her to Nicole. "Take good care of her. They're expecting her at the Mt. Auburn ER. They already have the paperwork from the last time."

"Hey, hold on," said Cindy. "Your head looks worse than mine, and you can barely talk. Nicole, don't you dare leave without him."

Fortunately, Nicole drove one of those boxy little wagons that sit high, and Craig was able to fold himself into the back seat—where she should have been, if she'd been thinking. She thanked Nicole as they rolled out to sit in traffic. The fatigue hit her then, and she was in a stupor for the ride to the hospital.

When the nurse helped her into the wheelchair, her headache blossomed, and she was seeing double. This time she was seen quickly by the same gray-haired doctor as last time, who ordered a shot that put her to sleep on the gurney.

PART III

3 4

Paul

Passing people stumbling around, pushing their IV bags on little pole carts, I finally find Cindy's room. A big woman clanks past me on her way out. Cambridge Police.

I'm surprised to see only one bed. Who gets a private room? Another surprise stops me short: there's a guy sitting on a chair close by. Ralph, trailing a little ways behind, bumps into my back. The guy's big, even sitting down, with a bandage covering his head and part of one cheek. He's got one of these big plastic splints on one leg, and he's wearing one of these hospital things that ties in the back, showing some of his white ass.

"Paul." She smiles, but it looks like it hurts. The side of her face is swollen, and her head is shaved on the right where she has a gauze patch taped on. Her right eye is all red and puffy. "Hey." Then, in a different tone: "Ralph." It comes out weak, but hard just the same.

"Good to see they kept you," I say, "before you could do any more damage."

She gives me a pained smile, says, "Don't make me laugh. My ribs are sore." Then she looks over at the guy. "Craig, this is my brother, Paul, and his friend Ralph." Ouch. Then, to us, "This is Craig Besler, the security guard at Back Door who rescued me."

When he stands I can see he's even bigger than I thought, and when he nods and says, "Nice to meet you," I can tell there's something bad going on with his mouth. Ralph winces, but he goes to shake the guy's hand, only it's all wrapped up, so they do this wave instead.

I figure I better do something to save the situation. "The cops going to help any?" I make a motion toward the uniform that just left.

"She said they'd try," says Cindy, "but I don't see how. Homeless guy, probably crazy."

That burns, but I've got to let it go. I guess Cindy can tell, though—she is my sister.

"I know, I know, but come on. What else could it be?"

That's when Ralph speaks up. "Someone doesn't want you poking around in that place, maybe? Someone with something to hide?"

He edges closer, just looking at her. The guy doesn't know how to play it cool, and you can see the emotions going over his face— worried, sad, angry. The other guy, Craig, moves over a little to let him in and looks at him.

"I don't know how I could be a threat to anyone," says Cindy. "I haven't gotten anywhere. I've probably been walking by this guy's camp, and he's paranoid about it."

Ralph, shaking his head, says, "There is no camp."

"How would you know?" Cindy's not making her annoyance a secret.

"Because I checked." He's looking like he just won something. That's the thing I don't get about Ralph: he's devoted to Cindy, would do anything for her, but he just can't seem to get her. He should know how pissed she would be, hearing that he was poking around where she works. The smart thing would be to make something up, but that's another thing about the man; he's always got to play it straight.

I can see in Cindy's eyes how offended she is, but they must have put her on something, because she's not yelling. Or maybe she doesn't want to make a scene in front of this other guy. Could be there's something going on between the two of them. She's just staring at Ralph. You'd think that would be enough to shut him up, but you'd be wrong.

"I went all through those woods," he says, "after the last time. It was the same this morning. No one's living in there."

The guy's looking at Ralph now—not hard, more like interested. I can see now, around his eyes, that he's in pain, and his jaw's wired shut, so when he speaks it's through clenched teeth. "Well, I'll be getting out later today. What about you?"

"Maybe later this afternoon. They say I have to have a CAT scan first, and they haven't told me when."

"Yeah," he says, "they're like the Army." I can see him start to laugh, then cut it off, like it hurts. "I should let you have your visit. Just wanted to see how you were doing."

"I think I'll live, but thanks for checking. And thanks again for coming to my rescue."

That snaps Ralph's head around. He's been looking down, forlorn, but now he turns to Craig. "I'll follow you out. I just wanted to say hello." He gives Cindy a long look. She just stares back at him, like she's happy to see him go.

"So, that's Craig." I guess I can't think what to say; so much went on just now, but it's stuff I don't want to discuss, and neither does my sister.

"He fought off the guy. I'd be dead if he hadn't come along when he did."

For my sister to say that—she would never want to worry me or Father; she'd be more likely to play it down—it must have been bad. And I can see it was, looking at her lying there. "This can't go on, Cindy. We've got to do something."

She doesn't say anything to that, and to be honest, I'm not sure what we can do anyway. That's when Ralph comes back in.

"Nice guy," he says. He looks almost happy. Weird.

"I was just saying how we've got to do something about this. Cindy could have been killed."

Might be a growl I hear from Cindy then; hard to tell.

"We're working on it," says Ralph. We are? "I talked to Grace, and she's going to start driving Cindy to work. She'll pick her up at seven to bring her back home. It should work out okay." Then he looks at Cindy. "You could come over on your way home, stay for dinner—there's always plenty."

She's shaking her head, not hard because of how it must hurt, but enough so he can see.

"Or she can just drop you home." He's looking smug now. He's got to know how mad that will make her, but I guess he can't help himself.

She manages, at last, to bring up some gratitude. "That's so nice. It will be good to see her again, and it will help for a few days. After that, I should be okay."

He nods. At least he's sharp enough to know that's as good as he's going to get.

"It's time we were heading out," I say. "I think we're tiring Cindy out. Besides, she's still got that scan."

I talked to the doctor, so I know she isn't getting out for a couple of days. I fill Ralph in on that as we walk down the hall.

Then I have to say, "It's awful nice of Grace to do that for Cindy."

"She's happy to do it," he says. "Besides, I told Billie I'd make a lasagna from scratch, with the real Italian sausage she likes from that butcher in the North End. Then I'm going to try osso bucco—using pork, though. I draw the line at veal. Anyhow, it did the trick."

Then he says, "What do you think of this guy Craig?"

I'm not sure what he means. We both saw the look she gave him, but he did save her life.

"She says he's a good guy. I think he was in the Marines or something, but that's about all I know."

Then he surprises me. "I like him. We're going to stay in touch."

Things didn't go so well for him just now, but he seems okay and, like I said, he's the kind you generally know how he's feeling.

We're walking past the nurse's station when I see a familiar form blocking most of the hallway—Father. And he's with someone, maybe one of the ladies from the church, but no one I recognize.

He stops in front of us. "How's she doing?"

Ralph speaks up first. "She's hurt, but I think she'll be okay."

Father looks relieved, then looks over at the woman. "This is my son, Paul, and Cindy's, uh, friend Ralph. This is Gloria Farrell from Back Door Technologies."

Okay, it's not that weird, someone from there coming, and I heard she visited after the murder, but something about the way they're standing together makes me think of the spring that's come back in Father's step. Damn!

"I, well, nice to meet you," I manage to get out. "I'm sure she'll be happy to see, uh, both of you."

Could Cindy know? No way. She would have said something. Oh boy.

"Well, Eugene, we'll have to make it a brief visit. Why don't you go in, and I'll see if I can find a nurse and scout up some information."

Wow. Smart lady! Called him Eugene.

Not bad looking, either.

• • •

I'm back home on familiar ground, and it's not like anyone's attacked me, but I'm on edge, more like I was when I ran out of that group home a couple years ago. Mt. Auburn Hospital isn't exactly relaxing. It always feels like you're in the way of the nurses. It's better than the place I need to be, though.

"How's he doing?" Phyllis means Johnnie. Her idea is I should be going to see him every couple of days, but I haven't been out there since that last time with Sam. It's not like anything bad happened then, but it still took me a few days to lose that clenched-up feeling in my gut, and with what happened to Cindy, it's back. There's this guy at work, Edmund (not Ed), who's always complaining that it gets too hectic in our section of Elder Affairs—I wonder what he'd think of this place, nurses moving back and forth, machines beeping. *Too much mustard*, that's what he says. Now I know what he means.

Besides, I don't know what to say to Johnnie. I'm scared for him, but now that he's got the Aryan Brotherhood on his side, where do I fit in? He's got to go deep into his own head to get by day to day, I know that much, but I worry that, after he's been there a while, he won't be able to find his way back out. If I'd been as unlucky as he was, I hate to think where I'd be now, and I had a family of my own growing up. Somehow, feeling bad for him makes it even harder to face the visits, so all I do is worry about it.

Father holds out the phone. "It's that lawyer, Shapiro."

It almost seems like he thinks I've got a thing going with her, but of course that's ridiculous. I can't blame him, though—a smart woman with a job, not White, not crazy.

"Mr. Abernathy?"

"Yeah, this is Paul."

"Listen, your sister isn't returning my calls"—no surprise there— "and I've got some news. It's something you should hear anyway. Could we meet?"

I'm thinking what a pain it was to take the subway out to her Malden office, but she goes on, "I've got a deposition on Congress Street tomorrow, and I'd like to visit the Stewart Center. Any chance we could meet there?"

"I've got work starting at noon; maybe in the morning?" Yeah, I got my job back. Turns out it wasn't Billie's call to Martin that did it. My supervisor over at Elder Affairs put up a stink, asked to speak to Sophie's supervisor, and it was Carolyn who caved. Sophie was put out with the way it happened, but happy for me, so I guess it worked out.

We settle on ten. Way too much mustard. Having a meeting to look forward to is enough to ruin my sleep. I keep thinking what news could this be? I'm assuming if it was good news, she would have shared it. I get maybe an hour or two before four. Then I'm awake, lying there until seven, when I give up.

They had these meetings at the group home for a time, maybe ten years ago, called Recovery Incorporated. The idea was, no matter how bad you feel, if you know what you have to do, you can move your muscles and get on with it, and if that doesn't make you feel better, at least it keeps your life from falling apart. That's what I do this morning—just make myself move to the bathroom, brush my teeth, make coffee, stare at the paper, whatever, until it's time to take the subway downtown.

Phyllis is in her usual place, the big clerical room downstairs, when I walk in.

"She's on a tour. Got here half an hour ago with all kinds of questions, so we got Mary to take her around, like she was in orientation. You might have to rescue her."

I'd go over and give her a hug and kiss, but I know she gets self-conscious when she's working. In here I'm all business with her, except maybe for a look that's likely wasted effort, but I hope not. We're getting together when I get off work this evening.

Sam and Mary are on the third floor when I catch up, in the job placement room, which is all crowded now that ConDo has pulled members off their jobs. The dirty looks I get from a few of them, I get it—what's so special about him, he gets to keep his job—but that doesn't make it feel any better. Most, though, are crowded around Sam, who's talking about discrimination and class action lawsuits. When she's finished she shakes my hand like she's glad to see me. Mary says they've been done with the tour for a while. It's crowded enough we have to go into the stairwell to talk. Taking Sam away earns me more dirty looks.

"All that time working at Bridgewater," she says, "I'd heard about places like this but never got to visit one. I can see that was a mistake."

"How come?" That's me, always ready with the smart riposte.

"All you see in those places is people in despair, and you associate that with the people, but here everyone is so calm and positive—"

"Huh. You should have been here last week. Folks aren't so happy about losing their jobs."

"You know what bothers me most about that? They're not as angry as they should be."

"Lots of us get used to that sort of thing."

"You mean, getting screwed?"

I do like the woman's spirit. "Yeah, that. And disappointment, setbacks in general. Sometimes it's the system, sometimes it's you falling apart—either way, it's something you can't control."

"I get it. Anyhow, I need to talk to you about Johnnie. You see, we've known about the apron . . ." She must have seen my blank look. "Oh. It was on the floor near the body, spattered with the victim's blood. It's got Johnnie's DNA. The thing is, he kept it on a hook in the kitchen. Anybody could have taken it and used it for the murder, so it's not determinative, but the knife . . . The DA's people said they couldn't identify prints from the handle—it's mostly wooden, and rough, from use I guess. But they got something off the metal part, up right next to the handle. It's a partial—they had to send an image off for analysis. It came back, and now they're ninety percent sure it's Johnnie's. I'll attack that, try to beat the number down, but it doesn't look good. If there's some reason his print is on that knife, I'd sure like to know about it."

"Well, he was the dishwasher."

"Maybe that's it. He's still not talking to me much, though. I wondered whether you could ask him."

Of course, I knew we'd be talking about Johnnie—why else would this lawyer talk to me? It still opens up the door, though, the cold draft, that place.

"He seems more comfortable talking when you're there," she says. "I could take you out there and back—tomorrow?"

I'd planned on visiting Cindy, still in Mt. Auburn, but it's hard to say no. Worst thing is, when I say I'll do it, she acts like there was never any question. We agree to meet here tomorrow at ten.

● ● ●

At least it's easier getting in this time, and they seem to be getting used to me. They're more relaxed around Johnnie too. They take off his handcuffs at just a hand motion from Sam. We sit, and she starts her questions. Sounds like they're ones she asks every time she visits—

how he's feeling, how have they been treating him, is he getting his medications, have any of the other inmates been bullying him. If he's bothered by anything, it doesn't show. I can tell he likes her, but there's something—a kind of dreamy vagueness around his face—seems off. He's got his fingers drumming and his lips are moving, like he's doing his rhymes. Only half of him is there in the room with us—maybe less.

"Uh, Johnnie," she starts, in a serious tone, slowly, brushing his hand with hers, "remember I said they didn't have any fingerprints on the knife, the one that, uh, killed Carlson?"

He shrugs and nods at the same time.

"Well, they found a partial print. They say it's yours." She pauses and stares at him, but if she can see anything there, she's better than me. "Now, maybe they're right, and maybe not. I'll work on that. But is there any reason your print should be on that knife?"

He looks at her with his mouth open. Hard to see whether he's getting much of what she's saying.

"I mean," she tries again, "could you have handled it, washed it, maybe, with the dishes?"

"I wear gloves when I do that. The water's hot."

I feel like beating my head against the wall, but Sam's patient.

"Okay. But did he lend it to you?"

"For what? I'm a dishwasher, not a cook."

Now I can see her shoulders slump, even though she's doing her best to stay cool. I can't blame her—it's not the answer she's looking for.

"Thing is," he says, and she perks up, "earlier that day, you know, when he asked me to stay around?"

Sam's riffling through the pages of her yellow notepad, but I think I can help.

"Johnnie, was that the thing you told me and Cindy when we were here?"

He just shrugs, so I say to Sam, "He told us that Carlson said he wanted to show him something. We never got any further—we'd just met him."

I say that last part because she's giving me this look, like *He said that, and you let it go? And never told me?* The kid saves me, though.

"How to get the bones out of a chicken."

Sam's staring at him now, all still like Cindy's dog Bruno when he sees a squirrel. Johnnie just keeps going, getting into his own world now.

"He said he had something to show me. We go into that special kitchen he has, and he has me stand next to him at the counter."

I look at Sam—this is a long speech compared to anything I've gotten out of the boy, and it's obviously been the same for her.

"He starts out by taking off his watch and handing it to me, says tell him when the second hand's on the twelve, time him. He pulls out this chicken, all floppy—raw, you know—along with that big knife. You can do everything you need to with the big one, he always says. It's the only one you'll ever need. I say go and he starts in."

The kid's smiling now, getting excited.

"Shoulda seen his hands—wicked fast. That big knife's flashing, he's flipping the chicken all around, and while he's at it, he's talking about it—*I cut here, then through here, you see where that's attached right there, you can feel it with your finger.* Then, when you think he's just been playing around and talking, you know, about chickens, he stops, says time. There's this pile of bones to the side, and he's got that bird all put back together. It looks like a chicken again, like before, only slumped over. It was like magic, so I'm clapping, you know, because it was such a show."

Johnnie, clapping—I try to picture it. I couldn't have come close until now, but with his face lit up like a third grader's first trip to the zoo . . .

"I never seen anything like it, the way his hands moved. He's just smiling, like it's no big deal, but he's proud, like he even cares that I'm impressed. Then he pulls out another chicken, puts his hand out for his watch and hands me the knife with the other, and I'm like, seriously?"

Sam and I are both staring now. *He* put the knife in the boy's hand?

"Whoa, was that thing sharp! I still couldn't do much with it, nothing like him, anyways. I made such a mess—I never was interested in cooking, but this was so cool, I wanted to learn how to do it. And that knife felt natural in my hand, like it belonged there. That's what he kept saying, *you're a natural, Johnnie*, and I'm thinking, like, well, maybe . . ."

Then his eyes turn down and his voice gets soft.

"I'm not, you know. He was just being nice, but . . . that's the way he was, always. Funny dude, but he was that way with me, like I could be something."

Right there, that breaks my heart, thinking how it was when I was his age and in trouble, how special it would be to have someone treat you well when everyone else is mad at you all the time, telling you what a fucked-up piece of trash you are. Saying he was good at something, a natural—it had to have meant a lot to the young man.

On the way out, there's a lot to be sad over, but I'm feeling okay, and not just because we get to leave the place.

"He explained it," I tell Sam. "That's great, right?"

She shakes her head.

"The only way I can introduce it is if I put him on the stand."

And I'm thinking, yeah, so?

"That means exposing him on cross. They'll eat him up. And the worst thing is, I can't predict what will come out of his mouth. I won't be prepared."

"Still, when you heard him tell that story—he liked the guy. You could tell."

"You could, and I could. But he knows us. It took us how many meetings to get it out of him? I go to court, say, 'Okay, Johnnie, tell your story,' in front of all those people, he'll freeze up. If he's all spacey and blank, like he is most of the time, people will figure he's cold, a killer. Worse, it'll come up late in the trial. What if they bait him until he gets mad? There'll be no time to undo the damage." She shakes her head. "No. Too much risk."

"But the prints on the knife—"

"Yeah, the prints on the knife. I don't know. If I can keep out the part about him wearing gloves for the dishwashing, maybe I can minimize the damage. I just don't know."

3 5

Cindy

Cindy's scan came up negative, but it took until her third day to get out and home. The headaches and blurred vision persisted, and her throat still hurt, but only a call from Gloria backing up her father and brother kept her home through the weekend. Now, after a ride from Grace that Monday morning, she managed to drag her body into the lobby at Back Door. For once, she resented the glass wall that let in the morning sun. It did lift her spirits when the figure of Craig standing behind the marble reception desk made it through her pained squint.

By the time she shuffled over, he had come around to the front of the desk. He took her arm and led her behind, lowering her carefully into his chair. "Gloria said you might be showing up." The words were forced out through his still-wired jaw.

If there was some way to respond, to show her good humor and pluck, the thought escaped her. A stupid half smile would have to do. "It's good to see you. I won't ask how you're feeling if you return the favor."

He was unable to smile, but there was humor in his eyes.

"My orders are to direct you to Steven's office—Gloria would like a word."

"Just like old times," she managed. Exhausted and shaky as she was, it felt good to be here.

"You just rest here a bit first."

She wanted to argue, but the walk in from the car had used up her reserves. The stabbing pain behind her right eye that had subsided yesterday afternoon was back, and sparkles danced at the edges of her vision.

"I have to thank you anyway," he said. "I won the pool on when you'd be back. Nicki bet on Wednesday."

"You're welcome. How about Gloria?"

"She wouldn't bet—said she had inside information."

"An honorable woman. What have I missed?"

"Well, Charlotte's on the warpath. Said if anything more happens to you, she'll outsource security."

"Hey, that's not fair. You saved my ass."

"Which was my job. Would have been better if I'd gotten there sooner."

"As it is, you got rained on by my cloud."

His eyes hardened. "I'm not superstitious. Just because we haven't figured out what's going on doesn't mean it's your fault. I'd say this place has been bad luck for you."

"Well, thanks. I think I'm ready for the next leg of my journey."

She reluctantly accepted his help to stand, only to find his arm supporting her on one side and his hip on the other as she made for the elevators. He whispered in her ear.

"I know you don't need this, but it's for show. Someone will report back to Charlotte."

She started giggling and then felt him wince as she lost her balance and bumped him.

"Your ribs too?"

"Yeah, we make quite the pair, don't we? And don't make me laugh—that hurts worse."

Once Cindy had a firm grasp on the railing in the elevator, Craig left her.

When the elevator doors opened, Gloria came in and helped her hobble toward Steven's office. He came bustling out and saw them.

"Oh my. Cindy, do you really think—"

Gloria cut him off with a raised hand and a sterner voice than Cindy had heard before. "I've got this. You go ahead."

He hesitated, then gave Cindy's arm a quick squeeze and moved toward the elevators.

"Some meeting or other. We'll have the office to ourselves," Gloria said in her normal voice.

Once she had dragged Cindy over to the couch and got her down without incident, Gloria excused herself. Cindy had no sense of time having passed, but Gloria was back, and there in front of Cindy sat a steaming mug of coffee and two Boston cream donuts. She must have been staring, because the other woman said, "Arthur said they're your favorite. You go ahead and eat both—seems like they've been getting smaller lately."

Right. "Thanks. Sure beats green Jell-O." Cindy couldn't remember anything tasting better. "I appreciate the welcome, but it's not like I'm helpless."

"No, just wounded. You need time to heal."

"I just wanted to get back to work. I'm sorry, I seem to be bringing bad luck wherever I go."

"No one blames you for any of this. That's the silliest thing I've heard yet."

"Well, you've been very patient, but I feel like, I don't know, this big distraction. You do important work here."

"Not you—we. We do important work, and we're good at it, because everybody here is important and gets respect. Including you. And don't think I don't respect you for dragging your sorry ass in here, but can you really work like—like this?"

Cindy sat up straighter. The sparklers were gone from her vision, and she felt some energy. Nothing like some emotional support, along with sugar, grease, and caffeine.

"Look, I've got to get to work."

"Oh no." The voice was back, along with a restraining hand. "When are you going to give yourself a break? Arthur loves your work, and his folks like you. You're smart and funny, and you care."

Cindy felt herself blushing.

"Doesn't mean you can scare me. Your father said—"

"Huh?"

"Yeah, I talked to him. I told him, just keep you home, and he acted like he couldn't handle you. Big man, huh!"

She was chuckling, shaking her head.

"He told me all about it—your mother, her plans for you. She was quite a lady, wasn't she?"

Now Cindy's head was spinning again, and she couldn't have walked out if she wanted to—and she did, badly.

"He told me what happened to you, working for the state. I remember, that case was in the news; a real shame. He told me what a thankless job it was, how it wore you down. And your momma not there anymore to buck you up."

"That's the thing, I—"

"You think that was your fault too, part of that little cloud you told Craig about?"

Was everybody talking about her? Didn't they have anything better to do?

"I've got no time for that nonsense. You did what you were supposed to do: did your best, then got back up and kept on trying. And here you are, after getting knocked down again—twice. Give yourself some credit, maybe even some love, and you'll be fine, you hear?"

And Cindy started to cry, right there. Gloria was beside her then, pulling her gently to her sideways, patting her head.

"That's better. That's more like it, child. There you go. That's what you need."

Then it dawned on Cindy, and she leaned away. "You talked to Father? When?" *And why?* she wanted to ask.

• • •

Cindy pushed off the elevator wall and stumbled into Morris, who guided her carefully toward Arthur's office. She managed to push him away when they reached his desk and continue on alone. As she made her way through the bullpen, supporting herself hand over hand on desks, the greeting was much warmer than usual, and a rush of gratitude overwhelmed her aches.

Something else struck her as she walked around the last desk before reaching the office. Of course—where was the beast guarding the gate? Elmer was absent. There was something else pecking at the back of her mind, but she didn't have time to pursue the thought. Arthur wasn't there, and two figures, she now realized, had been following behind her. Neerav took Arthur's chair, while Freddy leaned like a broomstick against the wall next to him.

"We wanted you to know," said Neerav, "all is taken care of."

"Handled, completely," added Freddy, his voice cracking on the second word while his hands made the sweep of the safe sign.

"Fully resolved, in fact," said Neerav.

They seemed to think repetition would make things clearer. Neerav figured it out first.

"We spoke to Charlotte. That is, Freddy told his mom about your little misunderstanding regarding Arthur, and she had a word with her old friend Charlotte, who in turn contacted us. Pffft—done. Resolved. Fully and completely."

"Okay, okay, I think I get it now," said Cindy.

Back to work, speed the old brain back up.

"But I still don't . . . How did Charlotte get that idea?"

"Ah, yes," Freddy said. "From our good friend Elmer, apparently." At this, he held his nose.

Wait. There it was again—that tickle. Something . . .

"Arthur is furious," added Neerav. "So Elmer is making himself scarce."

"Good idea," said Freddy. "Asshole!"

A minor stir drew their attention to Arthur's approach.

"Thanks, guys. I owe you," said Cindy.

"Aw shucks, little lady," drawled Neerav. When Arthur arrived, both coders gave him a thumbs-up and left. Cindy's boss gave her his usual neutral nod. "You're back," he said. "That's, uh, good." And that was it. Back to work.

It was difficult at first. Her mind seemed to slide around among the various pieces of the website, never lighting on any one thing for long enough to engage, and there were times it slid into dreams, random hospital images flashing by.

"Man is in the forest. Man is in the forest."

It was soft, but the second time she heard it clearly—Neerav. When she raised her eyes, no one was looking up as Vernon wound his way through with quick, efficient steps. Behind her, Arthur groaned.

"Arthur, a word." The little man's voice was imperious as he stood, hands on gray-suited hips, his prominent chin thrust forward.

"What is it now, Vernon?"

The intruder threw a glare toward Cindy, but Arthur motioned her to stay put, so Vernon turned back to her boss.

"I've certainly made it clear: this deadline is critical. It means everything to this company, to everything we're trying—"

"Yes, I understand, Vernon. You've been clear."

"So for me to hear—"

"We're working on it. I've told you that. I think we're almost there."

"You think. But you're not sure."

"We've been through this. Until it's done, we can't know if it works, and so . . . Wait. You hear? What are you talking about? Who told you . . . what?"

Now Arthur was angry. Cindy had never seen much emotion from him, but there was no mistaking his eyes as he pointed through the open door.

"That stinking shit pile Elmer told you. What, exactly?"

Vernon must have felt it. He pulled back and softened his tone to a whine.

"Never mind who . . ."

It clicked. There was more back and forth between the two, but Cindy didn't hear it. The smell. Elmer was absent, and so was his body odor. He smelled like a homeless guy. But her assailant had not, either time. His cloths had been frayed and stained, but he gripped her both times, breathed in her face, rubbed his cheek against hers—she shivered at the memory. But there was no strong smell. A homeless man would have left his stink on her. And Ralph had said there was no camp.

So, it wasn't some paranoid guy who thought she was invading his space. It could still be some crazy guy with a thing about her, but that didn't feel right anymore. Why dress up as homeless? It had to be something she wasn't seeing. Ralph's words came back to her—someone hiding something. Someone here, at Back Door.

Fucking Ralph!

"He's upset because I had to take him off it." She heard Arthur's voice as she surfaced. "Something's going on with him. His work was sloppy. It's never sloppy. It's not like him."

"We all hit a wall sometimes," said Vernon. "Perhaps this was his."

He had dropped his aggressive posture and turned thoughtful.

"Maybe," said Arthur, "but it's okay. I've got Milton and Irene working on his component. He messed up, and he doesn't want to admit it, that's all."

"So we're—"

"On schedule. Nearly, anyway. Really, Vernon. Now, please, you're wasting my time, distracting the team. Do you mind?"

He sat and turned to his monitors, which threw the smaller man back into a rage.

Vernon hissed at his back. "I will deal appropriately with anything or anyone who stands in the way of our mission. You forget that at your peril—all of you."

"Bye, Vernon. Stop by again soon," sang one of the coders, to general laughter. When the operations manager was gone, they burst into applause, and Arthur got up and gave them an awkward bow.

Cindy couldn't join in the fun. Close as she was, she'd seen the depth of Vernon's rage. When she tried to return to work, her hands shook on the keyboard, leaving her no choice but to sit and think through all the implications for her investigation. Should she trust the cold knot in her gut? If it took great passion to plunge a knife deep into a man's chest, Vernon had plenty. He might be small, but he was wound tight, and in that moment, he had looked like a killer.

But why Carlson? She didn't know, but it was a place to start.

Then another thought struck her. Craig—her friend—had been hired by Vernon, the friend of his CO. Could Craig be involved? She had always felt safe around him. Now it was something she had to explore.

Cindy's thoughts were interrupted by the ring of the telephone. Arthur grunted into it, then held it out to her. She realized that she should have been answering it all along. As little as she was accomplishing, it didn't make sense for him to be interrupted by her calls.

Susan, as usual, dispensed with formalities. "Charlotte wants to see you. Now."

• • •

The desk outside Charlotte's office was empty, but the door was open, and Cindy understood enough of the protocol by now to know she was expected to go on in. This time Susan was seated back against the wall, as she had been for Cindy's first time in the office, and Charlotte rose to greet her.

"Thank you for coming so quickly." Charlotte took her hand in both of hers, and Cindy had to steel herself so as not to flinch. If Charlotte detected how shaky she was, she didn't show it, but led her to the sofa and sat close, at ninety degrees, on one of the soft chairs.

"I have to apologize," Charlotte continued.

Cindy snuck a peek at Susan, but her face was stony.

"I was hasty in my conclusions, regarding your treatment of my son. I'll have to think about that."

Her manner reminded Cindy of her father, another strong personality unaccustomed to apology. "I'll have to pray on it," he would have said. Imagining the phrase coming from Charlotte forced Cindy to suppress a giggle. She managed a cough instead.

Charlotte didn't appear to notice.

"I was informed"—with the briefest glance at Susan—"that your behavior toward my son was unkind. Since we spoke, several of Arthur's team have come to me to vouch for you."

Neerav and Freddy.

"I should have checked before confronting you. That was inexcusable. I hope you can forgive me."

Tears blurred Cindy's vision, and she had to work hard to keep from crying. Of course, she accepted the apology, and barely managed to stumble through the rest of the blessedly brief conversation.

"I imagine it must be hard to go back to where we were before . . ." She waved her hand. *Before you ripped into me?* Apparently, Charlotte couldn't go that far.

"I should have listened to Susan here . . ."

Charlotte seemed unable to finish a thought, and Cindy felt uncomfortable for her, but it was hard to be sympathetic now that the flood of relief had passed. She stumbled out as soon as she could.

Susan's gaze was kind, her voice uncharacteristically soft.

"You see how quickly she can flip. She likes you again. Don't make the mistake of assuming it will last. It's just the way she is."

Susan's warning startled her, but Cindy was grateful to be brought back to earth.

"Thanks. I think I needed that. But who's the rat who accused me in the first place?"

"It was probably Elmer. He's Vernon's puppy. Arthur suspects him of running to Vernon with little tidbits. I guess he knows where the real power is around here. The thing is, once he got close to Vernon, there would be no escape. The man's ruthless."

Cindy thought about that.

"I saw how angry he can get, earlier today. He had quite the confrontation with Arthur. This deadline must be big."

"Look," said Susan, lowering her eyes along with her voice, "I shouldn't be telling you this, but Vernon came to us from the government—the NSA.

"Yes, you told me before."

"Did I? Well, the thing is, they've been a major customer of ours, thanks to him, but it's not always clear where his loyalties lie. I mean, can you ever truly leave an outfit like that?"

"That makes sense," said Cindy, thinking of the screens in his office monitoring activities all over the building.

"The other thing you need to keep in mind—he oversees all the nontechnical operations. He brought in the security people. He's got quite the network, eyes and ears everywhere."

"You mean, like Craig?"

The woman nodded. "Military men, both of them. If it wasn't for Charlotte, we'd all be calling him Colonel Crofter."

"How did Vernon feel about Carlson?"

It slipped out before Cindy could stop.

Susan paused. "A combination of things, I suppose, all negative. Carlson was gay, histrionic, artistic—I'm sure Vernon saw him as self-indulgent and undisciplined as well. All things he would despise. And weak, the unforgivable sin among manly men.

"If you could have seen his face when Arthur turned his back—I have the feeling he takes things very personally."

"You're right there. It's important to be careful around him. Speaking of which, I know Craig chased off your attacker in the subway, but I wouldn't count on him to watch your back. He's Vernon's man, all the way."

If Cindy couldn't trust Craig to protect her, who could she trust? Would Susan be enough? Then a horrifying thought popped into her mind. What if the whole scene at Alewife station, with the homeless guy and Craig's rescue, was a show? The guy just happened to know when to expect her, and Craig just happened along at the critical time. His injuries seemed real—but not severe enough for the hospital to keep him after that first night. If it was all a show, either it had gone a bit awry or they were taking pains—literally—to make it look real. Which would mean they were deadly serious.

Cindy hated that she had to mistrust both Craig and Nicole, but there was no choice.

3 6

Paul

Billie's meetings used to start around 6:30, but now that Grace is driving Cindy home, it's half past seven. We eat the takeout first. Billie grumbles that Ralph's cooking has fallen off lately, and they're doing takeout or precooked from the market. That's what it is tonight, chicken and ribs with coleslaw, potato salad and pickles, like a cookout in the middle of November. Paper plates; wine out of paper cups.

I'm sitting in the raggedy living room with Billie, Sophie, and Emma. Ralph comes in, then goes straight into the kitchen to forage for what's left, which is plenty, and comes back out with his hand under a plate he's trying to balance. It slews to the side, and he's just able to rescue it with his other hand. "Paper plates?"

Billie glares back. "Times are hard around here, in case you haven't noticed."

Ralph drops his head, starts eating. The mood is gloomy, with conversations that start and then just hang there.

"This sucks."

That's Emma, who's usually upbeat. She and Sophie have been telling us how the search for violent incidents in participants' clinical histories is grinding on.

"Damn right it does," Billie growls. "ConDo cocksuckers! You people are too young to remember the McCarthy hearings. Swap crazed killers for commies and it's the same old shit."

"But this time," says Ralph, through a mouthful, "it's us, the ones who are supposed to help people recover—we're the hunters."

Sophie is next. "All these members who were pulled off their jobs, sitting around the clubhouse. We can't give them any attention, we're so buried in record reviews. And we're not allowed to help them get back to work. After a few days, most of them stopped coming."

"They should stay away." Billie has lots of moods, and it isn't hard to guess how she's feeling, but I've never seen her hopeless. "It's not their place anymore. Not ours either."

"But sitting home worries me," says Sophie. "They need us."

"They need each other," adds Emma. "It's just as bad in the group homes. And I'm hoping I didn't make it worse."

Grace, who's just come in, says, "Oh, I'm sure you couldn't have, dear." Then, in answer to questioning looks, "Cindy's not coming."

This draws a snort from Billie, and Grace springs to her passenger's defense.

"She's exhausted. It's too soon for her to be back at work as it is, poor thing." With an angry wave at Billie, she stalks off into the kitchen.

Emma starts again. "I insisted that when they find something they think is bad—"

"Dr. Marsha's fucking red flags!" Billie.

". . . that they ask the person what happened. You can't trust those records to be accurate."

"Ha," Billie growls, "like Dr. Dachau would believe them anyhow."

Emma continues, "What happens now is when the staff do have any contact with residents, it's to ask them about bad things in their records, from years ago. It's all staff talks about with them, and it's humiliating. Emily Mattson was telling me that the week after she got out of the hospital, like, twelve years ago, she lit a cigarette and threw the match into a trash can, and it caught fire. Just a little smoke, really, but now they're saying she's got a history of arson."

"Ah," says Sophie, "so that's why she stopped coming."

Then she describes a scene at the Center from two days ago. I know the folks she's talking about. I can picture it.

"I had to suspend two members for fighting. In the kitchen. Florence just got back from her job at Muriel's, that nice cafe on Tremont. She's trying to show Jeffrey how to load the dishwasher rack, the way they taught her there, saying you can fit more on that way. He tells her to leave him alone—well, he's not very nice about it. And next thing they're wrestling, banging into things, people are screaming—"

"When was the last time you had a fight?" That's Ralph.

"I can't remember."

"I had Mary coming over to me," says Phyllis. "She's back from working at the bank. 'You got the right idea, lady,' she says. I've got no idea what she's talking about; she had to explain. 'We've got a good deal here. We're accepted. Out there, they pretend to think you're okay, you know, but they don't believe it. Now it's like, *we knew you shouldn't be here. You're not really one of us.*' She loved that job, too. Thought she was making friends."

"You see," says Sophie, "this is what I was afraid of."

"Well, I wanted to know what makes her so sure they don't accept her, you know, as one of them. And she goes like this"—Phyllis holds her palms up next to her shoulders—"and says, 'I'm here, aren't I?' I tell her it's not fair, she shouldn't have been caught up in this. You know what she says then? 'It's a good thing I didn't risk my disability check. Here I was, worried I could slip up and lose it all. I was so naive. All it took was some guy flipping out—that's all they needed. It wasn't up to me at all.'"

Sophie is going from looking angry to sad. "I try to tell them this is temporary, you'll be back on the job, it just takes time."

She shakes her head, pressing her lips together.

"But what?" Emma is Sophie's good friend. She can see there's something else.

"Florence won't be going back, at least not to the bank. It seems their human resource director called. She's been emailing Lu, but ConDo shut down her account—apparently IT doesn't realize how important our relationships are with employers, how hard we worked to establish them. Thank God the lady called to find out what was going on. I did my best to explain, but then she told me they would want their medical consultant to review Florence's medical records before she could return. 'We need our own expert to assess her condition' is the way they put it. They don't trust us. Caroline and Marsha are supporting us on that, at least. It would be illegal to share them anyway, even with Florence's consent—but of course, they want us to lose the placement."

"Bastards," said Billie. "You can't blame the bank, though, when ConDo puts out word that our people might be dangerous."

"It's just perpetuating the old myth," adds Emma. "What a disaster!"

Things go back and forth like that for a while, when Phyllis says, "Well, at least Cindy's working on it. If she can find a way to clear Johnnie, we might be able to turn things around."

Billie seems to perk up at that.

"I talked to Big Sal about it. And Gracie's driving her to and from. I don't see how they'll get at her now—whoever they are."

"I'm not so sure," says Ralph. "We're confident Johnnie didn't do it. That means it's got to be somebody else who works there. We don't have any idea who it could be, or why, so we can't rule anyone out. And she's there, every day, for more than ten hours. If she gets close to the truth, they'll know. And you want her to start rattling cages."

"What else can we do?" Billie is getting pissed now.

"I talked to this guy Craig. He's the guard at the front desk, knows everyone there. He and his girlfriend, Nicole, are friendly with Cindy, and he's concerned about her too."

Emma asks, "That the one fought the guy off in the subway?"

Ralph nods. "He said if I see anything on the outside, let him know. He'll watch from inside. Last night he walked me around the grounds there. It's like a park between Back Door and Pfizer; there's ponds with boardwalks across them, lots of dense brush. It's pretty, but there's lots of places to hide. I'm going to hang out around there as much as I can."

Sophie looks puzzled. "When do you have the time for that?"

Ralph shrugs.

Then Billie cuts in. "He doesn't. We're going to have to help out. Here's what I'm thinking . . ."

And the talk goes on for another hour after that, until everyone's too tired to keep going and Grace offers to drive Phyllis and me home.

3 7

Cindy

Late Friday afternoon, the now familiar hush led Cindy to look up as Susan wove through the desks in the bullpen. Why did her friend's presence inspire such a chill? The guys hated Vernon and weren't shy about it. The razzing they threw his way seemed more competitive and teasing, but then they probably didn't know about the cameras and the monitors in his office. Even so, it made their reaction to Susan more puzzling: she seemed to shut them down.

"Cindy, we've got to talk."

Susan waited silently. Apparently their talk wasn't going to happen here in the office. Cindy would have objected, but a week back at work had left her mostly healed. Though her body ached, her mind was clear, and the frequent memory flashes of the attack on the subway platform were less immediate. And something was different: steady, calm Susan was twitchy, crackling with energy. It seemed like an effort to contain herself until they stepped into the empty elevator.

"Marshall, the coder we talked about?"

Carlson's jilted lover. Cindy nodded.

Susan's eyes were bright, and her voice rose.

"He sent me an email, asking to meet. He read about our murder, said he might have something I should hear."

Our murder.

"Yeah, okay."

"It's all very mysterious, but he, uh, didn't leave on such good terms with some people here. I think he's afraid of Vernon. He agreed to meet somewhere away from the building, and I thought you would want to hear what he has to say. I think it could be the breakthrough we've been looking for."

Breakthrough? We? Had Susan seen through her? She wouldn't be the first, and Cindy could certainly use the help. And it seemed logical to fear Vernon.

"So, where?"

"There's this pond over on the other side of the brook." Seeing Cindy stop walking, Susan went on quickly. "I'll be there with you. I brought something, just in case." She patted her handbag, which had a lumpy look to it.

As usual, Susan ignored Craig as they walked past his desk on the way out, and Cindy met his concerned look with a shrug. Craig—Vernon's man. Then they were moving briskly down the dirt path. The darkness fell early and hard, the first Friday off daylight saving. The sky glowed orange gray on one side, and the last of the shadows were softening. Maybe this wasn't such a hot idea. Branches from bushes and stunted trees reached across the path, closer than those on the one that led to the station. Something else was different: there were no lights at all on this path.

Susan read her thoughts. "Don't worry," she said. "We can use the light on my phone to get back. I really think you need to talk to this guy."

The lights had done two things: they illuminated the path itself, which was useful for footing, and they reflected off the grasses and trees to either side, creating a tunnel. Anyone hiding behind would have been obscured. Without the lights, the weak illumination reflecting off the trees and undergrowth on one side had a similar effect, but the other side had more depth, allowing her to scan the woods. But there was another difference. Now the trees were bare, and didn't conceal much, but the grasses on this side were tall enough to shield someone, and close enough for that someone to emerge from the gloom and pounce.

She was being dramatic.

They passed over the little bridge and onto a familiar raised wooden walkway that traversed a swampy pond, well out of sight of the office complex. Dark clouds pressed down over them, and there was no light to reflect off the water, creating the sense they were high in the air, suspended over nothing. At least there were sturdy railings on either side.

Cindy was out of breath, trying to keep up with the other woman, and her hip and side ached. She was desperate to stop, but that would sound weak and foolish, and she couldn't bring herself to whine in front of Susan. Besides, every time she slowed her pace, Susan would start rattling on.

"I think Marshall might hold the key to the whole thing. It took Carlson a while to get over their breakup, when Marshall left so abruptly."

That didn't square with Kaz's version. Or Steven's. And how would Susan know that? Were they friends?

"I would have thought him capable of murder, but he's been gone for months."

And they were meeting him out here in the dark? That had better be a gun in Susan's purse.

"Still, I think he might have been close to Vernon. He kept saying how important it was not to run into him, or any of his people."

Like Craig? The pieces were beginning to fit together. Excitement bubbled up to join the fear in Cindy's throat. They were almost running down the trail now, and it was growing darker fast. A cramp bit into her side, forcing her to slow down, but Susan said, "We're almost there."

Kaz had been clear: Marshall was the one devastated when Carlson broke it off. The puzzle pieces were shifting again, sliding toward a different picture.

"I didn't realize," she said, as casually as she could manage, "you were that close to Carlson."

"Oh. I heard it from Charlotte. He was practically crying on her shoulder for a while. It was embarrassing to watch."

Something about the rhythm of this speech was different, off somehow.

"That's funny. Kaz had a different take; said Carlson broke it off— that for him, it was just a fling with a younger man."

"Kaz said that? Well, you have to understand, he's been lusting after Carlson's job for years. You can't trust what he says."

But Cindy was inclined to do just that. Susan's list of people to distrust was growing longer and longer, while on the other hand, she was supposed to trust Susan. What if Cindy flipped it? It would make everything much simpler.

At least Cindy had walked this way before, with Nicole. She could probably find her own way back, even in the dark. They turned right, following an offshoot through scrubby trees and onto the same oblong deck projecting out into the little pond. The benches on three sides were familiar, even in the dark—Nicole's secret place. The familiarity gave Cindy some comfort as she scanned the platform. It was unoccupied. Where was this guy? Susan led the way to the railing. Something about the place made a big puzzle piece thunk into place.

"Marshall isn't coming to meet us, is he, Susan? That's not what all this is about."

Cindy didn't know what compelled her to say it out loud. It might have been the anger that was jazzing her, from all the lies.

The woman let out a soft grunt and turned as Cindy stepped back. The slight shadow the gun made as Susan raised it to shoulder height dragged Cindy's gaze around against her will.

Back in Mt. Auburn hospital, Cindy had whined to Craig that she had done everything wrong in the subway, walking to the end of the platform with no escape, where the train would be moving at its fastest.

"Don't be too hard on yourself," he had said. "In the Rangers, they taught us when you're trapped and it looks like the end, you do whatever it takes to get to the next moment. Don't think too far ahead, just concentrate on living for that next step; draw it out if you can. It's your only option, and something good could happen in that next moment, if you can make it that far."

So, keep her talking.

"Who do you work for?"

For some reason, Cindy couldn't meet her eyes, looking just past her left shoulder instead, past the big black gun.

A snort. "Charlotte, of course." Then, with a smile: "Myself."

"Not limousine man?"

"Ash?"

"I saw you climb out of the back. You didn't look like you were having a meeting—at least, not of the minds. There was a lot of straightening going on. He seemed a bit old for that kind of action. Were you turned on by his power, or is it in your contract? And Nicole's the slut?"

"You just can't let it go, can you? What I can't figure is why. For that loser in the kitchen?"

Instinct told Cindy to go sideways, like a boxer.

"Did you really think I was getting anywhere? I didn't have a clue, but you couldn't shut up. You blew it with this little show. I mean, now what—you shoot me? How will you explain that?"

"Don't worry about that. There's always a way. You still think I'm nothing more than Charlotte's toady. There's a piece of work—thinks her shit's ice cream. Ash has what I want, and once I have the reins, I'll clean house, show what I can do. I'll be in for a payday that will set me up for life. I'm too close to let some do-gooder Nancy Drew get in my way."

She made little upward jerking sweeps with the gun.

"Climb on up."

Cindy backed away along the bench, but the other woman circled quickly to cut her off.

"Now!" Then, in a softer sing-song: "You've been so down lately, everyone's noticed. All those upsetting things that kept happening, it got to be too much, didn't it, sweetie?"

Get to the next moment. Cindy put her knees onto the bench.

"Stand up. You ready, Jason?"

"Anytime," came a man's voice from behind and below Cindy.

When Cindy turned reflexively toward the voice, she felt a strong hand under her butt, pushing her up. The railing struck her mid-thigh, but just as she grabbed for it, the gun slammed down on her fingers. Her arms groped air as she toppled over the railing, spinning over and down. Black water filled her vision, then slapped hard in her face and poured in.

3 8

Paul

I'm riding shotgun with Grace, which is tough because even though their old tank is as big as cars ever got, it has a bench front seat, and Grace has it up as far as it'll go so she can toe the pedals. I'm navigating with my knees scrunched up sideways. She's leaning so far forward her chest is on the wheel, and she can just about see over it, her fingers curled either side of her nose.

Billie's bad hip has left her to coordinate everything from the apartment and call in reinforcements if we need them. Ralph called to tell her something was going on—he heard it from Craig, the security guard—and Billie called me out of work early. Ralph's been hanging around in the bushes, keeping an eye on things: Mister Outside.

"Ralph says to meet him on the driveway," says Grace, "behind Pfizer, alongside the park."

Phyllis printed out a picture and map from Google Earth.

"Any idea why?" I ask.

"It backs up on this park, and Back Door is on the other side of that."

I have to turn the picture over, but then I can see what she means.

"He said he might need our help. I brought you a flashlight, just in case."

I look back to see a black metal thing a couple of feet long, the kind the cops beat you with. I can tell Grace is excited, because we're going over thirty on Fresh Pond Parkway, with only a few cars stacked up behind us. It's a tight, winding two lanes each way with no median, and we're taking up both of ours, but she's pushing that old bucket to the limit.

The building, when we get to it, is all lit up, but going around back, it turns dark in a hurry. We glide to a stop, and she kills the lights, then the engine. I can barely make out her little fingers drumming on the wheel as we listen to the engine tick.

"Woo!" Grace cuts off her little whoop as fast as she can, clamping her hand over her mouth as Ralph's face fills her side window.

"Jesus, Mary, and Joseph, you scared me," she giggles after she powers the window down.

"Sorry, Gracie." Then, seeing me, "Hey, Paul, thanks for coming. Listen"—all excited—"Craig just called. Cindy went outside with this woman Susan."

"Out by themselves," cries Grace, "in the dark? Lord have mercy!"

"Tell me about it! I've got to go find them. Just wait here, okay?"

"You got it, Ralph."

Grace manages to sound both excited and confident, like this is the best game ever. I'm neither. Cindy's out there, in the dark. Everything about this feels wrong.

3 9

Cindy

Cold, dark, choking—Cindy's mind couldn't catch up. What brought her around was breathing—she couldn't. Panic, wild, immense, her flailing arms hit underwater weeds, something hard—a post—then softer—a leg? Steely fingers held her hair in a painful grip, pushing her down. *No, no, no, no, no!* Then they dragged her up, and held her head back so she was looking at Susan's hate-contorted features leaning down toward her.

"You want to know what happened? A sad little suicide. The poor depressed girl couldn't get over all her failures. That pathetic jerk Marshall was supposed to get Carlson to fall in love, but all he got was laid. Of course, I had a backup plan, offered Carlson a share of the company. He could be back in charge of his own kitchen, no more Kaz, no more snooty Charlotte. You'd think the pathetic fairy would be thrilled, but no, he was loyal. Charlotte was getting ready to dump him, but he couldn't see it. He was going to rat me out. We're alone in the kitchen and he's telling me, like I'd let it happen." She shrugged. "I didn't."

Then her voice hardened. "Okay, finish."

In one motion, the hand turned Cindy's head to the right and slammed her face into the big boulder she'd seen during her visit with Nicole, then yanked her back to adjust the angle so that her forehead hit the rock the second time. Cindy barely felt that one and was out when he plunged her head back underwater and held it there.

4 0

Paul

The splash sounds faint, far away, but the yelling that follows is louder.

I look at Grace. "Paul, you better go."

I can't tell you what it is about Grace, but when she says that, any idea of not going leaves my mind. I grab the flashlight—damn, it's heavy—and I'm out of there, trying to get my stiff legs to work.

There was some light when we drove up, but I didn't notice a path then, and it's full dark now. I feel along the barrel of the flashlight for the switch to get the thing lit. When I do, it's got a strong beam, and I can see right away where the dirt path connects up with the wooden walkway. It crosses over the water, easier to follow than a trail, but noisier. As I pound along, I hear grunts and splashes, so when I get to the end, I know to turn left onto a dirt path. Following the sound, I'm back on boards again. There's a railing on each side, so no chance of falling in, but that splash flashes back on me, and I'm gripping the light tighter. I've been at the other end of the thing—it's a damn good weapon, and it feels good in my hand.

I'm making enough noise that I almost miss the footsteps clicking the other way—not as loud as mine, but there, unmistakable. The yelling, though, that's off to my left, and when I turn down that way, I pop out onto this open pier thing with benches: a dead end.

Splashing and grunting is coming from straight ahead, but I can't see anything. I get to the rail and point the light down there and can't figure out what it is I'm seeing. There's arms and heads, fast and violent, water splashing around. I don't know when I decide to yell, but I do: "Hey, HEY!!"

A big part of the pile separates and surges around to my right, then along the side. The dark, wide shape comes up the side bank with heavy, sloshing steps. He's moving slowly, and I'm hoping at first he's my size, maybe even smaller, but as his big head breaks out above the railing, it keeps on rising—turns out the guy's huge. Shit!

The good thing is, he doesn't see how close I am, and just as he steps onto the platform, his right hand levering him up, I lean back with my flashlight, swing as hard as I can, and get him a good one upside the head. I was hoping that would put him down, and it does make him stumble, but he wheels around so fast I don't have time to think of putting my hands up to block the backhand chop under my chin. I'm down hard on my rear end, and it's all I can do to hang on to the light when the back of my head hits the boards with a loud, sickening wham. Feet pound away, barely audible over the buzzing in my head.

Then I hear a woman's voice, weak but familiar. "Ralph? Ralph!" Cindy?

I follow the way the guy came out, down the slippery bank and into the water. It comes up to my chest, and I see my sister holding on to what looks like a big sack of something, which turns out, when I get the light on it, to be Ralph.

After pitching my flashlight up on the deck, I manage to drag him up the bank with my sister hanging on for the ride, then alongside the platform and up onto it. I'm down on my knees, grunting, but piece by piece I get him on one of the benches. My sister's in a little better shape, and I can get her half standing, so it's easier to help her onto the other one. Only now do I grab the flashlight and shine it on Cindy. Blood's coming down the side of her face, and she's coughing hard.

"You okay?"

She nods, coughs, points over at Ralph. I turn the light that way; he isn't moving at all. Even with my ear down on his face, I can't hear any breathing, and I'm trying to decide what to do next—I took CPR once, about a year ago. Airway, breaths . . .

I'm just getting him arranged, turning his face up and grabbing underneath his chin to cock his head back, check the airway, when his arm flops down and he yelps, then starts his own coughing. The light shows his arm crooked at the wrong angle off his elbow, and he's holding his side with the other one and whimpering when he coughs. His eyes are still closed, and he's sort of rolling back and forth.

Now that he's breathing, I go back to check Cindy. I figure I'm going to have to go back and forth between them while they cough and spit up brown water, but when I go back to Ralph, he's stopped moving again, and I can barely hear his moaning alternating with gurgling breaths.

Cindy's starting to groan more than cough when I hear footsteps pounding and this big guy—that's right, we're in the land of the giants—comes charging out onto the platform. I grab the flashlight and point it, but this guy's got a gun, yells, "Put it down. Now! Hands on your head. Kneel down. Do it now!"

I catch just a flash: white face, uniform, sounds like the law. I'm thinking there's worse things could happen right about now, so I do as he says. "I'm Paul, Cindy's brother. That's her over there. I just pulled them out of the water."

He's quick, I'll give him that. Then I realize—Craig, Cindy's friend, the security guard. I didn't recognize him at first either. He shines his own light over at Cindy—it's silly, but I notice mine's bigger and brighter than his—and seems to figure it out. "Paul. Right. Can you stay here? I'm going to clear the area, then go get help."

I'm feeling safe enough now to take my hands down so I can point. I want him to go after the guy, but I'm not sure which way he went.

Then he's gone. That guy, the one hit me, he could have gone the way I'd come, to where Gracie's parked. And suddenly I wonder about those footsteps I heard before I got here.

I'm starting to notice how soaked and slimy I am, and tired, when there's a car horn, a yelp, a guy yelling. I'm worried about Grace, but how can I leave Cindy and Ralph here, bleeding and moaning? Ralph's gone quiet, and that worries me, but Cindy's gasping, saying something.

41

Cindy

There was a lot to take in. Cindy was wet. She remembered going in headfirst, but somehow she was back on the deck. And there was her brother; and Ralph. *Fucking Ralph!* It was all crazy, but nothing compared to the fact that Susan had pulled a gun on her and pitched her over the railing.

"Gun. She's got a gun."

Did he even hear her croak?

Paul was next to her now, an arm around her, patting her shoulder and dabbing at her head—ouch! She felt like crap: throat burning, lungs aching, or was that her ribs? A headache came in overwhelming waves, knocking grunting moans out of her sore throat. Ralph, though, barely moved, his arm hanging down at an impossible angle. And he'd stopped moaning. Paul went over to him, calling his name, trying to bring him around.

Susan threw her over the railing, into the pond. And the guy who grabbed her, smashed her head, and held her under? From the other times, the same one. She didn't know how she knew—hadn't, after all, gotten a look at him—but those hands had held her before, she was sure.

Would it have been different if she had kept her mouth shut the moment she realized Susan was lying? No. Susan had an accomplice waiting in the pond. That, at least, felt better.

Morris, the guard from Arthur's area, came next, and he was leading four others, two for each rolling ambulance cot. There were questions about where it hurt, hands probing, and she heard the other two conferring as they poked at Ralph. He seemed disoriented and was trying to fight them off until Paul managed to calm him. They had an oxygen mask over his face and were putting a splint on his arm while they tried to get Cindy to mount the cot. When she refused, they actually laughed. That made it more embarrassing to resist than comply, and as they helped her onto it and strapped her down, she heard the other cart wheel Ralph away.

Before they could do the same with her, she grabbed Morris's sleeve. It wasn't much, just a tug before her fingers failed her, but enough to get his attention. "She threw me in," she croaked. "Susan. She has a gun." His eyes went wide and he nodded. *He heard me,* she thought, able to relax at last as they began bumping her way along the path, back the way she had come with Susan such a long time ago.

4 2

Paul

This guy in a tan uniform, a brother, middle aged and chunky like me—okay, bigger and stronger—came with the EMTs, and he's taken charge. Cindy's not great, but she's with it enough to go along. She seems to know the guy and calms down when she sees him. Ralph, though, is fighting them off, wild, frantic. It takes holding on to him and shouting, but once he recognizes me, he quiets down and lets them check him out. I have to stay with him until they get him onto the cot, then make sure Cindy goes too. She gives in after a little resistance, but has something to say to the guard first, too soft for me to hear. There's an EMT on either end of the cot, and the big guard follows them, thumbing a radio as he disappears down the path. I remember the car horn and the shouting and figure I should go check on Grace.

As soon as I get past the trees, I see all the blue lights flashing over the water and I know there's going to be lots of company. When I get close, I make sure to slow my pace—no brother with any sense goes running up out of the night onto a bunch of cops. Of course, the first one who sees me has his hand on my chest.

"Sir"—well, that's something—"you have to stay back."

"I'm with her, over there," I say, pointing toward Grace, as calm as I can manage.

She sees me and bustles over.

"That's my friend Paul, Officer. I need to see him."

She gets right up under him, shakes a finger under his nose. The guy steps back—probably went to Catholic school.

"Paul, are you alright? What's going on?"

I tell her about Cindy, Ralph, how they're being taken care of but the guy got away.

She gives me this twinkly little smile.

"Oh, I don't know about that."

She points over to one of the cars. There's cops standing all around it, and I think I recognize Craig with them. I can just make out someone hunched over in the back seat.

"I got him," she says. "He's in there."

I can see she's pleased with herself, but she doesn't offer any details.

Once the cops realize where I've just been, the guy's on his radio, and a few of them go marching back down to the pond with me. The guy in the tan uniform introduces himself as Morris, and they listen to him, then me. More cops come and I give them a statement right there, and they write it all down, names and everything. They're polite, but they make me go over it again and again. It's a long time before they let me go, and Grace is still in the lot, but without her car.

"I thought they'd never get done with you," she says. "They finished with me a while ago, but they wouldn't budge on the car. I figured they'd need it, but I hated to see them put my baby up on that truck and take her away. Tommy here"—she gestures toward a young officer standing to the side—"promised they'd take good care of her. He's going to take us home."

He just nods over and over, like he's her puppy, says, "Yes, Sister, sure thing, Sister." I have to stifle my laughter when she gives me her saintly innocence look as we sit together in back, my first time in quite a few years, this time without cuffs. There's so many things I want to ask her, but it's like this wave hits me; I'm so tired I have to drop my head back on the seat.

Somehow that wave missed Grace—maybe she ducked under it. She leans toward the front, keeps on at the guy during the whole ride.

"It took you people long enough to get here. You should have listened to me in the first place—then Paul wouldn't have had to get knocked into the water. At least you didn't let the guy get away. Of course, I made it easier, didn't I?"

"Yes, Sister Grace, you sure did, ma'am" is all he has to say.

I don't get what that's about until later.

4 3

Cindy

The lights bored into her brain. Hospitals were bright, noisy places full of frantic motion, and Cindy would have been exhausted by now even had she been well. The same policewoman as before had come to interview her in the emergency ward, with the same skeptical, long-suffering attitude. Cindy was a serial victim—obviously a low-life; probably a pervert. The good news was this time, she had a witness—Ralph. The bad news, other than the fact that it was Ralph, was that he was, according to the cop, in a medically induced coma, and might very well come out of it with no memory of the event.

Still, with Paul happening onto the scene later, they seemed inclined to take her more seriously this time. She would have to come to their station within the next few days to sign a formal statement. And don't leave town—no French Riviera for her.

After lying on her back for a long time with her good arm over her eyes, the waves of headache diminished, and she was able to sit up in the middle of the gurney. She was okay as long as she kept shielding her eyes from fluorescent glare. All the medical people seemed to forget her when more spectacular injuries arrived.

She threw me in. It was like a voice-over, narrating the memory loop of cold hands pushing her, lurching and tumbling, a wall of black water rushing at her, the panic as she fought without breath, over and over. Her stomach and throat burned, and the swamp still fouled her mouth, but she could think.

She threw me in. So, not her friend, not at all. Everything Susan had told her, so many things, about Craig, about Nicole—poor little Nickie; about Vernon; about Charlotte—especially about her—and Back Door. What was true? Anything? And Elmer—what about Elmer? That did it. "Hello. HELLO-O. I'M STILL HERE. HELLO." After she repeated that, as loud as she could—making her throat burn and bringing a stabbing pain behind her right eye—a nurse appeared.

"What?"

"I had a phone. I need it. Now."

"Not allowed. It's safe. It will be with your things when you're released."

"No, uh-uh. I need it now. It's urgent—you understand, an emergency." She was yelling, a hoarse cry she didn't recognize. She didn't care.

The nurse squinted at her. She affected a calm manner, but her eyes were angry, and she choked on her sweet voice. "No, dear. You're going to lie down now and rest. The doctor will be with you shortly."

How many times did she have to hear that line? Anyway, that didn't matter, not now. She spoke slowly, enunciating carefully, very loud: "I said I need the phone now. I don't give a fat fuck about your regulations; I need it now. NOW, GODDAMN IT!"

That was as loud as she had, and it hurt a lot, but the woman stormed out and came back with her phone in hand, slamming it down on the gurney and stalking back out without a word. The phone was wet but alive. She called Craig.

"Cindy, are you okay? Where are you?"

"I'm still in the ER at Mount Auburn, but I'll live. They've decided they have more urgent cases, so I'm just hanging out at the moment. Look, the battery's going to die on this thing, and the doctor may walk in. I called because I wanted to be sure you knew that it was Susan—"

"I know; Morris told me. She came in through the lobby. She said you seemed depressed, wanted to be alone. She looked, I don't know, off, so I called Morris to cover the desk and went to have a look. I heard splashing, was able to find you. They wanted it to look like suicide. I called Vernon on my way back to the building, and he called for the ambulance."

"So, what about Susan?" Was everybody dense?

"In custody. The funny thing is, she came to Vernon, all concerned about you, but Morris had already called him from the pier and told him what you said, her throwing you in. Morris called the cops while Vernon managed to stall her until they arrived. And they got the guy."

"The guy in the pond?" *Duh!* Maybe her brain wasn't so fine.

"Yeah. Same guy as attacked you at Alewife. I thought I recognized him. We served together in the Army; not in my unit, but the same Ranger battalion. I knew him to say hello."

"Wow. Listen, there's something else. There's a coder on Arthur's team, Elmer. He was feeding lies to Charlotte about me. He might have been involved in this too."

"Hm. That's something to follow up. I'll tell Vernon. He's all over this now, and he's like a terrier. You don't want him on your trail."

Cindy thought for a minute. "Look, Craig, that woman, she fed me so many lies, she had my head spinning. She managed to turn me against my friends. Like you, and Nicole. I'm sorry."

"Yeah, well, she's a piece of work. We'll get this straightened out, that's a promise. You just take care of yourself. How are you doing, really?"

"I'll live. I'll get out of here as soon as I can. After the scene I made getting my phone back, they can't wait to get rid of me."

Cindy's discharge didn't happen, at least not that day. Eventually a shockingly young doctor came in and asked a series of stupid questions. She almost told him the president was Jimmy Carter, just to see if he recognized the name, but decided she'd pissed off enough medical staff. When he took her phone on his way out, she regretted the missed opportunity. After another three hours of mostly sitting alone, they wheeled her down for another CAT scan before dumping her into a private room. She tried to sleep, but the ward was noisy all night, with nurses talking in the hall, the rattle and squeal of their carts, telephones ringing and machines beeping, an all-night parade of people checking on her. It was a relief when her father and brother arrived at nine the next morning.

"Get me out of here," she demanded, and they did.

• • •

ONE WEEK LATER

The phone rang and, as usual, Arthur picked it up and growled, "What? Oh, yeah—sorry. Uh, I think so, sure."

He turned to Cindy. "Mother would like a word—with both of us. There will be some others. Don't worry; it's nothing bad."

He rose and walked out. At least he waited for her at the elevators.

The chairs in Charlotte's office were arranged in a circle, with Charlotte and Steven the focal point on the sofa, Vernon in a chair on Charlotte's other side. Kaz was there as well, along with Nicole, Craig, and Morris, and, looking at ease, Sam. Charlotte motioned the new arrivals into two empty chairs between Nicole and Sam. The wince Cindy tried to suppress turned into a grunt as she lowered herself. Ribs, she'd been told, took a long time to heal, but luckily her head had escaped serious damage.

Everyone looked to Charlotte.

"Thank you all for coming, especially Ms. Shapiro. Sam, you obviously know Cindy. This is my son, Arthur, our chief technology officer."

Apparently, the other introductions had already been made.

"Pardon me for springing this on you, Cindy, but after all you've been through, I didn't want you worrying about the meeting." She turned to sweep her eyes around the room. "Cindy has the most visible wounds"—the reference to the stitches and her bald spot was embarrassing—"but we've all been hurt by this unfortunate episode, and I thought we needed to come together, to heal. This is a complicated story, and Vernon has done the most to unravel it."

They must have discussed the meeting in advance, because he nodded and began without hesitation in his clipped, confident voice.

"To understand this, you have to know our history. Back Door began when Arthur, age eleven, was caught hacking into a government network. I worked for NSA at the time, and we were upset, but also impressed. It was an opportunity to bring on board a rare talent, so we worked out an arrangement with his mother"—offering a graceful wave to Charlotte—"and Back Door Technologies was born. We were able to use off-books NSA money, along with Charlotte's personal funds, to get things rolling. Charlotte set things up so that our core staff, Steven, myself—I had left government service by then—and Carlson, were granted generous ownership shares. The company succeeded beyond expectations, and as more opportunities arose, it became clear that we needed more capital."

He paused and looked at Charlotte, who nodded and took over.

"My cousin, Ash Whitaker, controls a hedge fund, Winston Properties, and they provided us with the necessary funds in exchange for a substantial ownership share and a seat on our board. At the time it seemed a way to have the best of both worlds: we kept the company private and in the family, while getting the funds we needed to grow."

Vernon spoke in response to Charlotte's look. "As our success brought more opportunities, the need for funds only grew, and with it Winston's power, along with his share in the company. Lately our Mr. Whitaker has become more assertive, demanding that management cut spending and prioritize profits."

"He has expressed contempt," said Charlotte, "for everything we've tried to build. He refuses to see the link between our unique culture and our success."

Vernon said, "Charlotte's ideas may seem Utopian, but I've seen them produce results. People work hard, and they stay. Training new staff is expensive, making turnover costly. Of course, I bridled at some of her hires, including Carlson." He didn't have to add Nicole to the list. He just nodded in her direction, with what appeared to be an affectionate smile.

Charlotte picked up the narrative. "Ash came to me with what seemed like a constructive demand, though there was an undercurrent of threat. I should hire an executive assistant to help with details. Compared to his other suggestions, it seemed reasonable, a way to meet him halfway. And he had just such a person."

Steven looked visibly uncomfortable at this point.

"Yes," she said, putting a hand on his shoulder, "you warned me—as did Vernon—but I agreed to meet with Susan, and she charmed me."

Cindy felt like running for the door.

Charlotte must have sensed her unease. "She's a chameleon—that's the kindest way to put it."

"A manipulator," Steven said, with plenty of venom of his own. "A snake."

"A classic sociopath, I guess you would say," said Charlotte. "She had a way of planting ideas, suspicions, and when you expressed them, she'd argue half-heartedly against them. She would play the naive innocent, and allow you to be the smarter, worldly one."

"Quite brilliant, really," said Vernon. "She had young Elmer coming to me, telling me that Arthur's team was losing focus."

"He was an amazing coder," added Arthur, "one of a kind. Lately, when we kept finding errors; it took me months to trace them to him."

"Of course, when he shared that insight with me, I suspected Arthur of a cover-up, of persecuting the whistleblower—with some artful encouragement from Susan, who said she would never believe he would do such a thing," said Vernon.

"He's disappeared," said Arthur. "I think he's dead. He left me a note, as a pop-up on my screen. Classic Elmer. He had it programmed so that he had to actively cancel it every Monday morning or it would go into operation."

"A dead man's switch," said Craig.

"Exactly," said Vernon.

"You'd better read it aloud," said Charlotte to her son.

He pulled out a sheet of paper, cleared his throat, and began. It was strange; Cindy could almost hear Elmer's whine through Arthur's toneless delivery.

"Congratulations, asshole. Probably you'll never read this, but if you are, I am at least missing or more likely dead. Bummer writing this, but I don't trust Ash. I don't like the looks I get. Susan either. So here it is. Susan Hayes killed Carlson. Yeah, not the stupid dishwasher. Had to shut him up, she said. He figured something out or found out about her. She said making things crazy around here was a bonus. See, it's a takeover. She says if they make this place fail, they can take control. And that's where I come in. I built this place. You know it too. Even you said it. My codes are the best, period."

Arthur paused to shake his head and add, "I suppose," before resuming.

"So what. I am still out in the hall with all the noise, and all those kids think they are smarter and they are not. You got the office and everyone kisses your ass, and I take shit every day from the others. Not fair and you know it, but I never get respect. Susan said when they take over, that office is mine, and the job with it, and it should be. I thought I would start my own place, but why should I leave the place I built? You don't want to hear it, but your mother's shit is bringing us down. I hope you all just go away, but if you read this, it's me gone, which sucks. You are a smart guy, but you know I'm better. I am sorry I planted that fucked-up code, but it was part of their plan. Back Door will be better off now. But not if you read this. So, go to my desktop. There is a Susan icon. I made multiples. Go find them, asshole."

Arthur looked up, but nobody spoke for some time. Cindy looked around at downcast faces; only Sam met her eyes.

"I found the recording," said Arthur. "I'm not sure it proves anything—Susan was careful, the way she put things. The police have it now. Of course, it was digital, on our servers. They say it might be hard to use as evidence."

Cindy saw Sam make a note. Then Charlotte turned to Cindy. "It was with a show of reluctance that she sent Elmer to me, and he claimed you had been making fun of Arthur in front of the others. Of course, Susan told me not to believe him—she presented herself as your champion, but in such a way that she seemed to be acting only out of loyalty. And I fell for it. I'm sorry."

"Don't worry," Cindy said. "She had me convinced that you had this eugenics obsession, this scheme to improve the breed. And you brought in Nicole as some kind of sex instructor or surrogate."

Nicole put a hand on her hip, rotated it toward the group, and saucily rolled her shoulder back while she puckered her lips. Everyone laughed, and some tension left the room.

"Now, that," said Charlotte with a big smile, "is why I brought Nicole on board, and I haven't regretted it for a single day, even when Susan accused her of, well . . ."

"Were you a takeover target?" Sam Shapiro spoke quietly, but her voice carried, with a presence that probably served her well in the courtroom.

Vernon smiled. "Full points, Ms. Shapiro." The other woman nodded while a rustle of shifting bodies went around the circle. "I don't know whether it was a coincidence—this has made me even more cynical than before—but our NSA contract managers were ramping up the pressure to meet increasingly ambitious deadlines. You see, they have always been a critical part of our business, and Arthur's team handles their contracts."

Charlotte said, "After Neerav and Freddy came to disabuse me of my suspicions of Cindy, I brought Vernon and Arthur in, and we began trading notes."

"I did some research on Winston Properties," said Arthur.

"Something I should have done a long time ago," said Vernon, the muscles around his eyes tightening.

"They're takeover artists," said Arthur. "They buy into a company, then short sell it as a way to boost their equity share."

"But why did they need to murder Carlson?" asked Kaz.

"We're not sure," said Steven. "He came to me after the fling with Marshall ended, saying someone approached him with an offer to buy his shares while they were still worth something. He seemed excited, said he thought he had found a way to turn the tables—that was how he put it. It was all very mysterious, and I didn't know what to make of it." He sighed. "We weren't on the best of terms at that point, and I didn't want to pursue it. Now I think it must have come from Susan. Perhaps they felt he knew too much? Carlson was nobody's fool."

"Susan told me after she threw me in the water," said Cindy. That brought a gasp. "She offered Carlson a deal, and he turned her down, threatened to blow her cover."

"Susan isn't talking now," said Vernon. "Winston Properties is paying for her representation,"

"Malford Lyon and Crebbs, from New York—the best," said Sam. "They don't want her turning on them—not that it would help her much, but the DA might be willing to cut some kind of deal."

"I don't doubt it," said Vernon. "Whitaker was a generous campaign donor, to both parties."

"Well, we may never know the whole story," said Charlotte.

"Marshall, the coder who couldn't code," said Arthur, "has disappeared. I've been trying to track him down, as have the police, as a person of interest. Background documents go back about ten years, then stop. Probably phony, all of it. The same with Susan, by the way. I can't believe, Mother—"

"Yes, I know," said Charlotte, holding up her hand. "Susan tried to get me to stop Cindy's meetings with people, first as her protector, then her accuser. That finally made me stop and think. Yes, Arthur, I should have done my due diligence, but your father always trusted Ashton."

Craig added, "So, they tried to eliminate Cindy after they couldn't scare her away."

"Yes," said Charlotte. She faced Cindy directly, meeting her eyes. "We all owe you a lot for your courage." Then she turned to Sam. "What will this mean for Johnnie?"

"It's too early to say," said Sam. "You've said a lot that makes sense, but proving it will be hard. They'll have Susan on assault, possibly attempted murder, for throwing Cindy into the pond, but that may not be enough to clear Johnnie. The DA's office made a commitment to prosecute, and they'll have to be convinced. I'm meeting with the assistant DA in the judge's chambers later this week. We'll see."

Then it was time for everyone to return to work. As Cindy went to get up, Charlotte put a restraining hand on her arm.

"Stay a moment, would you, dear? I've something to discuss with you."

Cindy caught herself looking around for Susan—ridiculous.

"I want to discuss your future here. I find myself without the services of an assistant. It wasn't something I thought I needed, but I've found there are many benefits. At any rate, I was wondering whether you would consider that role for yourself."

Whoa. That wasn't what Cindy was expecting. It was an exciting prospect in so many ways. She would have to shake off all the poisons Susan had planted regarding her boss. Charlotte was still talking.

"... mistake to place my trust in that woman, but I have a different feeling about . . ."

She must have noticed that Cindy looked less than enthusiastic.

"You could try it out—a trial, for both of us."

Cindy didn't know how to respond, but Charlotte conspired to give her time to consider her words. She held up a finger, rose, and went to the electric tea kettle, moving slowly as she filled it, waited for it to heat up, and poured the hot water over fresh leaves. Was she sending a message?

Once they were seated together again, with fresh cups steaming in their hands, Cindy answered.

"I'm flattered, and honored, really, but I'm not sure it's what I want. I had this plan, a new career, and I feel like I'm just getting started. Working with Arthur and his team has been wonderful. I was hoping you would allow me—"

Charlotte held up her hand.

"Say no more. I understand. You were not made to be anyone's assistant. I should know you that well by now. And I'm very happy you like working with my son. He was very angry when I told him my plan to steal you away."

Cindy got out of there as fast as she could, before she could change her mind and grovel for a second chance at the job. It would have been a relief, not having to try to keep up with Arthur and his young geniuses.

A smiling Morris met her at the elevator, and he followed her into the bullpen, where everyone stood at their desks, cheered, and applauded. Neerav ran over and grabbed her in a big hug until she yelped in pain, then fended off the others who came around, crying, "Gentle, gentle please," as they patted her back and arms. Outside his office door, Arthur was almost smiling. Craig and Nicole flanked him, beaming.

"I tried to bet someone," Neerav shouted, "but no one believed you would leave us. Charlotte called Arthur just now to give him the news."

"And," said Freddy, "we're moving your things over. You're with us now, with your own phone, and two monitors." He grabbed her hand and dragged her over to the desk just outside the office, the one missing its usual occupant.

"It's all yours," said Freddy, with a bow and sweep of his long arm.

"The collective hygiene of our team is immediately improved," said Neerav.

"Nickie—I'm so sorry," Cindy said through tears. The other woman grabbed her into a hug and held her to a chorus of aws.

Arthur reached down onto the desk, now hers, to hand her a

wrapped package, which the group loudly demanded she open. An oddly shaped object emerged from the tissue paper: a diving mask and snorkel tube, spray-painted gold, mounted on a mahogany stand.

"'For Cindy,'" she read from the little plaque. "'Our love runs deep.' Guys—it's beautiful. I'll keep it on my desk, always."

Freddy took pictures of her with various groupings and promised to post them on the internal web page. Then Kaz wheeled in a big cake, and all hell broke loose.

4 5

Paul

We have our own celebration. It's Saturday night, and Father, Phyllis, and I are set to party when Cindy gets back from the Stewart Center with Bruno. When we're settled, Phyllis comes out of the kitchen, and we open some wine while the chicken rests out of the oven.

"He was so excited to go there," Cindy said, referring to the exhausted golden retriever. "I think he really missed it."

She had been taking him to the Center a couple times every week for a visit since I moved out of the group home, and they had kept on after I got my job, only stopping when Cindy started at Back Door. "It was good to see people again, even though the only reason some of them were there was they got pulled off their jobs. They needed a lift, and my sweetie's always good for that."

"Looks like you wore him out," says Father, looking at the pile of fur in the center of the room.

"I was wondering," says Phyllis, looking down at her hands, "what exactly happened, you know, in that pond."

Ralph's still in the hospital, in intensive care for more than a week now. We've both been by to visit, but he wasn't really aware of much. Phyllis has been firm that it wouldn't be fair to bother Cindy about it. She'll tell us when she's ready. Of course, if Phyllis can't wait, that's different.

Cindy seems okay with it, though, so we get the story. Phyllis has a way of sensing things with people—I should know by now.

4 6

Cindy

After the second blow to the head, she was only dimly aware of being back underwater until the need to breathe became desperate again and brought her partway back to consciousness, enough that she started to struggle. It was no more productive than the last time—the hands that held her were overwhelmingly strong, and the water made her blows mushy against his legs.

And then she was free and flailing her way to the surface, stumbling upright, gasping and coughing. All she could see was a roiling, jerking mass of dark shapes. The one in front of her was blocking the other, who began by reaching over toward her, then pushing the other aside only to be blocked again. Though out of the water, breathing wasn't as easy as she imagined it would be, and her head kept dropping when she retched up water. It hurt like hell when it was forced back up her nose, blinding her with tears. When her vision cleared, she could see the other, much larger figure chop away with the sides of his hands as he grunted with the effort.

The blows were drawing yelps of pain from the figure in front of her, but he wouldn't stay down or be moved aside. Then, after two devastating blows, he was down in the water, motionless, and the larger man was reaching for her through the gloom when a bright light from above blinded her. It stayed on them for a moment, and someone yelled something, but when it was gone, the other figure was retreating. She stumbled over to the prone figure, found a head of hair, and jerked it up out of the water.

It was Ralph. She must have said it aloud because she was suddenly aware how much the croak hurt. There was a crash above them on the deck, and soon a sloshing sound of someone approaching. She tried to hold Ralph's face above water as she pivoted his body around to her side to protect him from another assault, but the figure that approached was obviously smaller, and then the light was back.

"Cindy?" It was Paul, her brother. Ralph, now Paul—maybe she *had* drowned, and this was her last dream, the figures in her life dancing before her eyes. All she could do was hang on and be dragged around the side of the deck, up the bank and onto shore.

4 7

Paul

"Fucking Ralph," says my sister, by way of ending the story.

When we were young, Father could be stern, and when he got angry, you didn't want to challenge him. Of course, it got so I would goad him into it, but that's another story.

I haven't seen such dark storm clouds in years. "I've heard that out of your mouth one time too many. The man saved your life, and paid a heavy price."

I'm looking at Phyllis, hoping she won't jump into the middle to defend Cindy. I know she wants to, but I don't know what I'd do then, because he's right. I put my hand on hers, and she gives me a nod.

"I know," says Cindy. "I've been going there every evening after work."

Father looks at me. I didn't know that either.

"I talk to the nurse—my new friend," she says with a bitter laugh. "The dislocated elbow, broken ribs, the collapsed lung, the bruised spleen, she says all that is going to heal, but they're not sure about his brain."

"He did seem out of it." That's me, Mister Sensitive—earns me an angry glare from Phyllis.

"They're keeping him under sedation. She says it's his best chance."

"Was he hit that hard?" That's Father.

"It's about how long his brain went without oxygen, when he was underwater, and after, before Paul got him breathing again."

I didn't, exactly, but it's nice for my sister to say, and I'm getting used to hearing it.

"I'm sorry, Cindy," says Phyllis. "This was supposed to be a celebration."

"And so it shall be," says Father, raising his glass of wine. "To Cindy . . . and fucking Ralph!" And we repeat it together, our strange little family, minus one.

• • •

SIX MONTHS LATER

"The weird thing," says Cindy, "is that Susan could have left me alone. It's not like I was getting anywhere."

"Instead, she's in deep shit," says Billie.

It's Saturday, and the late-afternoon sun lights up the dust in Billie and Grace's living room. There's been talk of bringing in a cleaner—neither Billie nor Grace are much into housekeeping, and now they're getting older—but so far it hasn't happened. We're gathered at Grace and Billie's for a reunion of sorts, my sister and I, Sam, and Shep. Ralph is back, at least in body.

"That's typical, though," says Billie. "Sociopaths have so much confidence that they're smarter than everyone else, they can't help but manipulate."

"Besides," says Sam, "it was an opportunity to create more chaos, help with her mission."

"I'm still confused about that," says Billie. "What the hell was the point, anyway?"

"It's about the money, of course." Grace sounds more like the corporate accountant she used to be, before she took her vows. "They wanted the chaos, to divide the others so they could take control."

"But it's so destructive," says Cindy.

"It's how the bastards make money," says Shep, "piles of it."

Grace says, "To be fair, the rich people who invest in those hedge funds expect huge returns—twenty percent and up. The managers have to pull these maneuvers."

"And the investors know damn well what's going on," says Shep, "though they'll never admit it."

"But will it go any higher? To Susan's boss?" Billie asks.

"Ash, the man in the black limousine," says Cindy.

"Hard to say," says Sam. "Maybe if the state can show he had any role in creating the sham identities for Susan and this Marshall character, but it's still not that serious a charge. Unless Susan turns on him or they can uncover specific instructions to her."

"And Marshall and Elmer have vanished, so no help there," says Cindy. "We're not sure who Marshall was, but Elmer's father is still making noise, so that may keep some pressure on."

"It would help if they could find his body," says Sam.

"The bosses never go down," says Shep, who no longer works for ConDo. Earlier, he had asked Sam if ConDo could legally prevent him from visiting Johnnie. Her answer—"Only if you want to continue working for them"—made him realize he didn't want the job. Now he's an intern with the Committee for Public Counsel Services, in Sam's office, and waiting tables at night, saving up for UMass Boston's paralegal training. Good for him, but too bad for the folks he supported.

Lu's another loss. Folks who find jobs for others make a lot of contacts, and before long they end up making more money somewhere else. Lu's doing just fine working for a public relations outfit. Last week she stopped by the Center for a visit, and the guys are still talking about it.

Things aren't as clear for Ralph. He's lost weight, and one side of his face droops, which looks awful when he smiles. Cindy says the doctors won't say whether that will change. He walks like an old man, can't stay on his feet long. No one's saying when he'll be able to go back to work, and he's had to stop cooking for his ladies. Billie complains but gets dinners from the hot bar at the market, and they still eat together. Grace says it's God's will. Right now, he's leaning back in one of the cushiony chairs, mostly staring at the ceiling. He can talk, but only does if you ask him something. Mostly, it's like he's somewhere else.

Now that I'm living with Phyllis, we only see Cindy for weekend dinners with Father. For all my urging, if Phyllis ever decides to try employment, she'll point to my sister as her inspiration. Living together has cut her social security, so we could sure use the money, but I can tell she's more confident, and some of that's rubbed off on me. When I come by the Center, it's like I'm a star—the brother of the one who lifted the curse. It doesn't make sense, but it's nice just the same. Only about half the people got their jobs back, and they won't let Sophie hire a job developer to replace Lu; Doctor Marsha gets to put her nurse there instead. I'm afraid the place will never be the same.

I don't deserve to be a star. My job was to look after Johnnie. I tried, but maybe not hard enough. I could have gone back to the jail more often, even though it scared me. The day of his release, I could have been there with Sam to pick him up, but I thought, once he's out, there'll be lots of places to meet. It never happened, and now he's gone.

My old friend Harvey Salvanich, the social worker at the Berkeley Street shelter, says Johnnie's stays there off and on, and hears he's crashing with other young guys when he can and otherwise sleeping rough. He's worried Johnnie's going to keep sliding down until he's like the older guys I remember from my stay there, the ones got eaten up by all those years of no home and no hope. I hate to think that will happen, but I get it. He never had a family to stand by him, no one to come back to. If I'd grown up like he did, I'd have ended up just like those guys, drifting through my days one hour to the next, trying to stay warm and fed, getting old fast.

I got a glimpse of what that's like, and that was enough. It's like Ralph always says: you walk through this world, sooner or later it will break your heart. Cindy's got broken bad enough she had to run away. I get that now. I was going to continue my peer specialist training, but now I'm thinking I'll stay with Elder Affairs. Ralph just keeps on, like it's all he knows to do. We'll see if his brain lets him.

I wait until Cindy and I are alone; the others went into the kitchen after we put Ralph to bed. "You're seeing him again?" Her look confirms that this is dangerous territory.

"He needs me. When I needed him in that pond, he was there; you can see where it got him."

When I decide there isn't more coming, I say, "Phyllis was thrilled when Charlotte called her, not Sophie or the others. She's determined to get exchanges going between Back Door and the Center."

"You shouldn't be the only one who recognizes everything she does. Paid work isn't the only way to make a difference. And she's got more guts, to keep on getting back up, than Carolyn or Dr. Marsha will ever give her credit for."

"Amen to that, sister!"

What Cindy's leaving out is how she's behind the whole thing. In a funny way, this has healed her up from that disaster at child protection. It's like she had to scrape the wound open, get the pus out. Hurts like hell, but in the end, you're better off.

Afterword and Acknowledgments

People familiar with our world will recognize Center Club in Boston as the model for the Mary Stewart Center and the Pine Street Inn as the model for the Berkeley Street shelter. I can't say enough about those great institutions and the wonderful people who keep them alive.

The Cambridge Discovery Park exists on the grounds of the former Arthur D. Little campus, but Back Door Technologies and its building are entirely fictional. The swamp and paths between it and the Pfizer complex are largely as described, but I had to invent the footbridge linking the two.

I am deeply grateful to the members of my wonderful writer's group, the Sweetwater Draft Society—Evan Cole, Patrick Donahue, Monica Gribouski, Stephanie Machell, Barbara Sheehan, and Julia Todd—for their invaluable consultation and criticism of every scene. They never let me settle for less than the best I could produce.

Lynne Griffin provided an invaluable manuscript consultation. Thanks are due to Hannah Woodlan for her excellent editing, Lauren Sheldon for the cover design, Kellie Emery for the interior design and layout, and all the other folks at Koehler Books for bringing the book to the public.

Finally, as the story is told by a White heterosexual atheist from the perspective of African American characters with a religious background and includes gay and lesbian characters, I have to answer to the charge of cultural appropriation. Because I have always worked in mental health settings that included these kinds of diversity, I was never interested in telling stories that didn't reflect it. I am grateful to the sensitivity editing services of Dennis Norris II, who helped me avoid at least some of the pitfalls of my ignorance. I hope I have not offended too many people too badly. That was never my intention, but to those who think I should never have told my story in this way, I can certainly understand your objections and apologize for any offense, pain, or aggravation I may have engendered.

www.ingramcontent.com/pod-product-compliance
Lightning Source LLC
Chambersburg PA
CBHW030527120726
47904CB00005B/1660